HIS WICKED EMBRACE

"Do I detect a note of jealousy in your voice?" Barrett asked.

"Jealous? Hah!"

Barrett leaped in front of Meagan and made her pause near a column at the top of the steps. She darted behind it, but he was right there, blocking her way. "Tell me what you were going to say."

"No."

His arms shot out and captured her against the column. "I don't give up easily." He moved closer.

Meagan's back connected with the column. "Neither do I."

She met his gaze without a blink. She stared at the afternoon stubble on his square chin, at that unsettling curve on his lips, the determined gleam in his eyes.

"We shall see," he whispered. He bent and angled his lips against the edge of her mouth, barely touching it.

Meagan battled the urge to turn her mouth fully toward his. "You can stop now."

"I've just gotten started." He nibbled the corner of her mouth.

"Seducing me will not work."

"I love a challenge." He moved lower, barely touching his lips into the hollow of her throat.

Megan felt her body trembling all over, and before she knew it, she was kissing him . . . .

Books by Constance Hall

MY DARLING DUKE
MY DASHING EARL
MY REBELLIOUS BRIDE
MY WICKED MARQUESS

Published by Zebra Books

MY WICKED MARQUESS

CONSTANCE HALL

Zebra Books
Kensington Publishing Corp.

http://www.zebrabooks.com

ZEBRA BOOKS are published by

Kensington Publishing Corp.
850 Third Avenue
New York, NY 10022

First Printing: November, 1999
10 9 8 7 6 5 4 3 2 1

Printed in the United States of America

*To my sister Cathy and my niece Meagan.
May you find joy and love in everything you do.
This book is for you with all my love.*

CHAPTER ONE

London
December, 1823

Barrett Rothchild, the Marquess of Waterton, paused before the tent's entrance and read the sign:

THE SOCIETY FOR THE INDIGENT'S
TWELFTH ANNUAL CHRISTMAS BAZAAR

He wrinkled his brow, curious as to why Sir James Neville, his cousin and head of Foreign Affairs, wanted to meet in such a public place—especially since the note Barrett had received intimated it was a matter of national security.

Barrett passed several smiling gentlemen and stepped inside. Heat from two braziers burned his cold cheeks as he surveyed the booths lining the tent sides. An array of needlework, handmade rugs, pottery, watercolors, and baked goods littered the counters. Several groups of ladies hovered near them, but the most popular, by far, was a stall at the back of the tent.

Seven people—five gentleman and two ladies—stood in line at the booth's entrance. Mistletoe and red ribbons decorated the top and sides. Above the mistletoe, a large wooden sign proclaimed:

HAVE YOUR FORTUNE TOLD
BY THE WINTER PRINCESS—ONLY A SHILLING

Barrett raised his quizzing glass and dropped his gaze. Whoever had created the booth knew exactly how to add mystery and allure to it. A small tent filled the booth and a bright light burned on the inside, casting the "princess's" reflection and that of her patron onto the canvas.

A full-figured, middle-aged woman with blond hair and world-weary eyes stood at the front of the tent collecting the coin. She wore the black bombazine uniform and mob-cap of a maid. By the way the woman guarded the entrance with a sentinel's eye, it was obvious her mistress was the Winter Princess.

Barrett surveyed the princess's reflection closely. Her hair flowed down her back in curling waves. A scarf covered the top half of her head, and she wore a veil over the bottom half of her face. Her full bosom, clearly outlined by the light, claimed his attention; then his gaze dropped to a flat waist that flared and rounded to sensuously curved hips. His curiosity conjured all sorts of visions of what she must look like in person. The five gentlemen standing in line to have their fortunes told must have been thinking the same thing.

Barrett remembered why he was here and looked for his cousin's broad frame and raven hair among the bazaargoers. He spotted him coming out of the Winter Princess's tent. Before he dropped the tent flap, James turned and graced the princess with a charming smile. He stood there so long talking that the maid tapped him on the shoulder.

After a farewell to the princess and a quick look in the maid's direction, James left the tent. He strode toward Barrett, his smoky black eyes gleaming with amusement.

"Was getting your fortune told that amusing?" Barrett asked, watching another gentleman hand his shilling to the woman and step inside the tent.

"It is when the fortune-teller is as intelligent and alluring as the one in there." A grin twisted up one corner of James's mouth. After an assessing glance at Barrett, James changed the subject. "What took you so long, cousin? You were supposed to meet me here half an hour ago."

"I was waylaid at Tattersall's."

"Your stable is already full." James knew Barrett better than he knew himself, and he proved that now by asking, "Are you suffering that annual Christmas melancholy? Outbidding everyone at Tattersall's won't make it better."

"I needed some new hunters." Barrett kept his face impassive, easily covering the lie he'd just told.

"Sure you did." James's intuitive black eyes scrutinized Barrett.

Barrett would never admit to James that he had a feeling this Christmas would be more dismal than some of those during his childhood, and he had felt the need of a little reckless spending to cheer him. He saw James reading his thoughts and quickly changed the subject. "Why did you choose this place to meet?"

"I support this bazaar every year. Thought I'd kill two birds with one stone." James smiled.

"What was so urgent?" Barrett rested his cane over his arm and pulled out his snuffbox.

"I need your help on a case." A group of ladies strode past them, their silk gowns swishing. James lowered his voice. "I have to go outside of the Foreign Office this time. There's a traitor working for me, but I haven't yet discovered who it is.''

"Will I have to go to France again?"

"No. This time the case is here. I need you to put a spoke in Lord Fenwick's wheel.''

"Fenwick." Barrett tapped his gloved fingers on the top of his cane and frowned, deep in thought. "I've seen the gentleman about town. Got a reputation for being a reckless gamester. Plays for high stakes, I believe. Inherited a fortune several years back with his title.''

"Yes. Since Fenwick inherited, he's depleted his estate down to almost nothing. He owes everyone in town.''

"What's Fenwick done?''

"My sources tell me he's a member of the Devil's Advocates.''

"Quite a nasty group of radical extremists. Spawned from Thistlewood's group, weren't they?''

James nodded. "After the Cato Affair. Up until now, they've been fairly harmless.''

Barrett frowned and remembered the sensation Arthur Thistlewood had caused in 1820. He'd tried to assassinate the members of the cabinet and seize power, but he had been captured along with his twenty followers in a hayloft on Cato Street. Thistlewood and four others were hanged.

"What are they planning now?'' Barrett asked, keeping his gaze on the Winter Princess.

"I've learned they are plotting to murder someone high up in the government, but I'm not sure whom. We'll find that out from Fenwick.''

"It shouldn't be hard.'' With complete indifference, Barrett glanced back at the princess's reflection. She stared down at the gentleman's palm lying on the small table between them, her lips moving in soft waves as she spoke.

"Not for someone with your kind of ruthless charms. From what I gather, he's not very loyal to anything but the gaming tables." James cocked a brow at Barrett. "So will you do it?"

"Of course. I was growing rather bored of late."

"Capital. I knew I could count on you." James smacked Barrett on the back. "You'll let me know when it's done?"

"Yes." Barrett's gaze shifted to the Winter Princess's reflection.

James took a step to leave, saw that Barrett hadn't moved, and said, "Are you coming?"

"No. I have a date with my fortune." Barrett covered the length of the tent and stepped in line to have his fortune told. The princess's reflection intrigued him and he couldn't leave without seeing her in person.

On his way out of the bazaar, James cast a glance in Barrett's direction, his onyx eyes gleaming with satisfaction.

Fifteen minutes later, Barrett watched while a large woman as round as she was tall stepped out of the tent. Her ample cheeks radiated a smile. She saw Barrett was next in line and shook the tip of her parasol at him. "Oh, the princess is just splendid! Mark my words, she's well worth the shilling." Without waiting for his response, she strolled over to a booth selling pomanders, and pointed at one with her parasol.

Barrett handed his shilling to the maid, who eyed him with a watchdog light in her eyes. "You get five minutes, sir," she said, staring down at the shilling.

"That's all I need." He saw her frown as he stepped into the tent.

His gaze met the princess's. He realized his imagination had not done her justice. She wore a peasant dress, with a bright yellow shawl tied around her shoulders. Her hair was darker than he'd imagined, a rich sable brown, the color of dark mink. Burgundy highlighted her long curls, which were held back by a scarf. Wide hooped earbobs hung from her ears and brass bracelets dangled from her wrists.

A veil covered her nose and the bottom half of her face, but her eyes and brows showed. Long lashes hooded the deepest violet eyes Barrett had ever seen. A lantern sat on the table next to her, and the light flickered in the violet depths. All too quickly, she glanced away and looked disconcerted by his scrutiny. Was she truly shy or was she acting to increase the mystery surrounding her?

She turned over an hourglass that sat next to her. "Please. You may sit," she said in a husky voice. She motioned him to a chair opposite her.

Brushing aside his coattails, he sat across from her.

"Now, let me see your palms."

He set his hands on the table, eager for her to touch them.

She didn't. Her finely arched brows met over her nose and she narrowed her eyes at his upturned palms. "Hmm! What is it you wish to know?"

"You can start by telling me if you are free to dine with me this evening."

The small portion of her cheeks showing above her black veil turned bright red. She kept her eyes lowered in a coy manner. "Surely, you know princesses never dine with strangers." She continued to study his hands.

"Then tell me your name."

"No, no." She waved a hand through the air. "Not permitted. Now let me see if I can tell you something about yourself."

"Please do."

"Hmm!" She leaned forward, pointed her finger, and traced one of the lines in his palm without touching his hand. The many bracelets on her wrists jingled. The sound lured Barrett's gaze to her delicate feminine wrists. "I see you have troubles in your life."

"Really?" Barrett eyed a thick curl that had fallen over her shoulder and curved down over one high, proud breast. With fascination, he watched it quiver as she breathed.

"Oh, yes. Very big trouble. You have a restless soul. Sleep evades you."

Barrett stiffened slightly, hiding his surprise behind his usual mask of apathy. "How did you know I suffer from insomnia?"

"I see it here in your palm." She glanced up, feigned indignation in her eyes.

"What else do you see?"

Her veil moved as if she were smiling beneath it. "I see you are a man who likes to spend money, but it gives you little pleasure. You grow bored very easily."

Barrett felt the tension in his chest tighten. She could have easily guessed his wealth by his attire. The observation about his insomnia must also have been a guess. But how could she know that life held little pleasure for him and he was plagued by ennui? "What other aspects do you see of my character?" he asked, his voice laced with suspicion.

"You are particular in your choice of a tailor— Oh! And I see you have had a troubled past. Something still haunts you."

"Can you see what it is?"

"Hmm! The lines—they are fuzzy. Perhaps trouble with family members." She glanced up and studied his face for a moment. Then she said, "Perhaps a sibling or your parents."

Another presumption. She couldn't know about the estrangement with his father. This lady was not only alluring; she also had a very astute imagination. Still, he couldn't totally dismiss her uncanny ability to read him.

"Ah! I can tell by your face I was right." She glanced back down at his hand, then over at the last grains of sand draining through the hourglass. "I'm afraid that is all the princess can tell you. Time is up."

He stood and captured her hand. Then he ran his thumb over her warm, satiny skin, aware of her sweaty palm slick against his own skin. He could feel the slight tremor in her hand and he knew he unnerved her. "Tell me who you really are," he said, bending to press her hand to his lips. Her skin felt like down against his mouth. He wondered if her lips were as soft.

"I cannot." She kept her gaze lowered, her mink lashes casting long crescent shadows on her cheeks.

Barrett lowered his lips to her fingers. The shiver that went up her arm made him smile inwardly. "How can I persuade you?"

The maid opened the flap and peeked inside. She grimaced at Barrett. "Everything all right in here?"

"Yes, Mildred. The gentleman was just leaving."

When Barrett cast the princess one more glance and saw the determination in her eyes, he wanted her more than ever. She had aroused his curiosity and touched a cord deep within him that he couldn't sever.

A commotion outside forced their glances toward the front of the tent. Lord Collins—a tall, lean, raven-faced gentleman—staggered past Mildred and flipped her a shilling. He stood in the door, swaying, his breath reeking of alcohol. He bawled, "Where's the little fortune-teller?"

Collins's gaze fell on the princess. He grinned and winked at her. "I hope you do more than fortunes."

Barrett watched a humiliated blush spread across the princess's brow. Through his teeth, he said, "Leave, Collins. You're foxed."

Collins's eyes shifted to Barrett. The grin faded. "By God! Waterton! The things they let crawl around in this bazaar."

"I quite agree." Barrett leveled a look back at Collins. "Doing it up a bit tame, ain't you? Why are you here when you could be out destroying someone else's livelihood?"

"I knew you'd be here." Barrett clutched his cane in his hands to keep from striking Collins. "Now you've offended the lady, and I'm going to ask you again to leave."

"Ain't going. I paid my shilling."

Mildred slapped the coin in his hand. "Here, take your blunt and leave, sir. Only gentlemen are allowed in here."

Collins rolled his eyes at her. "Oh, that's how it is, is it? My money is as good as his." He hitched his thumb at Barrett, then raised his other hand to toss the coin back at Mildred.

"You really don't listen." Barrett grabbed Collins's hand and thrust him toward the tent opening.

Mildred held open the flap and Collins staggered back through it.

Barrett heard the princess gasp behind him as Collins charged back into the tent, his ravenish eyes boring into Barrett. He swung at Barrett's face.

Barrett jabbed Collins's ribs with his cane. Collins buckled a moment, then attacked again, swinging wildly.

Barrett ducked, raised his cane, and struck Collins beneath the chin. Before Collins fell back, Barrett used the curved end of the cane to hook the back of Collins's neck and jerk his face forward. He struck twice—on the chin, and the mouth.

His opponent stumbled back, hit the side of the tent, then slid down the heavy canvas. Large ripples fanned out from his body. Collins blinked his dazed eyes. Blood trickled from his nose.

Several of the other gentlemen in line hurried inside to help him stand.

Collins shoved them aside and shook his fist at Barrett. "I should kill you!"

"Name the place and time." Barrett draped his cane back over his arm; then he picked off a piece of lint from the cuff of his coat. He flicked it away and glanced at Collins.

For a moment, neither blinked. The tension between them sizzled in the silence. Barrett kept a deceptively bland impersonal expression on his face—a mask he'd mastered over many years to intimidate and humiliate.

Collins grimaced at Barrett's expression; frustration and anger were etched in every line on his face. He glanced away, then wiped the trickle of blood from his nose. "I'll not forget this," he said before staggering out of the tent.

Barrett turned and saw the Winter Princess wide-eyed in a corner. He strode over to her and asked, "Are you harmed?"

"I'm fine." As she nodded, her earbobs hit the sides of her face. Her composure quickly returned.

Barrett had a feeling that, in spite of the princess's obvious shyness, it took a lot to unnerve her. She was an enigma that he meant to unravel. He pulled his gaze from the princess and looked at Mildred. "And are you well?"

"It gave me a start, sir. That was a kind thing you did. Hard telling what he'd have done," she said, a touch of excitement in her voice.

The princess looked at Barrett. "Thanks to you, it is all over now."

Barrett noticed her voice held the same husky, seductive quality as before. "Allow me to escort you both home."

"That is very kind of you, but I promised to help with the bazaar."

"How much did you hope to make today?"

She shrugged. "I really do not know, sir. We hoped to at least make five and twenty pounds for the needy."

Barrett reached inside his coat and pulled out a hundred pound note. "Will this cover it?"

Her eyes widened. "You are too generous."

"Nonsense, madam. I'm many things, but never generous." Barrett cocked a brow at her. "I admit I only did it for your sake." He graced her with his most charming smile.

Her eyes twinkled coyly at him, while she nervously fingered the bracelets on her wrist. "That contemptible man doesn't seem to like you."

"Yes, well, he and I go way back."

"Please say you'll not duel with him on my account." She looked at him with worry in her eyes.

"You needn't concern yourself over me. When they were handing out backbones, Collins only got hot air."

Her veil moved and a smile touched her eyes.

Something in that smile moved Barrett as nothing had in a long time. "Enough about Collins, dear lady," he said. "Come. You must let me take you out of here."

Mildred flashed an ever vigilant glance at Barrett and handed the princess her reticule. "I'll see her home."

"No, Mildred. I can't leave. Mrs. Pool was counting on me."

A gray-haired woman with sallow skin entered the tent. She glided up to the princess and patted her arm. "Oh, such a stir! Have you ever in your life? You should go home, my dear. We can manage without you."

"But what about this booth, Mrs. Pool?"

"They'll just have to have their fortunes told by me." Mrs. Pool smiled and gave the princess a motherly pat.

"Here, Mrs. Pool." The princess handed her the hundred pound note.

The elderly woman looked at it and grimaced. "Oh, my. When I took over organizing this bazaar I never thought of security. We just cannot keep such a large sum here. After what just happened, I'm surprised no one has tried to rob us." Mrs. Pool grabbed her throat. "I must appeal to you, my dear. Please take this home with you. I will not be at ease unless I know it is out of here." She thrust the note at the princess. "I'll send my husband around to pick

it up"—she stared at the peasant dress, shawl, and veil—
"along with the clothes."

"If it eases your mind, Mrs. Pool."

"Oh, it shall."

The princess stuffed the note into her reticule. Her veil
moved against her mouth as she breathed. Barrett watched
the veil, wishing she'd remove it so he could glimpse the
bottom half of her face.

"I'll see she gets home safely." After Barrett bowed to
the elderly lady, he waited while Mildred threw a cape over
her mistress's shoulder. Then he laced his arm in the
princess's and guided her out the tent and past the booths.

He noticed the fallen faces on the gentleman standing
in line. A triumphant feeling stirred with him as he said,
"My carriage is but a short distance away."

"We have our own carriage, sir," the maid piped up,
her brown eyes narrowing on him.

"Then allow me the honor of escorting you to it."

"No. We have trespassed upon your kindness long
enough." The princess's eyes crinkled in a shy smile; then
she almost ran out of the tent, her maid at her side.

He realized the object of his desire was getting away and
followed her out to a rented hack parked on the street.
Before she stepped inside, he grabbed her arm. "You can't
just fly out of my life so easily, madam. At least, give me
your name."

"She ain't gonna, sir," Mildred snapped, slapping his
hand away from her mistress's arm. "It ain't the proper
thing to do after she was in that booth and you know it."

"Then allow me to be presumptuous and tell you
mine. . . . " Barrett paused as Mildred pushed her mistress
up into a waiting carriage and hopped in behind her. The
door slammed in Barrett's face.

"Lord Wat—"

The driver flicked the reins and the carriage sped down
the street.

Barrett clamped his mouth closed, the rest of his name and title dying on his lips. "Bloody hell!" he mumbled.

As he turned to run toward his carriage, he saw a vendor leave his gingerbread stand and grab a dog by the scruff of its neck and beat it with a belt. Barrett glanced at the hackney speeding off into the traffic, then at the man beating the dog. Follow the lady or save the dog—which would it be?

CHAPTER TWO

"Hell and damnation," Barrett said, running across the street toward the dog.

"I'll teach you to come around here beggin'." The man drew back to hit the dog again.

The animal cringed, all the while whining.

The pitiful wail went through Barrett like needles. In seconds he reached the vendor and thrust his cane at the man's chest and caught the dog in his arms. He glared at the buzzard-faced man. Greasy hair stuck out from beneath a brown cap, and not an ounce of compassion showed in the man's eyes.

"Here now! That scut comes around beggin' all the time. I've a right to tear up his hide." The man shook the belt at Barrett and sucked his toothless mouth.

"Not while I'm present. If I ever see you beating another animal, you'll get the same from me."

"Aye, me lord," the vender grumbled.

Barrett strode back toward his carriage. He stared down at the dog, which was still shivering in his arms. Large brown eyes, almost hidden by tufts of wiry gray-colored hair, gazed up at him.

"You needn't look at me like that." Barrett searched the street for the hack. Not a sign of it. "Indeed, she's gone, boy. I lost her." He patted the mutt's head and said, "But how hard could it be finding a young lady with a maid named Mildred?"

"I'm glad I remembered to call you Mildred." Lady Meagan Fenwick looked at her maid, Tessa; then she jerked the scarf off her head. Long sable curls sprang out around her face and shoulders. She pushed her curls behind her ear and stared out the window at the row of trees in St. James's Park, feeling the carriage rocking her head back and forth.

" 'Tis a good thing. I don't fancy Lord Watt will give up so easily in finding you."

"Lord Watt?"

"Aye, that's what the gentleman said his name was. Didn't you hear him?"

"I did not." In her haste to put distance between herself and the gentleman, Meagan hadn't heard a thing. He was too unsettling by half.

She rubbed her hand and recalled how Lord Watt had kissed it, how his lips had moved over her fingers, how his hot breath had sent tingles up her arm and caused her insides to quake.

Tessa's voice broke into Meagan's thoughts. "You ain't heard a word I said."

"I'm sorry."

"I said it was lucky Lord Watt was there to throw that Collins bloke out. There's always one in a crowd who has to kick up a stir."

"Yes." Meagan stared absently out the window, her mind on Lord Watt. In spite of knowing she must, she couldn't get him out of her thoughts. She stared out the window and saw a boy hawking cherries and nuts on a corner. "Why in the world I allowed Harold to force me to come to London and volunteer my services to the bazaar, I shall never know."

"Well, I don't approve of a lot things your brother does, but there wasn't no harm in coming to town and working the bazaar. You were in disguise, so no one recognized you. It's done you a world o' good to get outta the country—even if that Collins bloke ruined the day." Tessa tapped the side of her jaw. "And I don't approve of that Lord Watt. He had hungittery eyes."

" 'Hungittery eyes?' " Meagan raised a brow at Tessa.

"Aye, hungry and glittery. I saw him eyeing you like a piece of rump roast and following you out to your carriage, asking after your name like that." Tessa harrumped under her breath. "Well, he might be a gentleman, but I don't trust him. But there'll be others."

"I don't want others." Meagan realized she had over-emphasized her words.

"You're only twenty, and I know what you're thinking." Tessa shook her finger at Meagan. "Ain't no call to go throwing your life away because of your condition. You haven't had an attack in five years. It ain't likely to come back now that we know how to control it."

"I wasn't thinking of it." Meagan swallowed hard. Her condition always loomed in the back of her mind like a specter, forever lurking. It had ruined her life in ways from which she wasn't likely ever to recover. She frowned down at the hand Lord Watt had kissed. "I'm determined only the deepest love can induce me into marriage. I doubt any man is willing to take me with very little dowry or to put up with my penchant for books and scientific studies."

"Don't fool yourself. There's one out there."

"I'll not find him. You know how set in my ways I can be. And I'll not have a man who can't love me the way I am. Anyway, I'd rather not have a man underfoot, ordering me about." Meagan forced out the words with firm resignation.

Tessa looked askance at Meagan. "It ain't so bad being ordered about by a man who loves you. Then it doesn't seem like ordering at all."

Meagan waved her hand through the air in a dismissive gesture. "Let's speak no more of love. I shall go home directly." The thought of going home caused Meagan to frown down at the veil in her hands. Lately, she'd grown to resent the dullness in her life, but she would never admit that to Tessa.

"It'll be a shame if we don't stay a little longer." Tessa cut her eyes at Meagan, a moue on her lips.

"You just like the entertainments here."

"You should too. There's more to life than them books and gazing at the stars. And we ain't seen nothing but the museum and that Royal Society place. You spent two whole days there nosing around their library."

"Not just any library. Do you realize they have Sir William Herschel's papers in there and the design for his six-foot Newtonian telescope?"

"Don't matter. You can't build one."

"I saw the plans. That is all I could have hoped for." Meagan heard the delight in her own voice.

"I don't know what looking at papers does for you." Tessa shook her head, her expression saying she'd never understand her mistress. "You should forget about those stars. They'll be there forever, and you only live once. You should be enjoying yourself and going to balls and plays."

"I should go home, where I belong."

"You can't hide from people all your life."

Meagan knew Tessa's assertions were born out of caring and loyalty. Tessa had been her mother's abigail until that lady's death; then she'd become Meagan's. Tessa had always been treated as one of the family, but sometimes, like now, she could be exasperating.

Meagan frowned at Tessa. "You know how awkward I am around strangers. If I hadn't been in disguise, I would never have worked the fortune-telling booth so confidently. No, I function at my best alone in the country."

"Well, if that's the way you want it." Tessa shook her head, setting the sides of her mobcap flapping against her plump cheeks. "But it ain't right. It might be fine and all, losing yourself in the stars and reading about other people living their lives in a book, but it ain't the same as living life yourself. Now I've said my peace, I'll shut my gob."

Thankful for Tessa's silence, Meagan rode the rest of the way home in peace, though she didn't feel much peace. Lord Watt still loomed in her mind.

He was a fine figure of a man, with his stylish black suit and his wavy blond hair, a dynamic contrast. His hair had been parted in the middle and long enough to fall rakishly along the sides of his temples and down the back of his collar. She recalled his chiseled features, the sharp cheekbones, the proud square jaw, the wide mouth, and the slight hump in his aristocratic nose, as if it had been broken, which added to the gaunt harshness of his face.

But if she cared to admit it, his wicked handsomeness wasn't what drew her to him. It was the cool detachment in his eyes. She would never forget them: searing, predatory, and unyielding, as vivid blue as a summer sky and just as capable of a violent storm.

Though he'd tried to hide the emotion in them behind an impassive facade, there had been a moment when she'd unnerved him with her guesses about his parents and she'd reached something deep inside him. His eyes had softened, and she'd glimpsed the remoteness in the blue depths.

In that moment, she too had been nonplussed, for he had touched a compassionate part of her. She knew how it felt to be lonely and miserable, and for an instant, she had sympathized with him so much she could feel his pain. Nothing like that had ever happened to her—especially with a gentleman.

She rubbed the hand he'd kissed, recalling the way his blue eyes had seared her, how aware she was of his closeness and the heat that crept through her body at the mere touch of his hands on her bare skin. Warm, powerful, gentle hands. She'd never forget his touch. Not ever.

Lost in daydreams involving a pair of predatory blue eyes and a handsome face, Meagan almost missed their stop. She called up to the driver to let them off on Fenchurch Street and pulled her cape tightly together so no one could see the peasant dress beneath it.

The carriage finally rocked to a halt. Meagan stepped out and paid the driver. In case Tessa was correct and Lord Watt did try to pry into her identity, she waited until the hack disappeared into the flow of carriages. Then she and Tessa melted into the bustle of pedestrians along the walk. This wasn't the nicest part of Cheapside, evidenced by the peeling iron railings and thick film of soot that covered the unwashed windowsills and bricks.

A boy passed her throwing papers on her neighbors' stoops. A servant stood in front of one of the doors, hanging a Christmas wreath of holly. Number 12 stood in the middle of a row of rental houses that lined one side of the street. Not the best town house Harold, her brother, had ever leased, but it was at least a place to lay her head while in London.

They had long since given up the expensive luxury of employing a footman, and Reeves, their butler, rarely answered the door these days, so Meagan thought nothing of letting herself inside.

"Oh, my!" She bumped into Reeves and grabbed his arm to right him.

He stood hunched over his cane. He had a shawl around his shoulders, and his springy white hair stuck out from the sides of his balding head. He squinted past the cataracts in his eyes and said, "Ah, Miss Meagan, you are home. I've been worried."

"What are you doing out of bed, Reeves?"

"I'm feeling a touch better, my lady. I heard the door." He held out his trembling arm for her wrap.

It would be a strain for him, but she knew his pride was the only thing that kept him alive and moving. So she placed her cape gently over his arm, steadying it as the weight made him tremble. "Here you are."

"I'll go and get tea started, my lady." Tessa took off her own wrap, then strode down the hallway.

"The master"—Reeves drew out the word *master* as if it left a bitter taste in his mouth—" has been looking for you." Having served her father all his life, Reeves hadn't been able to accept the earl's death or the fact that Harold had inherited his title and land.

"Where is he?"

"Right here," Harold answered for Reeves. He strode down the hall with a wide smile on his face. The wainscoting, darkened and dingy from years of polish and wood smoke, stood stark against Harold's bright burgundy suit.

Harold was her half brother and William Fenwick's firstborn. After his first wife had died of a fever, her father had married Lady Lillian St. Clair. Meagan came of that union. Harold looked like their father, with his tawny blond hair and golden eyes. Unlike Meagan, who resembled her mother, with dark features and the violet eyes that ran in generation after generation of St. Clair ladies.

At four and twenty, Harold still had a boyish face that lent an innocent charm to his features. He knew how to use it too. He was the flawless child, the heir presumptive, the one who'd been pampered and spoiled by their parents. Meagan could never measure up—especially with the skin condition that had plagued her. She could have resented Harold, but he had a gregarious manner about him that made her love him.

Reeves struggled to keep his gait steady as he headed for the hall closet.

"New clothes?" She eyed Harold's expensive velvet suit, the yellow-striped silk waistcoat, and the starched white cravat, tied in such a way that he couldn't lower his chin.

"Of course. I can't be seen in my old suits here in town. Must keep up appearances."

"And where did you get the money for them? Don't you owe your tailor nine hundred pounds?"

"I had a good night at the tables," he said proudly. "I paid in gold for these." The frown on Meagan's face made him throw his arm around her shoulder. He teased her with one of his charming juvenile smiles. "Don't be like that, Meggie."

"You told me you were not going to gamble again."

"I know, but I thought just once more for old times. I'm glad I did. I won three hundred pounds. Enough about me." He eyed the peasant dress and shawl. "What are you doing in that getup?"

"I manned the fortune-telling booth."

"I can't believe old Mrs. Pool gave you that duty. How are you going to meet gentlemen dressed in those rags? You go from those governess rigs you wear all the time to this." He pointed his finger to her wrinkled brown dress. "I say, you'll never find a husband that way."

"Did it ever occur to you I don't wish to attract a husband?"

He acted as if he didn't hear her. "Of course you do. It ain't natural to want to be a spinster and rot away in the country."

"If you forced me to come to London to ferret out a husband, then I'd better tell you now you're wasting your time. I'm going home."

"You will not. I'd be shirking my responsibilities if I

didn't find you a husband. And it's your duty to marry. I can't support you all your life." Harold shook his finger at her. The crestfallen look on Meagan's face tempered his tone slightly. "You're not going home. Let's just drop it, shall we? Tell me how it went. You must have made some money for them."

Meagan glanced down at her reticule, aware arguing with Harold never got her anywhere. Sometimes he was as dense as wood. "I raised a hundred pounds."

Harold whistled, a hungry gleam passing over his eyes at the sound of money. He chanced a quick glance at her reticule. "That's a lot of fortune-telling."

Meagan shoved her purse behind her back. "There was a kind gentleman who donated it."

"I'll have to search him out and approach him. Perhaps he's interested in courting you. A man just doesn't plunk down one hundred pounds for no reason."

"He might already be married." Meagan frowned at her words. If he were married, she didn't want to know about it, nor did she want to see him again. When she'd met him under the garb of a gypsy disguise, her shyness had melted away. But the thought of facing him as herself mortified her, for he would be expecting an alluringly exotic woman he'd envisioned behind the veil. What he'd get would be a shy bluestocking spinster. "Please don't seek him out," she begged.

"All right, if you insist." Harold shrugged in his usual carefree way. "Well, I'm off to the club."

"Remember, you promised not to gamble."

"So I did, but I feel a lucky streak coming on."

"The last time you said that you ended up selling our family town house on St. James's Street."

"I'll get it back. Not to worry." Harold kissed her on the cheek and tweaked her nose to try to rout the pout off her lips. When it didn't work, he merely gave her his lighthearted grin, grabbed his coat, and sauntered out the door.

Meagan climbed the steps and stared down at her purse. She remembered the almost crazed gleam in Harold's eyes when she had mentioned the one hundred pounds, which was a small fortune.

She heard the steady tread of Tessa's footsteps and glanced up at her. Tessa carried a large tray before her, filled with cakes and a tea service.

"Why are you frowning like a nappcat that just got his tail rocked on?" Tessa's thick golden brows met over her nose.

"Nappcat?" Meagan asked, knowing she shouldn't.

"Aye, napping cat." Tessa looked at Meagan the way she might look at a dolt.

"Oh!" Meagan started up the steps, sliding her hand along the old oak banisters and feeling the scratches in the wood. She turned the conversation back to the matter at hand. "I think Harold knows I have this money. He's never taken money from me before, but that look in his eyes . . ." Her words trailed off.

"You'll have to keep it from him." Tessa shook her head. "You can sure tell he was spoiled rotten. Knew it was coming when the mistress doted on him. I tried to tell her—God rest her soul—but she didn't listen to me. Bad things happen when people don't listen to me. Now look. He's gambled away everything. Reeves and me ain't been paid in a year—not that I'm complaining, mind." Tessa paused.

"I'm sorry," Meagan said, frowning. She knew Harold was in arrears, but she didn't know he hadn't paid the servants in a year.

"Oh, ain't your fault."

Meagan couldn't find any words to smooth over the uncomfortable subject, so she remained silent, feeling provoked by Harold's selfish indulgences.

Frowning, Meagan said, "I'll take the tea up in my room, Tessa. Then I'm going to retire early—and find a good hiding place for this." She clutched the purse and strode into her room.

The clock on the mantel struck twelve. Harold froze in Meagan's chamber. She lay curled on her side, huddled beneath the covers, with only the top of her head showing. She didn't stir. He let out the breath he'd been holding.

Firelight from the hearth stirred shadows along the bed's canopy and the counterpane. Now to find the ready. He could sniff money out like a foxhound. The fact Meagan was a creature of habit would make the hunt go quickly.

He skulked around the room, picking up porcelain figurines, and looking beneath them. The lamps. Behind the heavy brocade curtains. His gaze glued on her, he moved toward the bed.

He checked all the usual spots. Ran his hands along the edge of the mattress. Looked beneath the bed. Along the two feather pillows. Careful not to wake her, he checked the pillow beneath her head. The dresser next. All the drawers. Nothing.

He eased open her closet door. The hinges creaked. His gaze snapped over to her. She didn't move. Usually, once she was asleep, it took a firing squad to wake her.

He thumbed through her dresses and petticoats. Searched through purses. Shoes. When he could find nothing, he plopped down on the tiny chair by her dressing table, propped his elbows on his knees, and rested his chin on his hands. The wood protested beneath his weight. Past caring, he didn't bother checking to see if Meagan had woken up. What had she done with the bloody money?

He shook his head, then raised it. A dark rectangular spot in the ruffled edge of the canopy caught his attention. The fireplace faced the foot of the bed, and the fire flicked light through the cheap muslin ruffle. Something definitely was sewn inside the material.

Harold whipped out his pocketknife. A tremor of excitement made every muscle in his body tense. Blood pounded in his ears with the same kind of intensity he experienced when he had a winning hand and he laid those cards down on the table, watching the other players' faces fall, one by one. That kind of exhilaration was better than reaching a climax with a woman or tasting that first sip of hundred-year-old scotch. Nothing matched the feeling of winning, of beating the odds, of outwitting worthy opponents—even if, as in this case, she happened to be his sleeping sister.

Grinning, he moved closer and examined the material. The face of the note shone through the scantily woven cloth. His grin widened as he cut a wide swatch out, careful not to slice through the note. Then he hurried from the room, positive Dame Fortune would be on his side tonight.

CHAPTER THREE

Through a haze of cigar smoke, Barrett glanced at Fenwick and knew his target's luck had run out. Beads of sweat dripped down Fenwick's temples. Half an hour ago he'd loosened his cravat and it hung down around his neck. His ill turn of the dice had caused him to drink heavily. A red flush painted his whole face. He crunched the dice in his hand, making a sound like nails grinding against glass.

A hush had settled over White's. Members had left their own games and circled Barrett's table. Even the waiters had paused and joined the crowd. Not an unusual occurrence when stakes ran high, and they usually did when Barrett was present.

Barrett had spent the night in every gaming hell in town looking for Fenwick. An hour ago he had discovered him here at White's. Barrett had been winning since he sat down, but his mind was not on the game. He couldn't get the princess out of his mind. Deep in thought, he tapped his finger against his crystal wine goblet. The high-pitched *ping* pierced the silence.

Fenwick glowered over at Barrett. "Stop that infernal noise. I can't concentrate."

Barrett toasted Fenwick with his glass, finished off the claret, then eyed his opponent over the top of his glass.

Lord Stockman spoke from the crowd, his deep baritone booming into the silence. "Balderdash, man! You don't need to concentrate on rolling the dice."

A peal of laughter went around the table.

Fenwick shot Stockman a look that could have curled the tips of his boots.

Too thick-skinned and arrogant to be bullied, the older gentleman puffed out his ruddy cheeks and crossed his arms over his protruding belly and stared back at Fenwick.

"Shall we up the stakes a bit on this roll?" Barrett asked, eager to be done with the whole business and his promise to James. All he wanted to do was put his energies into finding this mystic princess, who haunted his mind. He shoved the pile of chips before him out into the middle of the table.

Fenwick turned pale. "You can't bet that much. There's got to be fifty thousand pounds there."

"Too rich for your blood?" Barrett picked up his quizzing glass and eyed Fenwick through it. "Perhaps you should quit while you're ahead." Barrett lowered his gaze to the bare spot on the table before Fenwick, where only an hour ago it had held six columns of chips.

The disease of gambling exposed its harsher reality in Fenwick's eyes. He gaped at Barrett's mound of chips and licked his lips as if they were already his. "No, no. I'm sure I can win this time."

"What have you to bet?" Barrett dropped the monocle and stretched out his long legs beneath the table, crossing his ankles.

"I have my estate near Weymouth—that's worth a good thirty."

"What else?" Barrett asked, using his blandest tone.

Fenwick hedged and gripped the side of the table. "I have a small hunting lodge near Glasgow."

"I'll need something more. Property in Scotland isn't worth much these days."

Fenwick wiped his sweating brow with the back of his hand. "I'll throw in my sister's hand in marriage."

A wave of whispers broke out among the spectators:

"Ain't a reigning beauty, from what I hear."

"Heard tell she was so ugly her parents kept her locked up."

"Never seen the chit out in society."

"Wasn't it rumored she had some sort of skin disease that covered her body?"

"Heard she was a bluestocking."

"Got to be old-maid goods by now. What would Waterton want with her?"

Barrett wondered the very same thing, but he had learned never to give up any advantage over someone. James might find some use for the sister in plying the truth from Fenwick. Also she might be involved with the Devil's Advocates, a point James had failed to broach.

"Very well. Roll." Barrett motioned toward the dice.

Silence fell over the room. Stockman's stomach rumbled, melding with the sound of a waiter's wheezing breath.

Fenwick didn't take his eyes off the chips while he shook the dice. The crowd around the table leaned inward, their gaze on Fenwick's hand. Barrett kept his completely uninterested mien and picked off a piece of hair from his coat.

The dice hit the table.

Breath-stopping heaviness enveloped the silence.

Barrett gazed at the pair of sixes and a slow smile inched its way across his lips.

"Damn me, but he threw crabs." Stockman slapped

Barrett on the back. "Always knew you were a lucky bastard. Could have told him not to play against you. Blast me, they don't call you 'The Bear' for nothing. A fine joke, what. You being the richest of us all and always winning." He threw back his head and laughed.

Fenwick hadn't taken his eyes off the dice, his face twisted with disbelief and desolation. The hand that had thrown the dice was still frozen in place over the table.

Barrett usually enjoyed the excitement of gambling, but Fenwick had posed no challenge at all. He almost felt sorry for the puppy. Almost. Any gentleman who gambled away his last dime was a witless fish and deserved the hook in his mouth.

A waiter touched Fenwick's arm. "Can I get you something, sir?"

Fenwick shook his head, clearing the stunned expression from his face. He realized his awkward position and pulled back his hand; then he slid his fingers into his blond hair and rested his brow on his palms. In a barely audible voice, he said, "A scotch."

"Right away." The waiter bowed and left the circle of men.

Barrett could see the first rays of the rising sun gleaming through the windows in the room. "You can leave the marker at the desk." He took a step to leave, but Fenwick's voice stopped him.

"When do you wish to pay a call on my sister?"

"Perhaps this evening." Frowning, Barrett turned and strolled toward the door. The last thing he wanted to do was meet the sister. He had no intention of wasting his time with the sickly, reclusive old maid. Let James handle that end. Barrett had other fish to catch: the Winter Princess.

Outside, Barrett strode down the steps and onto the sidewalk. Brisk December air breezed across his face. Smoke spiraled from the ceaseless rows of chimneys rising up along the skyline. The aroma of fresh-baked bread drifted from a bakery across the street. His mouth watered, and he recalled he'd missed dinner last evening. He'd been busy at the Rawlings' ball, trying to find out the identity of the young lady who had so easily evaded him, but to no avail. Then he'd gone in search of Fenwick.

He headed toward his carriage, which was parked at the head of a long line of vehicles waiting in front of White's. Behind him, some of the other gentlemen were getting into their rigs.

"Barrett!"

He turned and saw James paying a cabby; then he hurried over to him. "Well, cousin, I thought I might find you here."

"Have you news?" James's eyes glistened with eagerness.

"He's ruined and at my mercy."

"I knew you could do it, and in such a short time. Now all we need is to squeeze him a little."

"Yes, well, I also have his sister's hand in marriage. You might be able to use that."

"Me?" James cocked a brow at Barrett, his dark eyes gleaming.

"Yes, you. I've done my duty."

"You can't quit now. I couldn't possibly bring in another man. You've got to see this thing through," James said, shooting Barrett a despairing look.

A deep scowl moved across Barrett's brow. After James's father's death five years ago, James had stepped into his position as head of the State Department's Secret Service. Since then, a dark, harsh side in him surfaced every now and then. Knowing James the way he did, Barrett was certain his cousin might be governed by that ruthless cunning side at the moment. But Barrett admired the work James did for his country and he couldn't bow out now. James knew that too.

In a skeptical tone, Barrett asked, "What do you want me to do?"

"Marry the sister."

Barrett paused and grasped the top of his cane. "You're not serious! I heard she was an old maid with a skin disease."

"I'm absolutely serious. It will provide the perfect cover to keep an eye on Fenwick and his sister."

"Do you suspect the sister is involved with the Devil's Advocates too?" Barrett couldn't keep the incredulous tone from his voice.

"I'm not sure. That's why I need you." James maintained his usual stoic expression—not a blink, not a movement of his brows, not a hint of emotion in his eyes.

"I still can't marry her. I have no intention of marrying anyone. You bloody well know how I feel about that."

"Still brooding over Lady Matilda, are we?" James looked askance at Barrett.

"I no longer think about her."

"I heard she's back from Bedlam."

Barrett remained silent, well aware of the news.

At Barrett's silence, James said, "You'll stay away from her if you know what's good for you."

"I have no intention of playing the fool as I did last time." Barrett wondered if the woman who had turned his heart to stone was cured or if her wealth had bought her release.

At Barrett's silence, James said, "You should think about setting up your nursery. You're three and thirty and you don't have an heir."

"I find it ludicrous that you counsel me on such things when you are three years my senior and have yet to tie the knot."

"I don't have a title, and I can't marry, not in my line of work." James sounded pleased by his fate. "Now will you help me get Fenwick or not?"

"Not if I have to marry the sister. When I decide upon a bride, she will be of my choosing, not a lady I have won in a game of hazard."

James thought a moment and rubbed his chin. "What if I arranged it so you do not have to marry the sister? Would you follow this through?"

"It all depends upon what you have in mind."

"Come. You can give me a ride to my office and I'll tell you what we have to do." James had the kind of face that never gave anything away. It was as opaque as a stone wall at the moment.

An image of the princess's dark eyes materialized in Barrett's mind. A frown moved across his brow. All last night he'd remembered her deep husky voice melting over him, her figure filling out the peasant dress, kissing her hand, running his lips over the soft warm skin. He pictured stripping off her clothes and veil, laying her across his satin sheets, and making love to her.

He realized his hunt for her identity would be hindered by this case. But no matter. When it came to acquiring things, he was a patient man. And he dearly loved a good chase.

Would he still want the princess when he caught her? His frown deepened at the thought. As with everything else in his life, it didn't take him long to grow bored with a mistress. He'd gone through two in the last year. He hoped, with the Winter Princess to warm his bed, he would find contentment for a while.

What time was it? Meagan stretched leisurely in her bed and glanced at the clock. Six. No matter how late Meagan went to bed, her internal clock woke her every morning at the same time. Not a minute past six. She listened to the chirping of sparrows outside her window and stretched, recalling the dream she'd had of the tall, blond lord with the piercing blue eyes. All night long, he'd held her, kissed her, and whispered sweet nothings in her ear.

She smiled at the memory. Reality set in and the smile faded. Up until meeting Lord Watt at the Christmas bazaar, she'd been perfectly content with her resolve. He made her aware of the loneliness in her life, no matter how hard she tried to erase it.

A ray of morning sun peeked in through the shutters and cut a swath over the edge of her dresser and across the door. For a moment, she frowned at the dust motes in the air; then she remembered the money. She gazed up at the canopy.

Her eyes widened. She flung back the covers and crawled over to the bed's edge. With trembling fingers, she touched the ruffle and the wide rectangular hole. Threads straggled down from the jagged material. She rubbed them between her fingers, hardly able to believe her eyes. A pit opened in her stomach, growing deeper and deeper by the second. If Harold had stabbed her in the back, she could not have felt any worse.

The sound of a carriage pulling up outside made her glance toward the window. When Harold gambled, he rarely returned home before morning.

The sight of the carriage prodded her into motion. She leaped out of bed and threw on her dressing gown. Male voices carried on the cold air outside. She hurried to the window and opened a shutter.

Two men paid a hack driver and waved to Harold, who was striding down the walk. Her brother's shoulders slouched. His pale face wore the same expression it had worn when he had lost the town house. To keep her hands from shaking, Meagan clenched her fists at her sides. Her gaze stayed glued on Harold while he waited for the two gentlemen to meet him. He didn't look at all pleased to see them.

Meagan had met the two gentlemen, who frequently

called on Harold. Mr. Walter Coburn, the younger of the two, had a thin face and droopy eyes. The other, Mr. Fields, looked about thirty. His brown hair, always slicked back with pomade, stuck to his head like a second skin. Both had cold eyes, and the look of men with a purpose and not an ounce of concern about how they accomplished it.

The two gentlemen followed Harold up the walkway toward the front door. Meagan bolted from her room and ran to the staircase. She took the steps two at a time, almost tripping over her gown. Their voices grew louder behind the door. The lock on the front door turned. Any moment they'd be inside the foyer . . .

CHAPTER FOUR

Meagan darted into an alcove beneath the stairs and heard the door creak open and shut. The men's footsteps clicked on the marble tiles in the foyer.

"My sister could come down at any moment," Harold said. "Let us go into the parlor. We can have some privacy there."

Meagan frowned and listened to their footsteps cross the foyer. She batted away a cobweb hanging from the molding along the alcove and peeked her head out into the hall. All clear. She eased out and crept down the hallway, her heart pounding in her chest. The floorboards creaked beneath her feet. Once. Twice. She froze near the entrance to the parlor and hoped the men hadn't heard her. The conversation continued:

"Can I get you anything to drink?" Harold asked.

"No, thank you. We just this minute left Brooks's and thought we'd catch you coming home." Mr. Coburn's deep voice had a hollow deadpan quality to it.

"How fortuitous," Harold said. "I was going to call on you later in the day."

"Were you?" Mr. Fields asked, an edge in his tone.

"Yes, gentlemen. I need to borrow two thousand."

"I'm afraid we cannot lend you any more, Fenwick. You already owe us twenty thousand pounds." Mr. Coburn sounded pleased.

Meagan clamped her hand over her mouth and stifled a gasp.

"What about a hundred then?" Harold asked, desperation in his voice.

A long pause. Meagan imagined Mr. Coburn and Mr. Fields were probably sharing a sly glance.

Mr. Fields finally spoke. "We'll see what we can do, but we need your help now."

"For what?"

"You've been one of us for six months now. It's time you proved your worth as a member," Mr. Coburn said.

"What do you want me to do?" Harold asked, his voice quavering slightly.

"We've gotten word from our leader. Our next target is a government official. We're all in on this one," Mr. Fields said, a threat in his voice directed at Harold.

"But—"

"No buts, Fenwick," Mr. Fields said. "You knew when you entered the fold that you had to follow the rest of the sheep."

"I never dreamed you'd be doing something like this," Harold cried.

"Damn it, man! Did you think we were a ladies' sewing circle? We're not called the Devil's Advocates for nothing."

"I know, but—"

"You're in, Fenwick. And let me remind you: There are an awful lot of hungry wolves out there looking for stray sheep," Mr. Coburn said.

Meagan's skin crawled at the menace in his voice. She bit her thumb and cringed in fear.

"Meet us at Hyde Park in two weeks. We'll have word by then on how to proceed."

Chairs creaked as the two men rose to leave.

Meagan turned and sneaked back down the hall, carefully avoiding the creaky floorboard. Her heart pounding in her chest, she darted back beneath the alcove.

"Good day to you both," Harold said and closed the door.

Before it latched completely, Meagan darted down the hallway and stood behind Harold. He turned and started. "Good God, Meagan! What the hell are you doing, sneaking up on me like that?"

"I don't think I'm the sneak in this family." She scowled at him and crossed her arms over her chest.

"I can explain about the money."

"There is no need for explanation—we both know what you did with it." Meagan lost control and blurted, "How could you? That money didn't belong to me. It belongs to the society. It was for charity. You had no right to take it!"

"I thought I could double it." He couldn't look her in the eye, so he stared down at the floor.

"Yes, you always think that."

"I'll pay it back."

"Not with the help of those horrible men who just left here. You already owe them twenty thousand pounds." The blood drained from Meagan's face when she thought of what a vast fortune that was.

"You eavesdropped on our conversation?" Harold's eyes widened in disbelief.

"I'm glad I did. How could you become indebted to those horrible men? Don't you see they are using your debt to force you to do terrible things? I knew the moment

I met them there was something wicked about those two. You cannot think to help them murder someone."

"You misunderstood." Harold forced his gaze up to meet her eyes, but the lie he'd just told her was evident in his expression. "They have these initiations and they make it seem as if you kill someone. You didn't think that they would, did you? It's all a joke, Meggie."

"It didn't sound that way to me." Meagan gave him a pointed look.

"It was."

"I don't care. I don't trust them. You must pay them off and get out of that club before it's too late."

"I can't. We're . . ." His words trailed off and his expression took on a tortured look.

"What? Tell me."

"We're under the hatches at the moment."

"We still have Fenwick Hall. You can take a loan out on the property."

Harold flinched as if her words had struck him. His dark gold brows made a straight line over his eyes. He leaned back and slumped against the door, speechless.

"Oh, no! Tell me you didn't lose my home. It belonged to me. My God! Papa knew I'd never marry and he put it in a trust for me. You gambled away something that didn't belong to you!" She wanted to pummel him with her fists. Instead, she grabbed his arms and shook him. "Tell me you didn't lose it! Tell me!"

He gazed up at her. He didn't have to utter a word; the answer shown on his face.

Meagan's knees grew weak. She dropped her hands and staggered away from him. Her back connected with the stair railing, and she gripped it to steady herself.

"I can explain." Harold gazed at her with pleading in his brown eyes.

Meagan stared straight at him, unable to find a drop of sympathy in her heart for him. "No, you can't explain.

You're sick. And because of your disease, we've lost everything. How could you be so selfish? How could you gamble away my home? Our livelihood? Did you not stop to think of me at all? Where shall I live?" Meagan sighed, then said, "I suppose I can live in the hunting lodge."

"You can't."

Meagan lost the thin hold on her temper. She flew at him and beat his chest with her fists. "That was where we always spent Christmas! We had so many memories there! I wanted to go there this year!" Her words became choked behind a lump in her throat. She stopped pounding Harold's chest and his face melted and ran behind her tears.

Her fondest memories of her father took place in that lodge. After her mother passed away from consumption five years ago, her father had lived only two years. For Meagan, those were the happiest two Christmases she'd spent in her life. Her mother could never come to terms with the fact her only child had a skin imperfection, and it had built a hidden wall of tension between them. Without that constant tension, Meagan had relaxed around her father. They had grown close before he died from the same disease that had taken her mother. All she had now were the memories of the lodge.

Before she said something she would regret the rest of her life, she started back up the stairs. "I'm going home to Fenwick Hall."

"You can't. It doesn't belong to us anymore."

She paused and dug her nails into the oak banister. "Until the owner comes to claim it, I'm going to stay there." She took another step, but Harold's voice stopped her.

"You can't leave. I've given your hand in marriage to the new owner of Fenwick Hall. You have to stay here and be courted by him."

She wheeled around, her face burning with indignation. "You had no right to do that without consulting me—

especially not to a gambling man I already despise for claiming our home in a bet." Her whole body shook, and she was forced to grip the stair railing tighter.

"It doesn't matter whether you approve of his character or not. He's rich—that's all that matters. As you know, Meagan, marriages are arranged. It's the way it's done. I was thinking of your welfare when I gave him your hand."

"Of course you were," she said, her voice filled with contempt.

They eyed each other in silence. She didn't have to say what she thought. They both knew he'd given her hand away because he'd had nothing else to wager. Unable to meet her gaze any longer, he frowned and glanced at her chin.

A perverse streak shot through Meagan, and she broke the stillness. "I don't care how it came about. I shall never marry the gentleman and that is final."

Harold jerked his hands through his blond hair as if to pull it out. "You will marry him. You have no choice."

"I have Lochlann."

"If he wanted you, he would have asked for your hand a long time ago. He'll never look on you as anything more than a friend."

"Because he is my friend, he'll never let you get away with this."

"He has no say in the matter. Until you turn one and twenty, I'm your legal guardian. You'll do as I order you."

"Thank God in two months I will turn of age. Then you will have no say so over me."

Harold's expression hardened into an unyielding mask. "Until then, I'm still your guardian."

"Some guardian you have been, losing my inheritance and forcing me to marry a stranger."

"He's one of the richest and most powerful men in London," Harold said, his contriteness melting beneath his anger. "You can't refuse him. You're damned lucky I

got him for you. You have very little dowry, no title, and—
let's face it—you're almost on the shelf. You're not much
of a prize with your nose always stuck in a book. What man
wants a bluestocking for a wife?''

Meagan flinched as if his words had stung her.

Oblivious to the pain he'd caused, he continued. ''You
have to marry Waterton—if he'll have you. If you become
his wife you'll have everything you've ever wanted in your
life.''

Her mouth dropped open at the name Waterton. She
recovered from the shock, clenched her jaw, and spoke
through her teeth. ''Is it the same Marquess of Waterton
I read about in the society columns?''

''The very same.'' Harold beamed with pride over his
catching Meagan such a treasure of a man.

''Why, he's a heartless rogue. A horrible beast! He's so
wretched he's acquired the nickname 'The Bear.' Why,
the rumors run rampant of his infamous duels. And they
always involve some gentleman's wife or sister. Just two
days ago at the Royal Society I heard two gentlemen dis-
cussing how Waterton snubbed Lord Dennison in a club
because he'd dueled with him earlier in the week. Now
people will not allow poor Dennison into their homes. It
is ludicrous. Waterton does whatever he likes because he's
rich and powerful. Yet his victims pay the price.''

''You don't know the particulars. I know Dennison. He's
not such a fine fellow himself.''

''I know what I've heard, and I despise the man. I'd
rather be a bone picker or a rag gatherer and live on
the streets than marry such a man.'' Meagan turned and
stomped up the steps.

''You will marry him! I'll make you!''

''You can try,'' Meagan said under her breath, feeling
the perverse streak in her getting wider by the moment.
Somehow she had to get home to Lochlann, her only
friend in the world. He would save her.

* * *

That evening Meagan sat in her chamber, knotting together the sheets that she'd taken off her bed. Her head perked up at the sound of loud voices echoing below in the foyer. They were muffled, but she could hear the anger in the voices. How she wished Lochlann were here. He would know how to get her out of this debacle.

A soft rap sounded at the door.

Meagan picked up the sheets to shove them beneath the bed.

"It's only me, my lady."

At the sound of Tessa's muffled voice, Meagan breathed a sigh of relief and hurried over to the door. She heard the key turn in the lock. Earlier Harold had locked Meagan in her room when she had tried to leave.

The door cracked open and Tessa peeked inside. "I got to hurry, or the master'll catch me. Here"—she handed Meagan a small bundle—"them's boys clothes. I borrowed 'em off the line from next door." Tessa's face reddened at her confession and she continued. "I thought you needed a different look when he came searching for you. I got a cabby like you said. He's waiting near the alley— Oh, and Reeves is all bent up stiff. Says he's comin' with us. He ain't staying here and taking care of his lordship." At Meagan's frown, she added, "You know he's never accepted him as the master, and after learning that he'd lost everything, well, Reeves is in a dreadful mope."

"Poor Reeves. Of course he can come with me, but you'll have to make sure he gets to the carriage."

"I will," Tessa said in her mother-hen tone. "And now's the time to go away from here. That Mrs. Pool and her husband are below stairs, looking for the money your brother stole. He's down there making up some lie." Tessa frowned.

"I shan't be able to hold my head up if word gets out. I've got to get that money back."

"Don't worry. Your friend, Mr. Burrows, will loan it to you."

"Of course, you are correct. I can ask Lochlann for a loan." The worried frown on Meagan's face dissolved.

They heard the door slam in the foyer, then Harold's footsteps on the stairs.

"Oh, no! He's coming. He'll check on the door."

"Lock it then. I'll find a way out."

Meagan quickly eased the door closed.

The key grated in the lock. Then the floorboards creaked as Tessa sneaked down the hall.

Meagan snatched up the bundle of clothes. In her haste to disrobe, she ripped the buttons off the back of her dress and tore her petticoat. The boy's pants and shirt were too tight, and she could hardly get them buttoned. She slipped into an old three-quarter-length coat that must have belonged to Reeves. The sleeves hung down past her hands. After rolling them up, she stuffed her hair beneath a cap and ran to the fireplace. She rubbed charcoal on her cheeks to complete her disguise.

Knock. Knock.

Harold banged so loud he rattled the door on its hinges.

Meagan froze. "Go away," she called, grabbing the end of the sheets and tying it to the bedpost.

"I need to speak to you, Meggie." He turned the key in the lock.

"Do not come in here! I don't want to see you! You have some nerve wanting to see me after locking me in here all afternoon." She snatched up a candlestick from the mantel and hurled it at the door.

It crashed against the oak, fell, and rolled next to the leg of her dresser.

"I did it for your own good. You're going to marry Waterton whether you like it or not!"

Meagan grabbed up a vase this time and flung it. It hit the door. Glass spewed out into the room and rained down on the floor and carpet.

Meagan hoped that might keep her brother out, but in case it didn't, she said, "I swear, if you come in here, I'll hurt you!" She ran over and grabbed the sheets, flinging the loose end out the open window.

"Very well. I'll wait until you calm down. But we have to discuss this. Lord Waterton sent a note around earlier today saying he'd be here at seven o'clock to meet you. You'll come down and receive him and be pleasant."

"Oh, yes, I'll be pleasant indeed." Meagan glanced at the mantel clock. It read quarter to seven. She darted over to the bed and pulled out a small valise that held a few of her clothes in it. To drive Harold farther away, she said, "Shall I beg him for the hundred pounds that belonged to the society's Christmas fund? I suppose Mrs. Pool is ready to hang me for thievery."

"I'll get that money back. You just make sure you're ready to receive Waterton. You've got ten minutes. If you're not presentable and out of there, I'll drag you out." Harold banged his fist one last time against the door. Then his muffled footsteps threaded down the hallway.

Relief flooded her. She slipped a scarf through the handle of the valise and tied it to her waist; then she headed for the window and opened the sash. Cold December air seared her face and lungs. Thousands of stars winked in the crisp dark sky overhead. She gazed at the ground, a good twenty-five feet below her. Stiffening her spine and her determination, she drew her legs up, grabbed the sheet, and eased herself out the window.

A few blocks away Barrett had his nose buried in the *Times* while sitting inside his carriage. The boon of owning a custom-built coach of his own design with the best springs made was that Barrett could read with a minimal amount of bouncing. Still, he couldn't keep his mind on the day's news. He wanted to be done with this introduction to Fenwick's sister so he could turn his attention toward finding the Winter Princess.

Nuisance, the mongrel Barrett had rescued, let out a staccato bark.

Barrett snapped down his paper. The dog hung out the window, his paws over the edge, his body convulsing with each bark.

"What is it this time, boy?" Barrett looked askance at the nerve-racking mutt. The whole ride, Nuisance had yipped at every carriage and person on the street, giving voice to his territorial instincts and generally living up to the name Barrett had chosen for him.

Over the top of Nuisance's furry head, Barrett glimpsed a dark figure running down an alley. It looked like a young boy with a satchel in his hands. No doubt one of the many footpads who prowled London.

"So it really is something this time." Barrett rapped three times on the ceiling's coach with his cane.

The carriage rocked to a halt.

Nuisance leaped out of the window, his incessant barking never missing a note.

"Idiotic canine," Barrett muttered, wondering if the dog had hurt himself.

Before the footmen could open the door, Barrett bolted out of the carriage and ran after Nuisance, who didn't seem at all in pain from his fearless leap. The animal darted past a hack parked near the street and raced down the alley, baying as if he were a bull mastiff on the scent.

When the thief spotted the dog and Barrett, he ran harder, his short legs pumping, his arms pushing.

"You there! Halt!" Barrett yelled over Nuisance's continuous yapping.

The young boy increased his pace.

Barrett decided he'd had enough of this waste of time. He passed Nuisance and came up behind the thief. The thrill of the chase made his heart pound and brought a smile to his lips. He lunged and grabbed the boy's arm.

Barrett pulled the thief around to face him. Dodging the little thief's fists, he easily captured the boy's arms at his sides. In the struggle the boy's cap slipped off. Long sable curls tumbled down around small shoulders, outlining a perfect feminine face. Enough moonlight shone for Barrett to see violet eyes and wide plump lips. The face was dirty, but there was no mistaking those eyes. He'd found his princess.

CHAPTER FIVE

"Get your dog off me," the princess cried, shaking her leg.

Barrett had been so overwhelmed by finding her, he hadn't noticed Nuisance's muffled growling. The pestering scamp had a death grip on the lady's pant leg, his head shaking as he tried to tear it to shreds.

"That is enough out of you, sir. Behave like a gentleman or go back to the carriage."

Nuisance instantly released the material and crouched back a step.

"Thank you." Her voice, breathless from running, had an excited husky quality to it that touched every nerve in Barrett's body.

"My pleasure," he said, gazing at her lips, watching her breath condense in the cold air. Each one of her hot breaths tantalized his face and neck as he held her close.

She warily glanced past Barrett's shoulder and tried to jerk out of his grasp. "I really have to go."

"I can't let you go now that I've found you again."

Barrett tightened his hold around her waist. "What is the matter? Why are you dressed like a boy and walking the streets alone at night? Tell me. I want to help you."

"I don't have time to get into it at the moment. If you would just let me go."

Nuisance barked.

Before Barrett could turn around, something struck the back of his head. Through a foggy blur, he made out the battle-ax of a maid with a board in her hand. Then everything went blank.

As he collapsed, Meagan held her breath and watched him. "Geminy, Tessa. You've killed him."

When Tessa saw who'd she'd hit, the board in her hand began to tremble. "Dear Lord! I thought he was attacking you."

Meagan's heart pounded as she dropped to her knees and felt his neck. Her fingers found the steady pulse in his neck, and she let out the breath she'd been holding. "He's alive."

"Thank the good Lord." Tessa tossed the board aside.

Meagan felt his head for injuries. "There's a big lump here, but no blood." Unable to pull away just yet, she ran her fingers over his soft flaxen hair, then along his cheek. Coarse brown stubble brushed her skin and sent a tingle up her arm as she said, "I'm sure he'll be fine."

Tessa sighed loud with relief.

Reeves petted the dog and stopped him from barking; then he staggered up to them and squinted. "We'd better go."

"Meagan!" Harold's voice echoed from the garden in back of their town house.

Tessa cried, "Oh, no, my lady! 'Tis the master. He knows we've gone. He'll find us for sure."

"Not if I can help it." Meagan cast one last glance at Lord Watt sprawled out on the cobblestones in his fine clothes, his white cravat and golden hair stark in the moonlight. It was a pity, but he would wake with a blistering headache. The idea of leaving Lord Watt wounded in the alley didn't sit well with her conscience, but some things couldn't be helped. What was he doing in this area anyway? Most likely visiting a mistress.

Her last thought lessened her guilt. She grabbed the cap that had fallen off her head, stuffed her hair beneath it, then ran and put her arm around Reeves's thin waist. "Come on."

"Hurry, my lady." Reeves squinted at her and tried to move as fast as he could, which was only a slow lope.

"Meagan!" Harold's voice grew angrier. The door to the garden creaked open.

Tessa took Reeves's arm and together they managed to guide the elderly man down the alley at a fast clip while staying in the shadows. Before they reached the entrance, two tall burly men in yellow livery came running up the alley.

"Now we're done for," Tessa mumbled. "They must be Lord Watt's servants. I'll surely go to jail for hitting him."

"No, you won't," Meagan whispered. "I'll head them off. We'll meet at the cab. Go that way. . . . "

Meagan shoved Tessa and Reeves through an opening into one of their neighbors' gardens. Two large hedges stood on either side of the gate, and she wasn't sure if the men had seen Tessa and Reeves. But she was sure they had spotted her. They ran straight at her.

She turned and darted down the alley back toward the house, hurtling past Lord Watt, who was still sprawled in the alley. His little dog jumped back and barked, but didn't follow her.

"You there! Stop!" one of the servants yelled.

She ran faster, her heart pounding in her ears. She chanced a quick glance over her shoulder and saw only one man behind her. The other man must have paused in the chase to see to his master. The man pursuing her gained on her. Any moment he would grab her.

Abruptly Harold darted out of the shadows. "Hey, you little urchin! Stop!" He lunged at her and snagged her arm.

She used her momentum to reel around Harold's back; then she shoved her brother at the man on her heels. The two men collided and tumbled to the ground like falling dominoes. Meagan stumbled a few steps, but kept her balance.

Loud groans and curses rang in her ears as she darted through a neighbor's yard. Past a line of boxwoods. Down a small path that ran between two row houses. This brought her back out on Fenchurch Street. She ran between another set of row houses and onto an adjacent street.

Finally she slowed down, with her breath coming in great gasps. She felt a stitch in her side, but she kept moving. She listened for footsteps, but heard none.

Lights burned in some of the windows. She remembered it must be seven, but it seemed like midnight. Dried leaves on the sidewalk crunched beneath her feet. Several bats swooped overhead; the flutter of their wings was barely audible.

Meagan reached the corner. Carriages and riders passed her in a steady stream. It seemed the traffic on London's main thoroughfares never slowed. She scanned the street for Tessa and Reeves, but she didn't see a hack anywhere. She saw only a black lacquered carriage and four with postilions in smart yellow livery and a lion crest emblazoned on the door.

She frowned. Something about the crest reminded her of Lord Watt. Perhaps it was his golden mane of hair that made her think of a lion. The carriage was parked near the entrance to the alley—a sure sign it belonged to Lord Watt. Her brows met over her nose in worry as she turned and hurried down the street in the opposite direction.

Abruptly, a cab pulled out of the flow of traffic and up to the curb. Moonlight illuminated the driver—a burly man with a cigar hanging from one side of his mouth. The whip in his hand snaked over the backs of two boney horses. The driver eyed Meagan; then his lips parted in a wide toothless grin.

She took a cautious step back, ready to run should the need arise, but Tessa stuck her head out the window and waved to Meagan.

Sighing with relief, she ran over and hopped inside. Stale perfume and unwashed bodies lingered inside the cab. She grimaced and collapsed next to Reeves.

"I see you got away from them, miss," Tessa said, sounding relieved. She opened her mouth to say more, but the carriage sped out into the street, knocking her back against the squab. "Ah! The rottiver! I could teach him a thing or two about driving."

Meagan knew better than to inquire, but Reeves's sense of the ridiculous made him ask, "Pray, what is a rottiver?" Reeves clutched the seat with his trembling hands to keep from being thrown from the seat. "I've lived for eighty years, and I've never heard such a word."

"Rotten driver."

"A very economical term." Reeves nodded in approval at Tessa while his ancient skin stretched in a smile.

Tessa turned to Meagan. "Where shall we stay? The master will surely find us if we go home."

"We'll stay at the inn in Weymouth until I speak to Lochlann."

"I would hurry 'cause the master will surely be on our tails." Tessa paused, then brushed back a lock of hair that had fallen from her mobcap. She said her next words with a hint of disgust. "That Lord Watt ain't likely to give up either. Mark my words, he'll find you. I bet he was on his way to see you when he spotted you."

Meagan had a feeling Tessa was correct. She remembered asking him to let her go and feeling his strong arms tighten around her waist. He wanted the mysterious fortune-teller, not the real Meagan. The part of her that was attracted to him wanted to see him again, yet there was another part that knew she could never measure up to the image of the mysterious Winter Princess. It would be better to go home and forget him.

She had other things to occupy her mind, like avoiding this horrible marriage Harold felt determined to thrust on her. A frown moved across her brow as she leaned back against the squab and let out a long breath.

Barrett couldn't believe his luck. His princess was kissing him. All over his face. Running her warm moist tongue over his nose, his chin, his cheeks, along his lips. He reached for her.

His fingers connected with her hair. Short. Wiry. Thin. He cracked open an eye . . .

A small black nose filled his vision. Whiskers. Round brown eyes peeked out behind clumps of gray hair. *Nuisance.*

"Bloody hell!" he murmured and shoved the dog away from his face. He clutched his pounding head.

"You all right, me lord?"

Stratton, one of his footmen, hovered over him. He grabbed Barrett's arm and helped him to stand. Barrett fought a wave of dizziness and said, "Never mind that, man. Did you see where she went?" Grimacing, Barrett wiped the dog kisses off his mouth with the back of his hand; then he felt the egg-size lump on the back of his head.

"Ran that way, me lord." Stratton pointed down the alley. "Hastings let her get away."

Hastings, who'd come walking up the alley, turned on

his fellow worker and snarled, "That's a lie. You let her get away."

"Did not!"

"Did!"

"You ran after her."

"Yeah, but she slipped through your hands like a greased pig."

"Enough." At Barrett's tightly coiled tone, both men clamped their mouths shut. "I hold you both equally responsible."

Stratton's brows furrowed. Then he blurted, "Pardon me speaking, me lord, but we shouldn't be blamed. We saw you talking to the miss and thought we shouldn't be intrudin'. Next time we checked, we saw you lyin' out flat and her running away. I figured she robbed you and ran. I stopped to see if you were dead and Hastings took after her."

"With the salary I pay both of you, the bloody least you could do is catch a scrap of a woman." Barrett gave them a cold stare. He was in no mood for excuses. His gaze shifted to Nuisance. "You could have earned your keep and followed her."

Nuisance cocked one ear as if he couldn't understand why he was being scolded.

"Waterton, are you all right?" Fenwick came striding toward him, his round face showered by moonlight.

"Quite. The only thing smarting is my pride." Barrett brushed the dirt off his coat and straightened his cravat.

"Can't believe you were accosted right in my own backyard," Fenwick muttered, brushing off his own coat. "We tried to stop the thief, but he got away."

"It was no thief, nor a male. She was a lady, and I met her at a Christmas bazaar." Barrett saw Fenwick flinch when he mentioned the bazaar. "Do you know a beautiful young woman with long sable hair, violet eyes, and rounded curves? She has a maid who would make an excellent infantry sergeant."

Fenwick's brows snapped together. In a tone laced with a taut edge, he said, "I'm sorry. We only moved into this area a month ago. We haven't really met all the neighbors."

"A pity. I was positive you knew her."

Fenwick was lying through his teeth. Most likely the woman was his mistress. But why had the lady been dressed like a boy? Probably to escape Fenwick and his cruel treatment of her. Barrett's fists tightened at his sides. It was all he could do not to grab Fenwick. But losing his patience might jeopardize the case, so he relaxed his fists.

"No, I don't." Fenwick said. "Perhaps it was just a coincidence she was here in my neighborhood. Perhaps the lady enjoys masquerading on the streets." Fenwick frowned.

"You may have a point, but she might still be hiding around here." Barrett faced his servants. "Stratton. Hasting. I want you to comb the neighborhood. I want her found."

"Aye, me lord." Hasting bowed. Then both men hurried off down the alley, grumbling about who'd let her get away.

"We'll wait at your home, Fenwick. And we can get the introduction to your sister out of the way."

Fenwick hedged and ran his hands through his hair as if to pull it out. Finally, he said, "I'm afraid I can't do that."

"Why?"

"She left for Fenwick Hall earlier."

"A bit reluctant, is she?" Barrett cocked a brow at him, sure that the sister had never been in London. If the sister was as ugly and deformed as the gossip Barrett had heard at the club, he doubted Fenwick would have let the lady come to town.

The side of Fenwick's cheek twitched nervously. "Oh, no. She is just shy. She has lived her life more or less like a recluse and doesn't take well to strangers."

"I do so love a challenge. Your sister has my interest piqued." Barrett's monotone belied his words. He didn't give a blink about the sister. He wanted the princess. "We shall go to Fenwick Hall directly to meet your sister. I have to survey my new property anyway."

Fenwick frowned at him. "May I ask a personal question?"

"It all depends on what it is." A dark object near a fence caught Barrett's eye, and he studied it.

"Are you seriously considering marrying my sister?"

"You wagered her hand, did you not?"

"But I never thought for a moment you'd marry her," Fenwick said more to himself than to his companion. Then he gave Barrett his full attention. "I have to be honest with you. She's never had a come-out and she has no connections. She also lacks a dowry."

"The usual conventions do not govern me, Fenwick. I keep them only if it pleases me," Barrett said with derision in his voice. He had to force out his next words. "All that matters to me in finding a wife is that she and I can abide well together. I'm sure your sister will do as well as any lady. Now please excuse me." Barrett strode over to the object he'd been eyeing. He bent over and picked up a valise with tapestry sides. It was definitely a lady's bag. He opened it and pulled out a lady's silk handkerchief.

"By Jove! Look at that. Someone left her clothes out here." Fenwick didn't sound at all surprised as his eyes shifted to Barrett.

"Not just someone. A *princess*." Barrett frowned and ran his fingers over the fine silk. He was convinced now the woman was Fenwick's mistress—a fact James had failed to mention at the bazaar. Barrett just needed to gain Fenwick's confidence and have him open up about his relationship with her. Then he'd find her and keep her safe from Fenwick.

CHAPTER SIX

Two hours later, Barrett sat in his coach next to James, feeling the silk handkerchief in his coat pocket and brooding over the fact that he hadn't been able to get Fenwick to talk about his mistress. Fenwick had the gall to even deny having a mistress.

James glanced over at Nuisance, who had his head on Barrett's knee. "Where did you find that bone gnawer?" he asked, grinning.

"Actually, he found me."

James's artful smile gave nothing away and it never touched his eyes. "You may appear a cynic to the world, but in actuality you're a sentimentalist. For as long as I can remember, you've never been able to resist a stray."

Barrett patted Nuisance's small head. "Thank you for analyzing my character so succinctly. But what about you? Are you as calculating and self-possessed as you seem? I haven't yet found a soft spot in you, but I'm sure one exists. Haven't you ever picked up any strays in your life?"

"Once." James grew silent as if he regretted his rare moment of candor.

"Oh, yes. I'd forgotten about your little spy, Lady Jaques."

"I really don't wish to discuss her. She's dead now."

"Dead? How?" Barrett's brows furrowed.

"She was shot crossing the border of France."

"I didn't know. I'm—"

"For God's sake, leave it alone. She's been dead a year. It's a closed book, so let's just drop it." James lapsed into silence, his expression as cryptic as ever.

Barrett glanced at James's profile. He had harbored suspicions James might have been in love with the lady, but he'd never been certain of it. James rarely spoke of Lady Jaques. And she had been shot in the line of duty. Surely James blamed himself for her death. He was the type of man who felt responsible for the lives of those who worked beneath him—especially those he loved.

A long silence stretched between them, the creak of the carriage and the rhythmic pounding of the horses' hooves the only sound filling the carriage.

After several miles, James moved and broke the stillness. He leaned past the heater in the carriage and poured himself a glass of claret from the dry bar. "This is the way to travel. You have all the comforts of home here. As a matter of fact, it's like being in the royal palace." He leaned back against the plush velvet squabs, sipped his wine, and smiled up at the cherubs painted on the gilded ceiling.

"Yes, it has all the luxuries, but it cannot take us to Fenwick Hall any faster than an ordinary hackney." A frown drew Barrett's brows together.

"You needn't scowl. We'll have this business over and done with soon enough." James yawned and pulled out his watch. "Eleven o'clock. You realize we may be rousing your bride from her bed."

"I want it settled and over with. Are you sure that Hibbert fellow knows what he's supposed to do?"

"Of course. He's one of my finest men. He's played the part of a clergyman many times." James took another sip and eyed Barrett over the top of the glass.

"And you are sure that we will not be married?"

"Positive. Hibbert is not a minister. All you need do is play the role of a husband—"

"And not consecrate the marriage and ruin the lady's honor," Barrett finished for him and frowned.

"Correct. Which shouldn't be so hard, come to think of it. All you need do is act your normal arrogant self around the lady." At Barrett's scowl, James smiled and continued. "And if she does succumb to your charms, you can stay in separate rooms and give her some excuse that prevents you from doing the dirty."

"I'm sure I'll have no trouble staying away from her." Barrett shot his cousin a baleful glance. He thought of the princess again and wanted to ask James about her, but he knew he'd get no help in that quarter.

James downed the rest of his wine. "Is Fenwick absolutely sure she will be there?"

"Ask him yourself when we stop at the next coaching inn." Barrett waved toward the carriage that followed them.

"If he had ridden with us, we might have been able to ply information out of him."

"I've found it will take more than a few hours in a coach with Fenwick to get him to disclose what he knows. Perhaps Hibbert can glean information from him."

"Has Fenwick lied to you about something?" James cocked a brow at Barrett.

"Yes, but I'll get the truth out of him sooner or later."

"I've no doubt you shall."

As usual Barrett had a hard time reading James's expression. Barrett thought he saw the barest hint of a smirk on his cousin's lips. Obviously his cousin knew the princess was Fenwick's mistress, and Barrett discovering this information entertained him. Barrett didn't find it the least bit amusing, but he wouldn't let James know that.

Ten miles away, Meagan strode past a small pond, listening to the night insects. Moonlight glistened along the surface like thousands of sapphires. A thin haze of fog seeped over the banks and just touched the edge of the water. Off in the distance the brick gables and Flemish lines of Oakwell Hall touched the edges of the moon behind it.

Closer to the house, a nighthawk screeched overhead in a willow. She grinned, remembering the ride home from London.

When they had left London, all the seats had been taken. Since Meagan had been dressed like a boy, the driver had stuck her on the roof. Tessa and Reeves had offered to ride up top, but Meagan, younger and better able to stand the cold, wouldn't hear of it. And if she wanted to travel incognito, she would also have had to act the part of a boy.

Never having ridden atop a post chaise, Meagan felt it was a reckless experience she would treasure, yet one she would not readily repeat. Most of the ten-hour journey from London she'd spent hanging on for dear life and listening to the driver and guard yelling in her ear. Her ears still rang.

Or was the bottle of brandy the driver had passed around responsible for the ringing? Meagan had refused the first offer. But after the first hour, she had felt chilled to the bone, so she'd accepted the fiery liquid, hoping it would keep her warm. She couldn't remember how many times they'd passed around the bottle, but by the time they reached home, Meagan felt a warm glow all the way to her toes.

She recalled staggering off the carriage, her voice raised in a bawdy song with the driver and guard. Tessa had berated Meagan all the way to the Weymouth Inn, which had sobered Meagan. But perhaps not enough.

She hummed that ditty now and trod up a paved walk, past a garden where, as a child, she had slain dragons, trounced pirates, and slaughtered many a Frenchmen with Lochlann. Though Lochlann was five years her senior, they had played well together, better than she and Harold.

She stopped humming and gazed out over the rows of manicured boxwoods, the fountain with Cupid in the center, and the row of yews on either side that made great lookouts to spy on pirates and dragons and Napoleon. Every time she passed this garden, she couldn't help but long for her childhood. And never more so than now since Harold was in trouble with some horrible men and he'd gambled away everything. Even her.

A few moments later, Meagan stood beneath Lochlann's chamber window. She didn't hesitate in grasping the trunk of an ancient English oak and climbing it. Spaced like steps on a ladder, the thick boughs made the going easy.

In no time she reached Lochlann's chamber window. He was a hot-blooded creature who always slept with his window open.

The blurry reflection of her face slithered across the windowpanes. Her cheeks were still covered with soot. Wisps of hair fell from beneath her cap. Perhaps she should have listened to Tessa and changed before she came here, but she had to speak to her friend. She shoved up the sash and slid inside.

Thump. Her feet hit the floor louder than she'd expected. She glanced at the bed. Enough moonlight pierced the chamber to illuminate the bed. Lochlann hadn't moved. He was lying on his belly, his feet dangling from beneath the covers. His bare arms were poised at odd angles near his body. A pillow covered his head.

Meagan tiptoed over, bent, and peeked beneath the pillow. "Lochlann," she whispered.

He didn't move.

"Lochlann." Meagan shoved his arm.

Not a muscle twitched.

"Lochlann." She shook him again.

He mumbled something unintelligible.

Meagan picked up the pillow and hit him with it several times.

He started awake and grabbed her arms.

"It's me. Meagan. You're hurting me." Meagan winced as she felt his fingers digging into her skin.

He dropped her arms and blinked at her. "What are you doing here? I thought you were in London." Looking uncomfortable at being caught in bed, Lochlann turned over and pulled the covers up around his chest.

Meagan stared at his dark curls sticking out all over his head and rubbed her bruised arms. "Oh, it was horrible. You just don't know what has happened." She plopped down on the edge of the bed.

"It must be something deuced wretched. You smell drunk."

"How does someone smell drunk?" Meagan leveled an indignant look at him.

"Good question. Let me clarify. You smell like a tavern wench who has helped herself to the stock."

"Yes, well, I have a good reason for the way I smell."

"Harold should never have forced you to go to London. I suppose it didn't go well." Lochlann leaned back against the headboard. He clasped his hands over his chest and waited patiently for her explanation, his pewter eyes gleaming at her from the shadows.

"It was dreadful." Meagan relayed everything that had happened, including the part about Harold being involved in the Devil's Advocates. She left out being attracted to Lord Watt and the way he made her nerve endings purr when she was near him. She ended by saying, "I just can't marry a man I already despise."

"You shouldn't have to." Lochlann patted her arm and grew incensed on her behalf. "I've heard of that Waterton fellow. He's a cad—a bounder with no principles but the ones he makes for himself."

"Quite right! You remember that day you came to me after your parents had that terrible row and your father struck your mother. Remember how we made a pact that day never to marry unless we love the person."

"Yes," Lochlann said, his tone pensive and faraway.

"I took that vow very seriously. I'll not marry a man I don't love. Anyway, I don't want to get married. I never wanted to marry. I'm happy with my life the way it is. I just want to be left alone to pursue my studies of the stars." An image rose up in her mind of a pair of piercing blue eyes, wide shoulders, and curling blond hair. Her last words had not been entirely true and she knew it, but she wouldn't admit it to Lochlann,

"You shouldn't give up hope of finding a gentleman who loves you, Meagan. You would make a fine mother. Mr. Wright is always telling me how good you are with the children at the school."

"He is just being kind." Mr. Wright was the elderly schoolmaster—a kinder, more considerate man did not exist. She helped him once a week at the school Lochlann had started to teach impoverished children how to read. Meagan admired Lochlann for his goodwill, but some of the other nearby landowners despised Lochlann for it. They believed the lower classes should be discouraged from learning to read; it only caused uprisings and strife.

"I'm sure he's not. He says he can hardly control the children when you come to give them their weekly lesson on the stars."

"They are easily excited over anything. They have little minds like traps. Some of them are so hungry for knowledge." Meagan's voice softened. "It breaks my heart to know that they have little more than the knowledge we impart to them."

"I would hate to lose your help at the school." Lochlann pulled himself straight up in bed. The covers fell, exposing his chest. He didn't notice as his expression grew determined. "I can't let Harold do this to you. I'll marry you before I'll let Waterton have you."

Meagan touched his arm. "I can't let you make that sacrifice. You don't love me, and you are supposed to marry your cousin."

"Nothing was ever signed, and I never once gave Lucinda any hint that I would wed her. No, I'll marry you."

"Would you do that for me, Lochlann?" Meagan felt a lump growing in her throat.

"Of course I would. We are friends." He reached out and squeezed her hand.

"I don't know what I would do without you. You were there with me through my whole childhood and my horrible condition." Meagan couldn't count the number of times she'd felt sorry for herself and cried on his shoulder. "You've been my strength for every catastrophe in my life. You are so good to me. I don't want you to have to make such a sacrifice. Perhaps we needn't make it binding. If this Waterton knows I'm already married, he'll leave me alone. In a few months we can get an annulment. But Fenwick Hall will be his. How I hate the thought of him owning my home."

"Don't worry. You can live here. And once we are married, we'll have no annulments."

"Thank you, Lochlann." Meagan threw her arms around his neck. "Do you think we can be happy as man and wife?"

"Of course." Lochlann pulled back and looked into her eyes. "I already love you, maybe not in the way a beau should, but I'm sure that will come."

For a moment, they gazed into each other's eyes. Lochlann bent toward her. Before his lips touched hers, Meagan pulled back. "I should go."

"Yes." He smiled reluctantly, showing his even white teeth.

Meagan had never looked at Lochlann with the eyes of a woman. His coal black hair curled around his long-jawed face. High cheekbones, a long Roman nose, and kind eyes added character to his features. Dark stubble covered his jaw. And she could see a dark mat of hair on his chest. Somehow he'd gone from gangly youth to handsome man without her noticing. But she still looked on him as a brother.

She stood and said, "I had better get back. Tessa is worried that she will be arrested for clubbing Lord Watt, and I left her and Reeves at the inn in the village."

"You should stay here. Harold might find you there."

"No, I tipped the innkeeper half a crown to remain silent."

"Very well. Make sure you are ready to leave for Gretna Green tomorrow night. I'll pick you up at the inn."

"I'll be ready."

"Let me dress and escort you to the inn."

"No, no, it's but half a mile. I'll be fine. The walk might do me good since I smell like a tavern wench." Meagan rolled her eyes, then turned toward the window.

"This room does have a door, you know," Lochlann said.

"Yes, but it's more fun this way." She shrugged and crawled out the window.

As she reached the ground, she realized the real reason she didn't want to kiss Lochlann. The romantic within her hadn't totally given up hope of finding a man who could accept and love her. It was a silly girlish hope. She should have given it up long ago. Now she would be marrying her best friend, kissing her best friend. She felt sure Lochlann loved her, but not in the way Meagan dreamed a husband should. When she thought of kissing someone it wasn't Lochlann, but Lord Watt. She wondered if she would ever get Lord Watt out of her mind.

The carriage rocked to a halt. Barrett glanced over at James, who jolted awake.

"Are we there?" James asked, blinking.

"I think not," Barrett remarked, using his cane to lift the leather window shade to peer out. The door to a small inn stood twenty feet from the carriage. Lights glowed from one of the windows, casting a globe of yellow light against the frosty glass panes.

Abruptly, the carriage door swung open and Fenwick appeared, his cheeks cherry colored from the cold.

"Why the devil have we stopped?" Barrett asked.

"I hope you don't mind. I had to use the privy."

"Where are we?" James asked, bending to peek out the window.

Fenwick waved his hand toward the inn behind him. "Weymouth."

A frown marred Barrett's brow. "Aren't we close to your estate?"

"Half a mile give or take, but I couldn't wait. You understand." Fenwick's gaze darted between Barrett and James. At Barrett's scowl, he added, "I'd better go in."

James waited until Fenwick walked away. "He's worse than a child. I'll go and keep an eye on him."

Nuisance lifted his nose. His nostrils flared at the smell of something. Then he growled, leaped past James, and bolted out the door.

As James stepped out, Barrett mumbled under his breath, "Bloody delays."

James started to go after Nuisance, but Barrett stayed

him with an arm to his shoulder. "I'll see to him. I need to stretch my legs."

Barrett stepped out of the carriage. Salty sea air stung his cheeks. Past a row of shops on the main thoroughfare, the harbor stretched out into an endless sea of shadows and rolling waves where ships bobbed and masts rocked. Moon rays touched the sky on the horizon and dimmed Virgo with an arc of indigo light.

Nuisance didn't pause to do his business as Barrett expected, but darted down the street toward a lone figure striding toward the inn. From the silhouette, the person appeared to be a young boy. Barrett whistled at Nuisance, but the insolent mutt paid him no mind.

"I should have left you where I found you," Barrett mumbled. He narrowed his eyes and strode after the hard-headed animal.

Nuisance cornered the boy on the sidewalk near a tavern and stood barking. The young lad bent and stretched out a hand. As if the dog knew the stranger, he became calm and allowed the boy to stroke his head.

At Barrett's approach, the lad straightened up and faced him. Barrett stared at the dark pants hugging a pair of shapely legs, the overlarge coat, the long strands of wavy sable hair hanging down from the cap. Shadows bathed the face, yet large violet siren eyes gleamed out at him, with their ability to pierce the darkest regions of his being. His heart banged against his ribs. He couldn't believe his good fortune. He'd found his princess again.

CHAPTER SEVEN

"Do you think it's fate that keeps bringing us together on dark streets?"

"Not fate. Your dog." Meagan smiled down at the small terrier mutt, busy sniffing a spot on the street.

"I had almost given up on his worth. I must reward him with a large bone," Barrett said, his voice filled with a velvety huskiness. He stared at her, his blue eyes shimmering, searing. He stepped toward her.

His gaze held her captive, stroked her as if he were touching her. Warmth melted over her. She leaned back and gazed up at his six-foot-four-inch frame. He radiated power, from his whipcord-muscled chest—clad by an impeccably tailored black coat—down to his lean, sinewy thighs—covered by a pair of black breeches that disappeared beneath shiny black Hessians.

Her eyes moved back up to his face. His thick blond hair curled around the brim of his high beaver hat and just touched his collar. Meagan remembered running her fingers through its softness, and she felt a blush burn her cheeks.

"I hope my maid did not hurt you earlier. She only meant to protect me," Meagan said, her voice unsteady. Her gaze dropped to his slightly crooked aquiline nose, to the firm generous mouth, to the dark brown stubble on his chiseled jaw.

"A pack of bull mastiffs could not have done a better job of it." He slid his hand in hers and pulled her close.

Meagan felt his strong arms around her, his hard chest pressing against hers. The brandy she had consumed magnified her senses and awareness of him. Where their bodies touched, heat flowed into her. Her shyness demanded she pull back, yet she could no more do that than stop the beat of her heart.

"I have this fear that I may have another encounter with your maid, and we will be parted again. . . . "

He bent and kissed her. The moment their lips touched, the feeling she was connected to him in some strange unfathomable way filled her, even as his fire engulfed her. She felt him slide off her cap and tangle his fingers in her long curls. Tingles shot down her neck and spine.

His mouth was hot and urgent against hers. Kissing was a new phenomenon for Meagan. The thrill far surpassed finding a new moon or following a shooting star with her telescope. Nothing she'd ever experienced came close. She relaxed and soared with the feeling until she felt as if she were flying.

"So sweet," he moaned against her lips. His hands slipped down beneath her jacket and cupped her bottom. Then he pulled her tighter to his hips and caressed her bottom.

He ran his tongue between her lips, along her teeth. Instinctively, she opened for him. He drove his tongue into the hot moist depths of her mouth, his tongue mating with hers.

Her fingers slid into his hair. She dipped her tongue into his mouth with a boldness that made him groan. His hands moved around and up inside her coat to caress her breasts.

Meagan arched her back and thought she would die.

"Tell me your name, my princess," he whispered against her lips.

"I say there!" Harold's voice rumbled through the silence and bounced off the buildings lining the street.

The spell cast over Meagan died in a flash. She broke the kiss and cried, "Oh, no!" She thrust Barrett away.

He grabbed her hand and wouldn't turn it loose. "What is the matter?"

"I have to hide."

"I assure you Fenwick will not harm you as long as I am here."

"You don't understand." Meagan jerked harder and saw Harold jogging toward them. "Let me go!"

"I can't, not after I've found you again." His grip on her hand tightened.

Harold ran up to them, heaving. His gaze landed on Meagan. At first it didn't register in his expression who she was; then fury gleamed in his eyes. "You! I should beat you senseless." He reached for her.

Meagan cringed.

Before Harold's hand touched her arm, Lord Watt attacked him. Once on the chin. In the nose. His fist moved fast.

Harold staggered back. His eyes rolled in his head; then he collapsed on the street.

Meagan ran to him and dropped to her knees. "Harold!" She shook him. His limp head lulled to the side; his eyes remained tightly closed.

She stared at Lord Watt. "You've hurt him!"

"I thought he meant to attack you. How do you know

him? Are you his mistress?" Something akin to jealousy tainted the gentleman's voice.

"I'm Meagan Fenwick, his sister." Meagan gently slapped the sides of Harold's face.

Meagan's words couldn't have had more of an impact if she had thrown scalding water on Barrett. His eyes widened. His jaw slackened, and he rocked back on his heels. After a moment, he said, "I'm the Marquess of Waterton."

Meagan's hand froze over Harold's cheek. Her breath caught while her pulse pounded against her temples. She felt the blood drain from her face as she blurted, "That can't be true."

"I should think I know my own name, madam." His voice held a touch of derision.

"I don't believe you."

"You'd better since we are to wed."

Wed . . . wed. The word flashed over and over in Meagan's mind as numbness flowed down her limbs. It took several moments for her to control the urge to scream.

She regained her sangfroid and forced herself to take several deep breaths. Then she said, "Do you think for one moment that I will marry you? You have taken every thing that matters to me and ruined my brother in the process. I'd rather be drawn and quartered than married to a contemptible villain like you. Should Prinny himself order me, I would refuse. If I were marched to the altar at gunpoint, I would—"

"I quite understand your feelings." His gaze cut into her face, his eyes turning a deep wintry blue.

Harold roused and frowned up at her, blurry-eyed. "Meggie, you have to listen." He reached out to her. "You will marry him."

"I'll not be dictated to by you"—Meagan jabbed her finger at Harold; then at Waterton—"or by the likes of him." She leaped up and wheeled around to leave.

"Not so fast, Miss Fenwick." A powerful hand clamped around her arm.

Her gaze locked with blue eyes that bored into her face. Harold had been easy to evade. As she looked into the hard, unyielding expression on Waterton's face, she knew he would not be so easily gainsaid.

The sound of footsteps made Meagan glance past Waterton's broad shoulders. A tall raven-haired gentleman came striding up, the edge of his coat whipping out around his legs. Behind the new arrival, an older, barrel-shaped gentleman with a balding head and sagging jowls puffed his way toward them.

Harold dragged himself up off the ground, holding his head.

"You can unhand me now." Meagan knocked Waterton's hand from her arm. He grinned and she realized he'd allowed her to do it.

The two strangers paused near them. Meagan noticed the older gentleman wore the white collar of a clergyman. The tall, dark one spoke first, eyeing Meagan. "Ah, what have we here?"

"I found my sister," Harold spoke, rubbing his jaw.

The tall dark one took in her boy's clothes and the charcoal on her face. He asked, "Does your sister always go about like this in the middle of the night?"

"I don't know what has gotten into her." Harold narrowed his eyes at Meagan. "I'll make sure she doesn't do this again."

Meagan fired a look that matched his own back at Harold.

"Miss Fenwick, allow me to introduce to you my cousin, Sir James Neville"—Waterton scowled at the tall, dark man; then he waved a hand at the clergyman—"and Mr. Hibbert."

The large, older man's gaze flitted between Meagan and

Waterton. He grunted in disapproval. "So you are to be the happy bride?"

"What gave you that idea, sir?" Meagan said in clipped tones; then she glanced at Waterton. "You were terribly sure of your suit, bringing along your own clergyman. It is a shame you have wasted Mr. Hibbert's time."

"I never waste my time or anyone else's." Waterton's expression turned unyielding and ruthless.

"This time you have."

"I'm not convinced of that."

"I am."

"I've dealt with quick-tempered skeptics before."

"Not this one."

"What happened to you, Fenwick?" Mr. Hibbert said, breaking the rapid-fire exchange between Meagan and Waterton.

"I hit him." Waterton shot Sir James a hard look. "I didn't know the lady was his sister."

"Really?" Sir James grinned so smoothly he barely ruffled the skin on his cheeks.

Megan took a step toward the inn. "If you'll excuse me, I'm in no mood for this arguing. I'm tired and hungry."

Harold snagged her arm. "You're going home, Meagan."

"I have no home now." She glowered at Waterton, who didn't flinch beneath her gaze. The unrelenting light in his eyes made her realize he could win any staring battle. She looked at his cravat. "I'll stay elsewhere."

"You're coming home with me." Harold's hand locked around her arm and he pulled her down the street.

Meagan dug her heels in and tried to break free of Harold's iron grip, but he dragged her anyway. "Let go of me!"

He looked at her, with a rare sensitive expression on his face. "No. You may think me an ogre now, but I'm only doing what is best for you."

"By forcing me to marry the man who took everything we owned. I could never be happy with him. Never!"

"He's rich. Money has a way of making happiness."

"You are so very wrong. Look at you. You had all of Papa's money. You're not very happy now, are you?"

Harold frowned at her and offered no retort.

They both knew she was right, though no amount of truth would change Harold's mind once it was set. She glanced toward the inn and saw the roaring-lion coat of arms on a sleek black carriage. The heartless eyes of the lion reminded her of Waterton's. A tight feeling of dread formed in the pit of her stomach. She had to find Lochlann.

As Harold and Meagan walked away, Barrett saw James take a step to leave and stepped in front of him. "You knew she was his sister."

"Yes. I was curious about her, so I went to the bazaar." James's expression remained stoical.

"Why didn't you tell me then?"

"I could have, but what difference would it have made?" James shrugged.

"A hell of a lot."

James studied Barrett for a moment. "I don't see why you're so vexed—unless of course you are attracted to her."

"That's the bloody trouble." Barrett ground his teeth, knowing he'd have a devil of time not bedding her.

"I didn't expect that. I thought your type was more in the line of Lady Matilda. If you like, we can make the marriage real." A trace of a grin touched James's lips.

"You know as well as I do I cannot marry her." Barrett meant to set up her as his mistress, but he wasn't prepared to marry her or any other lady.

Hibbert coughed, moonlight glistening off his bald head. "In my opinion you're putting the horse before the cart. It's obvious she hates you. You've got to woo her, or the marriage will not take place at all. The whole operation will be up in smoke."

"She'll marry me." Barrett stared down the street and watched Fenwick dragging her toward the carriage. He thought of the kiss they'd shared. She must have felt something for him or she wouldn't have responded to him with complete abandon. Her desire had made her shyness melt away. She'd turned into a wanton creature, taking as much as he had, driving him near madness with her passion. His loins still ached from wanting her. Oh, yes, she might say she hated him, but he knew better.

"Let's hope you can pull it off." Hibbert grunted and clasped his hands over his large belly.

"Did you get Fenwick to talk on the way here?" James asked Hibbert.

"He's got a mouth like a clam. Couldn't get two words out of him. So I napped." Hibbert bent and petted Nuisance. "I say, I wonder if we could impose upon Fenwick to feed us when we reach his estate. All this country air has given me a yearning for food."

"Damnation, can't you think of anything but your stomach?" Barrett grumbled.

"Just making a point." Hibbert aimed an indignant look Barrett's way.

As if he hadn't heard the exchange between Barrett and Hibbert, James rubbed his jaw. "Perhaps it was fortuitous to catch her unawares as we did. Barrett, you're going to have your hands full persuading her to marry you. So let's get to the hunt, shall we, gentleman?" James strode toward the carriage.

Barrett watched Hibbert follow James. He scowled at James's back and knew he had to go through with this feigned marriage. If Meagan Fenwick was indeed involved with the Devil's Advocates, Barrett had to make sure she was protected.

The thought intensified his frown. He called Nuisance.

The dog, in a rare moment of obedience, listened to his master. Side by side, they strode down the street.

Creak. Pop-pop. Creak.

Meagan opened her eyes at the noise and grimaced. She glanced through the darkness at the mantel clock as it gonged twice. Her gaze whipped back to the door.

Creak. Pop-pop. Creak.

For the past two hours, Meagan had listened to someone pacing in the hall. Every time he passed her door, the floorboard in her room squeaked. Too nervous to sleep anyway, she'd lain in bed, tortured by the incessant sound.

She threw back the covers and hopped out of bed. Dying embers barely smoldered in the fireplace. She strode to the door. Cold air poured over her bare feet and up her night rail. She jerked open the door and came face-to-face with Waterton. Meagan froze and sucked in her breath.

"Did you want something?" He leaned against the wall, inches from her, and crossed his arms over his chest.

She couldn't speak. Her eyes were on his shirt. The first four buttons were open, and the brown hair on his broad chest exposed. Her gaze rose to the dark layer of stubble covering his square chin. The stubble matched the nut brown hair on his chest. A blond curl fell rakishly over his forehead. His lean features looked as unyielding and ruthless as ever.

Meagan grew aware of his gaze slowly combing her body. She felt her insides heating as his eyes stripped off her nightgown. The memory of his hands on her bottom and breasts and his lips devouring hers burned in her mind. Blood infused her cheeks even as her wits returned.

She quickly stepped back behind the door and stuck her head around it to look at him. "Yes, I did want something. You must stop this pacing at once." She kept her voice low so as not to wake anyone who might have the good fortune to be asleep.

"Your prediction about me not being able to sleep is correct."

Meagan eyed the dark circles under his eyes. A thread of compassion stole into her voice. "Have you tried warm milk?"

"Doesn't work."

"What about brandy?"

"I've been plagued with insomnia most of my life. I've tried everything"—his gaze slid slowly down her body—"well, maybe not everything."

Her compassion left with her patience. "If you must pace, go below stairs. The floor does not creak down there."

"I have a better idea. Since you are unable to sleep as well, perhaps we can talk and get to know one another better. Who knows? You might change your opinion of me before we marry."

"My dislike of you is firm, and no amount of talking will change it. Furthermore, I'll never marry you. Now, if you don't mind, I'm going back to bed and I would appreciate a little silence." Meagan grabbed the door to slam it.

Thump. The door met with Waterton's boot.

"You didn't seem to dislike me when you kissed me earlier." He studied her face, his eyes alight with deliberate amusement.

"That was before I knew who you were."

"I'm still the same man who felt you kiss him back and moan when I touched you."

"I lost my head. I assure you it won't happen again."

"We shall see," he drawled, his gaze tracing her lips.

Meagan bit back a retort, aware of her disadvantage at the moment. She saw the determined gleam in his eyes; then she stared down at his foot in the door. "If you don't mind, I'd like to go to sleep now."

"Pleasant dreams." He pulled back his foot.

Meagan slammed the door and locked it. His deep laughter melded with the scrape of the key. "Insufferable lout!" she mumbled as she stomped back across the room. She jumped into bed, jerked up the covers, and lay there, her heart pounding.

Creak. Pop-pop. Creak.

Meagan pulled the pillow over her head and knew sleep would be a long time in coming. Her only solace was visualizing Waterton's face when he found out she had run away with Lochlann. She smiled and pulled the pillow tighter to her ears.

The next day, Meagan woke to loud voices outside her chamber door. For a moment she felt disoriented and thought she was back in London at the rented town house, but as she glanced around at the universe chart on the wall, the picture of Sir William Herschel near it, and the telescope perched near the window, she remembered what had happened. With clarity, she recalled her encounter with Waterton last night. Her face screwed up in a frown.

She glanced at the moon-faced clock on the mantel. Her eyes widened. The little hand just touched the moon's plump right cheek: three o'clock. She had slept the whole day away.

The voices out in the hall intensified. Meagan recognized one of them as Tessa's. She threw back the covers, left the bed, strode to the door, and opened it.

Tessa and a gentleman stood nose to nose, deep in an argument. Behind them, two footman, whom Meagan recognized from last night, stood holding the porcelain bathtub and frowning impatiently at the two combatants. None of them seemed to notice her.

Tessa was taller than her antagonist by several inches and she used the added height to intimidate him. The man was thin and black haired, with slanted eyes that suggested his Oriental lineage. He might have been shorter than Tessa, but he didn't look in the least cowed by her.

He raised his finger and said, "See here. My master needs that tub for a bath."

"My mistress needs it for hers. And since she owns the tub she'll use it first."

"Do you know who my master is?" The little man threw out his chest. If he'd been a peacock, his tail feathers would have opened.

"He could be the Prime Minister himself for all I care. My mistress gets this tub."

Meagan opened her mouth to intervene, but the door across the hall opened and Waterton appeared. She clamped her mouth closed as her gaze met his. They stared at each other while Tessa and the gentleman continued to fling words.

Meagan's gaze dropped to the wide V of skin exposed down the middle of his dressing gown. A thick patch of brown hair—much darker than his blond mane—splattered across his well-defined chest. Another thin line of hair grew down the middle of the taut, rippling muscles of his stomach and disappeared below the belt of his dressing gown.

The robe's hem stopped a good three inches above his ankles. A hint of the sinewy muscles in his calves showed beneath. Masculine brown hair covered his calves and bare feet. Like his fingers, his toes were long and slender, with wide, powerful tendons connecting them. The sight of so much bare masculinity made her palms sweat and her mouth go dry. She licked her lips and realized she was staring rudely. Her gaze snapped up.

A hint of a grin spread across his lips as if he enjoyed her perusal of his body. Then his gaze roamed freely down the length of her flannel night rail, undressing her with meticulous slowness, lingering over her breasts, her hips, the spot between her thighs. Up to her face again.

Meagan darted behind the door, aware she'd been standing there like a half-naked simpleton. "Tessa! For heaven's sake! Let him have the blessed tub."

All the servants in the hall paused and stared at her, then at Waterton. They looked too stunned to move.

Waterton had frowned when she'd spoken Tessa's name, as if it annoyed him in some way. Then an enigmatic mask settled over his face as he drawled, "I would gladly share it with you, madam." He punctuated his words with a wink.

"I'd sooner bathe with an alligator." Meagan pulled her head back and slammed the door. Her fists clenched and heart pounding, she stomped across her chamber.

"Insufferable . . . " She jerked a robe from her closet.

"Arrogant . . . " She jammed one arm into it.

"Man . . . " The other followed.

"Share it with me." She wasn't mumbling any longer, but growling as she grabbed the belt and yanked it together.

"Oooh!" She was marching back across the chamber to the washstand for a sponge bath when a knock sounded on the door.

" 'Tis me, miss."

"Come."

Tessa poked her head in the door and warily eyed Meagan. "I've your bath, miss."

"I don't want it."

"But he insists."

"Tell him to go to the devil. I'd rather keep the filth on me for the next fifty years than use that tub before him."

Abruptly, the door opened and Waterton breezed in. "Excuse me. I need a word with your mistress." In the blink of an eye, he shoved Tessa out the door and locked it.

"You can't do this!" Tessa pounded on the door. "Let me in!"

Waterton slipped the key from the lock and dropped it into his pocket. Looking pleased with himself, he stalked toward Meagan.

CHAPTER EIGHT

"Now that your warden is out of the way, we can be alone," Barrett said, hearing Tessa pounding on the locked door.

He watched Meagan's shapely bosom heaving as she took a step back into the sunlight streaming in through the window. Light set the burgundy highlights in her thick dark curls on fire.

"I hate you."

"Hate me all you like. It really doesn't matter in the grand scheme of things."

"You have no right to be in here—and you're half dressed." Her gaze flicked over his robe. An expression halfway between disgust and admiration moved over her face. "Get out!" She moved back, her violet eyes flashing.

"In due time," Barrett said, amused by her feisty temper. "You didn't hate me a few moments ago when you inspected my body from head to toe."

"I did no such thing. Now give me that key."

"Not yet." He glanced over at the telescope in front of

her window, then at the star chart near it. "Are you a stargazer?"

"That's none of your business."

"Everything about you concerns me. Do you know this is the first time I've seen your face without a veil or dirt on it?" Barrett eyed the flawless alabaster skin, the finely arched brows, the full rosebud lips, and the wide violet eyes hooded by thick black lashes. Not a hint of the condition spoken about by the members of the club rumors and by James. "You are as beautiful as Orion on a clear winter night."

"You won't impress me with your knowledge of the stars, and you can save your trite compliments. They won't change my mind about you."

He ignored her and took a step closer. "Would it impress you if I said Sir William Herschel was a particular friend of mine?"

"I don't believe you," she said over her maid's pounding as it grew louder.

"My father donated money so he could build his reflecting telescope in Slough."

"Really." She jammed her hands on her hips and didn't seem aware he was so close. She only eyed him suspiciously. "How tall is the telescope?"

"Forty feet."

"How big is the aperture?"

"Four feet."

Her disbelief turned to awe. "You *have* actually looked through it."

"Yes." He touched the side of her cheek, feeling her soft skin against the back of his hand. "I could perhaps arrange with his son so you can see it."

"Would you?"

Barrett stared at her in amazement. If he'd just handed her the universe, her face couldn't have glowed more. He'd never met a woman who preferred stargazing to diamonds and roses. "I warn you," Barrett said in a feigned ominous tone, "he's a bit stuffy and he picks his teeth at the oddest times."

Her face glowed with a smile. "I don't care what he does, as long as he lets me see through his father's telescope."

"I'll arrange it."

"Thank you." Meagan threw her arms around Barrett and squeezed his neck.

Barrett stiffened at the contact.

Bang. Bang. Bang.

He ignored the noise in the hallway, aware only of her soft breasts molded against his hard chest, the slender curve of her spine, her long hair brushing his forearm. Through her pink flannel robe, he felt each vertebra of her spine. A rosewater scent, blended with her own clean, feminine smell, filled his senses. His loins ached to have her.

One more second and he would ravish her. Marshaling every bit of will he possessed, he stepped back. . . .

The door burst open.

"What is the meaning of this?" Harold shouted.

Barrett gazed into her eyes and saw the truce between them had ended. Her expression turned wary. She stepped back from him as if she couldn't believe she'd hugged him.

One side of Barrett's mouth quirked; then he turned around. Fenwick stood in the doorway, wearing only breeches, his straw-colored hair wild about his head. Tessa loomed behind him with murder in her eyes. Lyng, Barrett's valet, had a pleased smug look on his face. The two footmen who'd been holding the tub peeked over Lyng's head, with grins on their faces.

Fenwick's gaze traveled from his sister to Barrett, then to Tessa. "I thought you said he was hurting her? He's done nothing to her."

"It ain't proper. He had no business being in here with her." Tessa glared at Barrett.

Barrett's gaze rested on Fenwick. "Your sister and I were just settling a little disagreement."

Meagan stepped away from the bed. "It is all right, Tessa We are done with our discussion. He was just leaving." She thrust her finger in the direction of the door.

Barrett noticed the slight tremble in her hand. "Always at your service, madam." He made a gallant bow, then strode from the room. Lyng and Barrett's footmen backed out of the door.

He listened to his footsteps echo in the hall and thought the interlude had gone better than he'd anticipated. A few more times alone with her and she would agree to marry him. The problem was reining his lust.

He prided himself on his self-control when it came to women. He mastered them with the same calculated focus that he handled everything in his life, but whenever he was near Miss Fenwick, she seemed to master him. With the same determination he'd used to conquer every other vulnerability within him, he would vanquish this power she had over him. He had to.

Aware of the ache in his groin, he strode into his room. Lyng hurried in behind him. "Will you shave before your bath, my lord?"

"I'll skip the bath. I want to be dressed before the lady finishes her toilet."

Lyng frowned at the interruption in Barrett's routine. "What a household this is. And that woman." He shuddered and blinked rapidly as he hurried over to pour water for Barrett.

"Yes, she is quite a woman."

Lyng turned in time to catch the twinkle in his master's eye. "Not that one—the other one. She can smite the gatekeepers of hell with her tongue."

"Yes. I'm counting on you to distract her while I court Miss Fenwick."

"Me?" Lyng squeezed his eyes closed until they were lost in the wrinkles lining his face.

"Yes, you. You seem to have a way with her."

Lyng grunted under his breath. "A fire-eating dragon could not have his way with her."

"With your resourcefulness, I'm sure you can manage." Barrett bent and petted Nuisance, who raised his head up off the mattress and licked Barrett's hand. He looked forward to spending the rest of the afternoon alone with Meagan, without her attack maid. He reached in his pocket and fingered the key to her chamber door.

Across the hall, Meagan watched the footmen set down the tub and leave her room. Her body still pulsed from hugging Waterton. How could he make every fiber in her body hum? She hated him, didn't she?

"Jolly good work, Meggie," Harold said, watching Tessa close the door behind the footmen.

"What do you mean?"

"You've managed to capture his interest. I never thought you had it in you."

"Thank you very much." Meagan folded her hands over her chest, feeling the sting of his words. No one was more aware of her lack of charms than she. Her parents had made her well aware of her imperfections all her life.

"You know what I mean," Harold said, sounding contrite.

"Unfortunately, I do."

"Don't be angry, Meggie. I was just trying to give you a compliment. And you deserve one. How on earth did you get him so interested in you?"

"It was very hard for a lady of my limited talents."

He ignored her quip. "It was a good sign he waltzed

into your chamber like that and locked the door. A very good sign. I believe he's set on marrying you now."

"I'm glad something came of having my privacy invaded."

"Had I planned it myself it couldn't have gone better. You'll see—it will all work out." He grinned at her and opened the door, then strode off down the hall.

"Why are you taking this so calmly?" Tessa returned from the closet and laid out a light blue morning dress on Meagan's bed.

"I'm tired of arguing with him. Let him think I'm resolved to marry Waterton. It will make my escape easier tonight."

Tessa's eyes widened. "Oh, miss, you're escaping alone?"

"No, with Lochlann. He and I are running away to Gretna Green." Meagan smiled at the thought.

"That's the best news I've heard in days." Tessa's round face stretched wide in a grin as she walked to the door and absently looked for the key in the lock. She couldn't find it and grimaced at Meagan.

"He's got it," Meagan said, motioning across the hall.

"Bet he wants to come back in here when the mood strikes him. We'll just see 'bout that." Tessa shoved the dresser over in front of the door with surprising ease. She brushed her hands together. "Now let's see him get through. Him and his hateful little valet. I'd like to grind that valet up and use his bones to fertilize the garden."

"This is his master's house now. He has every right to be here."

"That may be so, but it don't mean I gotta like it. This house has been in the Fenwick line for years. If I stay here, I won't be able to work for him." For all Tessa's bluster, her insecure side showed in her face.

"You're going to remain my maid at Oakwell," Meagan reassured Tessa.

"I wasn't sure, miss. Oh, thank you. I knew you wouldn't make me stay here." Tessa's face brightened.

"Speaking of staying here, I must find a way to get word to Lochlann. He'll go to the inn looking for me tonight."

"I'll sneak a note to him."

Meagan squeezed Tessa's arm. "I knew I could count on you."

"I always thought you and Mr. Burrows belonged together. He's good, kind, gentle. A right righter. He'll make you a proper husband. Nothing like that marquess, I'll tell you. If you married him, he'd end up hurting you for sure."

"You needn't worry, for I'll not be marrying him." Meagan slipped off her night rail and eased into the tub. Warm water washed over her, relaxing the tension that Waterton had caused. The image of his blue eyes formed in her mind. He was touching her breast again, making her quiver all over. Even now the water felt like the gentle caress of his hand against her breast. . . .

Meagan dropped the bar of soap. Water splashed in her face, ending her musings. She blushed, angry with herself for letting him invade her thoughts.

"You've got to stay on your guard around him, miss. And I'll be getting that key from him too."

"No use fighting over it. Lochlann is coming for me tonight." Meagan would give her eyeteeth to see Waterton's face when he discovered she'd found another husband.

Husband. Lochlann as a friend made her feel comfortable. Lochlann as a husband made her insides cringe.

The last rays of sunlight faded from the sky as Tessa hurried back along the path from Oakwell. A gust of December wind came from the north and whipped the hem of her skirt and cape around her legs. She shivered and gazed up at the darkening clouds overhead. They'd surely have hail or snow during the night.

The sound of a bark brought her gaze to the path. Waterton's drip of a valet strode toward her. The dog pranced at his side. The man paused before her and tipped his hat, exposing a mat of short-cropped straight black hair with a tiny bald spot at the top. His coat was of the finest quality, as was his suit beneath, but neither did anything to diminish Tessa's dislike of the man.

He pulled on the dog's leash, then double stepped up beside her. "Do you mind if we walk back with you, madam?" he asked in his foreign accent.

"I do." Tessa picked up her pace.

He ignored her and said, "It is a lovely time of evening for a walk."

"It's cold."

"Then why are you out?"

"You sure are nosy." Tessa eyed him with years of schooled suspicion.

"Just making conversation." He squinted his slanted eyes, as if something were in them.

"Being nosy is not makin' conversation. I'll be gettin' back now. If you'll excuse me," Tessa added in a tight voice that matched the small man's. Then she left him squinting at her and veered off the path.

A flock of roosting sparrows fluttered up to the sky from a nearby oak. She blazed a trail through the woods, shoving aside branches. Dry brown leaves crunched under her feet. Why had the little man been so affable? Well, she didn't want to have anything to do with him. She had a suspicion this wasn't a chance meeting. Most men couldn't be trusted—especially foreign ones who worked for that Lord Waterton.

* * *

Back at Fenwick Hall, Meagan peered through her telescope. She had chosen to place it in this chamber because it faced north and had a clear view of the eastern and western horizons—a good prospect for viewing the stars. Yet right now, her lens was trained on Tessa tramping through the woods.

A little to the left, Waterton's valet came into focus. He gazed at Tessa's back, his face screwed up in a grimace. The dog stopped to water a tree and the little man almost tripped over the leash.

Meagan's smile quickly faded. What if Tessa hadn't delivered the note to Oakwell? What if Lochlann didn't know where to find her? She had stayed in her room to avoid Waterton, using the excuse she had an ache in her head, but the walls were closing in on her.

After donning her cape, gloves, and bonnet, she opened the door and peeked out. No Waterton. She slipped out into the hallway and hurried down the stairs to the foyer. She found Reeves lighting the candles in the wall sconces.

Candlelight flickered along his bony face and the wrinkles of his paper-thin skin. His fingers trembled, and the taper in his hand shook. Wax dripped onto his wrist and the white cuffs of his shirt.

Without bothering to look at her, he replaced the globe and said, "That you, miss?"

"Yes."

"Thought those were your footsteps."

"I wish I had your sense of hearing and could tell who was coming by their footsteps."

He beamed from the praise. "My eyesight might be going, but I can hear as well as the day I was born."

"I've no doubt you can. Where is everyone?" Meagan kept her voice low as she glanced cautiously down the hallway that jutted off from the foyer.

"In the game room, miss."

"If anyone asks, you haven't seen me." Meagan started toward the door.

"You might want to listen in for a few moments, miss." Reeves stepped down off the stool and wobbled on his feet.

Meagan caught his arm before he fell. "Why?"

"They're speaking about you."

"Perhaps I should at that." Meagan patted his arm, aware Reeves knew she wasn't above eavesdropping—especially when it came to her future. "Thank you, Reeves."

"My pleasure." He shuffled over to another sconce.

Meagan left him to his job and sneaked down the hall. Harold's voice drifted down the hallway, mingling with the soft tread of her shoes.

"She is a bit headstrong."

"How did you know she would be here?"

Meagan recognized Waterton's voice and paused several feet from the game room's door.

"She's very close to Lochlann Burrows, a neighbor. They've been friends for an age. I knew she'd come to him for help."

"Do you think he'll be a problem?" This came from Sir James.

"Not likely. I believe my sister's resigned to her fate. You *do* still want to marry her, don't you?"

"Miss Fenwick will do as good as any for a wife."

Meagan grimaced at Waterton's self-assured drawl. He sounded as if he were picking out a mare at Tattersall's.

"Glad to hear it," Harold said. "I assume, since you brought your own vicar, you have no intention of going through a long engagement."

"I wish to get it over with as soon as possible."

"Have you set the date?"

"Got to be soon," Mr. Hibbert chimed in. "I must be back in London. My wife's relatives are coming for Christmas."

"Tomorrow at three," Waterton said, ignoring Hibbert.

"I'll inform, Meagan." Satisfaction rang in Harold's words.

Meagan had heard enough. She slipped away and as she drew near the foyer, she noticed Reeves had moved into another room.

Abruptly, the front door opened. Tessa stepped inside, a cold draft whipping the hem of her black skirt around her legs. She noticed Meagan and closed the door. Her cheeks glowed pink from the cold.

"Oh, miss." Tessa rubbed her arms to warm them. "What are you doing out of your room?"

"Shhh! Harold and the others are in the game room." Meagan pointed behind her. "I witnessed the encounter you had with Waterton's valet. Did you deliver the note?"

"Yes."

"Excellent. All that remains to be done is pack."

Tessa slipped the scarf from around her neck and surveyed her mistress. "What is the matter? You look irked enough to kick a dog."

"The only dog I wish to kick, Tessa, walks on two legs." Meagan stomped up the steps. An image of Waterton's bright blue eyes and arrogant grin formed in her mind. His words rang in her ears: *Miss Fenwick will do as good as any for a wife.* He'd soon learn she wouldn't do at all.

Ten minutes later, Barrett strode into his chamber and found Lyng polishing boots. Six pairs of black Hessians circled his feet. The valet started to jump up when he saw his master.

Barrett waved him back down. "Continue what you are doing. I can dress myself for dinner. Tell me: Did you follow the maid?" Barrett set down his cane on the dresser.

"I did. She went to Oakwell Hall."

"Ah, Mr. Burrows's abode, I presume." Barrett began to unbutton his coat.

"I checked with the staff. Oakwell is his home."

"I wonder what the lady is planning with Mr. Burrows?" Barrett's hand paused over a button as he frowned.

"The witch of a maid was hiding something, but getting her to speak of it was like stroking a cobra. I thought she might bite my head off at any moment. I did see her give the Oakwell butler a note."

"Good work, Lyng." Barrett spoke without thinking and immediately regretted it.

The self-effacing, humble part of Lyng that didn't do well with compliments came to light. He stared down at his reflection in the boot and remained silent.

Barrett tried to cover the awkward silence. "So Fenwick was wrong when he said Miss Fenwick was resigned to this marriage."

"I have a feeling he doesn't know his sister at all."

"He's so very young and naive."

"We all suffer from those maladies at one time in our lives." Lyng eyed his master.

Barrett knew Lyng was referring to Lady Matilda, his master's one crowning mistake. He frowned. "I suppose you are right. We all learn from our mistakes."

"Glad to hear it, my lord." Lyng buffed the leather harder.

"I predict tonight Miss Fenwick will finally consent to marry me, Lyng." Barrett rubbed his hands together as if he were about to open a present.

"How so, my lord?" Lyng glanced up and cocked his head.

"She's surely going to make a large mistake by underestimating me."

"A very large mistake."

"Indeed it is." Barrett pulled out the key to her bed-chamber from his pocket and fingered it.

"Shall I distract the witch—ah, I mean, the maid—again after dinner?"

"I might need your help. I'll let you know. Have Stratton go to Oakwell and watch the place."

"Yes, my lord."

"And have someone keep an eye on Miss Fenwick."

He thought of Meagan. Just how deeply was she involved with the Devil's Advocates? His brows furrowed. If she were tied to this unscrupulous group of blackguards, somehow he would make sure she didn't come to harm without exposing his cover. He had a feeling this would not be an easy task. There was one consolation though: With Meagan involved in this case, he wouldn't suffer an ounce of boredom. Restlessness and lust perhaps, but never boredom.

Bored stiff and alone, Barrett gazed out his chamber window. He flicked open his snuffbox with a practiced motion and snorted the special blend he had made for his own use. It tingled in his nostrils and throat as he gazed up at the clouds swirling around the edges of the moon. By its angle, he knew it must be well past midnight— perhaps close to two in the morning.

Dinner had been a tedious affair. James had hardly spoken two words. Fenwick rambled. And Hibbert stuffed his mouth and couldn't speak at all.

Meagan hadn't put in an appearance. She used the excuse that her head still hurt—a sure sign she was avoiding him and up to something. He took another snort and watched the white condensation of his breath mingle with the dark clouds in the sky.

He flicked closed his snuffbox and pocketed it. His hand brushed Meagan's silk handkerchief. Touching it reminded him of her soft skin and lips. He brought it up and took a deep whiff of her clean rosewater scent. He should probably give the article back to her; it only made his desire for her harder to control.

Someone rapped on the door.

"Come." Barrett jammed the handkerchief back in his pocket.

"Mr. Burrows is behind me, me lord," Stratton said, out of breath. "Looks like he's on his way here."

"How much time before he arrives?"

"A few minutes. He left his buggy at the gates and is sneakin' up the drive right now. I ran as fast as I could to tell you."

"Good. Watch Miss Fenwick's chamber door and stop her if she leaves. If Burrows tries to enter that way, cut him off."

"Aye."

Barrett picked up his cane and left the room, casting a glance at Miss Fenwick's door. Swinging his cane and whistling softly, he strode down the hallway.

On his way out the servant's entrance, he heard raised voices in the kitchen.

"I won that trick," Meagan's maid said with a vast amount of righteous indignation.

"You didn't," Lyng shot back. "It was not trump."

"Hearts are trump."

"Diamonds!"

"You're a blee-eater!"

"What is a blee-eater?" Lyng asked, confused.

"A bleeding cheater!"

Barrett caught a fleeting glimpse of Lyng and Miss Fenwick's maid sitting opposite each other at a table. The maid had her hand locked on a trick. Lyng gripped her wrist, his eyes squeezed tightly together in determination. Neither of them noticed him. Nuisance did. The dog lifted his head from his spot on a rug next to the hearth. The moment he spotted Barrett, he leaped to his feet and hurried to follow his master.

"Poor chap. I didn't realize what torture I was putting him through. I see you managed to escape."

Nuisance cocked his head at Barrett as if he understood him; then they both stepped outside. Crisp air stung Barrett's cheeks. The lawn glistened with a thick layer of frost, and his boots crunched across the icy blades. Nuisance caught a whiff of something in the air and took off running toward the garden behind the house.

Barrett gazed up at the long line of windows on the second floor. Only one window glowed with a shaft of light. A shadowy figure paced back and forth behind the panes. Miss Fenwick appeared at her window. She looked through her telescope. It wasn't aimed at the heavens, but at Oakwell.

Barrett stepped back near a yew, leaned against the trunk, and watched her. A wide-brimmed bonnet shadowed her face, and he could just make out the high neck of a blue morning dress. Her hair was pulled back, with small sable curls framing her oval face. She definitely wasn't dressed for bed.

Approaching footsteps brought Barrett's gaze around. A tall, dark-haired man prowled his way to Meagan's window. Mr. Burrows. Barrett had waited for this moment. A feral grin twisted up one side of his mouth as he watched Burrows pause below Miss Fenwick's window. He threw several stones at the glass.

Her face lit up with a smile. Barrett had never seen her smile like that. Awed by the dimples in her cheeks and the way her face glowed, he watched her step past the telescope, open the window, and lean out.

"Oh, Lochlann. I was so worried you wouldn't come," she whispered.

"I'm here. Can you get away?"

"Yes. Everyone is asleep."

Barrett stepped out into the open. "Not everyone."

CHAPTER NINE

Meagan gasped, dug her nails into the windowsill, and peeked over the edge at Waterton. He stood in the moonlight, his face shadowed, yet not enough that she couldn't see the searing blue in his eyes gleaming up at her. Dear Lord! She had misjudged just how cunning he could be.

Lochlann whipped around so quickly he stumbled. After staggering, he caught himself. Trying to look dignified, he squared his shoulders and said, "You're not stopping us."

"Pray, just what am I stopping you from doing?" Waterton picked up his cane and slowly ran his finger over the silver lion's head on its tip.

"We're going to Gretna Green."

Waterton studied his cane with obvious indifference. "It looks as if I will be stopping you."

"You have no claim on her."

"More than you, dear boy. You see, I won her hand in a card game. Technically she is mine." Waterton gazed up at Meagan with a ruthless expression on his face.

Meagan's fingernails dug deeper into the windowsill;

her breath came in rapid gasps. "I won't be wagered like a mare in a game of chance."

Waterton's gaze didn't waver from her face. "It is too late—it is already done."

"Surely, you do not expect her to honor that bet." Lochlann's normally low monotone voice grew impassioned.

"I do."

Flustered, Lochlann slapped his hands down at his sides. "I'll pay you for her hand."

"She's not for sale." Waterton set down his cane and turned his gaze on Lochlann.

"Then there is only one other thing to do. I'll meet you on the field at dawn."

"No!" Meagan screeched, her voice carrying into the night. "You can't fight him, Lochlann. He'll kill you! You've never been in a duel. For God's sake, stop this now!"

"I would listen to her, dear boy. I have no desire to kill you."

Lochlann turned and glared at Waterton. "Don't be so sure you'll win, you son of a bitch!"

Barrett narrowed his eyes. In a deadly tone, he said, "I've never lost one yet."

"There's always a first time."

"Lochlann, listen to him," Meagan cried from the window.

Lochlann gazed up at her, his face determined. "I'm going to do this for you. He can't make you marry him."

"Please. No! We'll think of another way."

"He's determined to marry you, and I'm determined he won't. There is no other way to settle it amicably."

"What if he kills you?"

"My mind is made up. I'm going to do this."

His voice thick with amusement, Waterton said, "This is all very touching, but—"

"Oh, shut up!" Meagan blurted, surprised by her outburst. She'd never told anyone to shut up before. "Listen to me, Lochlann—"

Her only friend in the world glared at Waterton. "Let me handle this, Meagan. I'll meet you at dawn near the pond on my estate." Lochlann turned to walk away.

Waterton's words stopped him. "I'm afraid that's up to Miss Fenwick. If she agrees to marry me, then I cannot duel with you."

Meagan's gaze darted frantically between Waterton and Lochlann. Her friend stared at her, seeming to hang on her next words. Her gaze landed back on Waterton, who looked confident he knew her answer. How she would love to tell him no. Lochlann would die. She would die if she had to marry Waterton.

She ground out the words. "I'll marry you."

"A wise choice." Waterton's gloating mien didn't waver.

Lochlann stiffened, his countenance brooding and hurt. He glared at Waterton. "This matter is not finished. I will have satisfaction." He wheeled around and trudged away with wooden steps.

"Lochlann!" Meagan called after him, but he wouldn't answer her. His moonlit form disappeared behind her tears. Without looking at Waterton, she slammed the window closed.

Meagan had waited an hour for Waterton to come to her room and gloat over his victory, but he hadn't yet put in an appearance. Tired of waiting, she decided to go to Lochlann and explain her decision. She'd never forget the hurt expression on his face.

She strode over and opened the door. One of Waterton's footmen bowed at her. " 'Evening, me lady."

She nodding curtly and slammed the door. How dared Waterton put a guard at her door? She ran back to the window and stuck out her head. All clear.

She stuffed her gown and petticoat up between her legs and secured them in the back with the sash from her dress. Then she opened the sash wider and crawled out on the sill. As she hooked her foot on the rose trellis below her window—something she'd done as a child many times—a knock sounded at the door. . . . Then her door opened.

Waterton came striding into the room.

Meagan's foot missed the trellis. Her fingers slid off the edge of the sill. She groped at air and screamed.

"Hold on!" His large hands clamped on to her wrists.

Meagan stared at the rose trellis in her face and prayed he wouldn't let go. Her heart banged in her chest until she thought it would break a rib.

"Don't worry. Rescuing damsels is one of my specialties. I'll have you up in a wink."

His arrogant drawl had never sounded so good. He pulled her up, careful to keep her arms and face from scraping against the bricks and trellis. The moment she cleared the window, he gripped her waist and set her down.

Then her trembling knees buckled.

"I got you." He pulled her into his arms.

"Thank you," she whispered.

Strange, but it felt pleasant to be bolstered by his strength. Her cheek rested against the crisp linen of his white shirt. The smell of starch, smoke, and his musk wafted beneath her senses. Her hands had landed against his chest when he had pulled her close, and she could feel the faint beat of his heart through his wool coat.

"Are you hurt?" he asked, a genuine tone of concern replacing the ever present derision in his voice.

"Just my dignity. I've climbed out that window a thousand times and never once fallen."

He leaned back, tilted her chin, and gazed into her eyes. His thumb stroked her jaw. "When I saw you tumble out the window, I thought I'd lost you. Are you sure you're unharmed?"

"Yes."

She gazed into his blue eyes. Behind the cool hardness, she saw a hint of warmth. The rare moment reminded of her of when she had told his fortune, and she had seen behind his mask. He touched something raw in her now, as he had done then. The odd feeling disconcerted her, for she sensed no evidence of the Marquess of Waterton in him, only the kind gentleman who had helped her at the Christmas bazaar, who'd held her and kissed her and made her want his touch until she ached from it.

To her dismay, he stepped back from her, the hard facade back in place. "From now on, you will use the front door when you go to see your friend, Lochlann."

"How did you—"

"I knew you'd try to go to him." The barest hint of jealousy flashed in his eyes and disappeared.

"I just wanted to explain to him. I would have kept my word and married you." Unable to bear his stare or his closeness, she strode over to her telescope. She ran her hand along the smooth brass, surprised to see her fingers were trembling.

"I'm glad to hear it." He studied her intently. "That is why I came in here. I wish to discuss the terms of our marriage."

Her brows snapped up in surprise. "I didn't think there were any terms to be discussed. I assumed you'd settled that with Harold."

"I'm not an ogre, Meagan. I'll not force you into a marriage without giving you some consolation."

"How very kind of you." She eyed him warily.

"Not really. It just makes for an easier relationship if we completely understand each other."

"I agree."

"Let me tell you what I expect of you. Then you can do likewise."

"Very well." Meagan folded her arms over her chest and braced herself.

"You will marry me tonight."

"Tonight? Can't it wait until the morn?"

"No. I want Burrows to realize you're mine. We'll marry tonight. Then we'll leave for London."

"Why so soon?"

"I have pressing business there."

She glanced at her reflection in the window. She was frowning. A curt edge slipped into her voice as she said, "If it is a social butterfly you are seeking in a wife, my lord, I'm afraid my wings do not extend that far. I never go out into society—especially not London society."

"I'm not asking you to go everywhere with me. Naturally we shall go our own ways, but occasionally we should be seen together."

"Naturally." Meagan had stiffened when he'd said they should go their own ways. Why didn't he just come right out and say he would continue to cavort with his mistresses? Well, it was common practice for husbands to have mistresses. And she had never expected to marry in the first place—much less have a husband who cared for her.

"I won't force you into my bed right away."

"You won't?" Her brows shot up in surprise and she almost felt disappointed. Almost.

"I want to get to know you better before I claim my conjugal rights. When I bed you, I want you to enjoy it. And you won't until you feel comfortable with me. I'm sure you agree."

Meagan couldn't meet those blue eyes that seemed to pierce right through her face. The casual indifference with which he spoke of their marriage bed made a blush burn down to the roots of her hair. She glanced down at his cravat and mumbled, "Yes."

"Now that we are clear on what I expect of you, what are your requirements?" He leaned back against the bed and crossed his arms over his chest, a curiously amused expression on his face.

It relaxed her a bit to know he didn't expect much from her. It also surprised and puzzled her that a man like Waterton had enough sensitivity not to force her to his bed right away. Perhaps she had misjudged his character in some small degree, but not enough to make her want to marry him.

Screwing up her courage, she looked directly into his fathomless blue eyes, meeting his gaze squarely. "My first requirement is that I must be allowed to pursue my scientific studies of the stars."

"Agreed." He motioned with lazy ease.

"I'll not alter my habits to please you," Meagan said, trying again to persuade him to change his mind about marrying her. "One of them is extensive reading. I can spend hours a day at it."

"So can I."

"I like to be alone when I look at the stars. It disturbs me when people flutter about." She continued to try to persuade him she would not do as his wife.

"Very well. I can leave you to your stargazing."

Would he ever stop being so agreeable? She tried again. "I want Fenwick Hall and the lodge in Scotland deeded to me and put into the hands of a trustee of my choosing. Also, I want five thousand pounds a year put into an account over which I have complete control."

His dark brows raised. "You surprise me with your business sense."

"When I watched my brother gamble away everything my family owned"—her gaze hardened on him—"I thought it would benefit me to learn these things."

"Very prudent of you."

"Thank you."

"Are there any other requirements?" He studied her, his gaze combing her body.

Meagan felt her cheeks burning at his frank perusal. She turned her back to him and glanced out the window. "Three more. Harold is ruined and unable to support himself. I want him to reside with me if he wishes." Meagan hoped to keep an eye on Harold and convince him to stay away from the Devil's Advocates.

"I have no objection to that." He looked pleased about something and said, "What are your other demands?"

"You must allow Reeves and Tessa to remain in your employ until such time as they wish to be pensioned off."

"Done. What else?"

"As soon as you can arrange it, I would like to meet Lord Herschel."

"I'll write him directly. Anything else?"

"That will do for now. If I think of anything more, I'll let you know," she said, her voice losing its businesslike tone. Something in the possessiveness of his eyes, the way he stripped off her clothes with just his gaze, quickened her breathing and warmed her down to her toes.

"I'm sure you shall." He looked amused and equally impressed by her as his eyes met hers.

"There is one other thing I would like to know?"

"What is that?"

"Why are you forcing this union? With your wealth, you could have the cream of the *ton,* someone titled with a large dowry, perhaps even someone who didn't dislike you. Why me?"

"That should be obvious." A sultry grin twisted up one side of his mouth as his gaze slid down her body. Seeing Meagan's discomfort, he adopted a satisfied expression and said, "I'll go rouse Hibbert and the others."

Warily, she watched his long-legged strides to the door, candlelight twinkling in the shiny leather of his boots. He was so broad shouldered, so tall, so commanding, his presence filled the entire room.

He turned, flashed a glance at her that dug deep into

her eyes, then left. The muffled tread of his boots faded away behind the closed door.

Meagan didn't know what to make of this agreeable side of him. Being married to him might not be as unpleasant as she first thought— What was she thinking? Of course it would be. After all, she was being forced into a loveless marriage.

"We are gathered here in the sight of God to join together this man and this woman . . . ."

Mr. Hibbert's words echoed through the small chapel at Fenwick Hall. But the ceremony had a hurried impatient quality to it that lacked eloquence or feeling.

Meagan heard his stomach rumbling between his words. He looked rumpled too, with his balding hair protruding from the sides of his head. But what could be expected of a vicar roused from his bed in the middle of the night to perform a wedding?

She plucked at the silk folds of her cream frock, the only dress Tessa could find in her closet that would suffice for a wedding dress on such short notice. She felt Waterton's long warm fingers entwined in her own. This was not how she'd supposed her wedding would be—not that she had ever wanted one.

Nuisance sat on the pew behind them, next to Sir James and Harold. She could hear the dog's panting keeping rhythm with the good vicar's stomach.

"Marriage is the partnership between two people, ordained by God . . . "

She glanced at the rose window above Mr. Hibbert's head. The Virgin stood holding her baby, tenderly gazing down at him, her face glowing with motherhood. Surely, children would come of this union. What sort of father would a callous person like Waterton make? She felt a lump growing in her throat.

"Marriage is not a union to be entered into lightly. . . . "

Lightly. Hibbert's word echoed in her mind. She glanced over at the stranger soon to be her husband. He towered at her side. His gaze was riveted on Hibbert, and he had no hint of emotion in his expression. He could have been standing in a line leading to an opera house.

Lightly. He certainly took the marriage lightly. Meagan gulped past the lump in her throat and felt her sweaty palm against his dry one. The air of deliberate indifference that emanated from Waterton caused her to glance frantically toward the door.

"If there is anyone present who believes this couple should not be joined together, let him speak now or hereafter hold his peace."

Meagan opened her mouth, ready to spew a thousand reasons why this union couldn't go on, but Waterton squeezed her hand and glanced down at her. Candlelight caught his eyes, the bright blue in them piercing her face. Unable to put two coherent thoughts or words together, she clamped her mouth closed.

Mr. Hibbert had been looking at his book, so he had missed the byplay completely. He continued. "I require and charge you both—in light of the answer you will give on the Day of Judgment, when the secret of all hearts shall be disclosed—that if either of you knows any impediment why you may not be lawfully joined in matrimony do confess it now."

Waterton's fingers tightened around her hand. Extra moistness flooded her skin, a sure sign he suffered with a bout of sweaty palms. She glanced at him and saw for the first time a hint of emotion in his face. He was scowling.

"Do you Lady Meagan Drina Beth Fenwick take Lord Waterton as your lawfully married husband?"

"Y—" The word wouldn't go past the lump in her throat. She cleared her voice and choked out, "Yes.

Mr. Hibbert examined his notes. "Do you Lord Barrett

Henry Wentworth Rothchild take Lady Meagan for your lawfully wedded wife?"

"I do." A hard edge came through in his voice.

"Then by the power vested in me, I pronounce you man and wife. You may kiss your bride."

Waterton grasped her arms and gazed deep into her eyes. She felt sure he would take her in his arms and kiss her now. He bent toward her. His lips veered off from her mouth; then he pecked her on the forehead.

"There now. That wasn't so hard," he whispered. He dropped his hands and stepped back.

She gazed at him in stunned silence. She couldn't rid herself of this feeling she'd been cheated out of a marriage kiss. Why did it matter to her? She should feel happy he hadn't forced his attentions on her.

A few moments later, the sound of crying met Meagan outside her chamber door. She pressed her ear against the oak, listened for a moment, then stepped into the room.

Tessa sat hunched on the bed, her face buried in her hands, each sob shaking her shoulders. Meagan closed the door and hurried over to her maid and friend. She touched Tessa's arm. "Goodness! What is the matter?"

Tessa glanced up; tears were streaming down her round face. She used the corner of her apron to wipe her eyes. "Oh, miss, I didn't want you to see me like this."

"What has distressed you so?"

"Oh, miss, I shouldn't say."

"Of course you should. Nothing has ever stopped you before from confiding what was bothering you. Now what is the matter?"

Tessa hiccuped and shoved back the ruffle of her mob-cap, which stuck to the side of her wet cheek. "Dearie me! It weren't never this serious before."

"Serious?"

"Aye, you've never ruined your life like this. I could kick myself for playing cards with that little blee-eater. None of this woulda happened if I'd been there and stopped you from agreeing to marry that Lord Waterton." Tessa frowned and mopped her puffy eyes with her apron.

Meagan pretended to know what a blee-eater was and said, "Are you speaking of Mr. Lyng?"

"The very one. He lured me into a game of all-fours. He knew that Mr. Burrows was coming and his master planned on trapping you both."

"No doubt you are correct, but it is over and done with now." Meagan tried to keep her voice confident, but it only managed to sound flat.

"It ain't right how it turned out. I just hate to see it. I wanted you to marry Mr. Burrows. He's right for you—but this other one. . ." Tessa shook her head in despair.

"It's not all that bad. I'm getting Fenwick Hall and the lodge back, and all of my dowry. If I truly cannot stand him, I can obtain an annulment and live very comfortably."

"Aye, but you give your heart too easily. He'll surely hurt you. I know it as well as I'm sitting and breathing. A man like him hasn't a care for anyone but himself. Mark my words, you'll rue this night."

Meagan studied the born skeptic in front of her. Tessa's pessimism ran bone deep, and usually Meagan tried to make her see a more optimistic side, but she couldn't find a bright side to this situation. She wasn't about to let Tessa know that and hear an "I told you so," so she said, "I promise you never to lose my heart to him—there, are you happy now? We need to pack. Lord Waterton wishes to leave for London tonight."

"Tonight?" Tessa screeched. "Doesn't he ever sleep?"

"Evidently not."

She frowned and pulled a copy of Gerguson's *Astronomy* from a shelf near her telescope. What irony. This was her wedding night. She should feel elated, in love, full of joyous buoyancy. All she felt was drained, dead, old. She dropped the book from nerveless fingers. Oh, Lord! What had she done?

Outside in the courtyard, Barrett thought the very same thing as he watched Mr. Hibbert gallop away, the sound of his horse's hooves echoing off the walls of the barn. James mounted the horse his groom had brought earlier in the day. The moon cast James's silhouette in shadow. His cousin's enigmatic features looked like some ghostly caricature that had no substance.

James looped the reins around his hand. "I didn't think you'd get it done so soon. I knew I'd chosen the right man for this case." James tipped his beaver.

"You can save your damned flattery."

"I can see your disposition is going to be surly while you're on this case. Not that I blame you. You've got this beautiful lady who thinks she's your wife and you can't bed her."

"You needn't point out the obvious." Barrett scowled up at James.

"Let me give you a little advice. I know you: You'd never allow yourself to become overly involved with a woman—especially one who might be a member of the Devil's Advocates and a traitor. Keep that in mind when you're forced to be alone with her. It might help to check your lust."

"Thank you for your rousing advice," Barrett said flatly.

"I wish I could offer more." James remained silent a moment; then a rakish grin spread across his mouth. "If you like, I could help watch her in town—perhaps take some of the burden off you."

"No, thank you." Barrett heard the tinge of jealousy in his own voice and frowned.

"Too bad." James sounded truly disappointed. "My men

will be watching Fenwick's every move outside the house. I'm sure you'll be too busy sporting your new *bride* around." His grin melted. "How do you think Lord Kensington will take the news of the marriage?"

Barrett thought of his father and their twelve-year estrangement. He wanted to tell James his father probably didn't give a damn whether he was married or not. Instead he said, "I'll deal with him if the need arises."

"Very well. I'll leave you to your wedding night." A ghost of a smile flitted back on James's face. Then he touched his riding crop to his hat and rode off.

Barrett watched him disappear into the darkness. A bitter wind blew through the courtyard; it pierced Barrett down to the marrow of his bones. Gooseflesh rose on the back of his neck. It wasn't the icy blast that had caused the reflex, he realized, but a feeling that someone was watching him.

CHAPTER TEN

Barrett wheeled around and saw a dark figure crouched near the stable. The person saw him and took off running. "Bloody hell!" Barrett cursed under his breath and gave chase.

His prey headed for the garden. The intruder, all in black, was dressed for spying at night. Even the man's hair blended into the darkness. And he sprinted with the stamina and agility of a man trained for spying.

The prowler headed straight for a hedge. Fifty more feet and Barrett would lose him in the cover of the garden. He pumped his legs harder. Harder. His heart pounded in his chest. His blood filled with the exhilaration of the chase. Closing in now. Thirty feet. Twenty. He was so close he heard the man's labored breathing.

Before Barrett had a chance to lunge, his prey whipped out a pistol and fired.

Barrett dove for the ground, the flash from the barrel vivid in his eyes. A bullet whizzed past his head.

He rose to go after the man, but the stranger had vanished. The whole case might be jeopardized. Hard telling how much the bastard had heard of Barrett's conversation with James. He had to get word to James.

He ran toward the hedge and wondered if the man might have been Fenwick. As if summoned by his thoughts, he heard the object of his suspicion call to him.

"I say, that you, Waterton?"

Barrett glanced at Fenwick, where he stood near the stable.

"Meagan says she'll be ready to leave in thirty minutes. Was that a shot I heard?"

"Yes." Barrett strolled up to him, still breathing heavily. "Someone was lurking out here and evidently didn't like it that I found him."

Fenwick wasn't out of breath. It could not have been him. "We ain't never had such a thing happen here in the country. I'll alert my groundskeeper." Fenwick grimaced and flicked a wary glance toward the garden.

"Never mind. I'll look for the person myself." Barrett frowned at Fenwick, then strode toward the garden.

Three hours later, Barrett ground his teeth and thought of all the time he'd wasted looking for the intruder. After searching the grounds for an hour in the dark, he had given up.

His gaze shifted to Meagan beside him on the seat. His frown melted. Her head rested between the seat and one side of the carriage. Sable curls hung over her shoulder, bouncing slightly as the carriage ate up the distance to London.

The whole journey, his gaze and concentration hadn't strayed far from her. He had studied the rise and fall of her chest, the way her lips parted slightly in sleep, the flutter of her lashes. He'd memorized the curve of her chin, the pert shape of her nose. Never a more tempting sight of femininity had lived and breathed. The fact Barrett couldn't touch her only added to her mystery and his perverse growing need to do just that.

Fenwick sprawled on the seat directly in front of Barrett, his jaw open. Loud snores boomed from his open mouth. Barrett listened to the ear-piercing sawing and scowled at Fenwick.

Meagan shifted. Her head fell forward and bobbed near her chest. Any moment she would tumble out of the seat. Barrett slipped past Nuisance—who had his head out the window, sniffing the night air—and slid over to Meagan. He eased his arm around her and pulled her over so her head rested on his shoulder.

"Show me the stars, Lord Herschel," she whispered in a husky voice, as she snuggled her face into the crux of his neck and slung her arm over his waist.

Barrett frowned down at the top of her head. He would like to show her a lot of things, but the stars weren't among them. For some strange reason, an unbidden wave of resentment for Sir William's son flowed over him. Perhaps he'd take his sweet time in keeping his promise to Meagan and contacting the gentleman.

Her lips touched his neck and his thoughts were diverted. He grew aware of her hot breath on his skin. He couldn't help but bend down and rub his cheek against the top of her head, feeling the satiny tresses stroking his face. The rosewater aroma of her hair and her own delicate womanly scent filled his senses.

The temptation to eavesdrop on her dreams made him whisper, "Can I kiss you?"

"Yes." Her lips pursed against his neck.

He stroked the side of her face and murmured, "Where would you like me to kiss you?"

"Sirius."

"If I could find Sirius on your face, I would definitely kiss it."

"Great dog."

"Yes, I know. Orion's dog, following on his heels and all that, but not on your body. Come back to earth for a moment and tell me where on your body you would like to be kissed by Lord Hershel?"

"Anywhere."

"That answer, Princess, is as limitless as the universe and infinitely more interesting." Barrett stroked her lips, fighting the desire to taste them.

She woke with a start. "Who! What!" she gasped, then shoved herself away from him. The sound of Fenwick's snoring brought her head around to him on the opposite seat. Recognition dawned on her face; then her violet eyes flashed at Barrett. "Did you kiss me?"

"No."

"But I could have sworn—"

"You were talking in your sleep."

"I did not."

"What of Lord Herschel?" Barrett raised a brow at her.

"You invaded my dreams. How could you?"

"I heard you speaking to him and answered you."

"You had no right. Dreams are private."

"You needn't fear I'll expose your wicked fantasies to anyone."

Her cheeks turned redder than the burgundy seats. "Why should I believe you? You are the last person I'd trust with any secret."

"Perhaps one day, I'll earn your trust." A note of sincerity slipped into Barrett's voice. It was foreign and disconcerting, and it had nothing to with his need to tap her for information. He stretched out his feet, crossed them at the ankles, and stared at the tips of his boots.

She eyed him as if she didn't know how to take his last statement. After a moment, she dismissed it totally by scooting as far away from him on the seat as possible.

"What time is it?" she asked, spreading her cape around her legs.

"About two A.M. We'll be in London soon."

"Have you slept at all?" Her brows furrowed with concern.

"No."

"Don't you ever get tired?"

"Rarely."

"But you must sleep sometimes."

"Two or three hours at most, and usually not before four in the morning."

"Is it your restless soul that keeps you awake?"

Barrett felt a growing unease at her ability to read him so well. He covered his discomfort behind a bland expression. "How can I sleep with that cannon fire coming from your brother?"

Her dimples beamed in a grin, but they disappeared as she glanced over at Fenwick. "Thank you for letting him ride with us. He sold our last carriage to pay for his gambling debts."

"He didn't inform me of that."

"He wouldn't. He's very astute at hiding his financial difficulties. I believe he's been living off credit for the past year, though he doesn't speak of it to me." She turned back to Barrett, wearing an unsure expression. Her eyes dug into his face as she said, "This brings me to something very uncomfortable I must ask of you."

"There is no need to feel discomfort. You can broach any subject with me."

She hedged a moment, reaching over to nervously stroke Nuisance's small head. "Harold owes a large debt he cannot pay. I was hoping you could clear it for him."

"Who does he owe?" Barrett eyed her closely.

"Some gentlemen friends."

"Are they your friends as well?" Barrett kept his face impassive.

"No, indeed. They are Harold's particular friends."

"Do I detect dislike in your voice?"

"I can't pretend to like them." Her hands twisted the handle on her reticule.

"Why not?"

She appeared to realize she'd said too much. "No particular reason. I just find it hard to be in their society."

"I see." Barrett wondered if these were members of the Devil's Advocates, or just moneylenders she detested.

She remained silent a moment, then said, "Will you pay his debt?"

"Of course."

"Thank you." Her eyes softened as she stared at him.

"How much does he owe?"

"Twenty thousand." Barrett didn't bat an eye at the sum. He'd lost more than that in one card game on a given night.

"That isn't too much money, is it?" Her brows furrowed in worry.

"No." Barrett gazed at her slender fingers stroking the dog's head. He realized how lucky the animal was.

"I'll never ask you to pay off his debts again, for I intend to put an end to his gambling."

"How do you intend to do that?" He smiled to himself at her indomitable spirit.

"I mean to see that no one lends him money."

"There are very unscrupulous moneylenders about. Someone will give him credit."

"Not if I speak to every one of them."

"I admire your spirit, but perhaps you should let me handle this."

"Would you?" She shot him a look divided by amazement and bemusement.

"Of course."

The carriage swayed gently to a halt. Nuisance perked

up his head and leaped down, barking anxiously at the door.

"Home at last," Barrett said, watching the anxiety on Meagan's face growing.

A thump sounded as the steps were let down. Then the door opened. Cold air whooshed through the warm carriage, making the embers in the stove flare. Nuisance bolted outside, yipping at nothing in particular.

Stratton appeared with Hastings at his side. Hastings accidentally hit his coworker's arm, and they elbowed each other over dirty looks.

Fenwick woke. "What? I say, are we here?" He threw his feet on the floor and sat up. One side of his curly blond locks stuck flat to his head from where he'd lain on the seat.

"Yes." Meagan's voice had a slight tremor in it.

Barrett stepped out of the carriage first and turned to help her down. "Come, Princess."

Meagan eyed Barrett's outstretched hand so long Fenwick said, "Are you getting out or not, Meggie?"

"Of course I am." She leveled a sharp look at Fenwick, then took Barrett's hand.

Barrett felt the warmth of her gloved hand seep into his skin as he helped her down. The brisk night air blew across Barrett's cheeks. Stars, blanketed by the thick veil of smoke, barely winked above the city. An odd quiet hovered over Wellington Road tonight, save for Nuisance, who only stopped barking long enough to cock his leg on a row of hedges that lined the front of the house. When he finished, he took off galloping around to the back of the house.

Abruptly, the front door opened and ten servants filed out and lined the walkway up to the porch.

Fenwick exited the carriage and whistled. "Some lair you got here." His jaw agape, he strode ahead of Barrett and Meagan past the line of servants.

Barrett watched Meagan's arched brows lower as she

gazed at the servants. "Oh, dear! Do your servants always come out in the middle of the night to greet you?"

"Only when I bring home a new wife," he said with studied indifference.

She smiled, but her expression was hardly more than a nervous little twitch of her lips. "Let us hope you don't bring home too many, for your servants will never get any sleep. Unlike you, they must require rest." Her eyes took in the sprawling lines of Pellam House, with its white Palladian facade and domed roof. The lights had been left burning. The staff were all well aware of Barrett's night owl hours. "This is a lovely home. It looks like a palace."

"It is a bit large," he said, aware he'd purchased one of the largest villas in St. John's Wood because he'd grown bored with his last residence. He'd been feeling restless that day and this was the largest house the agent had showed him. It hadn't really pleased him, and he didn't care for the house after he moved in, yet seeing the awe on her face now, knowing he'd be sharing it with her—if only for the length of this case—somehow gave him a strange feeling of contentment with the place. He found himself saying, "One of Prinny's architects built this home."

"Oh, my!" Her gaze scanned the eight towering Roman columns on the porch.

"Come. We'll get settled in."

She took his arm. As they passed the servants, she smiled and greeted them. When they reached the top step, Coates, a short stocky young man with a nervous twitch in his cheek, stepped up to her and swept a nervous bow before her. "My lady."

"Coates, this is the new Marchioness of Waterton. Princess, this is Coates, the butler," Barrett said.

Newly hired, Coates was apprehensive about his new position, and his uneasiness showed in the anxiousness in his eyes. Barrett had hired him because he had been fired by Lord Collins for accidentally breaking a priceless vase. Since he always searched for ways to vex Lord Collins, he'd hired Coates, knowing word would get back to Collins.

Meagan smiled at Coates, and in a friendly tone that would put anyone at ease, she said, "I must ask a favor of you, Coates."

"Anything, my lady."

"I'm very fond of Reeves, my butler, and he is on his way here"—she turned to look down the long drive—"though I don't think the carriage has arrived yet. Anyway, I would appreciate it if you would humor him. He's a very old man, and if not for his work, he would probably give up and not want to live any longer. I know it's not possible for him to take care of a house of this magnitude, but if you would allow him to help you, I would forever be in your debt."

Coates glowed radiantly. She had obviously found an admirer for life. "Yes, my lady. I would gladly do anything for you."

"Thank you, Coates."

"Come. I'll show you to your room." Barrett looked at her mouth as her tongue flicked out and moved nervously across her lips. The memory of the taste of her lips rushed back to him. When he recalled he would be escorting to the chamber next to his own, he groaned inwardly.

Meagan watched Barrett's long fingers curl around the knob and open it. As if he felt her eyes on him, he glanced at her. The blue in his eyes deepened with the same intensity she'd seen when he had kissed her on the street in Weymouth.

She had tried to repress the memory, but it flooded back to her now. With infinite clarity, she recalled every detail. The memory caused a fine sheen of sweat to break out all over her. If she cared to admit it, she wanted him to do it again. With trembling hands, she pulled off her gloves and cape and turned to face him.

Firm resolve hardened his expression. "I should let you get some rest."

"You're leaving?" Meagan glanced incredulously at Barrett.

"Yes. I have a little business to attend to."

"You have business at three in the morning?"

"Yes. I'll see you later." After one quick glance in her direction, he slammed the door on his way out.

Meagan brought her arms up, wrapped them around her waist, and stared at the closed connecting door. A memory from her childhood flooding back. . . .

Lights flickered in the hall at Fenwick Hall, dancing Meagan's shadow across the pink marble tiles. She eased closer to her father's study. Her nails dug into the door as she pressed her ear closer to it.

"I think we should give the girl a come-out. She'll be sixteen in two months." William Fenwick's tone retained its normal unflustered monotone—a stark difference to Lillian Fenwick's excitable twitter.

"You can't possibly think she'll ever find a gentleman who will take her," Lillian said.

"Of course she will."

"Not with that horrible rash all over her."

"She isn't broken out all the time."

"But enough to disgust any man. Can you imagine? We'd be the laughingstock of England if we tried to get her a voucher to Almack's. I can see it now. The moment I take her, she'll have another spell. Then what will poor Harold do? He'll not be able to show his face in society, nor shall I. It will ruin any prospects he might have of finding a bride."

"The boy is still in college—and doing very poorly, I might add."

"Oh, William, you must have patience with him. He's young."

Meagan screwed up her lips. Harold could do no wrong in her mother's eyes. He was her unblemished child. It didn't matter that he wasn't even her real son or that he had little common sense.

"I'm sure when he gets out of school he'll consider taking a wife. We can't let Meagan ruin his prospects. What on earth will the mothers of young debutantes say if they know his sister has this horrible condition? No. I'm sure this is one of the worst ideas you've conjured to date."

"You can be careful with her, my dear."

"I'm afraid since we don't know what causes her condition, I can't be. I'm sure 'tis far better not to get the child's hopes up. We should broach the subject with her now and resign her to the fact she will be a spinster." At William's silence, she continued. "You know I'm right. She has those horrid books and her interests to occupy her. And there is no use in getting her hopes up. No man will ever love her."

Meagan backed away from the door, her mother's words stabbing her. She wheeled and ran down the hallway, her footfalls melding with her sobs. . . .

Meagan rocked back and forth on her heels for a moment, feeling the pain as if it were yesterday. Swallowing hard, she sat down on one of two couches in her room. She glanced around the chamber. Fit for a queen and five times as large as her chamber back at Fenwick Hall, it was decorated in hues of gold, with filigree everywhere. Even gold leaf adorned her bed, which was a massive thing. With all this bright opulence and wealth surrounding her, she should have felt content. All she felt was the airy emptiness of the room.

Nuisance trotted out from beneath the bed, came over, and hopped up on her lap. He licked her face.

Meagan felt his whiskers and cold wet nose against her

chin, and she longed for a warmer, dryer nose and a coarser set of whiskers. "It looks as if I'm stuck with you on my wedding night."

His large, round eyes looked up at her as if to say, "That isn't so bad, is it?"

"I guess not." Meagan hugged the little dog to her breast.

Abruptly, a knock on the door sounded.

"Come."

Tessa entered, looking haggard, with dark circles under her eyes. "I came to check on you soon as our carriage arrived. I passed him in the hall as he left. I came straight-away to see if you were all right."

"I'm fine." Meagan set Nuisance down in her lap.

Tessa noticed Meagan's despondent look. She ran to her side and hugged her. "Oh, miss, something ain't right and you know it. Why'd he'd leave? Why you sittin' here alone, hugging his dog? It's your honeymoon night—or what's left of it," she added bitterly.

"He's gone, Tessa."

"Gone?" Tessa shook her head. "At this time of night?"

"He said he had business to see to." Meagan hid her disappointment behind feigned indifference. "It suits me just fine." By the look Tessa leveled her way, she realized she had overemphasized her words.

"Don't forget, my lady: This is Tessa you're talking to."

"How could I forget?"

"He'll be coming back, beatin' a path to your room," Tessa said, trying to sound cheerful.

"No, he won't." Meagan pulled back the hair from Nuisance's eyes and looked down into them.

"Sure he will." Tessa thrust her hands on her hips. "I saw those looks he was giving you."

"That's all they are: looks. He said he wouldn't force me into his bed until we knew each other better, which is fine with me." At Tessa's incredulous look, she added, "I'd just as soon forget this is my wedding night." She scooped Nuisance up in her arms and forced a cheerful note in her voice. "I have the only sleeping partner I need right here."

"All that thing will do is only put fleas in your bed."

"I'd rather have fleas in my bed than Lord Waterton," Meagan said with a forced casual air; then she strode over to her four-poster. "Go to bed now. It's late. I can undress myself."

Tessa cast her an assessing glance. Worry marred her brow as she left the room.

Meagan breathed a sigh of relief and began to undress. No matter what she told Tessa, it hurt that Barrett had left her on her wedding night and gone out—probably to his mistress. Again she heard her mother's words: *No man will ever love her.* Or, she supposed, want her on her wedding night.

She should have felt relieved Waterton had suggested they wait to get to know each other before he shared her bed, but she only felt a sharp pain over her heart that would not go away.

Across town, Barrett paced the length of James's bedroom floor, his boots thumping on a worn Chinese carpet. He paused, put his hand on the mantel and stared into the embers smoldering in the fireplace.

"Did I hear you correctly? You left her tonight?" James didn't bother opening his eyes as he spoke, as if he could care less that Barrett was standing in his bedroom in the middle of the night. In fact, Barrett had a key to James's house, and he used it at any ungodly hour that struck his fancy.

"Yes." Barrett turned away from the fire and glowered at his cousin sprawled on the bed, envious of the fact James could sleep.

"We do want this to seem real. You should have at least stayed and played the interested groom."

"I'll do it later. I had to ask you something." Barrett paced alongside James's bed, the thud of his boots melding with the ticking of a mantel clock.

"What?"

"Did you have a man watching Fenwick Hall?"

"No. You are the only person on this case so far."

"It may be jeopardized."

James opened his eyes and sat up. "What?"

"I caught someone listening to us after you left Fenwick Hall." Barrett told him what had happened, leaving out no detail. He watched James's expression for any sign he might be lying, but as usual James gave nothing away. After his cousin had failed to inform Barrett about Meagan being Fenwick's sister, Barrett wondered what else James might have failed to disclose. When Barrett finished he said, "I'm going to continue with the case."

"I don't know if that is such a good idea. If the Devil's Advocates are wise to you already, they could try to kill you."

"I have to keep her safe," Barrett said, more to himself than to his cousin.

"I take it you are becoming a bit more committed to this case than you'd anticipated."

Barrett realized he'd said more than he'd meant to. He quickly amended, "It's just I don't think she's guilty. She probably doesn't even know what her brother is up to."

"Can you be sure of that?"

Barrett recalled the guileless look on her face when he'd left her at her door. After working on cases with James, he could detect dissemblers after being in their company for a few moments. "There isn't a cunning bone in her body," he said with certainty.

"How can you be so sure?" James's brows made a sharp black line over his eyes; his distrustful side showed in his expression.

"She is an easy person to read."

James sat all the way up in bed and ran his hands through his black hair. "If you are wrong about her and she is an accomplice in a treasonous plot against the government, there is no way I can let her go. On the other hand, if she is the innocent in all of this, the scandal of having lived under your roof without a valid marriage license will destroy her reputation. You might consider marrying her."

"I don't want a wife." Barrett realized he'd added too much vehemence to his words and frowned. He began to pace again.

"So you've said." James's lips stretched with his usual maddening grin.

"Why are you being so insistent about me marrying her?"

"I was thinking of the lady."

"I'll not compromise her, and I'll find her a husband."

"I'm glad you've thought of everything."

Barrett remained silent. When he agreed to work on this case, he'd assumed she would be a member of the Devil's Advocates like her brother. But that was before she'd turned out to be his princess, before he'd felt an overwhelming desire to possess her, before he'd begun to care what happened to her.

At Barrett's silence, James said, "You know this new turn of events means I'm going to have to bring in some more men on this case. I've got to have agents watching your back."

"I don't need anyone skulking about. I can take care of myself." Barrett stopped pacing and draped the end of his cane over his arm.

"Nonetheless, for the sake of my own conscience, I'm going to bring in several men on this."

Barrett doubted the extent of James's conscience. A man as deeply involved in espionage as James had to be able to put aside his conscience when it suited him. It prompted Barrett to say, "Tell them to stay out of my way."

"They shall. I train all of my men. You'll never know they are around."

Something in James's words pricked the wary part of Barrett. He still had a feeling James wasn't telling him everything about the Devil's Advocates and this case.

He turned to leave, but James's voice stopped him. "Keep me informed."

"I shall." Barrett left, closing the door behind him. His thoughts turned to Meagan and her role in the case. If she were indeed innocent, as he believed, what would her reaction be when she realized his part in all of this? He tried not to think about that.

Something much worse plagued him: He had to go home, knowing his princess was sleeping in the chamber next to his own.

Meagan dreamed she was floating outside Pellam House. Holly wreaths and Christmas swags draped the windows and doors. Snow drifted up to the ledges of the windows. Icicles hung from the eaves like pickets on a fence. The sky overhead loomed murky and dark—an indistinguishable abyss that stretched as far as she could see.

Something about the house frightened her as she moved closer. Barrett called to her from inside. She tried to open the door, but an invisible barrier kept her from entering.

Barrett saw her and waved at her to come in. She could see their children, all four of them, lying on their bellies before the fire, playing with their toys. They could have been boys or girls—she couldn't make out their faces.

Barrett kept calling. Meagan tried to enter again, but she couldn't break through the barrier. His eyes were so cold and blue. If only they would warm up . . . if only the barrier might melt . . .

Meagan woke with a start and stared up into a pair of bright blue eyes.

CHAPTER ELEVEN

Meagan realized she was nose to nose with a little girl of about eight, not Barrett. Petite perfection molded her perfect oval face, rosy cheeks, and wide mouth. Her blond hair fell in long braids tied with a large blue bow.

"Hello." The little girl did not step back. She continued to stare directly into Meagan's eyes. "I'm Ann."

Something in the little girl's eyes disturbed Meagan, for they held a kind of sage understanding way beyond her years. As Meagan stared into the deep blue depths, she felt the little girl's perceptive gaze peering deep into her inner core. Meagan's fingers twisted nervously around the edge of the sheet.

At Meagan's silence, Ann said, "Something is wrong with you, isn't it?" She didn't wait for Meagan's reply. "My eyes used to look like yours when I couldn't walk—well, maybe mine were a little worse. You needn't fear I'll tell anyone your secret—well, maybe the fairies, but they already know. Perhaps I can help you." She leaned back, but her gaze didn't stray from Meagan's face.

Meagan wasn't about to discuss her situation with Ann, so she said, "Are you related to Lord Waterton?"

"Oh, no. He's a friend of my mama and papa's, but we call him Uncle Barrett. You must be the new marchioness. My mama— she's not my natural mama. My natural mama died a long time ago, but I like to think of Holly as my mama. My mama had quite given up on Uncle Barrett ever marrying anyone, you know. You are very pretty. Papa said Uncle Barrett would never find anyone but a desperate, hatchet-faced old prune to put up with him, but he was wrong. Papa is often wrong about things. We all had a good laugh teasing Papa when we found out Uncle Barrett had married. Papa swore you were ugly, so we came to call. He was wrong again. I can't wait to tell him so."

"Well, I'm glad you think he was wrong." Meagan slid up in bed and propped her back against the pillow and headboard. "He might think differently when he sees me."

"Oh, no. No one could find you wanting." Ann sat beside her on the bed. "I hope you don't mind my coming in here. I just wanted to have a peek at you."

"I don't mind at all."

"I let your dog out when I came inside. He barked at my brothers and chased them down the steps." An impish twinkle lit up Ann's eyes. "I'm glad he did. I didn't want them coming in here with me, you know."

"Yes, I'm quite aware how brothers can be."

"Mama is below stairs trying to talk Uncle Barrett into coming to our house for Christmas. Every year she invites him and every year he refuses."

"Why do you think that is?" Meagan waited eagerly for Ann's insight into Barrett's character.

"I think he likes brooding at Christmas. Some people like to feel sorry for themselves, especially lonely people." Ann's delicate brows furrowed. "Isn't it ironic? He's the richest, most powerful man in London, but the most lonely. It really is sad, don't you think?"

"Yes, I do." Meagan couldn't believe that this was a mere child speaking.

"You should come to our house and persuade Uncle Barrett to come too. We have a Christmas tree. My mama comes from America and her grandma was German and always had one. Have you ever seen one?"

"No."

"They're beautiful beyond words. You must come to our house when we light it."

"I would like that." Meagan noticed the bright light coming in through the curtains. "What time is it?"

"Close to noon."

"Noon?" Meagan almost shouted the word.

"What is wrong?"

"I never sleep past six." Since meeting Barrett, her life had been totally disrupted—even her internal clock was hopelessly befuddled.

"You did today." Ann grinned, her eyes twinkling.

A knock came at the door.

"Don't worry. I'll get it." Ann ran to the door and opened it.

A pretty woman, very much in the family way, with auburn hair and doelike brown eyes appeared at the door. When she saw Meagan, deep dimples appeared in her cheeks. "Hello. I must apologize for my daughter." She glanced at Ann.

Meagan liked the slow, mellow lilt of the lady's American accent. "It's quite all right," she said. "I enjoyed our little chat."

"I just wanted to have a peek at her to see if Papa was right." Ann's grin grew wider. "I'm afraid I woke her up, but I did invite her to our house for the tree lighting."

"I hope she'll come." Ann's mother smiled, then said, "We should let her get dressed now."

"That's quite all right. You're welcome to come in."

Meagan gave them a welcoming smile, already won over by the child and the lady.

Ann's mother waddled inside and extended her hand. "I'm Lady Upton, but please call me Holly. I dislike those stuffy English titles."

"And you may call me Meagan."

With an ease much like Ann's, Holly sat on the bed next to Meagan and touched Meagan's hand. "May I be frank with you?"

"Yes, of course."

"I'm thrilled Barrett's married. I'd given up hope of him finding anyone. I can see why he's fallen in love with you."

Meagan wanted to confide in someone, but she didn't know if she could speak in front of Ann.

As if Ann sensed Meagan's discomfort, she said in a perceptive voice, "I should go and see if the boys have murdered your poor dog yet." She smiled serenely, then left, closing the door behind her.

"She is such a marvel for a child," Meagan said, staring at the door.

"Yes. I like to call her my wise ancient. Now tell me what's on your mind." Holly rested her hands on top of her swollen belly.

Meagan didn't know why she wanted to pour her heart out to this stranger, but she felt a kindred spirit in her. "I was forced into marrying Barrett. He is not in love with me," Meagan said; then she told Holly all that had happened. She ended by saying, "I still don't know why he married me."

"That is very obvious to me. You are beautiful and kind. And knowing Barrett, he must care for you or he wouldn't have married you."

"I doubt it. He hasn't even shared my . . . " Her words trailed off.

"He hasn't?" Holly's intuitive brown eyes widened.

"Now that surprises me. As far as I know he has never had trouble in that area. There must be some reason. Would you like for me to quiz him?"

"Please don't." Meagan grabbed her arm. "He said he wanted to wait until we knew each other better."

Holly's expression took on a puzzled look. "Really? That is the last thing I would expect him to say. It really makes no sense at all. You can't get to really know him until you've shared the intimacy of his bed. Believe me, you learn so much about a man whey you're in bed with him." Holly's eyes glinted with a preoccupied look.

"He must have had his reasons." Meagan frowned and wondered if they were as gallant as she first thought they were.

Holly's faraway expression melted and she gave Meagan her full attention. "I believe a little shopping is in order."

"Shopping?"

"Yes. There's nothing like new clothes to make a husband notice you."

"I've never been shopping in London."

"Please say you will go with me."

"You're going out like that?" Meagan looked at Holly's belly.

"I know I should be in the country, sequestered away. I'm probably breaking every rule of propriety, but I have to do some Christmas shopping before we leave London and there is so much to do. Will you be ashamed to be seen with me? I promise to wear a cape that will cover this." Holly rubbed her swollen stomach.

Meagan laughed. "I'd be honored to be seen with you."

"Good. We'll talk more then." Holly eased into a standing position, then smoothed out the wrinkles of her deep blue morning dress.

A quick knock, and the door opened.

Barrett appeared with a two-year-old boy in his arms. He looked adorable holding the child. The baby twined his chubby little fingers through the fringe on a brightly colored scarf hanging around Barrett's neck. Meagan's mind conjured up a vision of him holding their own child: a little boy with Barrett's blond hair and brooding good looks. She remembered him leaving her last night and the vision vanished. She scowled at him.

"There you two are." Barrett's gaze traveled between Meagan and Holly.

"You have a delightful wife." Holly squeezed Meagan's hand.

"I know." Barrett's eyes glowed strangely at Meagan.

Warmth bloomed in Meagan at his words.

Holly didn't miss the byplay and she grinned. "I'm sure we'll be the best of friends."

"Anyone who meets my wife can't help but be her friend." Barrett spoke without taking his eyes off Meagan.

A handsome man appeared in the doorway beside Barrett. He was a brown-haired replica of Barrett. Just as tall and equally endowed with wide shoulders and lithe brawn. But his eyes were gold, not blue like Barrett's.

Holly lumbered over to him. "This is my husband, John. John, this is Meagan."

His eyes swept over Meagan, and he grinned. Meagan pulled the covers up around her shoulders. Not that anyone could see her body, covered as it was in her serviceable flannel gown. Still she blushed at being caught in bed by two men.

"A pleasure to meet you, my dear." John executed a dashing bow. "You'll have to forgive this intrusion, but I've come to retrieve my wife. We must be leaving." He elbowed Barrett. "I don't know how you did it, or why she would want to marry you, Waterton, but she's a diamond of the first water."

Barrett scowled while the baby patted his mouth. "Thank you. I was holding my breath for your approval."

"I pity you, my dear." John winked at Meagan; then he

took the child from Barrett. "Come on, baby Lawrence. We've seen what we came to see. It's time to go."

"Are you up for a round later at Jackson's, or have you gotten soft?" John raised a taunting brow at Barrett.

"The day I can't beat you in fisticuffs is the day they can shoot me and plant me."

Two boys peeked around the corner at Meagan. They looked around twelve and fourteen. "Is that her?" the eldest one said. He looked like his father, dark, golden eyed, with an unwavering expression that hinted he was not a young man to be taken lightly.

"She's not rat faced, Uncle Barrett. Good show." The younger one patted Barrett on the back. He was towheaded and green eyed, and he wore a worshipful expression as he gazed at Meagan.

"I'm glad you approve." A lazy smile spread over Barrett's lips.

Ann stepped between her brothers. She pointed to the eldest boy and said, "This is Dryden"—she put her hands on the blond curly locks of her other brother—"and this is Brock."

"Pleased to meet you," Meagan said, seeing a strangely adoring smile on Brock's face. He was obviously intrigued by the opposite sex even at his young age.

"I'm her favorite brother," Brock said, grinning.

"Are not!" Dryden shoved his brother.

"Am too!" Brock hit his brother on the side of the head and took off running down the hall, laughing.

Dryden took off after him.

Ann rolled her eyes. "See what I mean. They are wretched animals."

"If you'll excuse me, I'd better go knock some heads together," John said. "Come on, puss." He grabbed Ann's hand and strode down the hall.

"I'd better help him." Holly grinned at Meagan. "I'll bring the carriage around in two hours."

"Fine."

Barrett watched Holly leave; then he strode into her room. "I'm almost afraid to ask where you are going with Lady Upton."

"Shopping." Meagan stared at the strange-looking scarf around his neck. Large holes and bulges covered it from missed stitches in the crocheting. "What is that?"

The hardness in his eyes melted. His expression turned defensive as he said, "A gift from Ann. She tried to give it to me earlier, but I wasn't here." He touched the scarf as if it were the most precious thing in the world.

The strange connection she felt when his soft side surfaced pulled at her. She could almost forgive him for last night. Almost.

With more haughtiness in her voice than she felt, she said, "If you don't mind, I'd like to get dressed. Please leave."

He continued stroking the scarf and gave her a long curious glance. Finally, he said, "Very well."

Meagan watched him go and she thought of Holly's family and how happy they seemed. Deep emptiness filled her. Frowning, she threw back the covers and swung her legs to the floor.

Minutes later, Tessa sailed through the door, carrying a massive arrangement of tulips, roses, and orchids and a small box under her arm. "Look what just come for you."

"Who sent them?"

"Don't know. I was having a bit of lunch, and they arrived. I ran straight up with them."

Meagan pulled the card out of the arrangement. Scrawled in neat handwriting across the page were the words:

I hope you can forgive me for leaving you last night. I'll make it up to you.

Barrett

"Who're they from?"

"Barrett." Meagan bent and smelled the flowers. They smelled heavenly.

Tessa raised her brows in surprise. "Here, see what else he got you." Tessa thrust the small package at her.

Feeling like a little girl opening her first present, Meagan tore into the brown wrapping. She opened the box and stared down at a diamond necklace. A fortune in diamonds winked at her. They covered a choker and the teardrop pendant hanging from it.

"Lord be, miss. It's lovely," Tessa said. "I suppose he's trying to make up for how he acted last night."

"It appears so." Meagan picked up the choker and held it up to her throat. She looked in the mirror. "It's exquisite. I've never owned such an expensive bauble."

"Too fine to wear with that nightgown." Tessa grinned.

Meagan felt her heart soften toward Barrett. In his note he'd said he would make it up to her. Did that mean he had decided to take her to his bed? The idea caused her heart to slam against her chest.

"I want to wear my best morning dress, Tessa, the blue one."

"Don't let these baubles turn your head. Just remember why he sent them to you—leaving you like that on your wedding night." Tessa shook her head, setting the ruffle around her mobcap slapping against her plump cheeks.

"How can I forget?" Meagan wasn't about to let Tessa's pessimism ruin this glow. No, she couldn't wait to thank Barrett.

Half an hour later Barrett strode into his office, Nuisance's toenails clicking behind him. The dog had actually survived a frolic with Upton's two older sons, yet not without a certain expenditure of energy that showed as he plopped down on the rug near the fire.

Barrett flopped down in his chair and glowered at the stack of invitations and mail. His mind wasn't on opening the mail, but on a pair of flashing violet eyes and the cool way Meagan had turned him out of her bedroom. Naturally she would be angry with him for leaving her last night. He had expected as much.

A knock sounded.

He glanced toward the door. "Enter."

Fenwick strode through the door, his purple breeches and jacket clashing with his bright gold paisley waistcoat. Barrett groaned under his breath and frowned.

"Did you say something?" Fenwick asked.

"No." Barrett made a face at his jacket. "Have a seat."

Fenwick plopped down in the high-backed wing chair next to Barrett.

Nuisance raised his head from a cozy spot near the fire. He watched Harold's every move, the hair covering his eyes moving slightly.

"You sent for me?" Fenwick cast a nervous glance at Barrett.

"I wanted to speak to you about something that concerned my wife." At hearing the term *wife* come out of his mouth, Barrett frowned. He stretched out his long legs and crossed them at the ankles.

"What's that?"

"She asked that you be allowed to reside with us. I have no objection. You are welcome to stay in any of our homes." Barrett used his most gracious smile, but it didn't crease the corners of his eyes.

"Very kind of you indeed."

"She also asked that Fenwick Hall and the lodge in Scotland be deeded to her. I've written my man to have it taken care of."

"Oh." Fenwick's face turned the color of his crimson paisley vest. He couldn't meet Barrett's eyes as he said, "Well, that should make her happy. She was in high dudgeon when I lost it. Lady Luck wasn't on my side that night.''

"She hasn't been for some time, I gather."

"Not in the past six months." Fenwick stared pensively into the fire.

The flames popped and hissed in the silence.

Barrett pulled a check out of the desk drawer and slid it across to Fenwick. "Here."

Fenwick read the amount, and his eyes popped open. "This is for twenty thousand pounds."

"Indeed." Barrett leaned back in his desk and crossed his arms over his chest.

"But I can't accept this."

"It's only a loan to pay off your debts."

Fenwick's surprise melted behind a scowl. "Damn, Meggie. She asked you for this, didn't she?"

Barrett nodded.

"I didn't want to ask you for money, so . . . " Fenwick's voice faded. He stared pensively down at the check.

"You'll pay off your debts with the check. No gambling. Is that understood?"

Silence stretched between them. Barrett shot Fenwick a glance that made him look away and shove the check in his coat.

"Understood," Fenwick said, his voice as soft as a scolded child's.

Barrett steepled his fingers on his desk. "What are you planning to do with your life now?"

"I don't know." Fenwick glanced down at his hands, a lost expression on his face. "I had a few years of law at Oxford, before I was sent—I mean left."

"So you were sent down." Barrett used the words Harold could not.

Fenwick nodded, looking like a recalcitrant boy with his blond curls fringing his cheeks. His face screwed up in a grimace as he said, "I had one professor who hated me. I couldn't pass his class."

"I had one of those at Cambridge, but it wasn't the professor who failed me. It was the late nights of debauchery that did me in."

Fenwick remained silent, looking more despondent than the night at the gaming table when Barrett had ruined him.

"If you wanted to return, I could get you into Cambridge. I'm personally acquainted with the dean."

"You would do that for me?" Fenwick raised his head to look at Barrett.

"We are related now." Barrett felt a jab from his conscious. He had to gain Fenwick's trust. What better way than to appear the concerned brother-in-law? Barrett also remembered when he had been that young and reckless.

"Been meaning to ask you something." Harold cleared his throat. "I couldn't help but notice you went out last night. I heard some of the servants commenting on it this morning. They were saying you didn't visit Meggie's bed. Is there some reason for that?—I mean, when I saw you in her room at Fenwick Hall, I thought—"

"I know what you thought."

"If she's being difficult, I can have a word with her."

"You needn't," Barrett said in a firm tone that brought a frown to Fenwick's face.

He must have realized his mistake in bringing up such a touchy subject, for he gazed down at his hands and remained silent.

"I had business to attend to," Barrett offered, filling in the silence.

"I sent her the usual flowers and a bauble to make up for it."

"That'll do the trick. She's a woman, ain't she? Works for me every time."

Barrett felt another pair of eyes on him. He glanced

over Harold's head. Meagan stood in the door; the necklace he'd bought was sparkling around her neck. Her face was flushed, her eyes shooting darts at him, her jaw clenched. If she'd been a teakettle, steam would have been coming out of her mouth. A sick feeling rose in him.

"Meagan, I . . . "

She didn't wait for him to finish. She turned and fled down the hall.

"Damn it to hell!" Barrett mumbled, jumping up.

"Let her go. She'll get over it." Fenwick stood.

"Stay out of this." Barrett ran out of the room. Down the hall. Up the stairs. For a woman in a dress, she ran like a frightened doe. He didn't corner her until she bolted into her chamber.

"Let me explain," Barrett said. "I only wanted—"

"I know what you wanted."

A lamp flew at his head.

He ducked. It crashed against the wall behind him. "Now listen, Meagan."

"No!" She picked up a candlestick and hurled it.

He crouched and watched the candlestick sail by his face. It hit the door and joined the broken glass on the floor.

"I won't be bought with shallow gifts like the cheap harlots you may be used to." She reached for the vase of flowers.

Barrett made a dive for her and caught her before she picked up the vase. He wrestled her hands down by her sides. "I only wanted to make it up to you."

"Let me go!" She tried to wiggle her arms free.

"Not until you smile at me."

"Smile at you. I'd like to—"

He kissed her, cutting off her words. She kept her lips tightly together, her body stiff. Bent on getting that smile and feeling her surrender, Barrett stroked her mouth with his tongue and massaged her back. Her mouth finally softened and her body relaxed against him.

Barrett moved his hands up her spine, bunching the muslin of her dress along the feminine curve. He felt a shiver go through her. Smiling inwardly, he moved his hand along the back of her slender neck. His fingers tangled in the bun at her nape. Hairpins hit the floor like raindrops.

"Your tresses feel like silk," he said against her lips, threading his fingertips through her curls, the downy softness tantalizing his finger tips.

She opened her mouth. His tongue slid past her lips, plundering the deep recess. He told himself the reason he kissed her was to appear the attentive husband. But by the uncontrollable desire burning in him, he knew this had nothing to do with the case.

"Oh, Barrett . . . " she said against his lips, even as her arms slipped around his neck. Her fingers twined in his hair. Then she kissed him back with a brazenness that she could control no more than he could.

His hands moved down her back. Before his hands reached her bottom, he realized what he was doing. A sound halfway between a groan and a growl escaped him. Abruptly, he broke off the kiss, but he didn't step back.

She gazed up at him, her eyes dark with desire and disappointment. If only he could make love to her and have her look at him differently. He swallowed hard, quashing the urge to kiss her again. He ran his finger along her lips. "Are you going to throw something else at me if I turn you loose?"

"Most definitely." She teased him with a grin, her dimples showing.

"I'll have Coates clear this room of all hurling articles."

She laughed, a deep husky sound that oozed over Barrett and compelled him to taste her lips again. He forced himself to step back from her. Immediately, he felt the loss of her shapely body next to his.

Her expression straightened as she said, "I must thank you, my lord, for giving Harold the money to pay off his debts."

"You must have been at the study door long before I noticed you."

"I was. I saw you hand him the check. Anyway, I'm in your debt." Her eyes glowed with a soft light.

"Do you always hurl objects at people you are indebted to?" He lifted one side of his mouth in a wry grin.

"Not usually." She returned his grin. "I'm sorry. I lost my temper."

"Ahmm!" Someone cleared his throat near the door.

Barrett turned. Coates stood in the doorway, his face red from having disturbed them. "Begging your pardon, but Lady Upton is waiting on you, my lady."

"Thank you, Coates." Meagan smiled at him.

He grinned as if she'd given him a kiss; then he turned and strode away.

"Try to stay out trouble. Holly has a way of finding it."

"We're just going shopping."

"Hmm! There is no 'just' with Holly. She is all extremes. Take care you do not let her bankrupt me." Barrett winked at her and left her staring at him, a forlorn look on her face.

Barrett quit the room, feeling her eyes on his back. It was so easy to forget she was a suspect in this case. He kept trying to remind himself of that fact; still it was becoming imperative to him to see her face light up as it had when she thanked him for having given her brother the check. He couldn't very well give Fenwick money every day. Diamonds and flowers were out. He'd have to think of another way.

* * *

Two hours later, Meagan strode beside Holly along Mayfair Square. People, carriages, and vendors moved past them in a constant steady stream. Christmas wreaths of holly and boxwoods hung on shop doors, and pine roping waved along the tops of windowsills.

The activity hardly held Meagan's interest. She ran a gloved hand over her bottom lip and couldn't forget the way Barrett had kissed her. Her lips still tingled. Despite his shallow gifts, he could be so charming and irresistible at times. She could not help but wonder if he had put aside his chivalrous notions and decided they were acquainted enough to make love now. If she cared to admit it, the prospect made her insides flutter with anticipation. Holly's voice broke into her musings.

"John gets uncomfortable if I'm gone more than three hours—especially in this condition." She smiled down at her stomach. "Men can be such worrisome creatures. John acts as if I'll break if I move. I hate to say this, but it is such a pleasure getting away from him for a few hours." Holly casually glanced at a bonnet in a haberdashery's window.

"I'm so glad you suggested this." Meagan graced her with a smile. "You know, I've never had a female friend. You are my first."

"I'm honored." Holly's wide brown eyes overflowed with an inner warmth that seemed so much a part of her. "Since this is our first shopping trip together, I think we should make it one to remember. Perhaps we should stay out all day. What do you say?"

"It sounds lovely to me."

Meagan felt someone watching her. She glanced behind her and saw a short, thin man. A full red beard hid half his face, and red hair poked out of his cap. A pair of glasses covered his eyes, which looked slightly slanted behind the thick glass.

When he saw her looking at him, he paused to peer into a cobbler's shop window. Meagan turned to Holly. "Don't look now, but the man behind us has been following us for the past hour."

Holly pulled out a mirror from her reticule and pretended to pat her hair. "I don't see anyone."

Meagan turned around. The little man had disappeared. She scanned the sidewalks and the pedestrians, but couldn't see him anywhere. "He was just there near that shop."

"Well, he's gone now. Perhaps we'll see him again and you can point him out." Holly thrust her mirror back in her purse. "Come on. Here's where I wanted to take you."

Meagan followed Holly into a corsetiere's shop. A young woman wearing a bright platinum wig ran toward them. She smiled at Holly and Meagan. "Ah, Lady Upton, so glad you came in."

Holly grinned, flashing the woman a hint of her dimples. "We would like to see nightwear, something very sheer." Turning, she whispered to Meagan, "This will be my Christmas present to John."

The clerk thought for a moment, then said, "I have just the thing." She disappeared behind some curtains in the back of the store.

"I really don't think I should buy anything in here." Meagan looked at the skimpy see-through corsets and drawers displayed on the shelves.

"Of course you should. When Barrett gets one look at you in one of these"—Holly ran her hand over a sheer silk nightgown held together by three ties in the front—"you won't be able to get him out of your room."

"I don't know."

Holly locked arms with her. "Don't despair. Barrett can be very charming in spite of his shallow gifts. Just give him a chance. He's been a bachelor so long, I don't think he's ever put much thought into gift giving or pleasing anyone but himself."

The bell on the door jangled. A stunning dark-haired woman with ice blue eyes breezed into the shop, the silk of her lavender gown swishing. She exuded an air of grace and confidence.

The lady's gaze breezed over Meagan with casual indifference. Meagan stared down at her own worn cape, which was at least four years old, and at her simple gray muslin dress. Living in the country, she had not seen the need for spending money on a wardrobe that would impress no one—especially after Harold had fallen on hard times and stopped her allowance. Compared to this lady standing in front of her, Meagan felt like the gauche, unsophisticated dowd she was. If she had possessed half of this lady's elegance, refinement, and demeanor, Barrett might not have left her last night.

The lady eyed Holly. "How nice to see you again, Lady Upton." The woman's lips stretched in a thin smile.

Holly returned the smile, but the strain it cost her to do so showed in her face. "Hello, Lady Matilda."

"I hope Lord Upton is well?"

"He couldn't be better. Thank you for inquiring."

"I see you are expecting. Congratulations." Lady Matilda's gaze roamed over Holly's protruding belly, a hint of envy flashing in her eyes.

"Thank you," Holly said with strained politeness.

Lady Matilda's beautiful eyes turned Meagan's way. "And who might this be?"

"This is Lady Waterton."

Lady Matilda stiffened, and her smile vanished. "Yes, I read the announcement. I wish you luck in your marriage."

The door opened and a tall, lean, hawk-faced gentleman strode into the shop. His black eyes met Meagan. Her blood ran cold. She remembered the cruel black eyes from the Christmas bazaar. Lord Collins.

CHAPTER TWELVE

Lord Collins strode over to Meagan, never taking his eyes off her. "Ah, I knew I'd seen those wicked violet eyes before. The Winter Princess. You're even more comely without your veil." His gaze raked over her body.

Meagan felt her skin crawl. "You're mistaken, sir." As intoxicated as he had been the day of the bazaar, how could he have recognized her?

"Oh, no. I never forget a woman's eyes. You can learn so much about a lady from her eyes." His gaze snapped up and down her body. "You're the palm reader at the bazaar, all right. Did you know the gentlemen about town are taking bets on the lady's identity?"

"I'm surprised they have nothing better to occupy their minds." Meagan smelled brandy on his breath and realized he might be used to functioning while in his cups.

Collins smiled. "I must know your name, madam?"

Lady Matilda waved her hand airily through the air. "Allow me to introduce you to Lady Waterton. Lady Waterton, this is Lord Collins." She beamed a pleased smile at Meagan.

The blood drained from Holly's and Meagan's face at the same time.

"Well, well, well. Isn't this an interesting bit of news?" Lord Collins's pointed teeth gleamed in a smile.

"I do believe I'm done shopping. Would you be so kind as to escort me to my carriage?" Lady Matilda laced her arm in Lord Collins's, the pasty smile never leaving her lips.

"Delighted, my lady," Lord Collins said, his eyes boring into Meagan.

"Good day, ladies." Lady Matilda guided Lord Collins to the door.

He paused and turned to look at Meagan. "I look forward to meeting you again, Lady Waterton." He bowed, then led Lady Matilda out of the shop.

Meagan breathed a sigh of relief.

"Oh, my Lord! What have I done?" Holly grabbed her cheeks. "I told her who you were. Now Lord Collins knows."

"We would have crossed paths somewhere. No doubt, he would have recognized me. You needn't fret over it."

"But I'm afraid I've stirred up a hornet's nest." Holly squeezed her eyes closed. "Why, oh, why, did I even speak to her?"

"I sensed she wasn't pleased at meeting you."

"She shouldn't be. She had an infatuation with John, and when we announced our engagement, she tried to kill him."

"Really? I would never have guessed." Meagan glanced at Lady Matilda through the long window in the shop. The other woman twitched beside Lord Collins, her expensive red wool cloak swishing along her shapely figure. Lord Collins had his neck craned, because he was still looking at Meagan through the glass.

Their gazes locked. His black eyes bored into her. She quickly glanced away.

Holly saw the exchange and frowned. "Yes, she was arrested and sent to a mental institution. I can't believe they let her out." She gnawed on her bottom lip.

"Perhaps she's cured. She seems normal enough."

"Oh, she's good at hiding her feelings. She sent Barr—" Holly clamped her mouth closed and fingered a silk negligee near her.

"What were you going to say?"

"I shouldn't tell you this, but you'll probably find out soon enough. Barrett used to fancy himself in love with her for years."

Meagan's fists tightened at her side. In a voice that in no way hinted at the jealousy plaguing her, she said, "Is that so?"

"Yes. Luckily, she wouldn't have anything to do with him. But he was in love with her, or so he thought."

"Why would he love a woman who spurned his suit?"

"Don't ask me. You know men—you never can figure them out. They want what they can't have. Men are contrary, perverse creatures."

"Do you think he still loves her?" Meagan tensed while waiting for Holly's reply.

"He wouldn't have married you if he still loved Lady Matilda."

"He won my hand in a bet and probably married me to please his perverse side."

"He wouldn't have forced the marriage if he wasn't attracted to you."

Meagan let the subject drop. She would never understand why Barrett had married her, and she didn't think Holly would either.

At her silence, Holly said, "Stay as far away from Lord Collins as you can. He has a horrible reputation and he has been Barrett's enemy ever since he closed down Lord Collins's bordellos.''

"Why did Barrett involve himself?"

"Lord Collins was taking young girls, barely thirteen and fourteen, and turning them into prostitutes. Barrett found out about it and closed him down last year. Lord Collins has hated him ever since.''

"What a despicable man.''

"I hate to point this out, but you have become Lord Collins's enemy by association.''

Meagan frowned and glanced up at the sound of footsteps. The clerk appeared with an armload of boxes and laid them out on a counter. "Forgive me, ladies, but I had a delivery out back.''

They examined the colorful array of nightgowns and undergarments. Bright seductive reds. Mysterious midnight blues. Teasing, little-girl pinks. Diaphanous silks, gossamer satins, and transparent gauzes. All soft to the touch and wicked enough to stir any man's lust.

Meagan touched one black silk negligee. Lady Matilda's beautiful face materialized in her mind, her striking blue eyes twinkling. A territorial instinct that Meagan didn't know existed in her rose up like an awakening dragon.

Meagan pointed to the black negligee and an almost transparent silk chemise. "I'll take those— No!" She waved her hand at the boxes. "All of them.''

A pleased grin moved across Holly's face as she looked at Meagan. With the flourish of a pirate captain, she raised her fist in the air. "That's the way, Meagan. You lead the charge!''

Meagan charged up the steps of Pellam House, filled with a feminine confidence she'd never experienced before. A small battalion of five footmen followed behind her, their arms loaded with boxes that held a new wardrobe and an arsenal of seductive nightwear. She had never spent money so lavishly on herself. Doing so felt sinful. It felt wonderful.

Holly had even talked her into buying rouge and lip color. If Meagan could help it, Barrett would come to her bed tonight. Again she saw Lady Matilda's visage, poised, graceful, and ever so beautiful. Her brows snapped together, and she felt some of her confidence wane.

As she reached the top step Lochlann stepped out from behind one of the huge white columns.

"Geminy!" Meagan gasped. "You scared the life out of me."

"I had to see you."

Meagan turned to the footmen. "You can take the packages inside. Thank you." She waited until the door closed on the last one. "You shouldn't be here."

He grabbed her hand and looked hurt. "How could you marry him?"

She noticed the hurt in his eyes. "I did it to save you."

Lochlann dropped his hands to his sides in frustration. "I didn't need saving. Don't you see he manipulated you?"

"If he did, I've yet to learn the reason for it."

"You don't have to stay married to him, Meagan. You can get an annulment."

"I know that."

Lochlann grabbed her arms. His gaze dug into her eyes. "I can tell by looking at you that you're not happy. You'll never be happy with him."

"But I am."

I don't believe you."

"Believe her." Barrett's deep drawl came from behind them.

Meagan felt her blood freeze and glanced to her right. Barrett leaned indolently against one of the columns, his ankles crossed, his cane draped over his arm. He wore the scarf Ann had crocheted for him—a multicolored disaster against his perfectly tailored greatcoat and top hat. His humorless smile gave nothing away, though his eyes sparked blue fire.

"Do you always sneak up on people?" Meagan glowered at him.

"Only when it's to my advantage." He fixed Lochlann with a level stare. "Kindly remove your hands from my wife."

Lochlann dropped Meagan's arms and stepped back.

"Go into the house, Meagan. I wish to speak to Burrows alone."

"No!" Meagan cringed at the murderous coldness in Barrett's expression.

But it wasn't Barrett who made the first move of aggression. Lochlann strode toward Barrett. "She should hear what we have to say."

Lochlann paused several feet from Barrett. Broader in the shoulders and a head taller than her friend, Barrett towered over Lochlann; the high beaver hat he wore made him seem that much taller.

Lochlann held his ground. "You have some nerve standing there after what you've done to Meagan. You have no honor. I told you I would have satisfaction and I shall." Lochlann's eyes bulged with anger. He whipped a pistol out from beneath his coat and pointed it at Barrett. "If you don't agree to meet me at dawn, I'll shoot you right here."

"No!" Meagan cried and lunged at Lochlann.

The gun exploded.

The report hammered Meagan's eardrums. Something whizzed past her face. Silence hung heavily in the air.

Lochlann stared down at the gun, dumbfounded.

Barrett rushed to Meagan and grabbed her arms. "Are you all right?"

"Yes."

"Barely." Barrett reached up and stuck his finger

through a hole in the rim of her bonnet. He wheeled around and faced Lochlann. "You could have killed her."

Lochlann stiffened, suddenly on the defensive. He looked at Meagan, his eyes pleading. "I would never hurt you."

"I know." Meagan felt the small hole in her bonnet. Half an inch more and it would have hit her temple. Her stomach knotted at the thought.

"Leave while you still can." Barrett took a step toward Lochlann, a dangerous glint in his eyes.

"I'm not leaving until you agree to a duel." With a slight tremor in his hand, Lochlann shoved the gun back into the pocket of his coat.

Meagan stepped over to Lochlann and touched his arms. "Please just go."

"No, I won't." Lochlann laid his hand on Meagan's cheek.

With a proprietary gleam in his eye, Barrett stepped up to them and shoved Lochlann back from Meagan. "Dawn then. Battersea Park."

"Stop it! This is insane!" Meagan glared at both men.

Lochlann ignored her outburst and looked pleased by Barrett's assent. "At dawn then." He jammed his hands in the pockets of his coat, some of his bravado gone. "I'll see you later, Meagan."

"I don't think so," Barrett drawled, his voice laced with a deceptive calm.

"This is not over yet." After a final glance at Meagan that bespoke of Lochlann's embarrassment, resentment, and hurt—a look that said he wasn't about to give up on their friendship or his quest to save her from Barrett— her friend strode down the drive.

"You should have let me handle him," Meagan said, angry with herself for involving Lochlann in the whole debacle.

"You almost got yourself killed." Barrett stared at the hole in her bonnet.

"I know him—you don't. He's my friend."

"He doesn't look on you as a friend," he said, his voice deceptively bland.

"Of course he does."

"I saw him look at you and touch you. Friendship is the last thing on his mind."

Meagan thought Barrett might be correct. She'd never seen Lochlann look at her with such intense emotion. She quickly changed the subject. "I hope you were just humoring him by saying you'd meet him at dawn."

"I never humor people."

"But you can't face him. You'll kill him."

"No, I'll just teach him a lesson. I saw how crazed he is over you. He'll not stop until someone innocent gets killed. I hoped he'd cool down and come to his senses. I was wrong. Hotheads like Burrows can't see reason."

Barrett had a point. She'd never seen this side of Lochlann. "I shan't argue with you. I'll find a way to stop this duel." Barrett opened his mouth with a retort, but she blurted, "I met Lady Matilda today." She studied him closely for a reaction.

"Really?" His voice had been nonchalant, but a flicker of emotion flashed through his eyes and disappeared.

Her insides clenched. She had her answer. "I should have known you still—" She clamped her mouth closed before she could make a fool of herself. She grabbed the hem of her dress and stomped up the stairs.

Barrett caught up to her and asked, "What were you going to say?"

"Nothing."

"Did I detect a note of jealousy in your voice?"

"Jealous of you? Hah!"

Barrett leaped in front of her and made her pause near

a column at the top of the steps. She darted around behind the column.

He was right there blocking her way. "Tell me what you were going to say."

"No."

His arms shot out and captured her against the column. "I don't give up easily." He moved closer.

Meagan's back connected with the column. "Neither do I." She met his gaze without a blink.

She stared at the afternoon stubble on his square chin, at that unsettling curve on his lips, the determined gleam in his eyes. She sorely regretted the challenge in her last statement, for she was staring at the blond hair curling below his hat and her fingers itched to touch it.

"But I do . . . ." He pressed his body against hers.

"Never," she gasped.

"We shall see." He bent and angled his lips against the edge of her mouth, barely touching it.

Meagan battled the urge to turn her mouth fully toward his. "You can stop now."

"I've just gotten started." He nibbled the corner of her mouth, his hot breath searing her cold skin.

Tingles shot down Meagan's neck. In spite of the temperature being close to freezing, a fine sheen of sweat covered her body. "I'm warning you: Trying to seduce me will not work."

"I love a challenge." He moved lower, barely touching his lips into the hollow below her mouth.

Meagan felt her body trembling all over. Even her toes curled as she fought the desire. "You're wasting your time."

"Am I?" He brought his lips up to hers and held them a hairbreadth away.

They felt like the flutter of butterfly wings against her lips, working a spell over her mouth, drawing her lips toward his. Before she knew it, she was kissing him.

It was the surrender he'd been waiting for. He devoured her mouth. Meagan tried to resist the feel of his lips taunting her mouth, the way his tongue slid along her teeth. She tried not to give in to the strength of his arms as they circled her waist and pulled her tighter to him. She tried to ignore his broad chest, even though she felt all its hard contours and its heat seeping through her bulky wool cape and clothes.

The battle was lost. She opened her mouth and wrapped her arms around his neck. Her fingers tangled in his hair. The crisp silken mass tantalized her fingertips, and she grabbed large handfuls, inching his hat up, up . . . . *Plop*. His hat fell and hit the stoop.

He slid his tongue deep into her mouth. Somewhere in the back of her mind, she heard a carriage.

"Damnation!" Barrett mumbled and pulled back.

Her body still throbbing, Meagan glanced toward the drive. A shiny black town coach pulled by six identical grays rocked to a halt, the bright burgundy feathers on the horses' bridles flicking. Four outriders and six coachmen in bright burgundy-striped livery and white breeches scurried down. They made a line on either side of the door as if Prinny himself were alighting.

"Who is that?" Meagan asked, awed by the spectacle of the person's arrival. Her gaze fell on the crest on the door: a lion rampant, its teeth and claws bared.

"That, Princess, would be my father," Barrett said, his surprise barely hidden behind a scowl.

The ominous tone in Barrett's voice made Meagan's mouth go dry. She didn't want to meet Barrett's family, especially since she wasn't even sure of this marriage or Barrett. This wasn't fair.

One of the coachmen turned. With a loud nasal bluster that could cut through every tendon in a person's body and rattle the leaves on nearby trees, he announced, "The Duke of Kensington."

Meagan watched a cane appear first. A tall, well-formed man around fifty with thick white hair stuck out one shiny black boot, then another. He stepped on the ground and stretched to his full, stiff aristocratic height, his demeanor and address suggesting he was clearly aware of his own importance. Deep worry lines marred the duke's brow and his sagging jowls gave him the appearance of a blood-hound.

Hooded by the brim of a tall beaver, the duke's blue eyes surveyed the house and grounds. They were so much like Barrett's, stony and cynical, yet just below the surface was unveiled pain, loneliness, and indelible bitterness. Something in Lord Kensington's eyes touched Meagan's uncanny awareness of other people's pain. A tinge of regret and empathy for this stranger filled her.

His Grace glanced at Barrett, and his face wrinkled as if he'd just caught a whiff of a street sweeper's cart. Then his eyes raked Meagan, giving her a disapproving inspection.

Meagan felt Barrett slip his hand in hers. The gentle pressure of his fingers encouraged her not to look away or lower her eyes. She faced the Duke of Kensington knowing Barrett was there for her. For some unfathomable reason, it gave her comfort.

As he stood beside Meagan, Barrett held her hand and eyed his father. He had grown used to having his father's rancor being directed at him, but to see it focused on Meagan grated against every fiber in his body. Barely able to keep a civil tone, he asked, "I thought you were in France. To what do I owe this honor?"

"You know exactly why I'm here." Lord Kensington snapped his fingers and one of the footmen handed him a paper. He snatched it and shook it at Barrett. "This . . . this outrage! How dare you marry without my consent!"

The perverse side of Barrett that took great pleasure in irritating his father said, "And it's very good to see you too." He swept his father an exaggerated bow.

"Go ahead. Make light, but you've gone too far this time, by God! Damned insolent whelp!" The veins above his father's cravat popped out as he gritted his teeth.

"Please, Your Grace. You should go inside." Meagan aimed a reproachful glance at Barrett for deliberately vexing his father.

The duke fired a contemptuous glance Meagan's way, as if she had spoken out of turn. Then he said to Barrett, "I suppose this is the chit here?"

Barrett felt Meagan flinch at his father's harsh words. "Yes, this is Lady Meagan. I would appreciate you addressing her as such in a civil tone since she is my wife."

His father scorched Meagan with a look, then glanced back at Barrett. "We need to speak privately."

"Very well. Let's get this over with." Barrett waved his hand toward the front door. "How about the library? That's your favorite spot for my dressing downs."

"If you were not such a blight on my life, we wouldn't have need of these meetings." His father stormed past him, his cane clicking on the steps.

At that moment, another carriage rolled up the drive. Barrett and Meagan paused, as did the Duke of Kensington. They all watched Mrs. Pool and a gentleman step down from the carriage. The gentleman wore a white wig from a bygone era and peered at the world through a pair of thick spectacles. His belly protruded beneath his greatcoat and added to his bulk. The familiarity and ease with which he took Mrs. Pool's arm suggested he was well acquainted with the lady.

"Oh, no! I'd forgotten about Mrs. Pool. This is horrible. She's brought Mr. Pool," Meagan said under her breath.

Barrett felt her hand tighten around his and asked, "Is he so bad?"

"Mr. Pool takes some getting used to, and he's likely to vex your father." All the blood drained from Meagan's face.

As if Lord Kensington had heard Meagan, he leveled an intimidating glare at the newcomers.

"Lady Meagan, jolly good to find you home." Mr. Pool bowed slightly, then continued to ramble in his garrulous and heedless manner. "Don't know how elated we were to read about your marriage. Jolly good. I was just telling Mrs. Pool that you'd just forgotten about the money. I'm sure you didn't misplace a hundred pounds. No one misplaces a hundred pounds. Your brother said you'd misplaced it. What a whisker. Told Mrs. Pool right off the boy was misinformed." He seemed to notice Barrett now. "Damn me. You must be the happy groom. And you, sir— who might you be?"

Lord Kensington stared at Mr. Pool from behind lowered brows. He couldn't have looked more indignant that Mr. Pool dared to ask who he was without a formal introduction.

Barrett was enjoying the rise Mr. Pool had gotten out of his father, but Meagan wasn't. He heard her slight gasp beside him. Quickly, he said, "This is the happy groom's father, the Duke of Kensington. This, Father, is Mr. and Mrs. Pool."

"Your Grace." Mrs. Pool curtsied and had enough polish to blush for her husband. "My dear"—she grabbed her husband's arm—"perhaps we should call again another time."

"Nonsense. We're here. We'll get the money now."

"What money?" Barrett's father finally spoke.

Barrett felt Meagan stiffen; her fingernails dug into his palm.

"It ain't that we think she took it or anything," Mr. Pool said.

"Of course, she didn't take it." Mrs. Pool elbowed her husband, who looked oblivious to the nudge.

"Either she took the money or she didn't." Lord Kensington's gaze darted between Meagan and Mrs. Pool.

Barrett glared at his father. "I know she didn't take the bloody money."

"I'd like to hear what the chit has to say."

Meagan saw the disapproval on Lord Kensington's face. Her mortification showed in the redness of her face and the tears in her eyes. "It doesn't matter now!" She pulled away from Barrett and ran up the steps, the sound of her sobs following her.

Barrett cast his father an accusing look. "Well done of you indeed. But let me warn you: If you ever hurt her again, you'll pay dearly." He turned and ran after Meagan.

CHAPTER THIRTEEN

Barrett followed the trail made by Meagan's bonnet, cape, and gloves where she'd thrown them off as she ran down the hall into her room. He opened the door and found her lying across her bed, looking utterly adorable and vulnerable, with her face buried in her hands, her petticoats peeking out from beneath the bottom of her dress. He sidestepped three stacks of boxes and crawled up beside her.

"Go away! I want to mope in peace," she said between sobs.

"No."

"Haven't I suffered enough for one day?"

"I'm not here to make you suffer, Princess." Barrett slipped his arms around her. In spite of her rigid body, he pulled her over against him and eased his shoulder beneath her head. He'd never felt the need to comfort a woman before. He wasn't even sure he was doing it properly, but he was enjoying holding her. After a few moments, her sobs began to subside.

"Now tell me about the money you owe Mrs. Pool," he said, stroking her back and feeling the feminine curve of her spine.

"Harold took the bazaar money and gambled it away. I'd forgotten all about replacing it." She bit her thumb and a deep frown marred her brow. "Why, oh why, did Mrs. Pool come to get it today of all days?"

"Do not worry."

"It's so humiliating. Your father believes I'm a thief. He will never approve of me now,"

"It's not your fault." Barrett continued rubbing her back.

"But you know how first impressions affect people's opinions. Your father will detest me the rest of my days."

"He needs no reason to dislike you. It comes naturally to him to deplore everyone."

She inadvertently slid her hand over and played with the buttons on his shirt. "He might be different if you didn't try to anger him so."

He stared down at her fingers absently fondling his button and couldn't help but envy that button. "I don't try. He is in a perpetual state of anger when he's around me."

"But you shouldn't provoke him."

"That's not provoking him—that's what is called living up to my father's expectations. He expects it of me. And I'll tell you something else about him: If you show one hint of fear, he'll eat you alive. Remember that when you're forced to deal with him."

"Has he always been like that?"

"Always."

"I'm so sorry." She ran her hand along the edge of his shirt. "My parents were never quite that obvious about their feelings. On the surface they appeared kind, but every day I looked into their smiling faces and knew they only saw my shortcomings."

He brushed a curl from the corner of her lips. "I can't imagine you having any."

Meagan smiled sadly. "Oh, yes, and my mother was quite aware of them and quick to point them out. My father did so less toward the end of his life. One learns to live with it."

"Yes." Barrett rubbed his fingers along her cheek, and they shared a moment of silence, each aware of the other's pain. The clock ticked in the room, keeping rhythm with their breathing.

Meagan broke the silence. "I've never asked you this before, but do you have brothers and sisters?"

"A half sister and brother. They live in France."

"Do you ever see them?"

"No."

She rose up on her elbow and pursed her lips at him. "Why?"

"I don't think I've seen them above three times in my life, if that much. They are much younger than I, and when they were born, I lived here in England and they lived in France with my father and his wife. My father preferred it that way." A hint of emotion moved over Barrett's face as he stared into her eyes and ran his finger over her smooth lips.

"I'm sorry."

"Don't be." His expression grew hard. "I wasn't. James was all the family I needed. We shared a lot of the same boarding schools."

"I'm glad he was there for you." She grasped his hand and threaded her fingers through his. "You should go back down to your father."

"Very well." He stared down at the delicate smallness of her palm and her fingers, clasped against his own. Then he reluctantly dropped her hand, stood, and strode toward the door.

"Wait."

Her voice stopped him. He glanced at her as she stood and dug through the boxes. After a moment, she held a small package in her hand.

"What did you do? Buy the stores out?"

"I'm afraid I did." She smiled and handed him the box. "And I couldn't resist this." Sounding self-conscious all of a sudden, she said, "An early Christmas present."

Barrett stood there speechless. A strange, uncomfortable emotion welled up inside him. He took the box, opened it, and withdrew a gold fob. A medallion etched with a picture of the moon and the stars dangled from it.

"I didn't know if you needed a new one for your watch, but when I saw it I had to buy it. Do you like it?"

"Very much." After an intent glance at her, he excused himself, rubbing his finger over the gold chain.

He met Lyng in the hallway. Lyng bowed and said, "How did your day go, my lord?"

"Not very interesting."

"Any leads from Fenwick?"

"He spent the day at White's. I grew bored and left James's man to watch him. And you?"

"Lady Waterton"—Lyng squinted slightly as he said the name—"shopped all day with Lady Upton. It was uneventful—until they met Lord Collins and Lady Matilda."

"So Lady Matilda has sunk so low as to allow Collins to escort her," Barrett said more to himself than to his servant. His fists tightened at his sides as he thought of Meagan being near Collins. "Did Collins try to harm Lady Meagan?"

"No, but I did not like the way he looked at her."

"Keep a close eye on her."

"Yes, my lord."

Footsteps sounded in the hall, and Tessa appeared. She stooped to pick up the bonnet, gloves, and cape Meagan had discarded in the hall. "My lord." She curtsied to Barrett, then straightened up, snubbing Lyng all together. "Pardon me."

Barrett watched her go into Meagan's chamber and slam the door.

"That woman needs a new disposition." Lyng narrowed his eyes at the door.

"Perhaps you might give it to her."

"Not me. I'll not get close enough to change anything about her. Speaking of new dispositions, I saw your father below stairs."

"Yes. Time to face the dragon, Lyng."

"Some dragons are all smoke and no fire."

"Not this one." Barrett strode down the steps, scowling at the thought of the battle before him.

Peter Fields Sherman Rothchild, the tenth Duke of Kensington, sat in the library, glowering at the young butler with the twitch in his cheek. Peter didn't like twitches in his horse stock and he didn't like it in servants either. He drummed his fingers over the top of his cane and wondered when his son would put in an appearance. Barrett was probably taking his sweet time just to vex him.

"Can I get you anything, Your Grace?"

"My son. Where the hell is he?" Peter snarled at the intimidated expression on the young man's face. Just the way Peter wanted it.

"I believe he's with the Pools, Your Grace," he stuttered.

"Ha! Paying off the little thief's debts, no doubt."

"I wouldn't know." The young man's shoulders stiffened.

"Very well, very well." Peter waved his hand angrily through the air. "If I must wait, give me a brandy."

"Right away." The young man turned toward a table filled with decanters.

"You look decidedly young to be a butler. What is your name?"

"Coates, Your Grace." The moment the young man said his name the decanter slipped from his hand and crashed to the floor. Glass exploded across the room.

A piece hit the tip of Peter's shoe. He stared down at it; then his jowls shook with anger. "You incompetent fool!"

"I'm so sorry, Your Grace." Coates's face turned the color of the red Persian rug that had turned purple from the spilled brandy. He rushed over to pick up the large chunk of glass; then he pulled out a handkerchief and commenced wiping off Peter's boot.

"Get away, you imbecile." Peter poked him with his cane.

Coates cringed and backed away.

Abruptly, an ancient man hobbled into the room. He looked too old to have a heart that still pumped. By some physical miracle, he was still standing. His cataract-veiled eyes surveyed the damage and said, "We'll have it cleaned up in no time."

"Who the devil are you?"

"Reeves, Your Grace," the elderly man said with a wealth of pride in his voice.

"And what are you?"

"The butler, Your Grace."

"My son has two bloody butlers!"

"I'm Lady Meagan's butler. Coates and I share the responsibilities"

"That chit, huh." Peter snorted.

Coates stiffened and threw a large piece of glass into a wastebasket. The force behind the glass made it rattle against the brass.

"Begging your pardon, Your Grace, but she's not a chit." The bowed arch in Reeve's shoulders straightened slightly with indignation. He pursed his lips at Peter, stretching the wrinkles near the corners of his mouth. Then he said, "I watched her grow up. She's a fine young lady—the best there is."

Peter narrowed his brows at the ancient man. "If I want your opinion, I'll ask for it." Most likely, he had offended Coates and Reeves. They obviously felt some sort of loyalty to the bit of muslin who'd married Barrett. But why should he care? She'd be gone when he was done.

"Yes, Your Grace." Reeves clamped his lips together, and they disappeared into the wrinkles around his mouth.

"Can you get me a drink, or is that too much to ask?"

"Of course, Your Grace. Right away." Reeves shuffled past Coates, who was busy picking up the pieces of glass on the floor. He reached for a glass and a decanter, his hand trembling.

In a surprising amount of time, Reeves made it back to Peter's chair and held out the glass. Peter tried to grasp it, but the tremor in Reeve's hand made it impossible. After two tries, Peter captured the old man's hand with both of his and snatched the glass away.

Glowering at the elderly man, he held up the glass. "All right, pour the blessed stuff."

Reeves raised the decanter.

Peter tried desperately to get the glass beneath the lip, but the shaking in Reeves's hand made it impossible. Brandy dribbled down Peter's wrist, hand, and breeches, missing the glass entirely.

Peter jumped up and slammed the empty glass on the desk. "For the love of St. Michael! Forget the damned drink!"

"So sorry, Your Grace." Reeves tried to set down the decanter, but he appeared too flustered to locate the table. Groping at the air for several seconds, he finally found the table and set down the brandy with a loud plop.

Both Reeves and Coates attacked the duke's hand with their handkerchiefs.

He waved them away and growled, "Just get out!"

Barrett appeared in the doorway. He surveyed the scene with his usual indifference. "Are you having a little trouble here?"

"You'd better hire three butlers." Peter wiped his wrist with his own handkerchief. "These two incompetents can't get the job done."

"Leave us. You can clean this mess up later." Barrett motioned with his head toward the door.

Peter imagined he saw gloating grins on the two butlers' faces as they shared a look. Coates put a guiding hand on the elder's elbow and they left the room.

Barrett watched them close the door as Peter blurted, "What sort of ramshackle household are you running here?"

"The kind I like."

"You always were perverse in taking up with misfits and weeds."

"I feel a kindred spirit in them." Barrett sat behind the desk, propped his elbows on the arms of the chair, and steepled his fingers.

"You might be perverse as hell, but you were never a misfit or unwanted."

"Of course not. That is why you shipped me off to every boarding school you could find," Barrett said, his voice smooth with derision.

"If you hadn't resented Vedetta so much, you could have stayed. She tried to be a mother to you, but you wouldn't let her."

"Yes, she was a fine mother." Barrett's fingers tightened around the edge of his chair.

"I never understood why you hated her."

"And I never understood why you took your mistress into our home a month after Mother died." As usual when he broached this subject with his father, Barrett didn't see one hint of remorse or emotion. "Let's stop beating a dead horse, shall we? Say what you have to say."

His father picked up the cane he'd dropped near his side. "I want this marriage of yours annulled."

"No." Barrett's expression hardened with determination.

"She has no dowry and no connections, and I've looked into her background. She had some sort of skin disease in her early years. For God's sake! I don't want her tainted blood in my grandchildren."

"She has no condition now, nor does it matter to me what she had."

"I don't care. The fact is she did have it. It could come back for all you know. I can't believe you've gone and done something so damned stupid. Hanging after that loon Lady Matilda was bad enough, but this marriage tops it."

"What I do with my life is none of your business."

"It is my business. You've a duty to the bloodline."

Barrett laughed bitterly. "That is rich, coming from you. Correct me if I'm wrong, but Vedetta was nothing more than a Covent Garden abbess."

"I did my duty and married a lady first and sired you— God help me! You have been naught but an aggravation your whole bloody life. I won't let you ruin eight hundred years of our bloodline because of your perversity. You'll annul this marriage."

"I won't."

"You bloody ingrate!" His father stood, clutching his cane.

Barrett leaped up and leaned over his desk, matching the burning intensity of his father's stare. In the silence, they held each other in an embrace of hostility.

Barrett broke the silence. "Perhaps I'm not the prodigy you hoped for, but I've made my choice and I won't change it. Meagan will remain my wife."

"I doubt that. I'll give the chit a month with you. Then she'll be ready for an annulment." The Duke of Kensington shot Barrett a parting glare and stormed from the room.

Barrett watched his father leave, his hands trembling from the white knuckled grasp he had on the edge of his desk. He could have told his father he wasn't really married, but he wouldn't jeopardize the case in order to ease his father's mind.

He reached down and fingered the fob Meagan had bought him. He felt some of the anger drain out of him. When he had championed her against his father, he'd been caught up in the moment and had forgotten she wasn't actually his wife. It felt good defending her. What would it be like to have her as his wife?

His father's words rang in his ears. Barrett dashed the idea of marriage away. He wanted Meagan more than air to breathe, but he wasn't ready for that kind of commitment.

She deserved a man who could love her. His restlessness wouldn't allow him to love anyone. Barrett frowned down at his new fob and jammed it back in his pocket.

That evening after dinner, Meagan retired early, hoping Barrett would follow her lead, but he stayed down in the parlor speaking to Harold.

Nuisance had seemed to grow bored with Barrett and Harold's company and followed her above stairs. Of late, the fickle little creature seemed to prefer her company to Barrett's. He jumped up on her bed now and wagged his long, thin tail. She patted his head, feeling his wiry gray hair beneath her finger tips.

"You're a mighty fine pup." She touched her nose to his wet black one, then watched him flop down on the bed and give her a contented look.

"Now for tonight," Meagan said, hearing the excitement

and apprehension in her own voice. She turned and strode over to her closet.

Nuisance hung his small head over the edge of the mattress and he watched her.

"Hmm! I wonder if I can do this?" She stepped into the large closet, which was almost a quarter of the side of her chamber. Tessa had arranged all her dresses in order according to color; leaving the revealing new negligees Meagan had bought in the front.

The black one caught her eye. The black silk reminded her of Lady Matilda and her own vow to make Barrett forget that woman. Yes, she hoped the gown would give her the courage to seduce him. She pulled it off the hanger, stepped out of the closet, and laid it near Nuisance on the bed, watching the thin silk shimmer and wave.

The clock on the wall bonged twelve times. Barrett's door sounded as he entered his chamber. Nuisance glanced up and stared at the connecting door.

Any minute, he would come to her room. Her heart pounded against her chest with anticipation. When she heard his door shut and his footsteps die away in the hallway, her hand paused on the fourth hook . . . .

He wasn't coming.

Her heart sank. Tears burned her eyes. She wiped them away with the back of her hand; then her face contorted in an exasperated frown. What was so alluring about his mistress that he must leave Meagan alone and go to her? Gritting her teeth, she felt the blood throb in her temples.

"I shall see," she mumbled.

Nuisance perked up his ears at the tone in her voice.

She undressed, ripping at the eyes at the back of her dress. London streets at night were dangerous for a lady without an escort, so she found the breeches and shirt Tessa had pilfered for her. Making sure the bun at her nape was secured beneath a cap, she opened her door and stepped out into the hallway. Before Nuisance could follow her out, she quickly closed the door. With Nuisance following on her heels, she wouldn't be able to keep a low profile.

The cabbie let Meagan off a block from where Barrett's carriage had stopped. Since she'd left Pellam House, she couldn't throw off a feeling someone was watching her. The image of the redheaded man she'd seen with Holly appeared in her mind.

Her gaze swept the lamp-lit street. The dim light glowed along the cobblestone walk, casting eerie shadows along the line of trees that lined it. Nothing. Her imagination must be hard at work.

She caught sight of Barrett halfway down the block, his cane swinging at his side, his broad shoulders swaying as he walked. She made her way down Harcourt Street, her footsteps crunching softly against the gritty cobblestones.

She stayed well out of the light, keeping her eyes on Barrett, watching him let himself into a house near the end of the block. No doubt, his mistress's house. Was it Lady Matilda's residence? She could see Stratton and Hastings standing near the carriage and heard them arguing.

"You shoulda stepped up to the door quicker," Stratton said.

"I would o' if you hadn't barged in the way."

"I never barge. Can I help it if I'm quicker than you. You're slow as a sick mule. I'm surprised the master keeps you on."

"One of these days . . . "

Their voices died away as Meagan darted down the side of the town house next to the one Barrett had entered. Moonlight didn't pierce the small passageway between the buildings. In the pitch-blackness, she felt her way blindly through the darkness. Then she heard the barely audible sound of footsteps behind her melding with her own.

She paused.

The footsteps paused.

Could it be Barrett behind her? An overwhelming sense of danger kept her from calling out. A cold fist closed over her heart and her throat went dry. She could hear the person's breathing melding with her own. Forcing her trembling legs into motion, she ran.

The person followed.

Near the end of the alley, a dim beam of light burned from a gas lamp and cut into some of the pitch-darkness. She darted out into the alley and caught a fleeting glimpse of a dark figure behind her. Shadow obscured the man's face.

She bolted around the back courtyard of the house Barrett had entered, hearing the man's footfalls almost upon her, feeling his venomous smile piercing her back. A light burned in one of the windows and shot out into the night with a beacon's intensity. She headed for the light, the terror closing over her . . . .

The man lunged.

Meagan looked into the cruel black eyes of Lord Collins as she toppled forward.

Inside, in the parlor, Barrett watched James reading his mail and said, "Collins must be watched. Lyng saw him talking to Meagan."

"This probably isn't a good time to tell you this." James threw down a letter in the opened stack.

"What?"

"Collins was in White's today spreading the rumor that you met Lady Meagan at the bazaar. And a fellow by the name of Pool is going about the clubs saying you gave a small fortune to this same bazaar. Everyone is assuming it was to have carte blanche, with the Winter Princess. Then when you up and married her with such a short engagement— Well, you know what has happened." James shrugged. "They are taking bets at White's on the birth date of your heir."

"Bloody hell!" Barrett's fingers tightened around his cane.

"My sentiments exactly." James frowned absently down at an invitation in his hand.

"I'll kill Collins for this." The cane shook in Barrett's hand.

"No need to bother. He'll hang himself. I'm quite sure he's a member of the Devil's Advocates. One of my men spotted him in Hyde Park speaking to a Mr. Fields and Coburn, two of Fenwick's cronies."

"No doubt he's the ring leader."

James threw the invitation down on a third stack of mail. "I'd like to know how the bastard found out who she was so quickly."

"I had Lyng follow her today. She ran into him while shopping. He must have recognized her."

"He'll use her to get revenge on you."

"I should have given him to a press gang after I shut down his bordellos. Perhaps it's not too late."

"That's too good for him. I've been waiting a long time to see him swing. He will this time, along with all the other traitors in the Devil's Advocates." James ran his hands through his coal black hair. "So have you been able to avoid Lady Meagan's bed. I've got to be honest with you. As taking as she is, if it were me, I'd find it almost impossible."

"Well I'm not you." Barrett realized he'd overemphasized his words and grimaced.

James's lips stretched in his token impenetrable smile. "So you're having no problem remaining the celibate groom?"

"That's why you chose me for this case, isn't it? You know I'm a master at controlling my feelings."

"I'm glad to hear it."

A high-pitched scream split the air. At the same time, James and Barrett turned to look at the window.

"Bloody hell!" Barrett felt his gut tighten. That scream sounded awfully familiar. He bounded out the front door, ahead of James.

CHAPTER FOURTEEN

Barrett ran down the small walkway. James, Stratton and Hastings were close behind him. Stratton carried a lantern. In the swaying globe of light, Barrett spotted Meagan lying on her back in the alley. He let out the breath he'd been holding.

He ran to her and grabbed her arms. "What the hell are you doing here?"

"I'm-I . . . " She turned away from him, unable to speak.

He felt her body trembling and saw the tears gleaming in her eyes. His voice softened as he said, "Are you hurt?"

"No."

"What happened?"

"Lord Collins grabbed me."

At the sound of Lord Collins's name, Barrett's hands tightened around Meagan's arms. He saw her wince and loosened his hold. "Did he hurt you?"

Her lip trembled as she spoke. "I managed to bite him and scream, and when he heard you coming, he ran."

"I want an answer this time. What possessed you to come

here at this hour alone?" Had she been spying on him?
He was quite sure she wasn't involved with the Devil's
Advocates, yet she seemed to think nothing roaming about
at night in disguises. His gaze glided over her breeches—
which showed her shapely thighs—the bulky coat, and cap.

She didn't answer him. She just stared at the lantern
Stratton held.

"Well?" He felt like shaking her.

She glanced at James and the servants. "I really don't
want to get into it at the moment."

"Fine. We shall talk about it on the way home." Barrett
swept her up into his arms.

Meagan eyed James over Barrett's shoulder. "What is
James doing here?"

"He lives here."

"Oh!" Her brows rose in surprise. She stared over Barrett's shoulder at James, who wore an amused expression.

"Who did you think lived here?"

"No one." She clamped her lips tightly together in an
irritated manner.

Her reluctance to answer stiffened his strides. In six
steps, he reached the carriage. Hastings saw the black look
on his master's face and rushed to open the door. Barrett
stepped inside and set her down on the seat. He plopped
down beside her, watched Hastings close the door, and
stretched out his legs.

He looked at her and said, "Now, I want the truth. Why
did you follow me?"

"I thought you were going to see Lady . . . " Her voice
trailed off and she turned away from him.

"You thought I was going to see a lady? What lady?"
Some of Barrett's anxiety and anger dissipated at the
thought that she'd followed him because she was jealous.
He grabbed her chin, turned her face, and looked into
her eyes.

"I didn't say that."

"I'm beginning to be able to read your mind."

"What a horrible thought." Her lips pursed in a pout.

Wisps of hair escaped from her cap and brushed the back of his hands. He stared at her wide, full lips and asked, "What lady did you think I was going to see?"

"I don't know."

"Yes, you do."

"Lady Matilda. All right?" she blurted in frustration.

Barrett held back a pleased smile. "Let me put your mind at ease, Princess. Lady Matilda is the last lady I'd go to see."

"Then you don't love her?" Her gaze dug deep into his eyes.

"I thought I was in love with her once, but I realized since she wouldn't give me a second glance that it was my own perversity that made me think I was in love with her. I've never been in love with anyone, and I'm not likely ever going to be."

"Never?" she asked, her violet eyes searching his face.

"No." Barrett saw her eyelids flutter as if his answer had hit them; then he changed the subject. "So you thought I'd gone to see Lady Matilda last night too."

"I didn't give it a thought one way or the other," she said, a touch of acid in her voice belying the growing anguish on her face.

"Didn't you?" Something inside Barrett wanted to hear her admit her feelings.

"No!"

"I can see in your eyes it did."

"Why should it matter to me that you left me on our wedding night?" Tears spilled over her eyes and streamed down her cheeks. "Why should it bother me that you had to seek out your mistress's company? Why should I care that you don't wish to be with me?"

"Bloody hell!" He captured her face between his hands and stared deep in her misty eyes.

She gazed at him from behind spiked, wet lashes, the vulnerability and pain in her eyes cutting directly into him.

In a coarse voice he hardly recognized as his own, he whispered, "I've never met a woman I wanted to be with more than you . . . . "

He tipped up her face and kissed her, tasting her salty tears, hating himself for having hurt her. He made up for it now, pulling her over into his lap and placing kisses along the wet stream on her cheeks, over her nose, eyes, and chin.

Higher, he kissed her lips. The moment their mouths melded, Barrett lost himself in the need to show her how much he wanted her. He slid his tongue past her lips, tasting the sweet, hot depths of her mouth, while he pulled off her cap and threaded his fingers through her hair, unfurling her sable curls.

Her hands went to his chest and she kneaded the muscles there, while her tongue slid boldly into his mouth.

Barrett groaned at the feeling of her hands brushing over his nipples. With deft swiftness, he opened the buttons on the front of her coat. He untucked her shirt and eased his hand up inside. The heat of her body burned his finger-tips as he touched the skin along her belly, which was so smooth, so silken, it made him ache to kiss it.

Her chemise bunched along his skin as he moved a hand up to caress one of her breasts. He kneaded the perfect mound, feeling it fill his palm. He heard her sharp intake of breath as he leaned her back over his arm and suckled her nipple, teasing the hard little nub between his teeth.

A sound like a soft purr came from her. Her hands went to the back of his head, even as her back arched and she drew his face closer to her breast.

Splaying his fingers, he moved them down the softness of her belly. His finger connected with the waist of her breeches. He easily slid his hand inside and along her flat abdomen. Lower, he found the soft mound covered by feminine hair.

She clamped her legs together.

"Let me touch you, Meagan."

She relaxed her thighs. He slid his hand down between her legs, opening them wider. His finger dipped between her moist folds and penetrated her tight, moist heat; then he stroked the center of her pleasure.

"Oh, Barrett . . ." She clutched his arms as her hips moved against his hand.

"Let go, Princess."

"I've never felt this strange. I want to die it feels so good."

"Go with it, my sweet." He stroked her faster, watching her squeeze her eyes closed and the passion take over her expression. His own breathing grew ragged as he held back his raging lust.

She flung back her head as her hips undulated against his hand. "What are you doing to me . . . ?"

"Pleasuring you."

"Please, stop— Oh, Lord, what am I saying? Don't stop." She panted and writhed beneath his hand.

He felt her hips moving against his erection and it took every ounce of his will not to take her. He kissed her and took her scream into his mouth. Meagan collapsed against him, her heavy breaths filling the silence. Tiny shudders went through her as her thighs trembled against his hand.

"I like what you just did." She gazed innocently up at him, her eyes still dark with desire.

"That's only the beginning of making love." His voice cracked as he spoke past his barely controlled lust.

"Will you show me the rest?" She gave him an inviting smile.

"Perhaps later, when we know each other better." He eased his hands out of her breeches and stuffed her shirttail back inside.

"At times, I feel I know you better than I know myself," she said with disappointment in her voice.

Barrett tried to refine his lie. "I feel there are levels in a relationship that must be adhered to. We should stay on the first level for a while before proceeding to the next."

"Levels?" Her brows narrowed. "You mean like the rings of Saturn?"

"Yes, if you prefer that analogy."

"But there are no stationary objects in nature. Even the rings of Saturn shift." She kissed his chin and ran her tongue over his lips.

He groaned inwardly. "And we will move on to the next ring—just not so quickly."

The carriage swayed to a halt. Relief washed over Barrett. A few more moments alone with her and he might have lost control.

After getting out of the carriage, Barrett escorted Meagan to her chamber door. She looked over at Barrett and felt her face blushing for some reason. When he had pleasured her in the carriage, it had seemed like a luscious dream. Now, standing near her chamber door, the reality was quite real.

"Are you coming in?" she asked, searching his face.

His gaze raked her body, then moved up to her meet her eyes.

They stared at each other for a tense moment. Meagan felt a quickening deep inside her.

She sensed the struggle in him; then his desire melted behind firm resolve. "No, Princess. I should let you go to sleep."

"But I'd like it if we talked."

His gaze moved to her lips. "Unfortunately, I'm not in a talking mood."

What she really wanted was for him to move to the next

level and make love to her. She tried again. "Will you be able to sleep?"

"Most definitely not."

"I will gladly stay up with you."

"No use both of us losing sleep." He opened her door and pecked her on the forehead. "Sweet dreams, Princess," he said in a whispered drawl; then he turned and headed for his own chamber.

Reluctantly, she stepped inside. Nuisance's large brown eyes surveyed her from where he was lying on the bed.

She threw her cap on the bed next to him and frowned. "The way he touched me and held me, I'm certain he must feel something for me. But he said he would never love anyone. I hope that isn't true. What do you think?"

Nuisance barked and wagged his tail.

"I'm glad you think so too." She patted his head and felt encouraged. "If only he would move to the next level and come to my chamber."

Nuisance continued to stare at her and wag his tail.

"I know, I know. Patience. The stars in the heavens were not formed overnight."

She remembered how Barrett had stroked her, how he had made her burst inside, how she had longed to feel him touch her all over. A familiar quickening rose deep inside her and she frowned at the connecting door.

The next morning the sound of a door closing and footsteps in the hallway forced Meagan's eyes open. For a moment she thought it was still night and Barrett had decided to come to her room, but she glimpsed a ray of sunlight peeking through a crack in the curtains. The soft beam angled across the bottom of her golden counterpane.

"Oh, no, the duel!" she mumbled. She had meant to rise early and stop Lochlann from going, but Barrett's pacing had kept her awake and now she'd overslept.

Meagan threw back the covers and ran to the door. She caught a fleeting glimpse of a tall beaver hat and a black coat before Barrett disappeared down the steps. Lyng followed close on his heels. Nuisance shot out the door and followed them.

She slammed the door, ran to her closet, and snatched a day dress off its hanger. The scrapes on her elbows flashed as she hurriedly jerked on her petticoat; then she wiggled into the drab gray morning dress. She grabbed her riding boots and hopped toward the door while trying to get them on.

Success. She slammed the door with her foot and ran down the hall. She reached the front door in time to see Barrett's carriage racing down the drive. Taking the steps two at a time, she headed for the stable.

A large, arched walkway connected the stable to the house. The sun was just peeking over the top of the stable roof. The dew on the slate tiles sparkled like thousands of diamonds.

Squinting into the sunshine, she waited until a groom walked toward a tack room. Then she ran beneath the arch, hearing her footsteps echoing against the brick walls. The stable made a large U shape with a massive courtyard in the center.

As she hurried into the barn, the smells of hay, leather, and horse filled her senses. Twenty pairs of eyes stared at her from the stalls. Meagan wondered what Barrett needed with such a large stable. But she didn't ponder the matter long. She slipped into the tack room, grabbed a bridle, then stepped into the first stall she came to. A large roan with four white feet eyed her.

"You want some exercise, don't you?" She continued to speak softly while she bridled the animal. The warmth from the horse felt good against her hands.

Having no time to bother with a saddle, she snatched

up the hem of her dress and petticoat, then used the stall railings for a foothold and leaped on the roan's back.

He pranced several steps, then shot out of the stall without any urging. The cold air must have touched a frisky vein in the animal. Meagan dug her knees into his sides and hung on.

The groom stepped out of the tack room and dropped the bridle in his hands. He ran behind her yelling, "You can't ride that horse, my lady! Come back!"

Trees along the drive passed her in a blur. The horse headed straight for the closed iron gates that stretched across the drive. She jerked on the reins, but the animal ignored the bit as if it had a mouth made of iron.

Frantically, she glanced right, then left. All she saw was the wall that surrounded the property. Meagan was an expert rider, but she'd never attempted seven-foot fences without a saddle.

"Whoa!" Meagan jerked on the reins.

The horse barreled straight for the gates.

"What is wrong with you?" She kept pulling, her heart banging against her ribs. The gate was getting closer . . . closer . . . .

The horse jumped. His hooves seemed to sprout wings as they took flight.

"No!" Meagan screamed and felt her weight shift against the roan's sleek sides.

The horse cleared the fence and glided down onto the ground with the finesse of Pegasus.

Not so favored by fate, Meagan toppled over his neck and somersaulted through the air. On her way down, she decided if she lived, and if Barrett and Lochlann didn't kill themselves in the duel, she would take great pleasure in doing so for them.

*　*　*

Miles away in Battersea, Hastings opened the door for Barrett, who stepped out of his carriage. Nuisance leaped out behind him and took off after a squirrel.

The approach of riders brought Barrett's gaze around behind him. Burrows and another man with a moon-shaped face and a protruding brow dismounted and strode toward him. Their breath trailed white clouds in the crisp morning air.

Burrows paused before Barrett. "This is my second, Mr. Melton."

Barrett observed the pudgy gentleman with Burrows. He looked close to thirty. A thick mustache, worn in the Olympian style, fell down past the corners of his wide, plump lips. He eyed Barrett, suspicion and a marked amount of respect gleaming in his small eyes.

Barrett had never seen the gentleman before. Something in the stranger's manner pricked Barrett the wrong way.

"Waterton." Melton bowed stiffly. "I've heard of your abilities with a pistol. I look forward to this duel."

Burrows asked, "Where is the doctor?"

"Lyng is a doctor."

Burrows eyed Lyng with a marked amount of distrust.

"Shall we get this over with?" Barrett handed his cane to Lyng. "I've a busy schedule. The box, Hastings."

Hastings pulled a box from beneath a seat in the carriage and passed it to Lyng, who picked up the weapons and examined them.

Lyng nodded at Barrett. "They look ready." He handed the box to Melton.

Melton hefted one and narrowed an eye down the sight. "Ah! Gold plated. Nice piece."

"They are German made."

"I can tell."

"They work in a pinch." Barrett draped his cane over his arm and pulled out a snuffbox.

"I'm sure it doesn't take much aim to kill with these."
Melton raised the pistol and aimed it at a tree.

"Not much at all." Barrett looked askance at Burrows,
then snorted two pinches of snuff.

"Let's get on with it, shall we?" Burrows snatched the
gun out of his friend's hand.

Barrett noticed the slight tremor in Burrow's hand as
he held the gun. "Very well," Barrett said, taking the pistol
Lyng offered him.

Barrett strode several paces and stood back to back with
Burrows. He took up his normal stance, dropping the hand
holding the pistol to his side. He wore his usual indifferent
expression. If not for the gun dangling from his hand, he
might have been out for a morning stroll.

"Ten paces, then shoot," Lyng said.

Barrett and Burrows nodded.

"One . . . two . . . three . . ." Lyng counted.

They marched off the paces. Barrett visualized where he
wanted to shoot Burrows. He didn't want to kill him—
only to shoot the gun out of his hand and shock him
enough so that he'd stay away from Meagan and not jeopardize this case. He couldn't very well have Burrows trying
to persuade Meagan to annul the marriage and elope with
him, not when Barrett needed to keep up the sham marriage. And even if Meagan didn't want to admit it, Burrows
had almost killed her. Barrett wouldn't let the hothead get
away with that again, for he knew Burrows loved Meagan
enough not to give up until he had avenged his ego. Barrett
would settle this once and for all.

"Eight . . . nine . . . "

"Wait!"

Barrett heard Meagan's scream as he turned. Burrows
turned, the noise startling him. He fumbled with the gun.
As he tried to grab it, it discharged.

Pain tore through Barrett's upper arm with the piercing

force of a saber. He grabbed his arm and gritted his teeth against the white-hot searing feeling.

"Oh my God!" Meagan leaped off the back of Give 'em hell, a hunter Barrett had bought at Tattersall's on his birthday. The animal was said to be dangerous, unpredictable, and appropriately named. Barrett, always game for a challenge, had purchased the animal for far more than he was worth.

He took in Meagan's limp, the grass stains on her gray dress, her hair in disarray down to her waist, the leaves and twigs tangled in her dark curls. A smudge of dirt covered one side of her face. She grabbed his hand and said, "Are you all right?"

"It's just a graze. The question is, are you all right? What the hell are you doing riding that horse? He's dangerous."

"Believe me, I found that out." Her teeth chattered and he could barely understand her.

"This is no place for you." He pulled off his greatcoat and threw it over her shoulders, his annoyance taking precedence over the sharp pain in his arm.

"I had to stop you. Thank you." She smiled at him, her dimples beaming, and snuggled deeper into the coat.

"Meagan."

At the sound of Burrows's voice, her smile faded and she wheeled around to face her friend. "Don't you dare *Meagan* me! Do you realize you almost shot me once? Now you've shot Lord Waterton."

Burrows took a step toward her, his face screwed up in a grimace. "I was only trying to defend your honor."

"I don't need my honor defended." She snatched the pistol out of his hand and shook the handle at him. "I've had it with this nonsense. There'll be no more dueling and no more weapons. Do you hear me, Lochlann? No more!" She stomped her foot and winced.

Burrows wore the frown of a scolded child. "I just couldn't see you with him."

"Enough is enough. I'm his wife. I've accepted it—now you must. That's an end to it. Do you hear? An end! I'm ashamed of you. Do you hear? Sorely ashamed." She slapped the pistol into Lyng's hand. "Burn this."

She turned back to Barrett and tenderness filled her eyes. "Come on. We should get you home and look at your wound." She wrapped her arm around his waist.

"Perhaps I should be carrying you." Barrett gazed down at her limping foot.

"No, no. I just twisted it a bit. There's nothing wrong with it."

Melton strode over to Burrows. "Well, this was a waste of my time," he said, his voice sharp as a knife.

"If my friend hadn't ridden in here screaming her head off . . . "

Barrett watched the two men walk over to their horses and mount. Nuisance appeared from behind a tree and barked and growled at them. They ignored him and rode away.

Barrett whistled for Nuisance, then slipped his hand in Meagan's. "Come, Princess."

"Are you sure you're all right?" Meagan said, taking his hand. "You look pale. You need a doctor."

"Lyng will look at my wound." He stared down at the small hole on the upper edge of his sleeve. A tiny ring of blood oozed around the frayed edge.

"Lyng?" Her brows arched.

"Yes, he used to be a physician in China. I trust him implicitly."

Barrett wasn't worried about the wound at all. His mind was on the way her small hand molded so perfectly to his, the way her long sable curls curved down around her waist. The morning sun caught the highlight in her hair and danced past the twigs and leaves caught in it. His coat dragged on the ground near her ankles. He'd never seen her look so unkempt—or so fetching.

"How did you happen to find Lyng?" Meagan glanced over at Lyng and watched him climb up on the carriage with Hastings and Stratton.

"Something terrible happened to his wife in China, so he came here," Barrett said, keeping his voice low.

"Do you know what happened?"

"No, but I do know it pains him to think of them. He has never spoken of what happened, and I have never asked." They reached the carriage. Nuisance leaped up into the carriage first, his keen brown eyes peering out from behind veils of shaggy hair.

"You astound me sometimes." She bestowed a radiant grin on Barrett, the dimples in her cheeks beaming.

"Why?"

"Most people don't notice the pain of those around them—especially that of their servants."

"I would hope I don't go through life wearing blinders." With his good arm, Barrett helped Meagan inside.

"I would hope not either." She eyed him pointedly and squeezed his hand. "Are you sure you can make it home?" She stepped inside, the concern never leaving her eyes.

"Yes." Barrett smiled at her. No one had ever worried over him who didn't expect payment in return or want something from him. He had learned to gauge the sincerity in people. He could spot affectation with the greatest accuracy. Meagan's concern was sincere.

An uncomfortable possessiveness swelled inside him as he sat beside her in the carriage. In spite of trying to force it away, he could feel the power of it setting up camp inside him. His hands trembled slightly as he fought the desire to hold her. If he touched her at this moment, he would not let her go.

When this case ended he would have to let her go. He forced back the indifference that he'd survived with all his life, and he let it weave over his feelings.

* * *

"Is there anything I can do?" Meagan paused in her pacing and stepped in front of Lyng, who was leaving Barrett's chamber. Barrett had refused to allow her inside while Lyng looked at the wound. Something had happened to Barrett in the carriage—something that distanced her from him and made him hide behind his usual facade of indifference.

"I'm going to brew herb tea in which to bathe the wound." Lyng held up a pouch, and his black eyes sparkled with a strange light. "You could tear bandages, my lady."

"Anything to help."

"I left the sheets inside."

"Do you think his lordship will mind my going in there?" She glanced toward the door and frowned.

"No, no. If he does, he'll get over it." Lyng strode down the hall, his steps so light she couldn't hear them.

Meagan stared at him for a moment, remembering Barrett speaking of Lyng losing his wife. He was a strange little man; his reserved and unreadable demeanor gave away nothing. In a lot of ways, he resembled his master.

Not knowing what to expect, Meagan cautiously opened the door. Nuisance raced past her and down the hall, following Lyng.

She stepped inside Barrett's chamber, which was much larger than her room. Shades of blue decorated the walls, curtains, and upholstery. A huge four-poster bed sat on a dias that filled the middle of the room.

She found Barrett sitting on the side of the bed, unbuttoning his shirt. His presence filled the large room. Sunlight streamed in through the window, illuminating his blond hair. His shoulders, clad in a white linen shirt, dwarfed the frame of one of the largest beds she'd ever seen and made it seem puny. The moment she saw the bloodstain on his sleeve, she swallowed hard and ran to him.

"You shouldn't be in here." His light brown brows lowered over his eyes.

"Lyng said I could help. And it's a good thing. You shouldn't be doing that. Let me help you."

"I'm not helpless."

"I know—just witless." She knocked his hands away and finished unbuttoning his shirt.

He gazed up at her, yet allowed her to assist him. The usual indifferent mask he wore faded away, replaced by an unreadable expression that accentuated the sharp planes of his face. Without taking his eyes off her hands, he said, "I wish you wouldn't worry over me, Meagan."

She sensed something inside him that needed stroking with tenderness and kind words. She continued to unbutton his shirt and spoke to that part of him. "I'm sorry—it's too late. You're my husband, and I am entitled to care about you."

"One day you'll regret it," he said in a tone that was more honest and exposed than any he'd ever used before.

"Never." She looked deep into his hard blue eyes, her gaze never wavering, even though all her insecurities screamed for her to listen to him.

She ignored them and worked open the last button. She felt the back of her hands brushing his hard chest. The heat of his body seeped through his shirt, burning her skin through the fine linen.

His shirt fell open. Her gaze roamed down his neck. Along the tempered architecture of his chest. Muscles, rippling and sculpted, encased his chest and arms in lyrical perfectly formed beauty. A thick patch of maple brown hair tapered down his chest, along the middle of his waist and over the pleated sinew there. Then it thinned until it dipped below the waistband of his breeches. Power throbbed from his sleek brawn. What would it be like to

Take **4 FREE** Books!

Zebra created its convenient Home Subscription Service so you'll be sure to get the hottest new romances delivered each month right to your doorstep — usually before they are available in book stores. Just to show you how convenient Zebra Home Subscription Service is, we would like to send you 4 Zebra Historical Romances as a FREE gift. You receive a gift worth up to $24.96 — absolutely FREE. There's no extra charge for shipping and handling. There's no obligation to buy anything - ever!

Save Even More with Free Home Delivery!

Accept your FREE gift and each month we'll deliver 4 brand new titles as soon as they are published. They'll be yours to examine FREE for 10 days. Then if you decide to keep the books, you'll pay the preferred subscriber's price of just $4.20 per title. That's $16.80 for all 4 books for a savings of up to 32% off the publisher's price! Just add $1.50 to offset the cost of shipping and handling. Remember, you are under no obligation to buy any of these books at any time! If you are not delighted with them, simply return them and owe nothing. But if you enjoy Zebra Historical Romances as much as we think you will, pay the special preferred subscriber rate of only $16.80 each month and save over $8.00 off the bookstore price!

Check out our website at www.kensingtonbooks.com.

We have 4 FREE BOOKS for you as your introduction to
KENSINGTON CHOICE!

To get your FREE BOOKS,
worth up to $24.96, mail the card below.
or call TOLL-FREE 1-888-345-BOOK

Take 4 Zebra Historical Romances FREE!

MAIL TO: ZEBRA HOME SUBSCRIPTION SERVICE, INC.
120 BRIGHTON ROAD, P.O. BOX 5214,
CLIFTON, NEW JERSEY 07015-5214

♥ YES! Please send me my 4 FREE ZEBRA HISTORICAL ROMANCES (without obligation to purchase other books). Unless you hear from me after I receive my 4 FREE BOOKS, you may send me 4 new novels - as soon as they are published - to preview each month FREE for 10 days. If I am not satisfied, I may return them and owe nothing. Otherwise, I will pay the money-saving preferred subscriber's price of just $4.20 each... a total of $16.80 plus $1.50 for shipping and handling. That's a savings of over $8.00 each month. I may return any shipment within 10 days and owe nothing, and I may cancel any time I wish. In any case the 4 FREE books will be mine to keep.

KNH9A

Name _____

Address _____ Apt No _____

City _____ State _____ Zip _____

Telephone (   ) _____ Signature _____

(If under 18, parent or guardian must sign)

Terms, offer, and price subject to change. Orders subject to acceptance.
Offer valid in the U.S. only.

press her naked body to his? Meagan felt her heart pound in her chest. She licked her lips, aware of the ache growing in her to touch him.

"You shouldn't look at me like that," he said in a silken drawl that belied his words.

Meagan realized she'd been standing there like a simpleton, gripping the last button on his shirt. "I like looking at you. Perhaps you might let me do it when you are not shot."

She frowned and eased the shirt over the wound. Blood had dried around the small bright red gash on his upper arm. The wound wasn't as deep as she'd thought, and it looked like a surface burn. Surprisingly, the wound had stopped bleeding.

She bent to toss the shirt on the bed and glimpsed his back. Caught off guard by the white discolorations that slashed across his shoulders, she held her breath and felt the veins bulging in her temples.

"They are scars," he offered flatly.

"Who did this to you?" Meagan gasped, reaching out to touch him.

CHAPTER FIFTEEN

Before Meagan's fingertips touched the scars, Barrett leaped up, the white stripes rippling across his back. He turned and faced her. "It is in the past and of little matter."

Meagan took in the tight line of his lips, his proud jaw, and his cold blue eyes, and she knew without a doubt that the untold cruelty he'd suffered sometime in his life had made him the way he was.

She knew how it felt to harbor pain inside, to retreat from everything and everyone. Her condition had seen to that. Barrett had retreated behind a veil of wealth and indifference. In a blinding revelation that squeezed the deepest recesses of her heart, she realized she'd found a kindred spirit in Barrett. If he would let her, she could offer him solace, and in doing so, she could fill a void within her own life. He might never love her, but they could live comfortably together. She found herself saying, "It matters to me."

Without speaking, he strode to the window, the muscles in his back rippling. He leaned his good arm against the sill and looked out, squinting against the sunlight. He stood there for a full minute, staring off at some distant place, where he seemed to battle old demons. Finally, he said, "It is a part of my life I want to forget—"

"Did your father do this?"

Barrett opened his mouth to speak, but a quick rap on the door made him clamp his mouth closed. Lyng strolled into the room, carrying a pot of tea.

Meagan watched Barrett stare out the window again, withdrawing back into himself. Meagan cursed Lyng's timing. A few more moments and she might have coaxed the truth from Barrett. She could not stop the fierce dislike for the Duke of Kensington growing inside her.

Lyng's gaze darted between her and Barrett. He coughed nervously. "Perhaps I should have taken longer with the tea."

"No, no." Meagan tried to make him at ease. "You can set the tea here on the nightstand."

"Come, my lord. I'll bathe and dress the wound now." Lyng set the silver teapot down. "Would you help me, Lady Waterton?"

"Of course."

Barrett turned and frowned thoughtfully at her.

Meagan bestowed a dazzling smile on him. "Come, husband." She held her hand out to him.

He strode toward her like a reluctant child. Her lips stretched in an encouraging smile. When his warm fingers closed around her hand, she knew the same force that had created the universe and caused galaxies to form and stars to shine had brought them together for a reason. She might have a chance for happiness with Barrett.

He might even love her one day.

* * *

A little later, Meagan left Barrett brooding in Lyng's capable hands and headed toward her own room to have a bath drawn. She looked down at the tears in the hem of her dress and frowned.

As she touched the knob to go into her chamber the sound of footsteps made her pause.

"My lady."

"Yes." She turned at the sound of Reeves's quavering voice.

"I've a missive from the Duke of Kensington." Reeves's dislike for the duke came through in his voice. "It appears important. A boy is waiting for a response."

"Thank you, Reeves." Meagan picked up the letter and ran her fingers over the wax seal. A shiver of dread went through her. Her fingers trembled as she broke the seal and read the bold, flourishing strokes:

Miss Fenwick,

If it is convenient, I wish a private audience with you at eleven this morning in my home. Do not speak of it to my son. It would only cause trouble. I'm sure you do not want that.

The Duke of Kensington

Meagan frowned down at the use of her maiden name. It was obvious the duke couldn't bring himself to think of her as his daughter-in-law. She dreaded coming face-to-face with him. Still, hadn't he treated Barrett horribly as a child?

Armed with her indignation and resolve, Meagan entered her room and strode over to the desk. Without bothering to waste another piece of foolscap, she scribbled at the bottom of the letter:

Your Grace,

    I look forward to meeting you.

                     Lady Meagan Waterton

"Here, Reeves." Meagan placed the letter back on the tray.

In a concerned tone, Reeves said, "Begging your pardon, my lady, but I can't help but wonder what he wanted." Reeves squinted at the letter.

"A duel of sorts."

"A duel!" Reeves's bushy gray brows snapped together as he glanced up at her.

"Yes, one of wills." Meagan crossed her arms over her chest and ignored Reeves's severe scowl.

The wind came from the north. Thick clouds covered the sky like balls of cotton. As another cold gust blew past Meagan, she shivered and eyed the activity on Bruton Street.

Ladies and gentlemen hurried down the walks. Milkmaids and water carriers, their shoulders yoked with heavy buckets, deftly avoided the passersby. A gig draped with Christmas greenery and bows passed Meagan at a fast clip, the wheels crunching over frozen mud.

Meagan felt someone watching her and she turned in the sidesaddle and glanced behind her. She thought she saw the small bearded man she'd seen with Holly dart behind a building, but she couldn't be sure.

Frowning, she turned back around and glanced over at Stratton. "Did my husband happen to inquire about me before he left?"

"He didn't, me lady."

"Not one word?" Meagan couldn't keep the peevish tone from her voice. She thought she would have to avoid

Barrett in order to leave, but she had found he'd already gone out.

"No, me lady."

"Did he say where he might be going?" Meagan kept a tight grip on the reins. In spite of every groom's warning in the stable, pure perversity and determination made Meagan pick Give 'em hell to ride. Even if it killed her, she would master the animal. One day, she hoped, she would master Barrett as well.

"Didn't say a thing, me lady." Stratton looked anxiously over at Give 'em hell. "How's he behaving?"

"He has a bit of nasty blood in him, and he doesn't have a soft mouth at all. It may look as if I'm having to be heavy-handed, but he'll settle down."

"We should have taken the carriage."

"I needed the exercise." The truth was Meagan couldn't face the Duke of Kensington in a frilly dress if she hoped to maintain any degree of equanimity; she much preferred her new deep purple riding habit, boots, and crop.

"Begging your pardon, me lady. If you'd wanted exercise you should have ridden the mare I wanted you to ride. If the master gets wind of your ridin' Give 'em hell, he'll have all our hides."

"I'll make it plain to him that this will be my horse from now on."

She heard Stratton's skeptical grunt under his breath. Then her attention moved to the west side of the street and the houses lining it. Through the windows, she glimpsed the lavishly plastered interiors and grand staircases. Number 15, the largest on the block, rose some five stories into the air. Massive windows covered the front, each having a scrollwork cornice of lions over it.

Meagan looked at the two doormen on either side of the stoop, their faces dour and funereal. In spite of the chill in the air, her palms began to sweat beneath her leather gloves. She reined in, feeling her heart pounding.

She waited until Stratton held Give 'em hell's reins before she dismounted.

The horse danced to the side and cut his eyes at Meagan. She gave him a pat and said to Stratton, "I'll only be a moment."

The doormen eyed her with just enough haughtiness to make her feel unwelcome. Then they bowed and opened the double doors.

She stepped inside and faced the butler. He stood a head taller than Meagan, and she had to look up to see his long face. A tuft of flyaway brown hair stuck out from his head and reminded Meagan of duck fluff.

"May I help you?" The butler pursed his lips at her.

"I'm Lady Waterton. His Grace is expecting me." Meagan handed him one of Barrett's calling cards; she had ordered her own yesterday, but hadn't received them.

The butler looked at her and wrinkled his nose. "So he is. Please follow me."

Meagan listened to her footsteps echoing in the vastness of the foyer. In spite of the large windows adorning the front of the house, gloominess and oppressiveness stifled the place so that not even the morning sunshine could penetrate the rooms. Dark wainscoting covered the walls, blending with the black and green marble floor tiles. Even the paintings on the walls were Dutch and dreary and added little color or charm to the overall bleakness. To a great degree, the house resembled the personality of its owner. The silence was so heavy it squeezed every fiber in Meagan's body.

The butler reached a door, opened it, and announced, "Lady Meagan, Your Grace."

"Send her in," a gruff voice answered.

The butler waved her into the room.

Waves of acid churned in her belly. She could do this. Swallowing hard, she stepped past the butler into a study. Lord Kensington sat behind his desk, his white hair shimmering in the light streaming through the large window in the room. His overpowering presence saturated the air. He didn't bother standing when she entered, nor did the quill in his hand pause over a letter he was writing. He merely said, "Sit."

Meagan moved toward the seat farthest from the desk; then she remembered Barrett had told her to show no fear. Summoning up her courage, she sat in the high-backed chair directly in front of him.

For a few moments the only sound in the room was the scratching of the quill and the ticking of a clock on the wall. He continued to ignore her. Inadvertently, Meagan nervously banged her riding crop against her hand. Once . . . Twice . . .

"Stop that infernal noise!" He slammed the quill down on the desk.

She lost her patience and stood. "I can see you are too busy to see me. I'm sorry to have taken up your time." She started for the door.

"Wait!"

She glanced at him over her shoulder, aware she had a slight advantage now. With a sauciness that surprised her, she asked, "Why should I?"

"You are an impudent piece of baggage." His faded blue eyes narrowed at her through a pair of round spectacles.

"At least I'm not a gruff duke intent upon ruining the morning of everyone around him."

"Sit down."

Meagan turned the knob to leave.

"Please," he added in a begrudging tone.

Her brows rose at his request. By the tone in his voice, she could tell it went against his grain to even speak the word. She decided to give him another chance and strode back to her seat, aware of his blue eyes following her every move.

"I can tell you're not the type of woman to dilly-dally,

so I'll get straight to the point. Surely, you know why I wanted to speak to you." He sat back in his chair and steepled his fingers over his stomach.

"Yes, I think I have some idea."

"You must know you are unsuitable for my son."

"That is up to your son to decide."

"He's never made a sound decision in his whole life."

"Perhaps you should amend that, Your Grace, by qualifying they weren't decisions that pleased you."

"You little sauce box," he growled, though his eyes twinkled with respect for her.

"I'm just being honest."

"Just so." He drummed his fingers on the top of his desk. "Then let me get to my second point. I'll give you five thousand pounds to leave him and allow him to annul the marriage."

"That's not enough." Meagan stared squarely in his eyes.

"Ten."

"No."

"Fifteen."

Meagan shook her head, the feather on her riding hat bouncing near her ear.

"You drive a hard bargain. Twenty thousand and that's my final offer."

Meagan blinked at him and managed a convincingly insulted look. "No."

"Why, you little minx! That's a bloody fortune." He sounded vexed, but he wore the expression of a man enjoying himself at an auction.

"Indeed, sir, but it's not enough to induce me to leave your son." Barrett was right: The Duke of Kensington enjoyed a worthy opponent who showed no fear. Emboldened by this knowledge, she found it easier to look him in the eyes.

"How much do you want then?"

"Should you offer me all the gold in England it would in no way sway me."

"You love him then?" He shot her a dubious glance.

"That's none of your business, and I wouldn't admit it to you if I did."

"You little ingrate. No one has spoken to me like that since my Vedetta died." He stared pensively down at his hands, lost in thought.

Meagan looked at him. An emotion he was experiencing dragged down his face; every wound and grievance in his life came to the surface. It prompted her to ask, "Who was Vedetta?"

Lord Kensington glanced up at her, the cantankerous look back on his face. "She was my second wife. I would have thought my son would have told you all about her since he hated her so."

"He does not speak of anyone in his family."

He made a grumbling sound in his throat. "He would like to forget his half brother and sister and I exist."

"Where do they live?"

"In Nice."

"Then that is where you make your home?"

"Vedetta was from France. She wanted to live there and raise our children."

"What of Barrett?" Meagan gripped her riding crop.

"Unfortunately, Barrett flatly refused to be uprooted from his home and live in France. He was only eight at the time, yet already headstrong and belligerent. I knew that the resentment he felt for Vedetta would only make matters worse if I forced him to go, so I put him in boarding schools here." The duke cleared his throat and thought for a moment; then his voice grew unusually gruff. "It was for the best."

"I see." An image of Barrett as a little boy left all alone at boarding schools surfaced in her mind. She said in a soft voice, "Sometimes, when one thinks he is doing the right thing, it isn't necessarily the right choice at all."

His expression hardened. "How dare you sit there and judge my actions?"

"I wasn't judging you, Your Grace, merely making an observation." Under his critical eye, she tried not to fidget with her riding crop. "I believe Barrett acted the way he did only to get your attention. You see, in many ways, I was just like him as a child, but instead of being difficult, I tried desperately to please my parents to gain their love."

"How?" he asked, his gruff response laced with curiosity.

Meagan didn't want to reveal her painful past to him, for it might give him power over her. But he needed to hear about it in order to better understand Barrett, so she said, "Oh, I tried watercolors, embroidery, archery, riding, but all to no avail." She smiled, but the expression didn't touch her eyes. "A more blundering creature didn't exist. I barely passed at these things and only really mastered riding enough not to have my father scowl at me. Finally I realized no amount of talent would gain their approval. So I pursued my own passions, my love of books and the science of stars. I found solace there." She paused, her brow wrinkling deep in thought.

"And your point of this long narrative is?"

"Don't you see? Barrett must have found solace in making you and his stepmother angry."

"I'm sure he did." The Duke of Kensington's bushy gray brows dropped lower over his eyes.

"Perhaps you should have had more patience with him."

"I tried."

"Perhaps not as hard as you should have. I've always believed you get back the love you give in this world."

"Hah! It is he who spurns me. I've tried to give him everything—"

"But your patience and love."

He turned red in the face. "Who are you to counsel me

on how I should've raised my son? You know nothing of what went on."

Meagan twisted the riding crop in her hands. "I saw the scars on his back. You beat him."

"That is a lie!" Lord Kensington banged his fist on the desk.

Meagan jumped and stared at his large fist resting on a stack of papers. "Is it?"

"I never touched him. If he told you that—"

"He didn't. I just assumed you had."

"I would never harm my own son," he growled, his heavy jowls trembling from his indignation.

"Then who did?"

"I have no idea."

"Your son was beaten and you don't know who did it?" Meagan leveled a skeptical glance his way.

"I didn't even know he had scars on his back." A flash of regret moved over his face as he stared down at his clenched fists.

The clock in the room chimed once on the half hour.

Meagan stood. "I want to thank you for this meeting."

"You do?" He looked at Meagan the way her father used to look at her mother when he couldn't fathom her behavior.

"It helps me to understand Barrett so much better now."

"So you think you know him, do you?" Lord Kensington stood, stretching to his full height. "Well, I know my son. Let me tell you: He's more complicated a character than you could ever imagine. If you think he'll ever return your love, you are sorely mistaken. It isn't in Barrett to love anyone."

"Perhaps not, but I don't intend to give up as easily as you did." Meagan frowned at him. "Now if you'll excuse me."

"You can't leave yet. We've not concluded our business."

"It's concluded as far as I'm concerned." Meagan graced him with a perfect curtsy and walked out the door.

"I haven't given you leave to go! Don't you dare walk out on me!"

His bellow rang in her ears as she continued down the hallway and out the door. The butler looked at her, his expression one of awe and disbelief that she was walking away from an angry Duke of Kensington.

She stepped out onto the sidewalk and felt the incongruity of cold air and warm sun hitting her face. An overwhelming desire to hold Barrett washed over her. If he were standing before her, she would have run into his arms and held him—held the little boy who chose to be abandoned at boarding schools, the wounded man who hid behind a shield of callous indifference. She picked up her strides toward Stratton and Give 'em hell. She desperately needed to hold him.

At that moment, Barrett sat in his carriage, staring down at the gold chain Meagan had given him, rubbing his fingertips over it. It was getting harder and harder to look into her soulful violet eyes and not tell her the truth.

He shouldn't have pleasured her last night, but he couldn't bear to see the pain that he'd caused on her face, nor would he ever forget the miserable look in her eyes when he had left her at her door afterward.

It was all he could do to go to his room. Not one minute had passed last night when he did not recall slipping his finger into her hot, moist heat and touching her maidenhead, which he had no right to take. He kept telling himself that. Still, it had no effect on his lust. He had been forced to douse himself in cold water. Five times. When that didn't work, he tried drowning his lust in half a bottle of brandy. At dawn he'd fallen asleep, staring at the connecting door that separated them. Cold water and brandy wouldn't work again.

He frowned and felt the carriage stop. Nuisance perked up on the seat next to him and stuck his head out the window, barking. Before Hastings could get the door open, the dog leaped out of the carriage window.

"Little dimwit," Barrett said as Hastings opened the door.

Hastings's face scrunched up in an offended grimace.

"Not you," Barrett amended, "the dog."

"Oh! Aye, me lord." Hastings smiled. "I'll go after him."

Barrett stepped out onto Curzon Street and watched Hastings bolt after Nuisance. Hastings skirted a governess herding six children and whistled, but Nuisance paid him no mind.

Shaking his head in disgust, Barrett strolled toward number 17. A tall, burly man with a square face answered the door. "Aye, sir, what's your business?"

Barrett handed his card to the man. "Be so kind as to inform Collins that Lord Waterton is here to see him."

"Just a minute." The man slammed the door in Barrett's face.

At a leisurely pace, Barrett strode around to the back of the house, swinging his cane and whistling softly. After Collins had attacked Meagan, Barrett had had a Bow Street runner watching Collins's every move, and he'd received word Collins had just come home an hour ago.

Barrett noticed Slip, a young man with a nervous squint, peek around a nearby trash barrel. Slip stepped out from behind his hiding spot, wearing ragged clothes and a cap. Barrett had worked with him in France.

"You ain't supposed to be here," Slip whispered. "Sir James gave strict instructions not to let you near Collins."

"I'm just going to speak to him."

"I have my orders." The young man shoved his hands in his pockets and glowered at Barrett.

"You don't want to cross me on this." Barrett narrowed his eyes at Slip.

"Sir James ain't gonna like it—he ain't."

"Don't tell him then." Barrett reached into his pocket and threw the man a sovereign. "Go buy yourself a drink."

Slip looked at the coin glistening in his hand. He hesitated a moment, weighing the money; then his fist closed over it. "All right then, but don't kill him. Sir James needs him alive. You get five minutes."

"I'll only need one."

Barrett watched Slip pad down the alley. With the expertise born of his profession, he darted behind a coal bin and disappeared.

Barrett stepped up behind a brick wall that met a small garden in the rear of Collins's town house. He leaned his shoulder against it and waited near the gate.

After a few moments Barrett heard the door creak open. Footsteps came closer. The gate opened and Collins appeared.

Barrett thrust up his cane. "Going somewhere?"

Collins saw him, panicked, and whipped a gun out from inside his coat.

CHAPTER SIXTEEN

Before Collins could get off a shot, Barrett thrust out his cane and knocked the pistol from his adversary's hand. It hit the wall and slid across the cobblestones in the alley.

Collins dove for the gun.

Barrett grabbed him by the collar, thrust him up against a wall, and shoved his cane against Collins's throat, pinning him against the bricks. Barrett had the pleasure of seeing his eyes bulge with fear. "Now, we're going to have a little chat."

"You're going to regret this," Collins said through gritted teeth.

Barrett put more pressure on the cane and heard Collins gag. "I knew it was a mistake letting you live. You have been nothing but a thorn in my side. But you have crossed the line now."

"You're choking me," Collins rasped, his face turning the color of red Christmas ribbon.

Barrett forced himself to release his hold and step back. "Choking is too good for you."

He noticed Collins looking at the pistol. Barrett strode over to it. He used his cane and the side of his boot, and in one smooth motion kicked up the pistol and caught it. He stuffed it down into the waist of his breeches.

Collins rubbed his neck. Barrett's attack hadn't pierced the wealth of blatant insolence on his face. "You really need to get a little holiday spirit, Waterton," he said, his voice coarse.

"If you ever come near my wife again, or even look at her wrong, I'll show you just how much holiday spirit I have." A deceptive smile stretched Barrett's lips.

The soft pad of footsteps made Barrett glance to his right. Nuisance pranced down the alley, heading for Collins.

Collins smiled as if he'd just tasted pure table salt. "Come now, Waterton. No need to get so overwrought. You know I'd never do anything to your lovely wife."

"I know nothing of the sort." Barrett glanced down at Nuisance sniffing Collins's boots. Then the dog cocked his leg.

Collins jumped as urine hit his boots. "Ahh! Mangy bastard!" His face swelled with anger as he kicked at Nuisance.

The animal leaped back before Collins's boot touched him. Collins went for the little dog again, but Barrett stepped in between them and thrust his cane against Collins's chest. "That's my dog you're kicking."

"You owe me for a pair of boots."

"Believe me, you don't want the recompense I'd give you." Barrett smiled at the veins popping on Collins's neck.

For a long moment they stared into each other's eyes with equal hatred; then Collins backed away from Barrett. "Very well, take that scrawny bastard and leave."

"You cannot fault him for his Christmas spirit." Barrett

snatched Nuisance up in his arms, petted him, then strode away.

He felt the wound on his arm stinging and remembered the gentle touch of Meagan's hands as she'd bandaged his arm earlier. An overwhelming desire to feel her hands on him again plagued him. At the moment, he couldn't tell which smarted more: his arm or his loins.

Anxious to see Barrett, Meagan hurried into Pellam House. Coates and Reeves stood near the winding staircase, polishing the brass newels. The rag in Reeves hand trembled as if being blown by a gentle breeze. She hurried down the hallway toward them.

Her footsteps startled Coates. He dropped the tin of polish. It struck one of the steps and bounced. Meagan tried to catch the tin and missed. It hit a mahogany side table filled with crystal figurines.

The first figurine toppled over; then like dominoes the other five fell. Meagan made a mad dive and caught the last statue before it dropped to the floor.

An odd silence filled the foyer—the same sort of silence that followed gunfire. She stood there holding the statue and stared down at the broken pieces of crystal strewn across the floor.

Reeves squinted at the destruction and broke the silence. "A wonderful save, if I must say so, my lady."

"Thank you, Reeves." Meagan noticed Coates looked close to tears. "You needn't worry. I'm so sorry I startled you."

"Oh, I'm a bleeding disaster. I can't do a thing right." He turned and began to pick up pieces of glass off the floor. "I don't know why his lordship keeps me on."

Reeves patted him on the back. In a fatherly voice, he said, "Now don't worry. Once you get used to the job you'll feel more comfortable. Everyone breaks something every now and then. Isn't that right, my lady?" Reeves winked surreptitiously at Meagan.

"Of course. And we need you Coates. I've been meaning to speak to you about decorating for Christmas. I see it hasn't been done yet. I would like you to handle that."

"Me, my lady?" Coates asked, his tone incredulous.

"Yes, of course. And if you need help, Reeves knows all about decorating."

Reeves's wrinkled face beamed. "We'll get it done, my lady."

"And I'd like a Christmas tree."

Reeves and Coates shared a lost look. Then Coates asked, "What's that, my lady?"

"A German custom, I gather. You cut a tree and bring it inside to decorate with candles and such. Lady Upton's daughter was telling me about it." Meagan peeked into the parlor. "We'll need a good-size tree, I think."

"I hope we'll not be lighting it inside, my lady." Reeves's bushy silver brows narrowed. "That could burn down the house."

"We'll have to be extra careful, won't we?"

Coates nodded and smiled. "Yes, my lady."

"Is my husband home?" Meagan asked, aware that Coates looked more confident.

"No, my lady."

Meagan frowned.

At her grimace, some of the assurance left Coates's face. He tried again to please her. "But guests are here. Lord Fenwick has company awaiting him."

"This early?" Meagan knew Harold didn't rise before noon.

"Yes," Reeves said. "Mr. Fields and Mr. Coburn." His distaste for the gentlemen was apparent in the sagging wrinkles at the corners of his mouth and narrowed eyes. "They are in the east parlor."

"Thank you, Reeves." With everything that had happened to Meagan, she had forgotten about Harold's dreadful friends and the trouble he faced.

Meagan hurried down the maze of wide hallways. The house was so large she hadn't yet become familiar with all the rooms. She listened to her footsteps echo off the wainscoting in the hallway and passed a ballroom. A study. A game room.

She heard low voices and followed them to the parlor. Her back straight and shoulders squared, she steeled her courage and strode through the doorway.

Mr. Fields and Mr. Coburn sat near the fire at the opposite end of the room, their backs to her. They heard her footsteps and their low conversation quickly died.

In spite of the sun streaming in through the large windows, the warm tones of red on the walls and in the furnishings, and the blaze in the fireplace, a chill swirled in the air. She rubbed her arms and traversed the length of the room, her feet barely making a sound on the thick Oriental carpet. When she paused near them, Mr. Fields and Mr. Coburn stood and bowed.

"Lady Waterton." Mr. Coburn's flesh stretched across his thin face.

"Good morning." Meagan couldn't keep the coolness from her voice.

"I say, congratulations are in order." Mr. Coburn tried for levity, but his voice came out brusk and lifeless.

"Thank you."

"Quite a hurried affair, wasn't it?" Mr. Fields shared a knowing glance with his cohort.

"My husband did not want a long engagement." Tired of their snide innuendos, but determined to be polite, she quickly lied to them. "I'm sorry to say Harold is not home."

The men shared a surprised glance. Mr. Fields spoke first. "We were under the impression he was here."

"Yes, your butler said as much."

Meagan watched the firelight slither across Mr. Fields's

slicked-back hair. "I'm sorry, gentlemen." She shrugged. "You were misinformed."

"Did he say when he'd return?" Mr. Coburn eyed Meagan's bosom.

She felt her skin crawl and said, "He did not."

Abruptly, footsteps tramped down the hallway. Harold strode past the parlor door without looking inside.

"Wasn't that him?" Mr. Coburn blurted.

Harold's footsteps froze. Then he backed into the doorway and covered the length of the room. "Coburn. Fields. Jolly good to see you. So sorry. I get lost in this place." He saw Meagan and kissed her cheek. "Ah, Meggie, top of the morning to you."

"Good morning," Meagan grumbled.

Mr. Fields cut his eyes at Meagan, silently imparting to Harold he couldn't speak in front of her. "Your sister told us you'd left, and she didn't know if you were coming back." He narrowed his eyes at Meagan.

"Meagan, you know I sleep late." Harold frowned at her, looking for an explanation.

She didn't offer one. With strained politeness, she asked, "May I have a word with you?"

Harold and Meagan traded gazes for a moment. When she wouldn't look away, he said, "Very well. Make yourself at home, gentlemen. Help yourselves to a drink." He waved to a dry bar in the corner. "I'll be right back."

Meagan grabbed Harold's hand and practically pulled him out of the parlor. She didn't stop until she reached the ballroom. Her voice echoed in the vastness as she said, "I thought I told you to end your friendship with those men. Just being near them makes my skin crawl. I mean it, Harold. Stop socializing with them right now."

"I can handle my own affairs." Harold glowered at her. "Speaking of that, why the devil did you ask Waterton for money to pay my bloody gambling debts?" Harold ran his hands through his wheat-colored curls.

"I did it so you wouldn't be in debt to those horrible men."

"Now Waterton thinks I'm nothing but another weight around his neck. He's a real sharp blade. I don't want to appear the fool around him." A mask of self-deprecation slipped over Harold's face and he stared down at the floor.

"I'm sure he doesn't see you as a fool."

"Don't know why not. Any man who can't handle his own money affairs is a fool."

Meagan squeezed his shoulder. "It was the gambling."

He remained broodingly silent for a moment, then said, "Yes, well, I have flaws enough. What of you, Meggie?"

"Me?"

"Yes. I could tell how you resented having to marry Waterton, running away the way you did, and I know he hasn't shared your bed—"

"Does everyone in the country know this? First Tessa, now you. And I heard you approach Barrett about it in the study. You shouldn't have done that."

"I was just wondering if you were the cause. What is going on between you two?" Harold studied her.

"I don't know. Barrett said he wanted to wait until we got acquainted before we" —she paused—"you know."

Harold nodded, sending his golden curls flapping against his forehead. "Yes, I know."

Meagan realized they'd strayed from the immediate danger of Mr. Fields and Mr. Coburn. Harold had a way of shifting the conversation the way he wanted it to go, so she said, "About your visitors—"

"Don't worry. I have everything under control." He winked at her. "I'll deal with them."

"Just sever the acquaintance."

Acting as if he hadn't heard her, he strode out of the room, his footsteps ringing on the marble tiles.

Not completely convinced Harold would do what he said, she waited a few moments, watching the candles flicker across the blue crushed-velvet sofa. When she felt sure he'd had time to reach the parlor, she crept down the hall.

Just shy of the door, she paused and listened.

"What brings you gentlemen here so early?" Harold asked. A chair creaked as he sat down.

"We'd read the news of your good fortune," Mr. Fields said.

"Very fortunate for you," Mr. Coburn added.

"Yes, I suppose it is." Harold kept his voice even.

"Now that your sister is so well set, I suppose you won't be needing the money any longer." Mr. Fields's voice had a quality in it as slick as his hair.

"Actually I have a check for you."

Meagan heard the rustle of paper change hands.

"Twenty thousand," Mr. Fields said with surprise.

"Yes. That's all I owe you. And I have to tell you: I won't be able to attend meetings any longer. I'm going back to Oxford."

"Oxford?" Mr. Coburn sounded surprised.

"Yes, I've decided to pursue law."

Laughter rumbled from Mr. Coburn—an evil sound that filled the room. "As we told you, Fenwick, you're in the club for life."

"But I—"

"You can forget Oxford for now," Mr. Coburn continued. "You know the policy. We'll need you on this operation—the leader needs you. We'll give you instruction in Hyde Park on Friday."

Abruptly, Meagan grew aware of someone behind her. Before she could turn, a wide hand clamped over her mouth.

CHAPTER SEVENTEEN

Barrett bent close to her ear and whispered, "Is this a pastime of yours?" He grinned sardonically.

She frowned at him, feeling her lips against his warm, wide palm. His thick flaxen hair, parted in the middle, curled down the sides of his temples, just touching his maple brown sideburns. She could see a few hours' worth of stubble on his square jaw. Her heart skipped a beat, even as her face colored all the way down to the base of her throat. He dropped his hand from her mouth, and she realized she'd been standing there mesmerized.

"I-I broke a heel on my boot," Meagan managed to whisper, smoothing imaginary creases in the silk folds of her gown. "Do you always sneak up on people?"

"Absolutely." He let his gaze roam slowly down her body.

"Well, I wish you wouldn't." Still feeling her skin tingle where his palm had touched her mouth, she blushed and heard Harold and his guests talking.

Their conversation had turned to the possibility of snow

before Christmas. This might be a good time to tell Barrett about Harold's involvement with the Devil's Advocates, but she didn't know what her husband's reaction would be. It was bad enough she'd asked him to pay her brother's gambling debts.

"Where did you go?" she asked.

"I had business to attend to. And you, Princess—where have you been?"

"How did you know I'd gone?"

"I saw Hastings unsaddling Give 'em hell." A tinge of anger flared in his eyes. "I thought I told you to stay away from him."

"He behaved like an old mare this morning." Meagan hid the lie behind sweetly uttered words. "I wish to make him my horse."

"Absolutely not. He'll end up killing you."

"But I'm an expert rider, and I know how to take a tumble," she added with a grin.

"He's not a lady's mount. Why would you want such an animal?"

"I'm beginning to take great pleasure in taming beasts." Meagan eyed him with unmistakable bluntness.

"And you think you can tame this one?" He graced her with a charming grin that creased the corners of his eyes and softened the harsh blue of his eyes.

The natural warmth of the grin flowed into her body and pooled deep inside her. Her heart quickened, and a tingling sensation spread over her. In a ragged whisper she said, "Yes, I'm sure of it."

"One can never be sure of anything." The grin broadened. He reached for a curl that was sticking out beneath her riding bonnet. The back of his hand brushed her cheek as he picked up the sable ringlet and rubbed it between his fingers.

He was so close she could smell the starched scent of his clean shirt and cravat. Her breathing grew ragged.

"So where did you go?" he asked, his eyes never leaving her lips. He feathered the curl along her cheek, to her chin. His fingers paused at the base of her throat.

"I—ah . . . " Meagan shivered, feeling his knuckles rubbing her cheek. She couldn't tell him she'd been to see his father and open such a raw wound, so she said, "I went to see Lady Holly."

"Did you find our friend in good health?" he asked, a hint of amusement in his voice. He searched her eyes, as if he knew she'd lied and wanted to ply the truth out of her.

"She is well and still in a family way." Meagan twisted her hands in front of her, aware she'd have to tell Holly about the lie. She turned the conversation. "And you—where did you go?"

"I did a little shopping of my own."

"You shouldn't have gone out with your wounded shoulder."

"Were you worried?"

"Yes. I thought perhaps you'd gone to confront Lord Collins." Meagan thought she saw a strange twitch in Barrett's eyes, but she couldn't be sure. "Please stay away from him. I'm sure a man like him is capable of anything."

"You needn't worry about Collins. In fact he's the last thing on my mind." His eyes moved over her, darkening to the color of a stormy sea.

Every place his eyes skimmed her it felt as if he were actually touching her. She recalled the way he'd stroked her. Heat flared inside her. Her heart began to pound. A fine sheen of sweat covered her body.

A throat cleared behind them.

"I say, I thought I heard you two out here in the hall." Harold grinned at them.

Steely mastery slipped back into Barrett's expression, the indifferent mask in place. He held out his arm to Meagan. "Come, Princess. We should receive our guests."

Meagan almost resented Harold for the intrusion. Frowning, she placed her hand over Barrett's arm, and they followed Harold into the parlor. She felt the strength in Barrett's arm through his velvet jacket sleeve. The image of seeing his bare chest and arms and the waves of taught muscle there formed in her mind. It didn't help the throbbing still inside her.

Mr. Fields and Mr. Coburn rose immediately and bowed to Barrett.

Harold's face beamed as he said, "I'm sure you know Lord Waterton."

"Yes." Mr. Coburn smiled with the uneasy friendliness of a cat about to pounce.

"A pleasure to see you again, Waterton. Best wishes. You couldn't have picked a finer young lady to wife." Mr. Fields looked at Meagan, a hint of irony in his expression.

"I'm quite happy with her." Barrett swept the gentlemen with a cool glance; then he clasped his wife's hand and gazed down at her. A possessive gleam shadowed his eyes for a blink; then it quickly vanished behind a smooth detached grin.

"We were just going in to tea," Barrett said in a bored but gracious tone. "Will you join us?"

"That is very kind of you," Mr. Fields's lips thinned into a crafty smile.

Inadvertently, Meagan's fingers tightened around Barrett's arm. Their eyes met. The moment he noticed her scowl, he cocked a brow at her. She lowered one back.

"Let's go in." Harold rubbed his hands together. "I haven't broken the fast and I'm starved."

Barrett purposely held Meagan back until Harold and their guests had left the parlor.

She tried to pull her hand out of his. "I should go and change for tea."

"You look absolutely perfect." He tightened his hold

on her hand. "What is the matter, Princess? I get the impression you are unhappy with me."

"Whatever gave you that idea?"

"I don't know. Perhaps it was the glower you leveled at me."

"I have a toothache. You'll have to forgive me." Meagan wondered if he were one of them. Obviously he knew them.

He touched her cheek. "Sudden, isn't it?"

"I began to feel it only moments ago."

"I gather it became severe after I invited our guests to join us?" He studied her with his keen blue eyes and rubbed the top of her hand.

"It's just I had hoped to take tea with only you and Harold." At his touch, Meagan felt her pulse race and some of her irritation wane. "But I suppose since you are acquainted with them, you felt the need to invite them to tea. How well do you know them?"

"Very little. I've seen them at the clubs."

"Oh."

"And you, Princess? Do you know them very well?" He looked deep into her eyes as if to discover some hidden secret.

"I've only met them a few times."

"I see."

Meagan felt those searching blue eyes on her. The staid quality in his voice when he had said he didn't know them well gave her reason to believe him. Still, she wasn't ready to confide in him about Harold's involvement with them. What would he think of Harold—especially after he had to pay twenty thousand pounds for her brother's gaming debts? Somehow she had to keep Harold from harm, and she'd have to do it alone.

Quickly, Meagan changed the subject. "Would you object if I invited your father to dine with us?" Meagan looked over at him.

He stared at her a moment, an unreadable expression

on his face. "Why would you wish to bring such a dark cloud to our table?"

"Oh, Barrett, he's not so terribly bad."

"That's what we thought about Napoleon at first."

Meagan hit his arm. "You are terrible."

"Only honest." He grinned at her but no warmth touched his expression. "Even if you did ask him, he'll decline. He's probably leaving for France soon so he can spend Christmas with my half brother and sister and their families." Though he tried to keep his voice flat, a slight somber note slipped into his tone.

"Will you object if I ask him?"

"Truthfully, yes." An edge sharpened his voice. He turned and strode toward the dining room.

Meagan took giant steps to keep up with him, sensing the silent barrier he'd raised against his father and her. Though intangible, it stood between them like iron bars at the moment. She felt certain now his refusal to come to her bed was nothing more than emotional insulation, a way to envelop his heart in aloofness. She would find a way to scale those bars and reach his heart.

A few moments later, Barrett watched Fenwick and his friends and took a drink of tea. Over the top of his cup, he turned and eyed Meagan, who sat next to him on a sofa. He recalled the lie she'd told him. He had spoken to Stratton and knew she'd gone to see his father earlier. More than likely, his father had tried his browbeating tactics on her, which must not have worked since she was still here. Barrett had also overheard Fenwick's plan to meet in the park and would have to make of point of being there.

Barrett took a bite of a scone and couldn't draw his eyes from the slender curve of her throat, her creamy white skin stark against the deep purple riding habit she was wearing. Her bosom swelled against the tight bodice with each one of her breaths. He watched the voluptuous globes, remembering how they had felt in his hands . . . .

Reeves leaned over and blocked his view of Meagan.

"More tea, miss?"

"Thank you, Reeves."

The teapot in Reeves's hand shook. Tea spilled out of Meagan's cup and ran onto the saucer. She seemed not to notice and smiled over at Barrett.

As if Reeves and Coates were joined by an umbilical cord of ineptness, Coates dropped a tray of sandwiches. An array of colorful slices slid off the tray with the speed of greased sleds, bombarding Fields's legs.

"You idiot!" Mr. Fields leaped up, shaking the sandwiches onto the floor.

Nuisance, who'd been sniffing around Barrett's chair, flew over to the food and gobbled it down.

"I'm sorry, sir." Coates took out his handkerchief and began to clean the cucumber paste off Fields's breeches.

"Get away from me!" Mr. Fields knocked his hand away.

Before Barrett could come to Coates's defense, Meagan leaped up and said, "I'm sure there's no harm done."

At the indisputable tone in Meagan's voice, Fields seemed to gain control over his anger. Slowly he sat back down. "Of course you are correct, my lady. No harm done." He glowered at Coates and knocked some more crumbs off his leg.

Coates watched Nuisance wolf down the last sandwich. "I'll go replenish the tray."

"Thank you, Coates." Meagan smiled encouragingly at him. She glanced back at Fields with a satisfied expression on her face.

"Come on. I'll help you." Reeves patted Coates on the back as a father might; then he staggered out of the room at his side.

"Coates lacks confidence and it makes him just a little

clumsy," Meagan offered as way of an explanation, yet her voice held no contriteness for the mishap.

Her rosewater perfume teased Barrett as she sat back down. He found himself leaning closer to indulge in the scent.

"I say, are you two going to the Gledhills' ball this evening?" Harold asked, trying to fill an awkward gap in the conversation.

"Yes, we plan to," Mr. Coburn said, slurping his tea.

The sound went through Barrett like the bellow of a fishmonger's call. "Isn't that a pleasant surprise? I'm taking my wife there this evening." Barrett made the sudden decision so he could keep an eye on Harold and his friends.

"Jolly good!" Harold said.

"Quite," the other two men mumbled.

Barrett ignored Meagan's perplexed look and eyed Fields. The other man had managed to get one sandwich on his plate before the accident, and he commenced to eat it.

Unable to watch him chew, Barrett stared down at the gold ring on the gentleman's finger. The pentagram etched on the top shifted in the light, pulsing with its own strange heartbeat. Coburn and Fenwick wore identical rings.

Barrett glanced back at Fields and asked, "So how did you come to know Fenwick?"

Harold answered for him. "I went to hear James Mills speak, and they happened to be there."

"Isn't he a proponent of economic and political liberalism?" Meagan bent down and petted Nuisance, who'd come to beg at her feet.

Barrett's eyes widened slightly at her. "I didn't know you were interested in politics?"

"I'm not, but it is impossible to pick up a paper without reading something about Mr. Mills and his radical philosophical group."

"He's a good man," Mr. Coburn said, his tone defensive.

"I don't think causing uproar about government policy shows any sort of goodness at all." Meagan continued to pet Nuisance.

"Meggie, you don't know anything about the man. You've never heard him speak. Some of his theories are on the mark." Harold eyed Meagan over his teacup, then jammed a scone into his mouth.

"He just stirs up ignorant, hotheaded men who do not know right from wrong." Meagan narrowed her eyes at her brother, not budging from her position.

"Sometimes that's what it takes to have reform in government." Mr. Coburn entered the conversation, smiling at Meagan the way one would smile at an ignorant child who needed to be taught.

"It doesn't take revolution, Mr. Coburn. It takes logic and discussion and reaching the hearts of men who make and pass our laws. That is what our government is all about."

Barrett lost all interest in the scone on his plate. He set it down, steepled his fingers, sat back in his chair, and watched Meagan. Not only could she stir him as no other woman had ever done, but she was intelligent and insightful, and she could argue politics. A woman with those qualities would never bore him.

"When a government fails to make changes in antiquated laws, then revolution is the only way," Mr. Fields fired back at her.

"The only thing revolution has ever done is cause bloodshed, pestilence, and heartache." Meagan's face flushed as she warmed to her subject, yet her voice remained composed. "It is the women and children who suffer in revolution, not the zealous men who support ideas put into their minds by some radical visionary."

Mr. Coburn raised his glass and saluted Meagan. His aversion for all of her kind showed beneath his tight smile.

"I believe, gentlemen, we have a staunch Tory sitting here with us."

She smiled woodenly at him. "Thank you for so graciously pointing that out, Mr. Coburn, but I make no claim on any political group."

"Meggie, you have clearly taken the position of a Tory," Harold added.

"I've only taken a position against bloodshed and violence. There are aspects of the Tories I do not like. However, until I find a political group governed by cool heads and common sense, I prefer not to be labeled with any group."

"It is ridiculous to think of a woman in politics anyway." Mr. Fields sipped his tea.

"Hear, hear." Mr. Coburn raised his cup again.

"I'm sure you're correct. If we had women in office, there would be sewing parties instead of revolution. How horrid." The veins on Meagan's neck popped as she struggled to keep the tight smile on her face.

With her conservative views and her obvious dislike of Fields and Coburn, Barrett knew with absolute certainty his first impression of Meagan had been correct. She couldn't be involved with the Devil's Advocates. Every muscle in his body clenched at the thought. She was an innocent party in all of this.

Her gaze met his, boring straight into his eyes. If only he could get lost in those violet depths and forget this case and the lie he was forced to live with her. He wanted to tell her that they were not actually married. Instead he said, "You have a valid point, Princess."

"I'm glad you think so," she said, her voice husky. She glanced away and looked at Harold and his friends. "If you'll excuse me, I'll leave you to discuss politics."

She rose and strode toward the door. Nuisance perked up at her leaving and made a mad dash after her, his toenails clicking on the marble tiles.

Barrett felt the loss of her at his side. "Excuse me." He laid his cup and saucer on a table, stood, and followed her.

"I say, that is singular behavior," Coburn said, slurping up the last of his tea.

"Newlyweds." Harold shrugged and shared knowing glances with Fields and Coburn.

Coburn narrowed his eyes at Harold. "Just wanted to remind you to be in Hyde Park on Friday at noon. We'll know our plans then. Don't be late."

"I won't." Harold swallowed hard and frowned pensively down at his empty plate.

Above stairs, Meagan neared her chamber when Barrett caught up to her. He stepped in front of her and blocked her way.

Her gaze moved over his expertly tailored black coat and breeches, his white cravat stark against a black silk waistcoat. His cravat—perfectly tied in the mail coach style, without a wrinkle or crease in the wrong spot—looked almost as if it was made of wax. He looked dashing. Perfect. Still an enigma to her. She recalled how he had gazed at her below stairs, how his eyes had filled with so much regret. Her only thought had been he regretted marrying her.

"Why did you leave so abruptly?" His eyes searched her face.

"I really detest those men. I couldn't stand to stay in a room with them a moment longer." It wasn't a total lie.

"Are they the gentlemen to whom your brother owes so much money?"

"Yes." A frown marred her brows. His eyes bored into her as if he wanted her to say more. She thought of telling about Harold's involvement with the Devil's Advocates and dashed the idea away. "Did you follow me up here for a reason?"

"I wanted to confirm our date this evening for the Gledhills' ball."

Meagan felt all her old insecurities about crowds and strangers swell in her with tidal wave intensity. She wasn't insecure around people she knew, and since marrying Barrett she'd gained a certain amount of confidence. But a ball? If it were a masquerade ball and she could hide behind the veil of a gypsy she might not have minded. "But"—Meagan clapped her palm against her cheek—"I have a mighty toothache."

One side of his mouth curled in a lopsided grin. "I'll have Lyng brew up something for it."

Meagan frowned at him and asked in an almost defeated tone, "Must we go to this ball?"

"Yes. Unfortunately, our swift marriage has brought your reputation into question. Tonight I'm taking you out for your first appearance in society. When everyone gets a look at your beauty, they will see why I married you so quickly." His eyes darkened as he gazed at her.

Even as Meagan felt her body become warm from his gaze, she wondered why he had married her. She thought of the emotion she'd seen on his face below stairs. Had she been wrong about what he was thinking? Or was he just trying to coerce her into going with his kind words and heated glances?

"I'm sure it won't help," she said. "The damage has been done. And with your father's disapproval—"

"I don't need my father's blessing to have society accept you as my bride." Barrett's brows made a line across his forehead. "No one would dare snub you."

"You don't understand. I have never cared about going out in society, and I could care less about it now. I fully intend to make my home in the country." Meagan emphasized her words with a stubborn frown.

"You'll make your home where I am. And let me remind you that you agreed to be seen with me in London. It was part of the deal." In a tone that would suffer no argument, he added, "We are going, Princess."

Meagan looked at the determined expression on his face and knew she would have to go. "Very well, but know I shall dislike every moment of it."

"I'll see you do not." He brushed his finger across her cheek, then turned and left her.

Meagan grimaced and watched the sway of his wide shoulders a moment, still feeling her skin tingling from his touch.

At seven that evening, Barrett scowled at his reflection in the mirror as he expertly twisted his cravat into a perfect ballroom knot, feeling the crisp white linen stiff against his neck. "Lyng, the present."

Before Barrett could raise his hand all the way, Lyng placed a wrapped box in it. The servant's keen black eyes held a slightly reproachful gleam as he said, "No matter how fine the present, it will never be a substitute for a warm husband."

"Thank you for your bit of wisdom." Barrett's frown deepened as he thrust his arms into his coat.

"How much longer do you intend to deceive her?"

"As long as it takes to shut down the Devil's Advocates and find out who is behind them."

Lyng shook his head. "For her sake, I hope it is soon. I followed her as you asked. When she arrived at Lord Kensington's, I listened outside the window of the study. I heard her standing up to him and defending you. I think she cares very deeply for you."

"I know, Lyng." Barrett's hand tightened around the present; then he strode from the room, feeling Lyng's critical eyes on his back.

Barrett crossed the hall and pounded on the door harder than he'd meant to. The door rattled on its hinges.

"Who is it?" Meagan's muffled call came from behind the door.

Barrett stepped inside and froze. He crushed the package in his hand and gaped at Meagan, sitting at her dressing table. He took in the sleeveless red dressing gown that slithered along the top of her thighs. The diaphanous silk was so thin he could see through it. His mouth went dry.

Her shapely legs were crossed; nothing was on them save a pair of sheer silk stockings and garters. Her elbows rested on the table, while she stared at her reflection in the mirror and put on a pair of earbobs.

"You shouldn't be in here. I'm dressing." She spoke without looking at him and continued to gaze at her reflection in the mirror.

Barrett half listened to her, his gaze glued to her breasts exposed beneath an almost transparent chemise. She turned slightly, picked up a brush, and ran it through her long sable curls. He caught a glimpse of peach-tipped nipples, a flat waist, and a pair of drawers as sheer as the chemise. He saw the dark triangle of her woman's mound. His jaw dropped as his manhood rose. No matter how hard he tried to control it, a slight tremor shook his body. His fingers tightened against his sweaty palms. He could actually taste her on his lips.

"Are you all right? You look a bit pale." Meagan turned, ran her tongue slowly over her lips, then flashed an uncertain smile at him. A hint of her dimples showed on her bright red cheeks. She shifted nervously in her chair and stared at his reflection in the mirror.

"You know perfectly well what is wrong with me."

His gaze swept her enticing body, every nuance of it engraved in his mind.

CHAPTER EIGHTEEN

Meagan watched Barrett stride toward her, his eyes consuming her with blue fire. Her embarrassment at appearing before him wearing hardly anything gave way to the pounding of her heart and flutter of her stomach.

He paused near her side. Meagan held her breath, feeling her nipples pulling against the gauze chemise.

He gazed into her eyes and whispered, "Damnation." He reached for her . . . .

Meagan leaped up, avoiding his hands, and glanced toward her closet door. "Tessa, where is my dress?" She turned back to Barrett and asked, "Did you say something?"

He swallowed hard, his Adam's apple bobbing. His gaze froze on the spot between her thighs. "No," he choked out between his teeth.

Tessa appeared in the doorway of the closet, holding a new emerald green ball gown, the gossamer satin glinting in the candlelight. She eyed Barrett, saw his growing scowl, then lowered her gaze. "Begging your pardon, my lord. Shall I leave?"

Meagan piped up. "Oh, no, Tessa! I really should get dressed, or we'll be late." She tightened the sash on her robe—if the scanty material could be called that. "Did you come in here for some reason, my lord?"

He stared down at her cleavage, which the flimsy robe didn't hide. His expression turned tortured. He ignored her question and asked, "Where did you get what you're wearing?"

"I bought it when I went shopping with Holly."

"I should have guessed," he said ruefully. He held out the package. "I came in to give you this."

"Thank you." Meagan noticed the slight tremor in his hands and smiled inwardly.

"I'll wait for you downstairs," he grumbled and quit the room.

As soon as the door closed, Meagan and Tessa eyed each other and burst out laughing.

"Oh, Tessa, I thought I would die of embarrassment."

Tessa sobered and wore her usual serious mien. "Main thing was you didn't look it."

"Did you see his face?" Meagan gasped out.

"He'll surely bring you home early tonight." Tessa grimaced.

"I hope so, for I really don't want to go to this ball. I have a terrible feeling about it."

"O' course you do. It's your first ball and all. I always thought the mistress did wrong in not letting you have a come-out."

"You remember how mother was. She would never let me out for fear I would break out and embarrass the family."

"It weren't right. We knew how to control it by then."

"Yes, but it didn't matter." Meagan glanced down at the package in her hands, remembering all the nights she'd spent alone at home while her parents and Harold went out to balls, soirees, and dinners.

Tessa hugged Meagan. "You'll make up for it, my lady. You'll be the belle of the ball."

"I doubt it. I can't even dance."

"Just follow his lead. You'll learn in no time." Tessa scowled down at the package. "You going to look at that all night or open it?"

Meagan tore off the wrappings and fingered a copy of Ferguson's *Astronomy*. As if touching something precious, she gingerly opened the cover. It was a first printing, and priceless.

"It's lovely."

"Bless me, but I don't see how an old book slaps your happickle." Tessa shoved her hands on her hips, saw Meagan's curious look, and clarified, "Happy tickle."

"Oh." Meagan grinned and hugged the book to her breast. "It does slap my happickle, Tessa."

A thought occurred to her, and her joy took a quick turn. She stared down at the book, wondering if he intended not to come to her bed again tonight and this was his way of saying they would not progress past level one anytime soon. If that were the case, she hoped the sight of her practically naked had changed his mind.

An hour later, Barrett fingered the watch fob Meagan had given him and listened to Fenwick humming a tune that annoyed him, though it broke the tension hovering in the carriage. Barrett glanced over at the source of his tension: She sat directly opposite him, his feet mere inches from hers.

She looked good enough to eat in an emerald green ball gown and satin cape that matched it. Her hair was swept up and held back by a pearl comb. Five thick sable curls dangled over her shoulder, bouncing slightly near one plump breast. Indelibly etched in his mind was the image of her bosom stuffed inside the corset, of her woman's mound barely covered by her nonexistent drawers. He would have liked to strangle Holly for encouraging Meagan to buy such seductive undergarments. Thanks to her, he coveted Meagan's body until it seared him, wanted her more than he'd ever wanted anything in his whole existence.

As if Meagan felt his eyes on her, she glanced up, an apprehensive look on her face. "Are we almost there?"

"Soon," Barrett said, aware of her growing apprehension.

Meagan looked over at her brother. "Would you please stop that humming? It's grating against my nerves."

"Since when have you had nerves?" Fenwick asked, sounding indignant.

"Since you started humming." Meagan worried her hands in her lap.

"My, my, aren't we a bit on the grumbletonian side this evening?"

"Just because I dislike your humming, doesn't mean I'm cross, thank you very much."

"Forgive me, Meggie. I meant to say thank you for gracing us with your lovely disposition." Fenwick smiled derisively.

"I'm glad you qualified your statement. And there is absolutely nothing wrong with my disposition." Her fingers nervously twisted around the handle of her purse.

Barrett broke into their bickering. "Did you like your gift, Princess?"

"Very much." She graced him with a reticent smile— one that didn't bring her dimples to life. "It was very kind of you. You really didn't have to give me another gift. I did nothing to warrant it."

Harold frowned at his sister and spoke before Barrett

could. "A gentleman needn't have a reason to give his wife a gift."

"Frequent gift giving without a reason tends to make the wife wonder if the giving is out of the goodness of her husband's heart or if there is another meaning behind it." Meagan's gaze bored into Barrett's face.

"There was no other reason than I wanted to give you something." The lie rolled off Barrett's tongue smoothly.

"No other reason?" Meagan arched her brows at him.

"No."

She didn't answer him. She merely stared directly at him with an uncannily intuitive gleam in her dark eyes, a voyeur's gleam, as if she were looking into the deepest, darkest hollows of his being, into those places he hid from everyone.

He felt raw and split down the middle like a gutted fish. She knew he'd given her that book as recompense for not sharing her bed again tonight. For the first time in his life, Barrett realized he'd never given a gift out of the goodness of his heart, or because it felt good.

Fighting pangs of conscience, he drummed his fingers on the top of his cane. When the carriage rolled to a stop, he felt instant relief from the tension pulling at him.

The door opened and Hastings appeared, his face red from the cold night air.

Fenwick rose from his spot closest to the door and stepped out first. Barrett followed, the cold air welcome against his face. Thick dark clouds obscured the roundness of the moon and not a star winked in the sky.

While Meagan gathered up the hem of her dress, Fenwick turned to Barrett. In a disparaging tone, he whispered, "You'll have to forgive Meggie. She's not herself tonight. I've never seen her this cross."

"You needn't apologize for her."

Meagan appeared in the doorway. "I'll do my own apologizing, Harold, thank you very much."

"Then by all means go to it." Fenwick shot her an irritated glance, then looked at Barrett with a marked amount of sympathy. "Mind if I meet you inside?"

"Not at all." Barrett watched Fenwick stride past Hastings and hurry up the drive.

Light beamed through the frost-covered windowpanes of Gledhill House and touched the top of Fenwick's tall hat. Barrett turned to help Meagan down. The touch of her gloved hand brought another jab from his conscience.

"My brother feels I owe you an apology."

"You don't." He laced his arm through hers and escorted her past the line of carriages along the drive.

A thick, misty dew covered the granite gravel on the drive and made it shimmer. He listened to their footsteps crunching in unison on the gravel, mixing with the low conversation of the drivers and footmen standing watch near their masters' vehicles.

Her expression softened the slightest bit. "Perhaps I may have sounded as if I did not appreciate the book, but that is not so. I did. I'm just nervous about this ball."

"It will be all right."

Her gaze stayed glued to the Gledhill mansion, the color steadily draining from her face. The closer they moved to the door and the line of people waiting to be announced, the more her expression turned apprehensive. "I don't know if I can do this." She fidgeted with the frog on her cape.

"Yes, you can." He squeezed her hand.

"I have a confession to make. This is my first ball. I can't even dance. I've never gone out in high society. I'm sure the night will end in disaster. I should go home, where I belong." Meagan tried to bolt.

Barrett grabbed her and pulled her into his arms. He ran his hands over the soft velvet of her cape and whispered, "You're not going home. We'll do this together."

"Couldn't we just jump off a cliff together?" Meagan struggled to get out of his grasp.

"I might be able to manage it later, but first we're going inside."

She stopped struggling and a small grin tugged at the corners of her mouth. "Very well, but I shall dislike it. And if I make a fool of myself, I'm definitely jumping off that cliff afterward."

"Not without me."

Her face lit up in a real grin, with her dimples deep in her cheeks. He tried to glance away, but the glow on her face held him captive. If only he could run his tongue over her lips. More of this kind of thinking and they would never get to the ball.

He squeezed her fingers and gave her an encouraging smile. He'd taken advantage of her in every way, but he'd make it up to her by giving her the self-confidence she lacked. Yes, that was the least he could do. When he was done, she'd be the toast of the *ton*. He'd make sure of it.

A few minutes later, Meagan peered around a column at a rectangular-shaped ballroom so large she couldn't see the end of it for the dancers and the crush lining the perimeter. Swags of running cedar and pine rolled along the ceiling. Red bows surfed the tops of each evergreen wave, making the room look festive and Christmasy. Barrett nudged Meagan over to the doorman and handed the man his calling card.

In a thunderous voice that carried over the music and the roar of voices in the ballroom, the doorman announced, "Lord and Lady Waterton."

Their names took on a physical depth that pervaded the whole room. Every eye turned their way. Meagan felt the very air press in on her. The conversation trickled away. Only the soft notes of a waltz broke the hushed atmosphere. After a moment, even the melody ended.

Barrett leaned over and whispered, "Chin up, Princess. Let them know you are doing them a favor by being here."

"How am I to do that?" Meagan choked out.

"Never give too much away." Barrett pulled out his pocket watch, checked the time, then surveyed the crowd with schooled indifference.

Meagan couldn't help but smile. "You are very good at this acting business. I'm afraid to carry it off I'll need a watch and fob."

"I will definitely get you one if you feel the need of it, but you already have everything you require to conquer this crowd. You are five times more beautiful than any lady here and infinitely more amusing."

Meagan blushed and felt the region over her heart radiating with warmth from the compliment.

"You blush very becomingly, but I must warn you that is not allowed." With practiced ease he slid his watch back in his pocket and escorted her farther into the ballroom. "A princess never blushes. You must act polished, bland, impersonal, and extremely bored."

She almost giggled out loud.

"Dimples are never permitted if you are going to look weary of your present society." He grinned down at her.

His smile was a genuine one, with just enough candor in it to temper the harsh line of his mouth and the ice blue of his eyes. He'd never looked more dashing and attractive to Meagan. He wore all black, his cravat and white shirt so perfect and wrinkle free they seemed to be made of white paperboard.

His thick blond hair, brushed back from his face, curled around the edge of his collar in a way that made her want to run her hands through the silky mass. His brown sideburns dipped onto his cheeks, offsetting the squareness of his jaw and the hint of brown stubble beginning to sprout.

The orchestra struck up again as they passed a roaring

fireplace. An arrangement of lemons, apples, grapes, long springs of cinnamon sticks and "she" holly—so dubbed for being the nonprickly kind—covered the mantel. The scent of cinnamon, nutmeg, and cloves wafted through Meagan's senses.

Meagan noticed the ballgoers now and said, "Remarkable. They are no longer staring at us. I take that back. There is a group of dowagers against the wall who have their lorgnettes trained on me."

"They are easily toppled, Princess. The trick is to appear more disdainful of them than they are of you. It works every time." He gently squeezed her hand.

She felt the heat of his wide palm seeping through her silk gloves. The rigid sinew of his arm pressed against her fingertips. He was so close, the outside of his thigh brushed her dress. The rippling motion of the violet silk moved her silk petticoat and made it feel as if his hands were running along her legs. In spite of her apprehension, a burning hunger for him warmed her body all over.

"Shall we dance?" Before she could refuse, Barrett whisked Meagan out onto the dance floor to join the other waltzing couples.

He held her so tightly her feet barely touched the ground. Somehow she managed to step on his feet anyway. "Oh, I'm sorry."

"No need to be. I don't need my toes if we're going to jump off a cliff." She smiled at the devilish twinkle in his eye and he said, "Ah! You are actually smiling while dancing. See, you can do both at the same time. Now stop concentrating on the steps and let me guide you."

Meagan leaned against his hard chest and relaxed in his arms. She grew aware of his clean male scent, of his breath on her face, of his strong arms around her. The rest of the room melted away. It was only she and Barrett.

Round and round they twirled. Meagan let the beat of the waltz fill her and Barrett lead her. They became one with the rhythm of the dance. One with the moment. She grew light-headed, not from dancing for the first time in her life, but from the charming gentleman—her husband—holding her.

Suddenly the waltz ended. Meagan's skirt swirled around her legs and Barrett's as they halted.

He stared down at her, all the teasing gone from his eyes. "You were born to waltz, Princess."

"Thank you for teaching me."

"My pleasure." His face lit up in a smile. He laced his arm with hers and guided her off the floor.

Meagan gazed at all the people eyeing her and felt her confidence rising. She knew she had Barrett to thank for it. It wasn't as bad as she thought it would be. In fact, she'd never felt more alive or happier. She had missed so much in her life. Her parents had had no right to shelter her the way they had done.

Instead of smiling, she frowned slightly and let Barrett lead her over to a handsome couple. They looked in their forties and remarkably alike, with their black hair, wide smiles, and thick, dark brows. The woman's gold dress matched her husband's gold breeches and coat. They made a striking pair.

"Lord Waterton, so delighted you could come," the lady gushed and extended her hand to him. "And this must be your wife I've heard so much about. I'm so thrilled you chose my ball to introduce her to society."

"Quite lovely." The gentleman's gaze snapped over Meagan's figure.

Barrett possessively slipped his arm around Meagan's waist. "Lady Gledhill, meet my wife, Lady Waterton. Meagan, this is Lord and Lady Gledhill."

Meagan curtsied. "It is such a pleasure to meet you both."

A blond stepped up to Barrett, her white gown sparkling

over her perfect figure. She winked at him and touched
his arm. "It has been an age, Lord Waterton."

Meagan watched the beautiful woman stroke Barrett's
sleeve with her gloved fingers and held back the desire to
slap the lady's hand away.

Barrett noticed Meagan's frown and cleared his throat.
"Meagan, I'd like you to meet Lady Dennison."

"Ah, your little wife. I just couldn't believe you'd gone
and married." Lady Dennison's gaze swept over Meagan,
her eyes cold and assessing.

The name registered immediately with Meagan. She
couldn't help but say, "A pleasure. Your name sounds so
familiar to me."

"Probably because you heard the nasty gossip about
Barrett and my husband dueling over me." Lady Dennison
rolled her eyes and forced a little laugh. "None of it was
true, of course."

"Of course," Meagan echoed.

Lady Gledhill touched Meagan's arm, leaned close, and
whispered, "Don't believe half of the rumors about your
husband, my dear. He is not as naughty as he would have
the world believe."

"I'm sure he's not." Meagan scowled at Lady Dennison's
fingers still stroking Barrett's arm. She tried to surreptitiously jerk her hand out of Barrett's grasp. But she
couldn't break his iron grip and she only succeeded in
looking as if she had a nervous tic in her hand.

Lord and Lady Gledhill noticed it and frowned at each
other.

A brunette strolled up to them. Meagan frowned at the
woman. Everything about her bespoke of perfection, even
her teeth, which glistened in a seductive smile. She wore
a watered-down indigo dress that showed every curve of
her body.

The lady shot Barrett a come-hither smile, then commenced to mark her territory by eyeing Meagan and Lady

Dennison with feline contempt. "Well, my dear Barrett, I haven't seen you in an age." She stepped close to Barrett and touched the curve of his lapel.

"Hello, Mrs. Morris." Barrett hardly looked at her while he tried to snatch his hand back from Lady Dennison's fingers and hold on to Meagan's hand at the same time.

Meagan recalled hearing a rumor about the widow Morris being one of Barrett's mistresses he'd let go. She dug her nails into his palm until he turned her hand loose. "If you'll excuse me, I see my brother. I must speak to him. It's been a pleasure meeting you, Lord and Lady Gledhill. Mrs. Morris, Lady Dennison."

Barrett reached out to grab her hand, but Meagan wheeled around and crossed the room, her chest heaving. Of course she was bound to run into his mistresses, but a whole harem at once? It made her keenly aware she couldn't even foster enough lust in him to bring him to her bed.

Meagan hurried past a dancing couple and almost bumped into them. She quickly hopped back and spied Harold talking to a large group of young dandies, all looking as ridiculous as her brother, with their bright waistcoats and collars so high they could not turn their heads.

Some distance away, a lone tall gentleman stood near a potted fern, his black curls framing his square face, his pewter eyes gleaming.

"Dear Lord. Lochlann!" she gasped under her breath and turned to see if Barrett had seen her friend.

He had.

CHAPTER NINETEEN

Meagan skirted several dancers and attempted to reach Lochlann before another confrontation erupted. Lochlann noticed her and strode toward her. She tried to hurry past Harold, but he grabbed her arm, pulling her up short.

"Meggie, my friends are dying for an introduction."

Eight young dandies swarmed around Meagan. Peeking over the shoulder of a portly, bull-necked gentleman, Meagan half listened to Harold make introductions, while her gaze flitted between Lochlann and Barrett.

Harold sounded pleased that so many of his friends showed an interest in his sister. Of course, it probably didn't dawn on him that the gentlemen were only appeasing their curiosity about her since her reputation was the brunt of the latest scandal broth.

A short man edged his way past her admirers and grabbed her hand. "Dear, dear Lady Waterton. May I have this dance?"

"Forget it, Wallace. She'll definitely dance with me first," another gentleman said.

"No, I'll take that first dance with the Winter Princess."

"Not on your life," Lochlann said, elbowing his way through the crowd.

"Gentlemen, gentlemen! Please," Meagan said, afraid a fight might break out. She looked at Lochlann. "I will dance with—"

"Me." Barrett's arm clamped around her waist.

Lochlann's and Barrett's gazes locked. Meagan held her breath, thinking Lochlann's temper might flare. His expression turned brooding. Then he stepped back and allowed Barrett to escort her onto the dance floor.

Meagan breathed a sigh of relief and heard the dandies grumble as Barrett whisked her into the stream of waltzers. He held her so close, she could feel his sculpted chest pressing against her. The movement of his body hardened her nipples instantly.

"Please be patient with Lochlann," Meagan said, fighting the sensation his closeness caused in her.

"You forget, Princess, I'm not the aggressor. He is."

"I'm sure he will not cause trouble."

"If he does, I'll stop it." Barrett glanced over Meagan's head and narrowed his eyes at Lochlann, who stood in the corner near a fern wearing a chagrined look as he stared at Meagan.

"I wish you would forget about Lochlann. The evening was going so well."

He didn't answer her. He only eyed Lochlann as if he hadn't heard her.

"What is the use! You're not even listening to me. Why don't you go back to your *lady* friends?" Meagan snapped.

His gaze shifted from Lochlann to her would-be suitors huddled near Harold. Then he gazed down at her. The glitter in his eyes signaled he'd been listening to her all along. "What about your gentlemen friends? If that group hadn't been panting after you, I might not have had to intervene."

The hint of possessiveness in his voice pleased her, but she kept the irritation in her voice as she said, "I don't believe for a minute you would have minded if Lochlann hadn't been among them."

"Then you don't know me very well."

"You're absolutely correct. I don't know you at all." Meagan searched his eyes, but his gaze had dropped to her bosom. Too annoyed to blush, she said, "Sometimes I'm quite sure I might know your character. Then you go and do something that completely baffles me."

"A husband should always keep his wife off guard." His gaze roamed over the creamy white flesh of her neck and shoulders.

"The same could be said for a wife." She felt the heat of his gaze warming her down to her toes.

"Indeed. You disarm me at every turn, Princess. Especially with those underclothes you are wearing." He splayed his hand along the small of her back and rubbed his finger along the bottom edge of her corset.

Meagan felt his touch through her clothes. A shiver went down her spine. As Barrett twirled her around, she caught sight of Lady Dennison and Mrs. Morris, who were still speaking to the Gledhills and scorching her with their scornful glances.

Her brows met in a frown. "I suppose you say that to all the ladies you take to their first ball."

Barrett followed her gaze. "You have the wrong impression about Lady Dennison."

"I don't really care what happened." Meagan managed to keep her voice level.

"I have gouge marks on my hands to prove you do." He cocked a brow at her.

"Very well. I'm sure you want to tell me. Go ahead and do so," Meagan said, exasperated and a little dizzy from the way he whirled her around on the floor.

"Lady Dennison came to me and asked me to go along

with a plan to make her husband jealous, for she suspected he was taking her for granted. So I agreed. When I began paying court to her, it was all very innocent and above-board. Her husband grew enraged and challenged me to a duel."

"Naturally, you couldn't say no."

"Naturally. But he was a terrible shot and I didn't want to harm him, so I shot wide. And that was the end of it, but Lady Dennison bantered the story about to further her husband's jealousy."

"Then why is he not here?"

"Brooding, I believe."

"Does he treat her better?"

Barrett grinned. "I believe he will after he stops sulking."

"What of Mrs. Morris?" After the question slipped out, Meagan regretted asking it.

Barrett cast a casual glance in the lady's direction, his expression stoic. "She is an old mistress—that is all. There is nothing between us."

"How many ex-mistresses do you have? No, forget I asked. I don't want to know."

Amusement flickered in the blue depths of his eyes. "Are you sure?"

"Yes, I'm sure. And since I'm forced to meet your legion of mistresses, you must allow me to speak to Lochlann tonight without your interference. He is, after all, my friend and not an old lover." Meagan glanced up at him.

His amusement turned to a scowl, and his eyes turned a stormy blue gray. "You'll stay away from him."

"But I—"

"I said stay away from him."

Meagan gave him her best indignant scowl, aware arguing with him would do her no good. She heard the music end and stepped stiffly back from him.

"Remember what I said." He shot a warning glance at

her, then one at Lochlann, who was speaking to one of Harold's friends.

A young man strode up to her and bowed. "May I have the next dance, Lady Waterton?"

Barrett shot her a glance that said, "Remember what I said." Then he strode away, scowling. The young man took her hand and led her down a line forming for a country dance. Meagan watched Barrett pause near the Gledhills and Lady Dennison, and she wanted to throw something at him. Then she realized she didn't know the steps to the country dance. Her anger quickly turned to chagrin.

Half an hour later, Meagan left the necessary and someone touched her shoulder. She jumped and turned to see Lochlann. "Oh, Lord! You scared me."

Lochlann's expression softened as he reached out and touched her hand. "I wanted to speak to you."

"Why? So you could cause trouble again?" Meagan searched the hallway for any sign of Barrett. All she needed was for Barrett to find her speaking to Lochlann.

"I see you're still irritated with me."

"Irritation hardly describes how I feel." Meagan eased her hand out of his grasp.

"Please give me another chance, Meagan. I realize now we'll never be married, but I want to stay your friend. I miss talking with you. You can't throw away a lifetime of friendship."

Meagan's voice lost its sternness. "Oh, Lochlann, I'll never forget our friendship."

He smiled sadly. "Do you think your husband will let me call on you?"

"Not after all the trouble you've caused."

"Would it help to apologize to him?"

Meagan saw the strained look on his face and knew it must be hard for someone as proud and principled as

Lochlann to apologize to Barrett just to remain her friend. It was a noble gesture she admired. She wasn't about to let Barrett destroy her friendship with Lochlann.

"I could perhaps speak to him and tell him how you feel," she said, knowing she had to try to persuade Barrett to change his mind.

Footsteps made her glance up and she saw Mr. Fields. Nodding stiffly to Meagan, he passed them. She waited until he strode out of hearing range and said, "Remember me telling you about those men Harold was involved with?"

"Yes."

"That was one of them who just walked past us."

Lochlann frowned. "I've seen him in the clubs."

"Harold is supposed to meet him and Mr. Coburn in the park on Friday. Would you help me keep an eye on him—I mean, so he doesn't get in trouble?"

"I don't mind, Meagan, but isn't it up to Waterton to do that? He is, after all, your husband. He should help Harold."

"I haven't told him what I know. I don't know how he would react. Will you help me?"

"You know I can't refuse you anything." Lochlann smiled the first genuine smile she'd seen from him since she'd married Barrett. "But you mustn't tell Waterton. I won't have him taking the credit after I save Harold."

"I won't." Meagan glanced toward the ballroom. "Perhaps you should go and speak to them now. See what you can learn. I'll write you and let you know what Barrett says about allowing you to visit."

"Very well. It will be like old times." His grin broadened.

"Thank you." She squeezed his hand. It would be all right. She knew Lochlann would eventually come to his senses. He'd apologize and she'd have her dear friend back—if she could persuade Barrett to listen to Lochlann.

* * *

A few moments later, Meagan strode back into the ballroom and saw Barrett speaking to several dowagers. Barrett glanced at her and frowned. She decided to wait to broach the subject of Lochlann.

One of her many admirers strode toward her, a young man with a protruding brow. Meagan started to turn and bolt, but Sir James strode up to her and bowed slightly.

As he rose, Meagan watched the candlelight gleaming blue in his pitch-black hair. She could see the resemblance to Barrett, but James had a darker, more severe look about him, with his chiseled hawkish features and deep-set black-eyes.

"Shall I rescue you?" he asked, taking her hand.

"Yes," Meagan said with relief. She saw the dandy pause, frown at James, then turn and stride back across the ballroom.

Meagan let Sir James guide her out onto the dance floor. Then they joined the other dancing couples.

"For just having learned to dance, you have mastered the art," James said.

"How could you tell? Did I step on your toes?" Meagan's cheeks burned.

"No, but I saw how you concentrated on the country dance steps."

Meagan frowned. "You are just being kind. You must have seen me bump into my partner twice."

"Yes, but afterward you sailed right through." A grin eased across his lips. He twirled her around the dance floor, and his face sobered as he changed subjects. "I say, my dear, how are you and my cousin getting along?"

"Do you want the truth, Sir James, or the standard line?"

"Always the truth."

"Not very well." Meagan glanced past James's broad shoulder toward Barrett, who stood talking to a group of dowagers, their turbans rocking as he made them laugh.

"Ah, yes. He hasn't performed his husbandly duties."

"Does everyone in England know about this?" Blood rushed to Meagan's cheeks.

"He did come to my house, so naturally I knew." He smiled at her, his expression void of derision.

"Naturally." He had an austere, priestly composure about him, as if he'd heard many a dying man's confession. She felt she could confide in him. After a slight hesitation, her blush traveled down her neck as she said, "He said he didn't want to . . . you know . . . before we went to the next level."

"Level?" Sir James's black brows rose.

"Yes, he said there were levels in a relationship and we should stay on the first one for a while." She lowered her voice. "Quite frankly, I want to progress to the second."

Sir James kept the same schooled expression. "I believe Barrett didn't want to force you into his bed before you felt comfortable with him."

"Are you sure that's all there is to it? I can't help but think he might still be in love with Lady Matilda?"

"So you know about her, do you?"

"Yes."

He eased her along the dance floor. "If you tell Barrett what I'm about to say, I'll deny it—"

"I wouldn't divulge a confidence."

Sir James grinned, a prosaic expression that didn't touch his eyes. "Well, then, I'll tell you about Barrett. My cousin hasn't an inkling of what it's like to love a woman." A flash of sadness glinted in James's eyes—evidence of a heartache that still plagued him—then it disappeared with a blink.

The waltz ended and James whisked Meagan to a halt.

A footman's voice broke over the low roar in the ballroom. "Lady Rawlings."

Meagan clamped her mouth closed, gulped hard, and watched Lady Matilda float into the room.

CHAPTER TWENTY

Lady Matilda's gown hardly moved beneath her stiff posture. She looked radiant in a shimmering midnight blue silk gown that had been watered down to cling to her body. Meagan stared down at her own jade green ball gown. It wasn't half as alluring as Lady Matilda's, nor did Meagan have her hourglass curves and striking beauty.

Lady Matilda lit up the whole room when she walked into it. Meagan couldn't even start a fire. The self-confidence Barrett had instilled in her earlier melted away into a growing empty pit inside of her.

Lady Matilda noticed Barrett and eyed him with contemptuous haughtiness, even as a curious smile touched her lips.

Meagan's gaze shifted to Barrett. He strode toward Lady Matilda without taking his eyes off her. Pausing in front of the lady, he said something to her.

She shot daggers at him with her blue eyes, yet she wore an intrigued grin.

Barrett grinned back, his eyes glistening with a strangely amused light, an almost begging quality in them.

Seeing them together made it perfectly plain how Barrett felt about Lady Matilda. He said he had thought himself in love with Lady Matilda at one time, but no longer. Now Meagan could plainly see he had been fooling himself: He still loved her.

Sir James's words echoed in her mind: *My cousin hasn't an inkling of what it's like to love a woman.* But he did. He loved Lady Matilda, with all her perfection and beauty.

A pain stabbed her heart. She bit her trembling lip, feeling it ache like her insides. She saw a man with a protruding brow striding toward her, his bright fuchsia breeches stark against his white stockings. The amount of calm in her voice surprised her as she said, "If you'll excuse me, Sir James, I think I'd better go hide. I see another one of Harold's friends approaching."

Sir James frowned at her, but she hurried across the ballroom and blended into the crowd. The gentleman still followed her. A sudden pounding in her temples and a spinning in her head made her duck into a doorway and hide behind the door. His footsteps died away in the hallway.

Meagan stepped out from behind the door and noticed she stood inside a parlor. A table had been set up in the center, where an array of colorful appetizers and sweets beckoned. She approached the table. In her mind she again saw the look on Barrett's face as he spoke to Lady Matilda.

Tears stung her eyes. Long rivulets streamed down her cheeks.

He loved Lady Matilda.

She picked up a spiced shrimp canape and bit into it.

Of course he did. Lady Matilda was everything perfect and beautiful.

Meagan sampled a crab-filled puff pastry and a stuffed mushroom.

How could she have ever thought she could make Barrett forget Lady Matilda?

She kept eating canapés. She wasn't hungry, but the food made her feel better. It wasn't until she had made her way around the long table and sampled everything that she heard a deep, predatory voice issue from the hallway. It made her freeze. Lord Collins.

He must have come early and been in the card room all this time. She heard Mr. Fields's voice too.

She crept closer to the doorway to listen.

"We're meeting Fenwick in the park on Friday," Mr. Fields's slick voice said. "Are you coming?"

"Can we trust him?"

"I don't know. Waterton gave him the money to pay off his loan, but we made it quite plain to him that if he betrays us he dies." Mr. Fields chuckled softly.

Meagan gulped past a knot in her throat and clutched her chest, suddenly afraid. It was easy to believe Lord Collins was involved with the Devil's Advocates.

"We'll see you there then?"

"Yes."

Meagan saw the large, raised welts breaking out on her arms, hands, and chest. She'd never had such a bad case of them and she knew the strain of seeing Barrett with Lady Matilda and realizing he loved her had made them worse. She had to leave and quickly.

She waited until the men's footsteps died away; then she poked her head out the door to check the hallway. She saw the back of Mr. Fields's and Lord Collins's heads blend into the crowd. She turned and ran in the opposite direction.

Her skin burned everywhere. She could feel her tongue beginning to swell. Pretty soon, she would have hives all over her. If Barrett saw her like this, she wouldn't be able to bear it. She hurried past the game room, catching a fleeting glimpse of the card tables filled with ladies and gentlemen. Then she slipped through another door.

Her footsteps pounded on the Italian tiles and seemed to thunder in the empty hallway. The striped wallpaper on the walls blurred behind her tears.

She rounded several corners and finally found the back way out of the mansion. She stepped out into the cold air. It soothed her stinging skin. In the moonlight she could see the hives beginning to rise on her chest and the small swatch of skin where her gloves met her sleeves.

She ran past a cropped hedge of hollies that bordered one side of the mansion. Light from the windows beamed across the tops, making the red berries glisten. The drive rose up before her. A long line of carriages stretched before her. The drivers huddled nearby, their voices carrying in the night air and seeming to pound in her ears.

No one must see her like this.

She wheeled around to run in the opposite direction and plowed into a hard chest.

"Here now. What is the meaning of this?"

Meagan looked up into Lord Kensington's forbidding visage. It was the last vestige of humiliation she could stand. Sobs burst from her chest. She covered her face with her hands and wanted to die.

He cleared his throat. With uncomfortable gruffness, he said, "See here. 'Tis nothing to cry about."

She felt his arms go around her; then he patted her back. His kindness took Meagan off guard and she bawled louder.

"See here now, child. Nothing is worth all this upset. I suppose my son is responsible for it. I knew it wouldn't take him long to hurt you."

"It wasn't him so much— Oh, yes, it was. If not for him I would have watched what I was eating." She hiccuped and let out a loud sob.

"Come, come. Let me take you home and you can tell me about it."

"Would you?"

"Yes, I'm not an ogre. Here." He handed her a handkerchief.

She hiccuped into it and blew her nose.

"You must be freezing." He pulled off his cape and threw it over her shoulders. "My carriage is this way."

"I can't let anyone see me," she said, keeping her face down.

"You needn't worry about the tears, child. It's understood ladies cry."

She burst out into sobs again. Lord Kensington shook his head, mumbled something about never understanding impassioned young chits, and escorted her to his carriage.

Back in the ballroom, Lady Matilda said, "I met your wife. I pity the poor girl."

"I wouldn't waste your sympathy. She's quite content." Barrett glanced about the ballroom for Meagan. To prove to himself he was over Lady Matilda, he had engaged her in conversation. He had been so astonished by his complete indifference to her that he hadn't been watching Meagan as closely as he should have. Now he didn't see her anywhere.

"If you'll excuse me." Barrett bowed to Lady Matilda.

"You just can't walk away like that," she said, bristling.

"Our conversation has ended." He left her with her hands on her hips and her face red with anger. He strode toward James, watching him whirl Lady Gledhill around the floor, her gold gown glittering against James's dark suit.

Barrett tapped James on the shoulder.

James whisked his partner out of the dance and asked, "What is it?"

"Have you seen Meagan?"

"The last time I looked she was heading for the ladies' room."

Barrett thought she might be with Burrows. His gaze scanned the ballroom and alighted on Burrows speaking to Fenwick and his friends.

Lady Gledhill saw the worry on Barrett's face. "I'm sure she's about. Shall I check the ladies' room?"

Barrett nodded. "Thank you." He waited until she left. Then he said, "I'm going to look for her."

James followed on his heels. "She's here somewhere. I wouldn't worry."

"I don't like it. Where could she be?"

At that moment, he saw Collins in a corner speaking to Lady Dennison. He nodded stiffly to Barrett, a Machiavellian smile spreading across his lips.

"When did that bastard get here?" Barrett narrowed his eyes at Collins.

"He's been in the card room."

Barrett started toward Collins, but James pulled him back. "Don't let him goad you."

"He might know where Meagan is."

"I've got a man watching him. He doesn't know. We'll find her."

Lady Gledhill strode up to them, a worried look on her face. "I didn't see her in the ladies' room."

"Thank you," Barrett mumbled absently and hurried to check the rest of the mansion, the muscles in his stomach knotting.

CHAPTER TWENTY-ONE

Halfway home, Meagan wiped her tears away with her handkerchief. She had used Lord Kensington's shoulder to cry on, and she straightened up now, feeling embarrassed. "I'm so sorry. I didn't want anyone to see me like this."

"There is nothing to be sorry for, child." He tipped her face up and looked down at the bright red splotches, which were clear in the lantern light. His eyes widened. "I say! Your face."

She pulled away and hung her head. "It's my condition. I break out every time I eat mushrooms. It lasts for a day or two. It's horrible. I've lived with this all my life. It wasn't until I was fifteen and our old cook died and we'd gotten a new one that I realized the mushrooms were doing it. Thankfully the new cook didn't like them."

"Well, 'tis perhaps fortuitous you found out what was the matter." Lord Kensington looked relieved.

"I should have been careful," Meagan said, her voice barely audible. "Barrett will loathe the very sight of me. I can't let him see me like this."

"Then you must come to my house."

"You would do that for me?"

"I won't lie to you, child." He picked up her hand and squeezed it. "I have ulterior motives. I admit, when I first met you, I thought you unsuitable for my son, but I have come to believe he is unsuitable for you." He paused and his eyes misted as he spoke his next words. "You remind me too much of my Vedetta for me to let my son ruin your life, and sure as I'm sitting beside you now, he will make you miserable. I'm convinced he cannot care about anyone. He's a lost cause. Unfortunately, he's what I made him." Pain and regret etched every wrinkle in Lord Kensington's face.

Meagan felt his pain. She wanted to say something that would change the past and the years of animosity that had risen up like a wall between Barrett and his father. But no words on earth could do that. So she squeezed his hand and said, "You needn't worry about my getting hurt. I had no expectations when we married." Tears came to Meagan's eyes, and she had to blink them away.

Two hours later, Meagan glanced around her chamber in Lord Kensington's home. The rosewood bed wasn't half as large as the one at Pellam House, but the chamber was cozy like her room at Fenwick Hall. Only a sofa and a dressing table cluttered the light blue walls. It would do nicely until the hives faded and she could go home. Would Barrett even notice she wasn't there? Would he care?

Oh, he threw compliments and gifts at her and kissed her, and there had been real hunger in those kisses— especially when he'd stroked that center of her desire and shown her what real lust felt like. But Meagan knew he'd only touched her because she'd poured out her heart to him and told him he'd hurt her. It was his way of easing his conscience—just like the gifts he'd given her.

She strode over to the window and pressed her nose to the glass. A nearby oak blocked most of her view of the sky. She squinted past the gnarled, grasping branches and could see only clouds. No matter how hard she looked, she could not see one star or the moon, nor could she get her bearings. When she couldn't see the stars, she felt adrift, like a lost sea captain searching for a sign in the heavens. During her lonely childhood the stars had been her only comfort. There would be no comfort tonight when she needed it most.

Grimacing, she saw her reflection in the glass. Large blistery welts covered her face, neck, and arms. There didn't seem to be a place on her body that wasn't blemished. A memory flashed back to Meagan . . . .

It was the day of her parents' annual Christmas ball. Excitement filled the house. Servants ran back and forth like army ants. Smells of cooking cider, cinnamon, and plum pudding pervaded every corner of the house.

Up in her chamber on the third floor, Meagan looked out of her telescope. It was a perfect day for a Christmas rout. Thick white clouds molded the sky. By nightfall, it would be snowing.

Before Meagan turned away from the window, she paused and stared at her reflection in the glass. She didn't see a twelve-year-old girl with sable curls and violet eyes; all she saw was the hideous red splotches on her face. It occurred to her why there wasn't a mirror in her room. Frowning, she stepped away and walked to the bookcase.

She read the spines of the books. None of the titles held any interest for her. She'd had the hives for a week now. She'd read almost every book she was allowed to read. Would the hives ever go away? She longed to see Lochlann and play with him, but her mother wouldn't allow her to leave the house in her condition.

Footsteps sounded behind her. Meagan watched her mother glide into the room wearing a deep indigo gown.

She was a beautiful woman, dark, shapely, with perfect white skin so flawless it looked like the face on one of Meagan's porcelain dolls. Her mother had often remarked that she had such flawless skin no one could guess her age of forty.

"My dear." She patted Meagan on the head and her lips thinned in a sympathetic smile.

She never kissed or held Meagan when she broke out. Pats—that was all Meagan ever received, as if her mother was afraid she might be infected by Meagan's splotches.

"Yes, Mama," Meagan said, watching her mother drop her hand and step back.

"I just came up to say how sorry I am you won't be able to join in the festivities this evening."

"But I missed last year's ball too."

"I know, my dear, but we can't very well let you out in society. People can be very cruel, you know. We've tried very hard to keep your condition a secret."

"Why?"

"Well, it will ruin your brother's prospects for getting married. You wouldn't want that, now would you?"

"No, Mama." Meagan shook her head, sending her long curls bouncing against her back.

"That's my daughter. Now stay in your room like a good child." Her mother smiled at her and patted Meagan's shoulder.

"Yes, Mama." Meagan looked down at her pinafore and couldn't help but wonder if her mother really wanted Harold to make a good match or if she was just ashamed of her daughter.

"I've instructed Tessa to let you stay up late."

"Thank you, Mama."

"I'd better go. It's time to start getting ready. We'll miss you." Her mother blew a kiss and floated out of the room.

Meagan stared at the empty doorway, not really caring about the ball. She didn't want anyone to see her face like this anyway. But just once Meagan wanted her mother to hold her when she had her condition. Just once . . .

Released from her memory, Meagan turned from the window and strode toward the bed, a lump growing in her throat. Trying very hard not to cry again, she shoved the rolled-up sleeves of the dressing gown she'd borrowed from Lord Kensington and began to climb into bed when she heard loud shouts below stairs.

There was no mistaking the angry voice. Barrett. She glanced around, then ran to the dresser. Heaving as hard as she could, she shoved it against the door.

"You can't disturb her!" Meagan recognized Lord Kensington's bellow.

"The bloody hell I can't! She's my wife!" Meagan had never heard Barrett's voice raised in such seething rage.

"You don't deserve a wife."

"Do you realize I've gone half out of my mind looking for her? The least you could have done was let me know she was here. Where is she?"

Doors banged open.

Meagan jumped every time one hit a wall. "Dear Lord!" she mumbled and bit her lip.

"Now see here!" Lord Kensington growled.

"Stay out of this."

Barrett reached her door and shook it. "Meagan, I know you're in there. Open this bloody door!"

"No! I don't want to talk to you. Go away!" He couldn't see her like this. She'd rather die first. Frantically she glanced around for an escape route and ran to the window.

The door rattled on its hinges. "I mean it, Meagan! Open up or I'll tear this bloody door down!"

"I don't want to talk to you." Meagan raised the sash of the window.

"What are you doing?" Lord Kensington bellowed. "Don't use that statue. It's an antique!"

Bang. The door splintered near the top, the side of a marble bust poking through the oak.

Meagan gathered up the hem of her nightgown and crawled out onto a tree limb. Cold air burned her face and swished up her night rail. Through chattering teeth, she took a deep breath and continued to crawl.

Another crash from the chamber.

She cringed and reached the trunk, dug her toes in the bark, and climbed down. Bark scrapped her knees and shins.

The moment her feet touched the ground, Barrett poked his head out the window and yelled, "Bloody hell! Come back here, Meagan!"

Meagan saw him leaning out the window, his face in dark relief. She pressed her body back against the tree, her chest heaving, her bare feet almost frozen to the ground.

"Meagan!" His frustrated growl echoed out into the night and rolled along the black iron fence that divided Lord Kensington's town house from his neighbor's property.

Meagan heard him move away from the window; then she bolted around to the garden. Meagan hurried past a row of hedges and darted into the carriage house. Shivering, her teeth chattering, she closed the door behind her. The smell of horse, leather, and axle grease permeated the air.

She darted past three carriages looming in the darkness in their berths and found a corner piled high with straw. A horse blanket left behind by a lazy stable hand lay in a heap on the brick floor. Meagan scooped it up, buried her body down in the straw, and pulled the blanket over her, feeling the coarse wool abrading her hives.

She could hide here. Hopefully he wouldn't find her . . . .

The door to the carriage house burst open. She could hear Barrett heaving.

"I know you're in here, Meagan. I can sense you." Some of the anger left his voice. "You can't hide from me. You sent me on a merry chase, and I do so enjoy merry chases, but not when I've gone half out of my mind looking for you. It's time to come out, Meagan."

Meagan snorted under her breath, not believing him for one little minute. She crouched down, and as quietly as she could, she piled straw on top of her. Before she covered her face, she heard steel strike flint. Lantern light filled the carriage house. She burrowed deeper and heard his footsteps.

Closer . . . closer . . .

He paused before the pile of straw.

Meagan held her breath, her heart pounding against her ribs.

She heard a plop as he set the lantern down. Then he stroked the tip of her big toe. Meagan jumped and realized half her foot stuck out of the straw.

"This toe looks very familiar, and it feels quite nice and warm." He stroked her foot with his thumb; then his hands slipped deeper to caress her ankle. "I remember this ankle well. Come out, Meagan."

She fought a tingle shooting up her leg and stayed buried in the straw. "I don't want to see you or speak to you. Go away!"

"I have no intentions of leaving." He paused and stopped stroking her ankle. His voice turned velvety with regret. "I wanted you to remember your first ball with fondness. I'm afraid I failed you, Princess. Can you forgive me?"

At the forlorn note in his voice, Meagan felt an overwhelming urge to touch him. She sat up and reached for him. The blanket and straw fell from her face and shoulders.

His eyes widened as they took in her face. He couldn't

have looked more surprised if she had kicked him in the stomach. Too late, she realized what she'd done.

"What happened?" He touched her chin and gently ran his fingertips along the edge.

"Don't touch me." Tears welled up in her eyes and she covered her face in her hands and blubbered, "I ate mushrooms. They do this to me. God knows, I didn't want you to see me like this. I tried to be careful, but when I saw you with Lady Matilda— Oh, I wish we'd never married. I wish I was at home in the country where I belong, and Harold hadn't been so stupid and gambled away everything and me. I shouldn't be around anyone. I know you love Lady Matilda and that's the reason you've never come to my bed. Well, you can have her. I intend to get an annulment and you can go to her. I just want to be left alone. I was all right when I was in the country. I can't even—"

Meagan's woes were cut off by Barrett's lips. He wrapped his arms around her and pulled her into his lap without breaking the kiss. His lips slid across her mouth, and she tasted her own tears on his mouth.

He said against her lips, "You're beautiful to me any way you look, Princess."

"I don't believe you. I look horrible."

"Would I do this to someone who disgusted me?" He placed tiny kisses over her face and neck while his fingers dipped into the long tresses that flowed down her back.

"Barrett . . . "

She could not believe he was actually touching her. All her life, people had shunned her—even her own parents. So many times when she'd been forced to stay in her room because of her hives, she had wanted to be accepted by someone, just wanted someone to touch her and make her feel wanted, flaws and all. Barrett gave her unconditional affection for the first time in her life. More tears streamed down her face.

He raised his head and gazed into her eyes. He pushed

back a curl from her brow and kissed the tears streaming down the corners of her eyes. "Don't cry, Princess."

"I can't believe you want me." She bit her trembling lip and gazed into the dark blue intensity of his eyes.

"I do want you, and I'll prove it."

He rolled over and eased her back into the straw, his mouth devouring hers, the kiss growing urgent and demanding. The musky scent of his aftershave blended with the starch of his shirt and his own maleness. It filled her starved senses, making her dizzy. Breathing deeply of him, she ran her hands along the hard planes of his back, reveling in the feel of him touching her. She never wanted him to stop.

His tongue made a deep foray into her mouth, while he cupped her breast. He kneaded and teased, turning her nipple into a hard, little numb. Meagan moaned and arched her back.

"Sweet . . . sweet Princess," he murmured, then kissed a line down her throat.

"Barrett . . . " Her voice trailed off as she felt his thigh ease between her legs; then he settled against her.

His hips moved in a slow undulating, dance, his erection pressing against her, hard and prodding, touching a secret place inside her that only he could touch.

Meagan writhed beneath him, feeling a hot yearning driving her. He kissed her again with longing and an urgency that made her toes curl against the back of his sinewy calves.

Emboldened by his desire, she jerked his shirttail out of his breeches and ran her hands up under the linen and caressed his bare skin. She could feel the small scars on his back against her fingertips, his body trembling slightly with need.

"Forgive me, Princess. I must have you . . . . " He jerked up the hem of her nightgown and made quick work of the buttons on his breeches. He freed his erection, lifted her hips, and thrust into her.

Meagan felt him break through her maidenhead and stiffened. Though it stung slightly, it was a wonderful feeling—something she'd waited and prayed to feel. He was finally inside her; she was finally his wife in all ways. He completed her in ways she'd never dreamed possible, nor had she ever felt closer to any other person in her life. She hugged him as tight as she could, feeling him moving inside her, his hard flesh thrusting deep inside her.

"Bloody hell, you feel good," he groaned, then kissed her hard.

Meagan's nails dug into his back, her body crying out for release. She found it with him. They both cried out. He thrust one last time and shuddered.

"Oh, God . . . " He collapsed on top of her.

"Is something wrong?" Meagan asked, beginning to feel self-conscious again.

He rose up and kissed her gently on the mouth, as if savoring the taste. "Everything is too right," he whispered against her lips.

"I don't understand."

"Barrett!" Lord Kensington bawled outside the carriage house.

"Damnation!"

Barrett buttoned his breeches while Meagan pulled down her dressing gown. Barrett threw the blanket over her and swept her up into his arms, as Lord Kensington stepped through the door. He stood there, his dressing gown hanging open, his nightcap askew on his head.

"There you are," Lord Kensington blurted and took in Barrett's mussed hair, the straw sticking to his coat and breeches, and the desire still burning in his eyes. His gaze moved over Meagan as she blew a piece of straw out of her mouth. "I see I'm too late."

"I'd say your timing was perfect." Barrett flashed a gloating look at his father. "Now if you don't mind, I'm taking my wife home, where she belongs."

Lord Kensington bristled and crossed his arms over his large chest. For a moment, he battled Barrett in a silent war, their gazes locked by blue fire.

"It is truly all right, Your Grace," Meagan blurted, afraid they might fight over her.

"I'm sorry, child," Lord Kensington said, his expression full of regret and irritation. "I should have stopped him sooner."

"It will all work out." Meagan didn't know if she believed that, but she managed a reassuring smile. "Will you be in town for Christmas, Your Grace?"

Barrett stiffened. "I'm sure he'll be going back to France."

"As a matter of fact, I won't. I've decided to stay here for the holidays."

"Then you must join us for Christmas dinner, Your Grace?"

"I look forward to it." Lord Kensington smiled at his son, wearing an expression remarkably similar to one of Barrett's basking grins.

"Good night," Barrett grumbled, striding past his father and out of the carriage house, Meagan still in his arms.

"You could be nicer to him." Meagan nuzzled his neck.

"I know what you're doing, Meagan, and it won't work. You'll not change how we feel about each other."

"I've always believed it's impossible not to love one's close relatives. After all, you share the same blood. You have to love your father—just a little."

"I'm convinced I can't love anyone—especially my father."

Meagan prayed he was wrong. He had to be. It must be the wounded side of him talking.

* * *

A little while later, Barrett set Meagan down at her chamber door. "Aren't you coming in?" She glanced up at him, her expression hopeful.

He stared into her dark eyes, hooded by long mink lashes, and guilt stabbed him. He'd lost his head and taken her. She would despise him when he told her they were not really married. If he went into her chamber, he'd want her again, so he said, "I'll keep you up with my insomnia. It's best I do not share your room. Good night." He took a step to leave.

Meagan grabbed his arm. "Oh, no. You'll not get away that easily." She wrapped her arms around his neck and pulled his head down for a kiss.

Barrett kissed her back, quickly becoming the aggressor. He ran his hands through her long hair, kissing her until her breath came in gasps and he throbbed with wanting her again. Finally, he pulled back. It took every ounce of self-control for him to say, "Go to bed now, Princess."

She smiled a seductive smile, her dimples beaming. "I hope you find a cure for your insomnia, because I don't intend to sleep alone the rest of my life, Barrett. What good is a husband if he can't even keep you warm on a cold night? I might as well have married a warming pan."

The sultry look appeared almost comical with the hives on her face. Still, Barrett thought her the most attractive woman he'd ever gazed upon. "You'll find husbands have more uses than warming pans, Princess." He playfully smacked her on the bottom. "Now get to bed."

"Very well." Her lips puckered in a moue as she stepped into her chamber.

He closed the door and started when he almost bumped into Lyng. "Must you sneak up on me like that?"

"I wasn't sneaking." Lyng surveyed Barrett, his eyes disappearing into slits in a knowing look. "It appears, my lord, you are deeper in mud than anticipated."

"No need to point it out, Lyng."

"When are you going to tell her the truth?"

"That's my concern," Barrett snapped. "Is there something else you wanted?"

"Yes. Sir James waits on you in the upper parlor."

Barrett found James stretched out on a couch by the fireplace, a glass of brandy in one hand and a cheroot in the other.

"What brings you here?" Barrett said, striding farther into the room.

James took a puff off his cigar. "I wondered if you found your wife?" His brow cocked at the word "wife."

"I found her."

"Where?"

"At my father's house." Barrett sat down on the couch beside James.

James never missed minute details, and he didn't miss the straw sticking to the cuff of Barrett's coat. He picked it off and examined it. "Your father keeping the stable in his house now?"

"I found her in the carriage house."

"And?" James looked askance at him.

"I made love to her. There. I said it." Barrett felt surprisingly better after getting it off his chest.

James puffed on his cheroot and blew a smoke ring toward the ceiling. He pointedly eyed Barrett through the smoke. "You know this complicates matters."

"I know. It just bloody happened."

"Just happened, huh?" One side of James's lip twitched in a skeptical grin.

"Yes, but it won't happen again."

"Is that right?" James cocked a dubious brow at him.

"You needn't look at me like that. I mean what I say."

"Of course you do."

Barrett scowled at his cousin, which immediately made James's grin broaden.

Down the hall, Tessa gazed at the fading hives on Meagan's face. "Oh, miss. You wasn't careful at the ball."

"No, I was not, but I left before anyone saw me."

"Did he see you?" Tessa motioned toward Barrett's chamber.

"Absolutely. And you know what, Tessa? He didn't react at all as I expected. He was actually kind and understanding." Meagan graced her with a brilliant smile.

Tessa paused near the bed, shoved her hands on her ample hips, and studied Meagan. "I can see he finally took up his husbandly duties—a bit late, if you ask me. Causing you all that worrying— Oh, and that look on your face. You love him, don't you? Sure as I'm wearing drawers, you do."

"Yes, Tessa. I think he will come around and make a good husband."

"I hope you're right, miss. I do. Up to now, he ain't been so good at it. I'll just go and draw you a soda bath. It will ease your itching. Be right back."

Tessa frowned at the pensive look on her mistress's face. It wasn't the look of happiness a new bride should be wearing, but one of uncertainty.

Tessa slipped out into the hallway. She saw his lordship bidding Sir James good night and slowed down. Then Lord Waterton turned and strode toward her. He looked tired and mighty formidable with a dark scowl on his face.

Tessa wasn't about to let that stop her. Screwing up her courage, she said, "My lord, may I have a word."

He paused and stared down at her. "Yes."

"You may think it impertinent of me, but I have to speak to you."

"By all means." He waved a hand at her. "You have my ear."

"I beg of you not to hurt my mistress. I know she's in love with you. Promise me you won't hurt her. She knows nothing of the ways of the world, having been sheltered all her life, and she gets her heart broken very easily 'cause she feels things more than most. She tries not to show it, but she does. Please say you won't hurt her." Tessa watched his expression harden.

"You don't like me, do you?" His penetrating blue eyes bored into her face.

"I have to be honest and say I don't." Tessa shifted beneath his scrutiny.

"Why is that?"

"Because you forced marriage on my mistress when you didn't love her. I haven't yet figured out why 'cause she didn't have a dowry, but I figure it will all come out in the tallying." She met his gaze squarely and saw a hint of emotion in those cold blue eyes. "But you ain't promised me yet, my lord. Make this promise to me and swear you won't hurt my mistress."

Regret flashed in his eyes for a moment, then disappeared behind a hard veneer. "I would never intentionally hurt her."

" 'Intentionally.' What does that mean, my lord? That's just a fancy way of saying you'll hurt her?"

"If you excuse me, it's late." He strode around her toward his chamber.

Tears streamed down Tessa's face as she wheeled around and grumbled, "Dear Lord, I just knew it. He's gonna hurt my lady."

CHAPTER
TWENTY-TWO

The next morning Meagan went in search of Barrett. She had ached to have him near her last night, yet he hadn't come to her room and she didn't feel bold enough yet to go to his—especially with her hives.

Thankfully, they were fading and with a little powder they didn't look all that noticeable. As she strode down the stairs she passed two huge paintings, a Rubens and a Titian. The somber eyes of their subjects followed her progress down the stairs.

In the foyer Coates stood on a ladder, putting up pine garland along the entrance to the library. Below him, Reeves held one end of the garland.

The strong woody scent of the pine filled her senses as she watched the pine rope trembling in Reeves's hand. "Good morning. I see we are decorating."

"Yes, my lady." Coates smiled down at her. "We hope you approve."

"It looks lovely and festive." Meagan surveyed the roping draped along the entrance. "Is his lordship at home?"

Abruptly Barrett's voice boomed down the hall. "What are you doing here?"

"Geminy! Who's made him mad?" Meagan glanced down the hall.

"Mr. Burrows is here." Reeves grimaced.

"He arrived only moments ago." Coates, paying more attention to the conversation than his task, leaned too far over on the ladder.

"Watch out!" Meagan grabbed the tipping ladder.

Coates still lost his balance. His arms groped the air.

With surprising speed for a man his age, Reeves grabbed Coates around the thighs and shoved him forward. "Got you!" Reeves blurted, looking pleased with his save, his wrinkled skin stretching in a smile.

"Thank you." Coates smiled nervously down at him, his face drained of any color.

Satisfied one disaster had been averted, Meagan ran to the other. She followed the loud voices to the morning room and found Barrett and Lochlann nose to nose. Barrett held Lochlann by his cravat. Lochlann's face was red from the stranglehold.

"Barrett! Stop it!" Meagan shouted.

"Why?" He glared into Lochlann's eyes.

"He asked me last night if he could apologize to you," she blurted, then grimaced at Lochlann. "I meant to tell you, but with everything that happened it slipped my mind. Please let him go!"

When Barrett stepped back, Lochlann sucked in a breath and rubbed his throat. When he spoke, his voice sounded hoarse. "I should go."

"I'll walk you out." Meagan shot Barrett a reproachful glance, which didn't quell the storm brewing in his eyes.

Barrett grabbed her hand. "He can see himself out."

"No need to announce us."

Meagan recognized Lord Upton's deep baritone echo

out in the hallway. She sighed with relief at the welcome interruption.

The moment Holly and John entered the morning room, Holly took in the sour looks on Lochlann's and Barrett's face; then she shared a sympathetic glance with Meagan. "Ah, I see we are intruding. You must forgive us."

"You're not intruding," Meagan said. "Please come in."

When he saw Holly, Barrett's expression lightened slightly. "Mr. Burrows was just leaving, weren't you?" Barrett eyed Lochlann.

"Yes." Lochlann's expression fell.

"I'll walk you out." Meagan fired a scalding glance at Barrett.

Barrett opened his mouth to say something, and Holly grasped his arm. "Dear Barrett, you must tell me everything that happened at the ball last night. I heard so much about it."

Meagan smiled to herself and knew Holly would do her best to distract Barrett. She followed Lochlann out of the room and noticed he looked particularly fine in his blue velvet breeches and jacket. Her gaze moved over several wrinkles marring his sleeve. She thought of Barrett and how his attire was always immaculate. But of course, she'd never met a gentleman who was so fastidious about his appearance. The image of how he'd looked after he had made love to her in the straw formed in her mind. A slow grin spread across her lips.

"I don't know how you tolerate him, Meagan." Lochlann's voice wiped the smile off her face.

"He's not as bad as he seems. And you should not have come here. I told you I'd send you a note."

"I know, and I waited. I know you rise at dawn, and when I didn't hear from you, I thought it would be all right to call."

"I slept in this morning." She'd been so tired and sated

after making love to Barrett that she'd overslept. A blush rose to her cheeks.

Lochlann noticed the blush. He sounded hurt as he asked, "You're in love with him, aren't you?" He took her hand. "Never in a million years would I have thought you'd fall in love with a man like him. He's all wrong for you."

"Please don't lecture me." She jerked her hand out of his. "I had hoped you'd gotten over all that. I intend to make this marriage work. If you can't accept that, then we can't be friends."

Lochlann grabbed her hand. "I'm sorry."

He looked so forlorn she patted his shoulder. "Very well. I forgive you. We'll make a pact, not to speak of my marriage, and I won't quiz you about your love life." She tried for a smile and remembered something. "Now tell me, what did you learn about Mr. Fields and Mr. Coburn?"

"Not much." Lochlann frowned. "I tried to hint around. I even took Harold aside at the ball and questioned him about his relationship with Fields and Coburn. He only gave me evasive answers and asked me to stay away from you and not cause trouble between you and your husband."

"I hope you told him you never meant to do any such thing." Meagan leveled a chiding look at him.

"Believe me, Meagan, I don't want to cause you any pain. Now that I know you're resigned to this marriage, I just want to be your friend."

Meagan remained silent a moment, then said, "I want that too."

"If you desire, I'll work on Fields and Coburn and perhaps they'll let me into this group. If so, I could make sure Harold doesn't get into trouble."

"Would you, Lochlann? Thank you so much. " Without thinking, Meagan hugged him.

Suddenly a man cleared his throat behind them. Swallowing hard, Meagan stepped back from Lochlann. She glanced over his shoulder at Barrett. Her mouth went dry. How long had he been standing there?

She blurted, "I was just saying good-bye to Lochlann."

"I can see that."

"Leave, Lochlann." Meagan waved him away. She stepped in front of Barrett, blocking his way.

For once in their twenty-year friendship, Lochlann obeyed Meagan without question. He strode down the hallway.

Meagan saw Barrett watching Lochlann and threw her arms around his waist. "Please don't scowl at me like that." She quickly rose up on tiptoe and kissed him, pressing her body against his.

His heavy breath brushed her face. She could feel the sculpted muscles of his chest still tensed for a fight. Meagan wasn't about to give up yet. She continued to kiss the harsh line of his lips and ran her hands along his back, feeling the velvet of his black coat covering the rigid planes of his shoulders.

After a moment, his lips softened; then he wrapped his arms around her and kissed her back. Meagan reveled in her ability to ignite such desire in him. It was the one weapon she could use to breach that part of him he kept well guarded from her.

Footsteps sounded behind them. Barrett groaned and broke the kiss.

"No, no, keep at it," Holly said, grinning. "We were just leaving. You will join us tomorrow afternoon at St. James's Park for ice-skating. I won't be able to skate, but we are taking the children. Ann expressly charged me to say to both of you that she expected you to be there."

"We cannot disappoint Ann." Meagan grinned. "We'll be there."

"Very good." Holly grabbed John's hand. "Come, my darling. We've overstayed our welcome."

"When you get the chance"—John looked at Meagan,

then grinned at Barrett—"I'm still looking for you at Jackson's."

"Come along, dear. The last thing on Barrett's mind is fisticuffs." Holly managed to drag her husband down the hall in spite of her heavy belly and awkward waddle.

"I know what's on his mind." John bent and nuzzled Holly's neck, making her giggle.

Meagan listened to their loverlike banter and felt a tinge of envy as she turned back to Barrett. His expression was anything but loverlike. The grin melted from her face.

He gazed down at her and frowned. "I don't want Burrows in this house again."

"But—"

"I mean it, Princess." He turned and yelled down the hall toward the foyer. "Wait, John. I'm ready for that match now."

"Wouldn't miss it."

Meagan stood there and watched Barrett follow them, his wide shoulders swaying. Just like that, he was leaving her while her body still burned for him. He still wanted her, for Meagan had seen it in the dark desire in his eyes. She'd never understand him. Tonight he wouldn't get away, she promised herself.

Meagan strode to the top of the steps and found Tessa and Lyng. Tessa scowled at him, while he shook a polishing rag at her.

"You don't know my master."

"I know him well enough."

"He is an honorable man."

Tessa snorted under her breath.

They saw her and they both clamped their mouths shut. In order to have a little peace in the family, Meagan said, "We are going skating tomorrow with Lord and Lady Upton. I expect you and Lyng to join us."

"What?" Tessa and Lyng cried at the same time.

"You heard me." Meagan strode into her chamber. A small package sat on her pillow.

She walked over and tore the wrapping off. Her finger dipped into the box and she withdrew a gold fob watch with diamonds embedded around the face. A card inside said:

Princess,
  I thought you might be in need of one of these the next time we go out in society.

                                               Barrett

Meagan stared at the hastily scribbled signature. No loving salutation. Just *Barrett*. She would have that endearment one day. He had made love to her. It gave her hope again.

Jackson's seemed empty for an afternoon. Barrett and John were the only two inside a ring. A few other gentlemen pounded the bags on the sidelines, while a trainer urged them by taunting, "You're smacking the leather like ladies."

The smell of sweat and smoke permeated the air, but hardly penetrated Barrett senses. All he could smell was the lingering scent of Meagan's rosewater cologne and all he could taste was her lips still singeing his mouth. Another memory of Meagan confiding in Burrows flooded his mind. It galled Barrett to think she didn't trust him enough to ask him to help her brother. Of course, he didn't deserve her trust, but she didn't know that. He threw another punch at John, who dodged it and caught Barrett's chin.

Barrett staggered back a step and shook the blow off. "Bloody lucky punch. Bet you can't do that again, dear boy."

"Bet I can. Your mind is elsewhere. Why the hell did you

leave her and come here?" John danced around Barrett, looking for an opening.

"I could ask the same thing of you," Barrett said, getting a clean shot at John's ribs.

He buckled a moment. "I can't touch Holly—doctor's orders. What's your bloody excuse, man?"

"I can't touch Meagan either."

"I saw evidence of a rash on her face. Does she have something contagious?"

"No, nothing like that. It's much worse."

"Worse?" John's dark brows furrowed.

"Yes." Barrett needed to unburden his soul, and John was the only person in the world he trusted besides James— and sometimes he wondered about James.

Oh, he had acquaintances, but they were shallow, mercenary gentlemen who hoped to gain something from their relationship with him. But John couldn't be bought by wealth and Barrett held him in high esteem for it. Though they contrived a mutual pretense of discord between them, deep down they were the closest of friends. So Barrett continued to pound on John while he told the whole story.

By the time he ended, he was so tired he found it hard to lift his arms and said, "I really don't know what to do."

"You've got yourself in a real pickle. This is just my opinion—and I might add, I've yet to figure out the workings of the female mind—but I see only one way out."

"Indeed. Enlighten me." Barrett barely dodged a left from John.

"Tell her the truth. Be forceful and stress the fact you forged the wedding certificate with honorable intentions—after all, the welfare of our whole government is at stake and you did think she was a member of this group. She cannot argue with honor, especially if you get down on your knees and humble the hell out of yourself. Then marry her."

Barrett mulled the idea over in his mind. Honor

demanded he marry her now that he'd taken her virginity. Common sense told him he would break her heart. It was true he cared for her, wanted her more than he'd wanted any woman in his life, but he didn't believe he could love her—or anyone.

John saw Barrett's concentration wane and continued. "No lady should have to put up with you"—John grinned—"but you might surprise yourself and her." He used the last of his energy and pounded Barrett's ribs.

Barrett came across with a right. Both men went down and landed on the mat at the same time.

"Damn me, but that felt good," John groaned out. "But it's a poor substitute for making love."

"Bloody right." Barrett grinned at him and clutched his ribs.

That night, Meagan put aside a copy of Pasacoff Bayer's star atlas. She couldn't keep her mind on it. Nuisance perked up his head. She stroked his ears, feeling his soft whiskers tickling her skin through the thin silk negligee she'd picked out to entice Barrett. Almost as bold as the transparent chemise and drawers she'd worn before, it opened down in the center and only two frogs held it together near her bosom.

She stroked Nuisance and sighed. "I love you, you know, but I'm sorry to say you do not come close to your master."

The small dog didn't move his head; he only looked at her with his large astute eyes.

"So tell me: Why do you think he preferred to play cards all night with Harold rather than join me? I'm quite sure he's in his room and has been there for the past hour. I believe I must make the first move. What do you say?"

Nuisance lifted his head and barked.

"Yes, I quite agree." Feeling bolder this evening since her hives had nearly faded, she crawled out of bed. Nuisance leaped down behind her and begged to be let out of her chamber.

"Very well. But if you must desert me, wish me luck."

Nuisance barked again.

She petted him and let him out, then watched him prance down the hallway until he disappeared into the darkness. She wheeled and glanced at the connecting door.

A thin ray of light shone beneath it. She tried the knob and found the door wasn't locked. The hinges creaked slightly as she opened it and peeked inside. Meagan scanned the room and spotted Barrett stretched out on a sofa by the fire, a book in one hand, a snifter of brandy in the other.

He wore only a dark blue dressing gown. Candlelight flicked off the wide V of skin exposed on his chest. Meagan stared at his chest and remembered the feel of the coarse hair there and the contours of his rigid muscles beneath her fingertips. Her gaze traveled to his long, powerful fingers holding the book. With searing accuracy, she recalled how they'd caressed her breasts and grasped her hips as he thrust into her. A wave of heat poured over her body and filled her with such longing she had to catch her breath and still the pounding of her heart.

He glanced up. His gaze slid down her body, stopping at her breasts, which were almost falling out of the low bodice of the negligee. Then his eyes went lower along her flat waist until they paused at the spot between her thighs. "Don't you have any nightclothes that cover you better than that?" he asked, gulping hard.

"You don't like it?"

"How could I not?" He dragged his gaze up her body. His eyes turned dark blue, glistening with the intensity of a comet.

From his reaction, she assumed he was more than pleased with her. She strode toward him, paused behind the sofa, and frowned down at the book. It was Aristotle's

Organon in a Latin translation. "Did you know you're reading your book upside down?"

"I get bored very easily. Adds a bit of a challenge." He frowned at her. "Would you like to try it?"

"No, I prefer the dull way." She grinned down at him and slipped her hands over his shoulders.

He stiffened. "I really think you should go back to bed."

"I couldn't sleep without you."

"I would just keep you awake with my insomnia. 'Tis best you sleep alone."

Meagan ignored him and said, "You are very tense." She kneaded the muscles on his shoulders, remembering running her hands beneath his shirt when they'd made love.

After a moment, he relaxed and dropped the book on the sofa, groaning softly. "Your fingers are sweet torture. Where did you learn to give back rubs?"

"I used to rub my father's neck when he was ill. It helped him relax." Meagan kneaded the tensed muscles along his neck. She felt the scars beneath the silk of his dressing gown and said, "You don't have to tell me this if you don't wish, and it may sound prying—"

"You can ask me anything, Princess. We have no secrets between us, do we?" He turned and gazed pointedly up at her.

Meagan thought of her secret about Harold and frowned.

"Something wrong, Princess?"

"No, no." She absently plied her fingers into his muscles.

He turned and dropped his head to the side. She moved her hands over to work on his left shoulder.

Meagan decided it was wise to change the subject of secrets and get back to her question. "How did you get the scars on your back?" She recalled how she'd mistakenly accused his father of doing the deed and her frown deepened.

Barrett remained silent a moment. His shoulder tightened slightly. "I had one particular headmaster, Mr. Loveless, who liked to take out his frustrations with a stick."

"Why didn't you tell your father?"

"I knew my father didn't want to be bothered, and he probably would have thought I deserved it. You see, I wasn't a very good pupil. I tested every headmaster's patience to the limit. It became a game for me." He grinned devilishly. "I went through boarding schools as fast as one goes through snuff."

"Why?" Meagan felt a tightening in her heart as she thought of Barrett, the boy, all alone, raised at boarding schools by intolerant headmasters and causing trouble to get attention.

"I never thought about why I did it." He raised his glass, downed the contents, and set the glass on a side table.

"You must have had a reason." Meagan continued to stroke the muscles he'd tightened when he'd spoken of his scars.

"I suppose I wanted to irritate my father as much as I could—I succeeded very well at it too." He grinned halfheartedly and said more to himself than to Meagan, "Every headmaster I ever had called me an incorrigible blighter—well, they used much more eloquently scathing terms. I wouldn't have been admitted into Cambridge if not for my father knowing someone on the board."

"But you turned out perfectly well. You are one of the wealthiest men in England."

"I have my father to thank for that. When I was twenty and flunking out of Cambridge, he came to England to lecture me on disgracing him and our good name. I remember his exact words. 'You're no better than the proverbial bad penny. You've disgraced the Rothchild name and every ancestor who bore it before you. You may be my heir, but by God, this is the end of it. Do you hear! The end of it! I wash my hands of you. From this day forward your allowance will be terminated. I'll not fork out money and watch you use it for your sordid debauchery.' " Barrett's voice took on a hard quality. "As I watched him storm out of the study, I swore I would prove him wrong."

"How did you go about it?"

"I inherited a small fortune from a trust my mother left me. I studied the stock exchange and turned my energies from trying to plague my father into investing and became rich—richer than my father ever was or shall be. I never asked him for a farthing." Barrett tried to sound pleased by his accomplishment, but a lonely quality in his voice masked his pride.

"There is more to life than money."

"No one knows that better than I." He captured her hands and pressed them against his shoulders, rubbing his thumbs over the back of her skin.

Heat from his touch rose up her arms and pooled in her breast. She bent, splayed her fingers, and ran them down the front of his chest. His heartbeat pounded beneath her fingertips. With infinite slowness, she moved lower, learning each ripple along his corded stomach.

He sucked in his breath. His hands were still on top of hers and he grabbed them before she could go lower. "You should go to your room," he said, his voice ragged.

Her lips were a hairbreadth from his ear as she whispered, "You don't sound as if you really want me to go."

"Meagan . . ." He whispered her name in an agonizing plea even as his whole body grew taut.

"I want you, Barrett." She kissed the ridge along his jaw, then whispered against his neck, "Make love to me."

"Damn . . ." he murmured. Then his fingers tangled in the hair at the back of her head and he pulled her mouth to his for a kiss.

CHAPTER
TWENTY-THREE

Barrett knew he was a lost man from the moment she had stepped into his chamber. He had to kiss her. Touch her. Feel her body next to his. Without breaking the kiss, he drew her around the couch.

With swift, deft movements, he had her negligee up and over her breasts. The thin silk dropped and pooled on the floor as he pulled her down into his lap.

His gaze moved over her body. Her sable hair waved down to her waist and covered one full breast. Candlelight flicked over her flat belly and along her rounded hips. Her woman's mound was a thing of beauty, dark as her sable hair, a flawless triangle nestled between her thighs. He'd had many women, but none had made him ache with such intensity.

"You are spectacular," he said, bending down to kiss her, even as her breasts filled his palms. He moved lower, splaying his hands along her stomach.

She tensed and wrapped her arms around his neck, her

fingers slipping below the collar of his robe to caress his back.

The heat of her hands sent a shudder down his spine. His heart raced. A fine sheen of sweat broke out on his body. He moved his hand lower, tangling his fingers in her woman's mound.

He dipped his finger into her warm moist folds, found the center of her pleasure, and stroked her while he kissed a line down her throat. He suckled one breast, running his tongue over one peach nipple, feeling it harden in his mouth.

"So luscious," he said, feeling her writhe beneath his hand.

He felt her hands move around to his chest and dip beneath his dressing gown. She twined her fingers in the hair on his chest, kissing him with wild abandon.

Her passion drove him wild. He mated his tongue with hers, while he slid his finger into her hot sheath. "You're ready for me," he whispered against her nipple.

"I was ready when I walked through the door," she murmured and moved her fingers over his nipples, caressing his breasts as he had done to hers. He stiffened, hardly able to breathe for the fire raging in him.

"Come here, Princess . . . ," He maneuvered her hips until she straddled him on the couch.

Her soft, moist folds brushed his hard flesh. He began moving against her, slowly, the sweet agony of her heat setting him on fire.

Her hips followed his. She moaned as she discovered her own pleasure.

If he didn't have her soon, he'd burst. He entered her and groaned at the tight, hot feel of her.

"Kiss me, Barrett," she murmured.

He kissed her and thrust into her. They found a perfect rhythm together. They both reached their release and cried out at the same time.

He clung to her and realized he was trembling like a young boy taking his first woman. In a way she was his first: the first woman he'd ever bedded and cared for at the same time. It was a new experience for Barrett, this caring for someone.

She brushed back the hair that had fallen over her face and smiled down at him. "That was an interesting position. Are there many more ways to make love?"

"Indeed, numerous ways," he said, nibbling her lip. "And I would like to show you them all, but . . . that will have to wait. It is late. You should be in bed."

"May I sleep with you?" She looked at him from behind thick lashes and ran her fingertips over his lips.

"If you stay, you won't get much sleep," he whispered against her mouth.

"Good."

Barrett couldn't bear to part with her yet. He stood and supported her bottom, feeling her arms tighten around his neck and her thighs wrap around his hips. He could feel her breasts rubbing against his chest, her woman's mound moist and hot against his loins. When he laid her on his bed, he was already hard for her again.

The next afternoon in Hyde Park, Meagan warmed her hands over a fire burning in an iron barrel. Ice-skaters slid past her and made a wide circle on the Serpentine, a lake constructed for Queen Caroline a century before.

Barrett came down the ice, holding Ann's hand. They swished past several boys who'd just learned to skate and came toward Meagan. Ann laughed at something Barrett told her.

"Hello, Lady Meagan!" Ann called and waved as they glided past her.

"Hello!" Meagan waved back.

Barrett smiled and winked at Meagan. The brightly colored scarf Ann had made for him flapped against his great coat. It struck Meagan what an attentive father he'd make. He looked so natural holding Ann's hand, seeming to hang on her every word.

Meagan watched them skate behind a crowd of people and couldn't help but remember last night. It could have gone better. She'd fallen asleep in his arms, but she'd awakened to find Barrett had put her back in her own chamber. The sound of footsteps broke into her musings.

Holly waddled up to her and stood near the fire. Her cheeks were bright pink from the cold, and she panted from walking.

"Are you all right?" Meagan asked.

"Yes, it's just a bit hard getting around these days. I wish I could join in the fun with the rest of them." Holly looked at her brood, smiled, then studied Meagan's face. "Things must have changed. You have the glow."

"Glow?" Meagan shot her a lost look.

"Yes, John's grandmother taught me all about it. It's that look ladies have when they've been bedded by the man they love."

Meagan felt blood rush to her cheeks, causing an odd warm sensation in her cold cheeks. "Yes, he's made love to me."

"I knew he would." A pleased grin brightened Holly's face. She glanced at John racing Dryden and Brock on the ice. John's younger brother Teddy, a handsome man with striking brown eyes and tawny blond curls, joined them. Brock elbowed his brother and Teddy, then raced past them.

"I'll get you for that!" Teddy skated after Brock.

"Not if I get him first," Dryden said, pumping his skates hard to catch them.

John gave up, shrugged, then leveled such an intense look of love at Holly that Meagan felt a tinge of jealousy. Would Barrett ever look at her that way?

John skated over to them and hooked his arm through Holly's. "What do you say I take these skates off and we'll take a little walk in the park, my sweet?"

"Have you given up trying to race the boys?"

"I didn't have a chance. I much prefer sitting out for a while with you and the little one." He patted her swollen stomach and kissed her on the lips.

Meagan felt like an intruder upon the intimate moment. Would Barrett be so attentive if she were in the family way? Swallowing hard, she said, "I'd better get back out on the ice. If you'll excuse me." Meagan turned and skated off.

Across the lake Tessa watched Lyng. The little man skated as if he had been born on the ice; he was even skating backward. Not so Tessa. Her ineptness was apparent for all to see, including Lyng. To make matters worse, he kept eyeing her strangely, a slight grin on his face that didn't touch his eyes.

Of late, Tessa wanted to be happy for her mistress, but the feeling that Lord Waterton meant to hurt her nagged at Tessa, and anything connected to the high and mighty gentleman irritated her, including his valet. Whenever they chanced to meet, she snapped at the irritating little man— especially when he tried to defend his master's character. That angered her the most. So she'd taken to avoiding and ignoring him as best as she could. But it was nigh to impossible to ignore him at the moment.

Since Tessa had her eyes on Lyng, she bumped into a couple. At the impact, the gentleman grabbed his partner and steadied her. Tessa wasn't so lucky and hit the ice. She slid five feet on her bottom and landed right at Lyng's feet. Of all the people skating, why him?

"Are you hurt?"

"No."

"Very good." He bent, grabbed her arm, and helped her to stand.

Tessa meant to knock his hand away, but the gloating was gone from his expression. A mask of genuine concern covered his face. And her bottom was killing her. "Thank you," she said gratefully.

"Here, lean on me. I'll help you sit." Lyng put his arm around her waist.

Feeling chagrined by his show of kindness, she blushed and allowed him to help her. Something else surprised her too: She felt comfortable in his arms. The strange scent of his aftershave, an Oriental fragrance of herbs and spices, filled her senses. It was an exotic smell, heady, fascinating.

"Here you are, Miss Tessa." He helped her to sit, not missing Tessa's grimace. He took a seat beside her and said, "You should let me look at the wound."

"No, thank you." Tessa saw a strange glitter in his eye. She wasn't ignorant of the ways of men; she'd had a few in her day. What was in Lyng's eyes was more than just concern. Odd, but it didn't seem like such a horrible thing that he might be interested in her. She found her voice softening as she asked, "How did you come to this country?"

He grimaced and his eyes narrowed. A look of pain washed over his face. "An evil emperor saw my wife and desired her. He took her for a concubine. I went to get her back. We ran down the river, but guards caught us." He paused, and his eyes misted over. "My wife took my sword and killed herself rather than go back. I killed the guards and got on a ship and left for good."

"That's horrible. You must have loved her." Tessa felt his sadness and found herself touching his forearm.

He smiled sadly over at her and placed his hand on hers. He stroked the back of her hand with his thumb. "I did, but love does not die. It is like a river: It takes different winding paths. May I take you to a play tonight, Miss Tessa?"

No one had ever treated her like such a lady. Tessa found herself blushing and saying, "Yes."

From some distance away, Meagan studied Tessa and Lyng. She could hardly believe her eyes. They appeared deep in conversation, their heads bent close in an intimate manner.

Grinning, she moved up beside Harold, who skated alone and seemed preoccupied. Her grin faded as she locked arms with him. "What are you thinking about?"

"What? Oh, nothing." He looked over at her with his boyish face.

"I just want to say how terribly proud I am of you."

"For what?"

"For keeping your word and staying home and not gambling. You've been particularly good about it."

He didn't say anything for a moment, the scraping of their ice skates and the chatter of people that passed them the only sound between them. His expression grew solemn. "I've been thinking about my life lately."

"And?" Meagan looked hopefully over at him. Could he finally be growing up and taking responsibility? She had waited years for this moment and she had Barrett to thank for it.

"I've turned over a new leaf. No more gambling for me. I realize I've been an abominable brother to you. I gambled away Father's fortune. You know, Mother and Father always treated me better than you and thought I was so perfect, but you were the levelheaded one. I never had your intellect and common sense. You were the perfect one."

Meagan felt tears sting her eyes and blinked them back. "Thank you for saying that."

"It's the truth. I wouldn't be surprised if you hated me—

especially for making you marry someone you didn't love."
He glanced ruefully over at Barrett, who glided along on
the other side of the ice next to Ann.

"That is one thing you should not bemoan."

"Then you are happy? I thought—"

"I know. But my feelings for him have changed greatly."

"Then he has—"

"Yes," Meagan said, feeling her face blush. Her sense
of the ridiculous made her wonder how long it would take
for everyone in England to know her husband had finally
bedded her.

"Ah! Well, I'm glad for you, Meggie. I knew he'd get
around to it sometime."

Meagan quickly changed the subject. "Since you are
turning over a new leaf, do you intend to meet Mr. Fields
and Mr. Coburn today?"

"How did you know about that?"

"I overheard you."

Harold frowned at her. "You needn't worry."

"I am worried. I don't like those men."

"I'll deal with them."

Meagan saw Barrett and Ann skate up to them. Barrett
looked at Meagan, his eyes gleaming with a strangely
unreadable light; then he patted Ann on the head. "Would
you mind very much, Puss, if I changed partners?"

"Oh, no," Ann said with the casual air of a lady twice
her age. "Would you mind, Lord Fenwick?"

Some of the worry left Harold's face. He looked at her
and extended his arm. "It would be my honor."

She hooked her arm in his. "You look as if something
is worrying you, Lord Fenwick."

Harold's mouth dropped open slightly. He looked warily
at her, as if almost afraid of her; then he clamped his
mouth closed. "Nothing is worrying me," he said.

"Perhaps you'd like to talk about it later," Ann said

airily and shrugged. "Did you know miracles really do exist?"

"No."

"Well, you should. I have experienced one before . . ."

Their voices faded as they glided off.

Barrett took Meagan's arm and they followed behind them. Meagan thought of telling Barrett about Harold, but she decided to wait. "Have you seen Lyng and Tessa? I believe they have found each other."

"Indeed." He glanced at them on the bench, deep in conversation, their heads together. "I would never have dreamed such a attraction could happen."

"That could be said of us."

He remained silent, his jaw hardening the slightest bit.

Meagan broke the awkward moment and said, "After seeing Holly, I wanted to—"

"Please do not tell me you've planned another shopping trip."

She grinned at him. "No, I was just thinking about children. We've never discussed them, but we should, now that we could be having one."

His brows furrowed. "We shouldn't discuss the matter until the need arises."

"But surely since we'll have the rest of our lives together, we should talk about children." She felt his arm stiffen beneath her hand. "I've given the matter a lot of thought, and I want a large family."

"How large?"

"Five will do."

"Five!" Barrett blurted out the number and lost his stride. His skates tangled, but he managed to catch himself before he went down.

Meagan grabbed his arm, laughing. "Perhaps we should speak of this while we're not on the ice." Slipping her hand in his, she pulled him over to the bank and climbed it, careful not to turn her ankle in the skates.

Behind a large tree, away from the prying eyes of the crowd, she stepped up to him and wrapped her arms around his neck. Windblown strands of curly blond hair fell over his brow. An afternoon shadow darkened his proud square chin. His handsomeness took her breath away.

She nibbled on his bottom lip, feeling the coarse stubble on his chin brushing her soft skin. She watched his eyes darken, felt his breathing grow rapid as if he were fighting something. "Now we can talk about it," she whispered.

"The last thing I want to do at the moment is talk." He lost the battle. He drew her close and kissed her.

She reveled in the feel of his arms holding her. She remembered the feel of his hands on her naked body last night, the way he'd felt inside her, the wild pleasure he'd given her. With longing so powerful it made her knees weak and her toes curl in her skates, she kissed him back.

He pulled back, a tortured expression on his face. "If we don't stop this, I'm going to take you right here." He stepped back from her, his blue eyes glinting with a hard light. "Come on. We should join the others." He grabbed her hand.

"But we haven't finished talking about children."

"Let's leave it alone for now," he said, a final note in his voice. He turned and urged her down the bank toward the ice.

The sudden withdrawn expression on his face made her shoulders sag with disappointment. One day they would have to speak of children, for she wanted them desperately and hoped he did too. But she realized today would not be the day. Perhaps she'd broached the subject too soon. She sighed and stepped back down onto the ice.

Half an hour later, Meagan watched Harold put on his boots and stride away from the Serpentine. She followed him, being extremely careful not to let Barrett see her.

He appeared preoccupied, sipping hot cider and eating cookies with Holly and John near the fire. Every now and then he'd throw a cookie to Nuisance.

All the way to Rotten Row, she stalked Harold, ducking behind trees and hedges. As she kept her eyes on him and lifted her foot to step out from behind a privet hedge, the sound of riders approaching stilled her. Crouching low, she peeked around the hedge at Mr. Coburn and Mr. Fields. Even though clouds blocked out the sun, Mr. Fields's black hair glistened like greasy coal. They dismounted and strode up to Harold, holding the reins to their mounts.

"I say, Fenwick, you made it." Mr. Fields eyed Harold.

"Yes," Harold said, his tone uneasy. "I came to say I want out."

Mr. Coburn grabbed Harold by the throat. "You don't get out of this club until they bury you."

Meagan held her breath and saw the blood drain from Harold's face.

When a choking sound came from Harold, Mr. Coburn dropped the strangle hold he had on his throat. He patted Harold's chest. "Hope I didn't hurt you too much, but I had to make a point."

"Now you're in, and you're going to help us." Mr. Fields shot Harold a warning glance.

Horses hooves pounded the ground behind them. All three men turned to watch Lord Collins dismount. At the sight of him, Meagan cringed.

Something jumped on her leg.

Meagan stifled a scream and gazed down at Nuisance. She glanced around and looked for Barrett, but didn't see him. Quickly picking up the small dog, she silently berated him for following her.

"Well, gentlemen, I see I'm late. What did I miss?" Lord Collins rubbed his hands together.

"We were just setting Fenwick straight here." Mr.

Coburn leveled an evil glance at Harold. "He wanted out, but we explained again he's a member for life."

"Jolly good you got that out of the way. Have you word from our illustrious leader?"

Meagan raised her brows. She could have sworn that Collins was the master plotter of the group. The small smirk on his lips suggested he could very well be the leader and hid his role for some reason.

"Yes, I got a missive this morning," Mr. Fields said. "We're to kill someone at the Royal Holiday Ball. I don't know the target yet. The leader said he'd be there and let us know. We are all to be there precisely at seven." He shot Harold a threatening look. "That means you too. We're counting on you to do your part."

"Very well, but how are we to get inside the ball?"

"We have a member who's inside the Foreign Office," Mr. Coburn said. "He'll get the invitations we need."

Meagan couldn't breathe for the foreboding gnawing at her. Lochlann couldn't possibly save Harold from these men. Where was he? She'd told him about the meeting. More than likely he'd forgotten his promise and was off somewhere nursing his ego, pining over the fact he'd lost her. Lochlann might have grown into a man, but in a lot of ways he was still as irresponsible as a boy.

Meagan felt someone's eyes on her, and she glanced around the park. When she saw no one, her mind turned back to Harold. She sighed, knowing she had only one recourse to save him. Barrett. She had to find him and quickly.

Meagan held Nuisance tight to her chest, crouched low, staying below the bushes, and took a step back . . . .

Crack. A twig snapped beneath her foot.

She froze.

"Did you hear that?" Coburn's voice carried through the park.

"I think it came from over there," Collins said.

"Someone might be lurking about. I'll go and check," Mr. Fields said.

His footsteps came closer.

Meagan put Nuisance down. "Go on. Let them see you," she whispered and nudged him out from the hedge. He wouldn't budge; he only stared at her.

"Stubborn creature, just like your master," she said.

She kept low, backed around the hedge, and plowed into something hard. A hand clamped over her mouth, stifling a gasp.

CHAPTER
TWENTY-FOUR

"It's me, Princess," Barrett whispered near her ear and slipped a gingerbread cookie from his pocket. He let Nuisance get a whiff of it, then tossed it through the hedge.

With the speed of a bolt of lightning, the little dog scrambled through the thick foliage, his gray tail disappearing into the leaves. Barrett kept his hand over Meagan's mouth and held her tightly, feeling her hot breath brushing his hand. Together they huddled behind the bushes.

Barrett heard Mr. Fields's footsteps pause on the other side of the hedge. "Bloody dog!" he mumbled.

"What was it?" Lord Collins asked.

"A bleeding mutt," Mr. Fields said as he strode away from the hedge.

"We'd better conclude our business," Collins said. "We'll meet again at the Royal Holiday Ball."

The men broke up. Harold strode right past Meagan and Barrett huddled behind the hedge. He headed back for the Serpentine, while the rest of the group mounted their horses and galloped away.

Barrett didn't move until he was sure they wouldn't be spotted. He slipped his hand in Meagan's. "Come on. We should get back."

Nuisance followed close on their heels.

As they approached the Serpentine, Meagan broke the silence between them. "It was lucky you had a cookie in your pocket."

"He likes them." Barrett glanced at Nuisance prancing beside him.

"Even so, you acted as if you're used to being in such situations."

"I'm rather good at thinking on my feet." Barrett wondered if she would lie to him now or confide in him. He watched her worry her lower lip as he asked, "What were you doing here?"

"I have to tell you something," she blurted. "I hope you will not think ill of Harold. He'll be at your complete mercy when I tell you this. He really has changed, if that might sway you. You have been such a good influence on him. And I know I should have told you sooner, but I didn't know what you'd do. I'm sure you'll treat Harold fairly—"

"What is it?" he said impatiently.

"It's just horrible. Harold is involved in a group called the Devil's Advocates. They are planning to kill someone at the Royal Holiday Ball. We can't let them. Harold tried to get out of the group, but they will kill him if he tries to leave. Oh, he really is in a coil. You're my only hope." She squeezed his hand and gazed up at him with imploring eyes.

When she looked at him with those long-lashed dark eyes in just such a way, he could forgive her just about anything—even not trusting him. He found himself saying, "I'll take care of it."

"I'm so glad. You're the only person I feel who can truly help Harold."

"The only person?" Barrett eyed her pointedly.

She hedged a moment. "Well, I did confide in Lochlann and ask him to help, but I know now I should have come to you. Are you angry with me?"

"Not at all." A kind of contentment he'd never experienced before filled him. She trusted him. At last. He thought of his own duplicity and the feeling quickly faded.

That evening, Barrett watched Fenwick enter his office at Pellam House. He looked pale. Worry lines etched his boyish features, adding years to his countenance.

"Have a seat." Barrett waved a hand toward a chair in front of his desk.

Fenwick sat, looking preoccupied. He stared at a hunting picture behind Barrett and spoke. "You wanted to see me?"

"Yes. Your sister told me about the Devil's Advocates."

Fenwick tensed and gave Barrett his full attention. "She had no right! I told her I could handle my own affairs."

"It appears you can't. You've underestimated the caliber of the people with whom you are dealing."

"You speak as if you know them."

"I've heard rumors of their existence." Barrett let the lie roll off his tongue.

"I thought it was a secret society. What rumors have you heard?"

"That is immaterial. The important thing is I'm willing to help you. But you have to be honest with me."

Some of the defensiveness left Fenwick's expression. He remained silent, studying Barrett, weighing whether he could trust his brother-in-law or not. Finally he rubbed his temples and said, "I tried to leave, but they threatened to kill me. No one can help me."

"You're wrong there. I know someone who can. I'll take you to him, but he'll expect you to name all the members and where they meet and anything else you know about the group."

"They'll kill me if I spill the soup."

"Look at it this way: You can take your chances and let me help you, or you'll be at the mercy of half-crazed fanatics willing to die for a cause."

Harold hedged, then mumbled, "Very well."

"Good." Barrett stood up and crossed the room. "We'll go now while it's dark. We'll have to take the utmost care. Since they are not sure of your loyalty, they may be keeping an eye on you."

Barrett opened the door and caught Meagan rising from where she'd been listening at the door. She blushed becomingly and smoothed the wrinkles from her dress. "I was just looking for you."

"One usually knocks and enters a room in that case." Barrett couldn't help but grin at her. He wanted to kiss the blush off her cheeks.

"Well, all right. You caught me." She flapped her hand in a frustrated gesture. "I was listening. Please, I want to go with you. Where are you taking Harold?"

"That is none of your concern. I don't want you involved in this. The less you know the better." Barrett leveled his sternest look at her.

"But I'll be worried. You have to let me come."

"You'll stay here where you're safe."

"Please."

"No."

" 'Tis best you don't come, Meggie." Harold stepped past her, wearing an expression of a man going to his own hanging.

"Stay here and don't worry." Barrett kissed her pouting lips, then followed Fenwick, aware of the mutinous mask growing on Meagan's face.

At Barrett's request Lyng stood waiting for him at the servants' entrance, their coats in his hand.

Barrett paused and whispered to Lyng, "Watch her, and don't let her leave this house."

"Yes, my lord." Lyng bowed, wearing a strangely contented grin. "She won't get out of my sight."

Lyng kept one eye on Lady Meagan, who stood in the hallway, her arms crossed, frowning, and one eye on his master and Mr. Fenwick. They hurried out the door.

Lyng heard footsteps behind him and saw Tessa trudging down the hallway, Nuisance jerking on his leash. The sight of her brought a smile to Lyng's lips.

"Hello there," Tessa purred in a soft voice. "Would you like to help me walk this mutt?"

"I can't. I—" Lyng remembered his charge and glanced behind him. He froze. An empty hallway greeted him. He felt the blood drain from his face.

"Something wrong?" Tessa frowned at his pale face.

"Everything." Lyng turned and ran down the hallway, leaving Tessa frowning at his back.

Shadows loomed along the Foreign Office building. Meagan lurked in one of those shadows, trying to control her pounding heart and rapid breaths.

It had been hard enough escaping the house before Lyng had found her. She had to sneak out through a basement window and couldn't find Barrett and Harold right away. Luckily she spotted them getting into a cab.

They had taken several hacks across town, stopping in various places to change them. Then they'd walked six blocks to get here, weaving through alleys, always looking behind them. Meagan had a devil of time following them without being seen. She'd lost them twice. Only by chance had she found them and stayed with them.

She held the stitch in her side and watched them walk

inside, Barrett swinging his cane, wearing an indifferent expression, while Harold clenched his fists and tensed his jaw.

She glanced up. A hint of the moon showed in the firmament, veiled by a thick layer of smoke that endlessly swirled over the city. The image looked like a reflection on water, wavy and hazy. Not a bit of starlight braced the sphere or gave it direction. Something in the lost sight of it bothered Meagan. She glanced uneasily around her and rubbed her arms, unable to shake a feeling something dreadful was about to happen.

The door banged closed.

The noise drew her attention. She crept along the side of the building, the frost on the lawn crunching beneath her shoes. After several minutes, she carefully opened the door so the hinges wouldn't signal her arrival.

She stepped inside a long hallway. A musty institutional smell mixed with cigar smoke filled her senses. She could hear Barrett's deep voice. He spoke barely above a whisper, and she couldn't hear what he was saying.

Her footsteps echoed softly as she turned down another long corridor, staying well behind Barrett and Harold. Drab white paint covered the ceiling and walls. Cracks veined the plaster and formed distorted faces in the corners.

They turned right again. Meagan heard a door open. She peeked around the corner and watched them go into an office. The words etched in a brass plate on the door caught her attention:

CHIEF EXECUTIVE OF FOREIGN AFFAIRS
SIR JAMES NEVILLE

Meagan frowned at the sign. Barrett hadn't told her James worked for the Foreign Office. She pressed her ear to the door. Nothing. She twisted the doorknob . . . .

Someone tapped her on the shoulder. "Have you come for a visit, my dear?"

She jumped, grabbed her heart, and faced Sir James standing behind her. "Egad! You gave me fright! Does sneaking up on people run in your family?"

He grinned. "I was just going into my office. Would you care to join me?"

Before she could protest, he locked his arm with hers, opened the door, and guided her into his office. The room, smaller than she'd imagined, held shelves of books that lined three of the walls. The other one held maps of the world. Tiny pins with blue or black flags on the end protruded from cities on every continent. Stacks of papers filled a large mahogany desk. It could have been a command post for the military.

Barrett looked like a weathered general as he turned toward her, not a bit of surprise on his face, only fury. "I see you went against my wishes." He gripped his cane as though he wanted to use it on her bottom.

She stared at the cane. "I told you I was worried. I couldn't just stay home." She turned to Sir James. "You won't arrest Harold, will you?"

The casual demeanor melted from Sir James's face. His eyes took on the same hard glint in Barrett's as he looked at Harold. "That all depends on your brother. If he cooperates, I'm sure the Chief Justice will let him off with just a slap on the wrist."

"He'll cooperate. Won't you, Harold?"

Harold nodded and proceeded to tell them about the murder that was to take place at the Royal Holiday Ball. James listened, his expression growing harder.

When Harold finished, James said, "So they haven't named the target."

"No." Harold grimaced.

"What do you know of the leader?"

"Nothing." Harold jerked his hands through his blond

hair. "No one in the group has seen him. He sends missives and directives by way of Coburn and Fields."

"Where do you meet?" Barrett asked, still clutching the cane and shooting annoyed glances at Meagan.

"We meet at different places. Fields's and Coburn's apartments. Once at Collins's. We've even met at the hells, like the Pigeon Hole and Two Sevens. Never the same place twice in a row. 'Tis always different."

"I know all this." James leaned back in his chair and eyed Harold. "Tell me something I don't know."

Meagan grimaced. How did James know so much about the Devil's Advocates? Later, she would question Barrett, but not now, considering the way he strangled his cane and fixed her with his smoldering glances.

"I don't know what you want me to say," Harold said, growing defensive.

"You must have heard something about the leader. Any hint as to his name or initials or where he resides. Something!"

"Nothing."

Not appeased by Harold's answer, James continued. "What of the members? Have you seen all of them?"

"Not all, but I can give you the names of the ones I've met."

James shoved parchment and a quill at him. "Write them, and don't leave anyone out. It might mean the difference of saving a life or not."

Meagan heard the quill scratch across the page and watched Harold form the letters. Lord Collins. The first name on the list. She stared at the name, an ominous feeling something was going to happen rising up to haunt her again.

After the interview ended, Barrett watched James pull a cord. Moments later, two stern-faced gentlemen with little warmth or any hint of personality in their demeanors entered the room.

"Make sure Mr. Fenwick is escorted to a safe place. You're not to leave him for an instant. Do I make myself clear? I want no mishaps."

Both men nodded.

A semblance of relief washed over Meagan's face as she watched the two men escort Harold out of the room. She glanced at James and took his hand. "Where will they take my brother?"

"Probably to Scotland." He saw the worried look on Meagan's face and added, "He'll be safe there."

"Thank you. I'll never forget how you've helped Harold."

James bent and kissed her hand. "It was my pleasure, my lady."

Barrett stepped between. "We should go."

James grinned at him. "Don't be too hard on her for following you, Cousin."

"She's my wife. I'll treat her the way I like."

James's brow darted up at the word "wife." They both eyed each other for a moment. Barrett realized he'd used the term too freely and with too much possessiveness. James was aware of that too and his grin widened. "Far be it from me to interfere in a domestic squabble."

"That's right. This is none of your concern." Barrett led Meagan out into the hall.

"That was very rude of you," she said, keeping her voice down so Harold and the other two men in front of them couldn't hear her.

"James is used to my rudeness."

"Still—"

"Still nothing."

"Must you growl like that?"

"I'm afraid I must," he said softly between his teeth. "You don't have any inkling of the kind of danger you could have put yourself in by coming here."

"If you had told me you were taking Harold to James I

would not have worried so much. And speaking of James, why didn't you tell me he was head of the Foreign Office?"

"I thought you knew."

"I didn't." Meagan saw Barrett's hand tighten around his cane and she wondered if he was being entirely honest with her.

They came to the door and stepped outside. Harold waited for them near a carriage. He turned to Barrett and said, "How can I thank you?"

"You can thank me by never getting involved with such a group again."

"I've learned my lesson. You'll never have to bail me out again."

"I'm counting on it."

Fenwick turned to Meagan and took her hand. "Goodbye, Meggie."

"You must write me every day," she said, hugging him.

Barrett watched Fenwick peck Meagan on the cheek and felt a sudden feeling of danger prick his senses. He turned and scanned the shadows lining Downing Street and the Foreign Office building. Movement near an upper window caught his eye. The sash was up, the form of a person visible. Moonlight glinted off the barrel of a rifle pointed at Meagan and Harold.

"Watch out!"

Barrett dove for them as a shot rang out.

CHAPTER
TWENTY-FIVE

Using his weight to tackle them, Barrett careened into Harold and Meagan. The bullet whizzed past his head and hit something close to him.

Everything seemed to slow down. Barrett counted the seconds, feeling weightless as he fell toward the ground. He landed between Fenwick and Meagan, his arms over both of them. He heard the two men go after the shooter. Fenwick cursed and rolled over. Fenwick seemed unharmed. What about Meagan?

His heart banged against his chest so hard it felt as if it were boring a hole through his ribs. He felt a little of him steadily dying. In that moment he realized that if he ever lost her, he would lose a part of himself. Not until he turned toward her and watched her eyes blink open did he let out the breath he'd been holding.

"Are you all right?" He crushed her to his chest.

"I will be as soon as you let me breathe." She smiled at him, her dimples beaming.

Barrett felt that grin down in the pit of his stomach. He

didn't realize he'd had such a tight hold on her. "Stay here." He pulled back and leaped to his feet, ready to go after the shooter.

Suddenly both men ran out another door at the opposite end of the building. They stuffed their pistols inside their coats and strode toward Barrett and Meagan and Harold.

"Did you find him?" Barrett asked.

The man shook his head. "Not a sign of him. It's as if he disappeared into thin air."

The door behind them opened and James ran out. "What the bloody hell happened? I heard a shot."

"Someone tried to kill Harold," Meagan blurted.

James glanced at Barrett. "They must have anticipated you'd bring Fenwick here and alerted the traitor inside my own organization. Damn it to hell!"

"I second that," Barrett said, helping Meagan up. That was when he saw the bullet hole in the side of the carriage.

"I'm sorry, Barrett," Meagan said in a contrite voice, her gaze also on the bullet hole. "You were right. I didn't think of the danger."

"I know."

"I promise to listen to you from now on."

"Forgive me, Princess, but I don't believe that for a moment. Neither do you." Barrett looked askance at her.

She flashed her dark eyes at him, trying to look coy. "Let me say I'll try my best to be an obedient wife."

"That's better."

James frowned at Fenwick. "Come on. I'll see you safely away myself."

"Be careful." Meagan touched her brother's arm and kissed him on the cheek.

"I shall."

As Barrett watched Fenwick and James stride toward the carriage, he wondered how the shooter could have gotten away so easily. He watched Fenwick and the other two men step into a carriage. Then James. Barrett couldn't help but wonder if James knew who the mole was inside the Foreign Office and wasn't sharing that information. What if James had ordered his men to let the shooter escape in order to have him tracked? He probably had more men out at this very moment following the shooter. James had no scruples when it came to criminals and hunting them; that was what bothered Barrett most about his cousin.

"Wait here a moment," Barrett said to Meagan; then he strode up the carriage. "Since your men haven't kept Fenwick out of harm's way, I'll see to his safety myself."

James's expression darkened. "Are you saying I'm incapable of doing my job?"

"No, I'm saying you don't know who the traitor is in your own organization."

Relief filled Fenwick's pale face. "That sounds like a good idea to me."

James glanced Fenwick's way. "If you go with him, I can't be responsible for your safety."

"Forgive me, but I'd rather take my chances with him." Harold gazed trustingly at Barrett.

Meagan strode toward them. "What is the matter?"

"I'll tell you later, Princess. Right now, we have to get your brother to safety."

"But—"

"Trust me." Barrett turned to James and the other gentlemen. "Now if you don't mind, I'm borrowing your carriage."

They glowered at him, then stepped out. Barrett saw Meagan and Fenwick safely seated inside and slammed the carriage door. He walked around and looked at the driver, a middle-aged man with a beard and a pipe hanging out of his mouth. "That means you too, Tea Leaf."

"Well, if that ain't a rub on the arse." Tea Leaf took out his pipe, spat over the backs of the horses, and climbed down, grumbling, "Drove for the sir all me life. Ain't never been accused of being a traitor. Ain't gonna stand for it, me lord. I tell ya ... "

Barrett listened to his grumbling and climbed up onto the driver's perch. He picked up the reins and whip and drove the barouche out of the drive, leaving Tea Leaf grumbling and James glowering after him.

Hardly before they reached the outskirts of London, Barrett noticed two men on horseback following them. Keeping a quarter mile back, they wore dark clothes and rode black mounts. Still, Barrett caught glimpses of them in the moonlight.

He waited for a deserted stretch of road, then leaned over and yelled, "Fenwick!"

Fenwick stuck his head out of the window. "What's afoot?"

"We've picked up some friends."

Meagan's face appeared beside her brother's. "What do you mean to do?" Meagan frowned up at him, her dark eyes gleaming in the moonlight, her hair blowing wildly around her face. "Can't we just stop the carriage?"

"Don't worry, Princess," Barrett yelled over the road noise. "Can you do it, Fenwick?"

"I'm game. Move, Meagan!" Fenwick pushed her aside and edged his way out the window. He sat on the side, gripping the edge.

Barrett heard Meagan arguing with Fenwick. Keeping one eye on the road, he secured the reins to his thigh and leaned over the seat. "Grab my hand."

Fenwick reached out.

Barrett's fingers couldn't quite touch him. He stretched farther.

Fenwick tried again. He lost his balance and groped at the air. In one smooth movement Barrett lunged, caught Fenwick's hand, and jerked him on the seat.

"Whoa!" Fenwick yelled, exhilarated. "Damned close. My heart's still pumping. Ain't never had so much fun, Waterton." He slapped Barrett on the back.

"Fun's over." Barrett unwrapped the reins from his leg and picked up his cane. "Keep the team at the same pace."

"What do you mean to do?"

"Jump. Wait a few minutes and stop the team. I'll catch up to you."

"But you can't jump at this clipping pace—"

Before Fewnick could finish, Barrett leaped off the moving carriage. He tucked his body and rolled down into the ditch. Tufts of frozen grass battered his back and rocks gouged his knees. He hit bottom and crouched there, waiting, his heart pumping, his eyes glued on the approaching men. The excitement of the hunt flowed through his veins and sharpened his senses.

Barrett waited until they were almost upon him and lunged. He knocked one of the men off his horse with his cane. The second rider pulled back so hard on the reins his mount reared.

Barrett attacked the fallen rider with such speed the man didn't have a chance to rise. One right to his face and the man crumpled in the road.

The second rider whipped his horse around to ride away, but Barrett grabbed the reins. The disoriented animal reared again. Using his cane like a bat, he hit the man square in the chest.

As he rolled off the back of the horse, Barrett grabbed him, hit him once in the jaw, then held on to his collar. "Tell me who sent you to follow me."

"Nobody."

Barrett raised his cane and held it over the man's face.

"All right! Sir James."

"I thought as much."

Barrett brought the cane down against the man's head hard enough to knock him out. He collapsed, his chin bobbing down on his chest. Barrett dragged both men over to the side of the road, rounded up both horses, then mounted one. With the other in tow, he rode toward the carriage. He should have guessed James would send someone to trail them. His cousin didn't like to be left in the dark about anything. If he didn't have complete control of a situation he wasn't content.

He saw Meagan running toward him. "Barrett! Are you all right? I saw you jump. I thought you were dead."

"I'm fine." To prove it, he bent and kissed her on the lips, then pulled her up before him.

"Barrett, when will all this stop?"

"Do not worry. Your brother will be safe."

"Those horrible men in the Devil's Advocates will not give up. I heard what you said to Sir James. There is a traitor in his ranks. And what about the person they mean to kill? It's all so horrible."

"Trust me. There will be no murder and your brother will be safe. We have a week before the ball. I'm sure James is busy going down the list of names your brother gave him. It will be all right." Barrett kept his voice convincing, though he had his doubts about the murder. With a traitor inside James's ranks, the members of the Devil's Advocates could easily slip into the ball.

"Exactly what does your cousin do? I know he's more than the head of the Foreign Office."

"Let's just say he has his finger on the pulse of the security of our commonwealth."

"That's a nice way of saying he's in charge of spying for our country."

"In essence, yes."

She cocked her head and eyed Barrett suspiciously. "Why did he come with you the night you came to claim my hand?"

"I wanted him as my best man. After all, he is my cousin. Now forget him." Barrett bent and kissed her.

He felt her melt in his arms and knew she'd forgotten about James. But for how long? The truth would eventually come out. He didn't look forward to that moment.

Deep in the throes of a dream, Meagan was a child again. Lochlann ran behind her, brandishing a sword. They reached a beach, where a thick fog rose from the water.

Sir James called to her, "Come into the mist. You'll be safe. Your brother is here. Come on."

She stepped toward the thick haze. "I'm coming."

Abruptly, hands formed from the fog. Swirling gray fingers reached out to grab her.

She screamed, darted away, and turned to warn Lochlann. Right before her eyes Lochlann's face changed. A patch slid out of his eye and covered it, a beard grew from his chin. His voice deepened. Suddenly, she was staring at Lord Collins.

"I'll get you this time." He thrust his sword at her . . . .

The carriage rattled to a stop. Meagan woke with a start, trembling, in a cold sweat. Darkness surrounded her. For a moment she cringed at the thought of the dream. Outside, two solid thumps hit the ground. Then two more. She recalled what had happened and that Harold had stayed up top to keep Barrett company.

The door opened and Barrett filled the doorway. His hair stuck out in strange, windblown angles and he'd pulled the muffler Ann had made him up around his neck, crushing his cravat. His nose and cheeks were red from the cold.

"We're staying here tonight." He smiled at her, a curious glow in his eyes, as if he couldn't get enough of looking at her.

"Where is here?" she asked.

"Slough."

She heard Harold whistle at something outside. "Would you look at that? Meggie will be in star heaven."

"What does he mean?" Meagan asked.

"You'll see." Barrett extended his hand and helped Meagan alight from the carriage.

A rambling house stood in front of her surrounded by oaks and yews. One light burned in a first floor window. Something loomed to her right. She turned and froze.

"My Lord . . ." Meagan murmured, gazing at Sir William Herschel's telescope. Her jaw dropped open. For a moment she couldn't believe the sight before her. She blinked, afraid the image would fade, but it didn't.

With the awestruck eyes of a child getting her first glimpse of Father Christmas, she walked toward the telescope and drank in the sight. None of the drawings she'd ever seen could have done it justice. Bending her head back, she followed its cylindrical form forty feet into the air. Above the observatory, the massive pyramid-shaped scaffolding held the wondrous miracle in place. Gemini gleamed just beyond the aperture, so bright, so bold, the cluster seemed to cry out to be viewed.

Barrett stepped up behind her and slipped his arms around her waist. "You like my early Christmas gift?"

Meagan felt tears come to her eyes. She turned in his arms to face him. "I shall never want for another gift as long as I live. How can I ever thank you?"

"I can think of several ways." He bent and kissed her, snatching her breath, making her insides melt.

He'd never kissed her with such searing passion. All thoughts of the telescope left her. She grew aware of the quaking he caused deep inside her, his lips moving over hers, the possessive way he crushed her in his arms, the feel of his warm body against her.

Harold cleared his throat. "I say, I'll just go on to the house."

Barrett pulled back and whispered, "We'll continue this later."

"I'll hold you to that," she said, feeling her ear and

neck tingling from his hot breath. Reluctantly, Meagan dropped her arms from around his neck and caught Harold grinning at them.

The front door to the house opened and a man carrying a lantern strode toward them. He raised the light above his head and squinted at them. "Ah, Lord Waterton. Lord Herschel said you'd be arriving. We did not expect you until Christmas Day."

"I was forced to change my plans slightly, Stubbing." Barrett glanced over at Harold and worried his brows. "We have an extra guest in the party."

"Quite all right, my lord."

"You've been planning this all along without telling me?" Meagan cut her eyes at Barrett.

He tweaked her nose. "Yes. I wrote Sir John earlier. I knew you'd be beside yourself if you knew. And I wanted it to be my Christmas gift to you."

"I suppose I can forgive you." She smiled at him and squeezed his hand.

"Please come in." Stubbing motioned them inside. "I can show you to your rooms."

"Is Lord Herschel here?" Barrett slipped his hand in Meagan's and followed Harold inside.

It was a dark house, with mahogany wainscoting in the foyer. Large portraits filled the walls. Meagan recognized one as Sir William Herschel, Sir John's deceased father.

"I'm sorry. I'm afraid the master is not home. He's in London doing further study with Mr. South."

"I heard they were working on the orbital motion of binary stars." Meagan's awe seeped through her voice. She took off her cape and gloves and laid them in Stubbing's outstretched hands.

Stubbing grinned at her. "Ah, so you are interested in the master's work."

"Interested!" Harold piped up, taking off his own coat. "You don't know my sister. All she speaks of is Sir William

Herschel did this and Sir John did that. Rather a nuisance
she is about the Herschels and this star business."

"Sir William was a brilliant man." Meagan shot Harold
an impatient look. He'd never understood her attraction
for the heavens and wasn't ever likely to. "And Sir John
is equally as bright as his father. I wish Sir John could have
been here. I do so look forward to meeting him."

"I'll arrange an interview later," Barrett said impatiently.
He handed his hat and coat to Stubbing. "Right now, let's
get settled in. I could use a drink."

"Forgive me, my lord." Stubbing frowned, taking in
Barrett's red nose and cheeks and Harold's. "I didn't
notice you were minus a driver and footmen."

"Yes, well, something came up and warranted leaving
them behind." Barrett's gaze darted over to Harold, then
back to Stubbing.

"I'll get all of you a hot buttered rum. Nothing like it
to take the chill off."

Harold rubbed his hands together. "That will do nicely."

Stubbing led them up the stairs, their cloaks bumping
his long legs. "If you'll follow me . . ."

Meagan grabbed Barrett's hand and let Harold go ahead
of them before she whispered, "Will it be all right if we
look at the stars before we turn in?"

"I know you wouldn't have it any other way. But I warn
you, if you try to stay out there all night looking at stars,
you might be in danger."

Meagan's bows snapped together. "In danger?"

"Of my kidnapping you and carrying you to my bed and
making love to you until you are writhing beneath me and
those stars are the last thing on your mind."

"I doubt that could ever happen." She teased him with
a grin.

"I can be quite ruthless where you are concerned." He
stared down at her, the blue in his eyes so intense, so
radiant, it was like looking directly into a sunlit ocean.

He had never looked at her in quite the same way. It took her breath away. A minute passed before she could speak. "I always knew you had a mercenary side. I'm sure I can learn to appreciate it."

He slipped his arm around her waist and led her up the stairs. She wouldn't have to seduce Barrett tonight. What had come over him? Something had changed the vigilant restraint in his eyes, as if a floodgate of emotion had broken free inside him. Could she dare hope that he cared for her as much as she cared for him? Only time would tell if that were so.

An hour and a half later, Meagan stood in the observatory, peering through the lenses of the telescope, feeling Barrett's eyes on her.

He lounged on the bottom step that led up to the aperture, his feet crossed at the ankles, his hands twirling his cane. Moonlight streamed in through a window near the ceiling and turned his hair a light silver gray.

She heard him fidget for the third time in two minutes. "I'll be done in a moment." Meagan couldn't take her eyes off the moons of Jupiter.

He pulled out his pocket watch and flicked it open with his thumb. "You said that exactly half an hour ago." He snapped the watch shut.

"Did I?"

"Yes."

"But I've never seen the sky so clearly. Do you know I actually caught a glimpse of Titania? This is a perfect night for viewing and this telescope is magnificent."

"I'm afraid the satellites of Uranus do not interest me, Princess." She could feel his eyes on her. "But other things do."

"Please, just a few more moments. Then I promise to go to bed."

"You said that too thirty minutes ago."

"I mean it this time."

"We can come again." She heard his boot steps on the plank flooring.

"I know but—"

He slipped his hands around her waist, then cupped her breasts, cutting off her words. "Later, my sweet. Don't make me turn ruthless."

"Seems to me you have passed ruthless," she said impishly. She stepped back and turned to face him, feeling a quickening deep inside her. She hoped to gain more time, but he began pulling the pins out of her hair and running his fingers through it while he kissed her neck.

"This is unfair," she moaned, moving her head so he could have free rain of her neck.

"It is the only way I can drag you from your stargazing." He raised his head, shot her a sultry grin, then swept up in his arms. "I've waited as long as I'm going to wait. I'm taking you to bed now."

CHAPTER
TWENTY-SIX

"I wasn't going to protest," she said, nuzzling his neck.

"It wouldn't have done you any good." He swept her up into his arms and carried her out of the observatory.

Meagan leaned her head on his shoulder and stared at the sky. The stars made a patchwork overhead. A kestrel cawed from a tree near the front of Sir John's house. Its mate answered in the distance.

She basked in the feel of his strong arms carrying her and asked, "Did you hear that?"

"Yes."

"This is a glorious night for lovers, isn't it?"

"It will be soon as I get you into my bed." Barrett opened the servants' door and shut it with his foot.

"Could we pretend this is our honeymoon night? For some strange reason I feel it will be."

He gazed down at her, without a hint of the guarded mask he usually wore around her on his face, only intense possessiveness and need. "In a way it is, for I'm going to make love to you as I have never done before."

His velvet-edged words caused her insides to tremble with anticipation. She listened to his boot steps echo in the stairwell as he climbed the stairs. Meagan nuzzled his neck and whispered, "Can you go any faster?"

His expression lit up and a wicked grin moved across his face. "I aim to please, my lady." He took the stairs two at a time.

By the time they reached his chamber, Meagan was giggling, and Barrett was panting. He laid her on the bed, then joined her. Barrett reached up and pulled off his boots, tossing them carelessly across the room. Then he turned on his side and faced her.

Their gazes locked. The teasing smiles left their faces. At the same time, they reached for each other. Their lips met. The moment they touched, heat erupted in Meagan.

She tore at the buttons on his waistcoat and pulled the garment off. Luckily he'd shed his cravat and coat earlier. She concentrated on the buttons of his shirt, while he opened the hooks at the back of her dress. In moments he pulled her dress and petticoat over her head and tossed it onto the floor.

His gaze moved over her pink velvet drawers and corset, along her white silk stockings held up by pink garters. She'd worn them to entice him, but by the look in his eyes he needed no enticement tonight.

"Do I have Holly to thank for what you are wearing?" he whispered against her chin, then trailed tiny kisses along her neck.

"Actually I picked these out," she said, her voice thick with wanting.

He reached the hollow of her throat and kept his mouth there for a moment. She felt his lips touching the pulse there; then his tongue flicked out.

"Barrett," she murmured and ran her fingers over the hard contours of his chest, feeling his heartbeat pounding beneath her palm.

"I want to savor you," he whispered, trailing his lips down her chest.

He paused and buried his mouth in the hollow between her breasts. His tongue flicked out, tasting her; then he trailed his lips over to her right breast. He ran his mouth along the edge of the corset where it touched her breast. The corset was so low, the top of her nipple just touched the edge. When she felt the sensation of his hot lips there, she could barely stand the ache it caused. It grew worse as he nipped her nipple through the velvet and suckled.

Meagan arched her back and writhed beneath him. "Barrett, you really are being merciless."

"Yes, and enjoying every moment of it." With a few deft moves, he unlaced her corset enough to urge her breast out.

He caught her hardened nipple between his teeth. The coarseness of his tongue tantalized her, and she wanted to melt from it. He untied the corset all the way and kissed his way over to her other breast, giving it equal attention.

Meagan wanted him inside her; she thought she would burn up if she didn't feel him soon. She slid her hand boldly down the inside of his breeches, touching his rigid manhood.

He stiffened and grabbed her hand. "Oh, no. You'll not sway me. I'm taking my time." He drew back.

Meagan couldn't keep her hand where she wanted it. She groaned.

"Be patient." He splayed his hands and moved them along her belly.

As his fingers glided over her skin, every muscle in her belly tensed. She felt him reach the top of her drawers. A fine sheen of perspiration broke out on her body as he paused and placed a kiss over her belly button, then eased down her drawers.

Her hips lifted of their own accord. He slid the velvet down over her hips, caressing her skin with it, kissing her abdomen. When Meagan felt his mouth getting closer to the center of her desire, she realized what he was about and stiffened.

"No, Barrett," she murmured, trying to pull him back up to kiss her.

"Yes." He slid her drawers down to her knees, then used his foot and eased them off. "Relax for me, my love."

His tongue slid between her soft, moist folds and stroked the center of her desire. Meagan dug her fingers into the sheet and felt her toes curl. Never had she dreamed a man and woman could share such intimacy. It was beyond anything. The power of it took her to the stars and back. Her hips moved, matching the rhythm of his tongue. When she couldn't stand it any longer, she cried out and found her release.

He raised his head and peered at her. "Now that was fair, wasn't it?"

"Far from it."

Meagan grabbed his shoulders and pulled him up to her. "I want to feel you inside me."

"You will."

She kissed him with all the passion within her. He worked the buttons on his breeches and slipped them off. When he eased down on top of her and their flesh met, she moaned and felt the alluring weight of his body settle along the length of her.

She ran her hands over his back, feeling the scars that no longer stood between them, and wrapped her legs around his hips. He kissed her and eased into her. She experienced a closeness that bound her to him, a happiness that she never wanted to end.

It lasted only a moment; then a strange sensation, as if this happiness wouldn't last, plagued her. It was a feeling that wouldn't leave her, not since that dream she'd had earlier in the carriage.

It melted away beneath his deep thrusts. The searing

heat took over and all she could think of was Barrett inside
her, filling her. She clung to him as they were both swept
away in release.

Barrett made love to her again before he collapsed on
top of her, panting, his body trembling. "Unbelievable,"
he said in a contented voice.

Meagan ran her hands through the hair on his chest.
"I know."

Barrett reveled in the feeling of her soft hands stroking
him and the affection she so effortlessly bestowed on him.
He grew aware just how empty and incomplete his life had
been without her. Before meeting her, he had paid for
affection, and he could never discern whether his mistresses truly cared for him or if it was just an act. He knew
this wasn't an act with Meagan.

After a moment of nuzzling her neck and feeling her
soft hair brushing his cheek, he pulled out of her and
reached over and snuffed the candle.

"What are you doing?" she asked.

"Going to sleep." He threw the covers over both of
them and pulled Meagan close.

"You're actually sleepy?"

"Yes."

She sighed with satisfaction and snuggled her bottom
close to his hips and her back to his chest. "What about
your insomnia?"

"I'll sleep tonight, believe me." He kissed the back of
her head, feeling her round bottom fitting perfectly against
him. A warm glow burned deep inside him, a sensation of
contentment, a euphoria the like of which he'd never
experienced. Restlessness no longer stirred in him. He was
totally and utterly at peace.

"Barrett?"

"Hmm?"

"Let's stay here forever."

"For a few days. Then we must get back. James will need my help at the ball."

"Do you help him on cases all the time?"

"I have in the past."

"How often?"

"I've never kept track." Barrett felt her hand slip over his; then she threaded her fingers through his.

"I don't want you to help him any longer. It is too dangerous."

"I'll stop after the Devil's Advocates are stopped," Barrett said, his eyes closing.

"Why did you start helping James on his cases?"

"Ennui, but I'll not suffer that with you by my side. Never that." He could feel the warm intimacy of holding her melting over him, taking him away. And he did something he hadn't done in years, he fell into a deep blissful sleep.

Meagan woke with the warmth of the sun on her face and the feel of Barrett's body cocooned around her, his chest perfectly molded to her back. She felt his hand cupped around her breast, his thigh resting on hers.

She committed to memory every sensation, the way his breath brushed her neck, the coarseness of his chin stubble against her cheek, the ridges and valleys of his sculpted chest muscles pressed along her spin, the hair on his legs brushing her skin.

In his arms she felt truly beautiful and accepted. She'd realized her dream of finding a man who could look past her flaws and want her for who she was. The impossible had happened: She had fallen madly in love with the Marquess of Waterton.

Barrett's arms tighten around her; then he kissed her neck. "Good morning," he said in a velvety drawl.

"Good morning yourself." She turned to face him as he pulled her close.

Meagan studied his face and saw the dark circles under his eyes fading. "You look as if you've slept well."

"Never better. It looks as if I've found my cure for insomnia."

"What is it?"

"You." He looked directly into her eyes.

"Promise me something," she said, losing herself in the liquid depths of his blue eyes.

"What?"

"Promise me we will always sleep together like this. I want to wake up in your arms every morning."

He hesitated. Uncertainty passed over his expression; then it quickly faded behind a grin. "I wouldn't have it any other way." He kissed her and eased on top of her.

The second of the hesitation disturbed her, but Meagan forgot all about it as Barrett made love to her again.

A few days later, Meagan and Barrett said their good-byes to Harold. Barrett handed him money and instructed him to go to Scotland for a few weeks and disappear into the countryside, just until the Devil's Advocates were arrested. Meagan had been worried about Harold, but Barrett assured her he would be safe. After extracting a promise from Harold to write her every day, she watched him get on a mail coach bound for Glasgow.

They reached London in a little over two hours. Now, she listened to the steady rhythm of the team's hooves hitting the paved drive of Pellam House. A part of her resented this intrusion into her happiness with Barrett. The two of them had set the nights on fire with their passion, making love until they were both spent. The mornings were even better since she woke up enveloped by the warmth of his arms and his kisses.

Such happiness she had only dreamed of possessing. Now that she had it, she clung to it, savored it, guarded it from all the nagging feelings that it would be snatched from her. Perhaps that feeling would go away once the Devil's Advocates were stopped and the leader found.

Barrett opened the door. He looked cold and wind-blown, his lips blue. He noticed the frown on her face and asked, "Are you still pouting about leaving Slough?"

"No, I'm just disappointed." Meagan smiled weakly and took his hand and allowed him to help her out of the carriage.

He pulled her close. "I'll make it up to you. After this is over, I'm taking you away on that honeymoon we've never had."

"Can we go back to Lord Herschel's?" Meagan said hopefully.

"No, I'm not sharing you with the stars or with some puffed-up astronomer for whom you have an infatuation."

"I wouldn't call it an infatuation. I admire him for his scientific caliber—that is all."

"I'm still not sharing you with the jemmy." Barrett pulled her close and kissed her.

She felt his cold lips and chin against hers while she wrapped her arms around his neck and kissed him back.

Running footsteps sounded behind them.

Barrett groaned and murmured against her lips. "I'm definitely taking you to some deserted place where we can be alone."

"Begging your pardon, my lord, but there's a fire in the north parlor," Hastings said, running past them with a bucket in his hands, Stratton right behind him.

"Bloody hell! Hurry! Get more water," Barrett said, grabbing the buckets from Stratton and darting up the steps.

Meagan hiked up her skirt and ran up the steps behind him, her heart pounding.

CHAPTER
TWENTY-SEVEN

Meagan raced through a cloud of smoke into the parlor. The heat hit her face. She coughed and saw Lyng, Tessa, Coates, and Reeves beat at the flames leaping from the Christmas tree. The pine lay on its side, a massive thing, a good twenty-five feet tall with branches stretching half way across the room. Flames leaped along the length of it.

"Get out of the way!" Barrett shoved Reeves back and emptied both buckets of water on the tree.

Half of the flames died. Stratton and Hastings dashed into the room and threw more water on the tree. Smoke spiraled up from the charred boughs, but no flames. Tessa and Lyng froze and dropped the small rugs with which they had been hitting the fire.

Reeves looked as if he might collapse and Meagan grabbed his arm. The elderly man coughed and caught his breath.

"What the bloody hell happened?" Barrett growled, eyeing all the servants.

Tessa spoke first. "Weren't me or Lyng, my lord. We smelled the smoke and came running." She brushed back a lock of blond hair that had fallen from her mobcap and looked at Hastings and Stratton.

"She is correct," Lyng said, narrowing his eyes at the footmen.

"Weren't us either." Hastings threw back his shoulders and shot the Oriental man an indignant look.

Stratton looked pleased that his coworker had taken up for him and added, "Aye, we heard Coates and Reeves yelling fire and ran in here and found the tree a-blazing." Stratton stared at Coates and Reeves.

Black smoke covered Coates's face. Only the whites of his eyes showed, along with a guilty expression. "I did it—"

"No, I did," Reeves said, raising a trembling hand and pointing to the tree.

"Who did it?" Barrett growled in an impatient tone.

Coates turned to Reeves. "I can't let you take the blame for me. Everything I touch turns into a disaster." He glanced at Barrett. "I'm sorry, my lord."

"Stratton, Hastings, get it out of here." Barrett glanced at the burned tree, the smoke still spiraling up from it.

"Right away, me lord." Hastings started to step in front of Stratton, but he stopped and allowed Stratton to go first.

Taken aback by the gesture, Stratton smiled and handed him the rug Lyng had thrown down. "Here, better use this so you won't get burned."

Meagan watched them wrap the rugs around the trunk and the top and carry it out, a trail of smoke following them.

Barrett looked at Coates. "I want to know exactly what happened."

"Reeves and I were trying to set up the tree. I suppose I got it a little too close to the fireplace and it just"—

Coates made a flaming gesture with his hands—"went up in flames."

"That's not true. It was my fault," Reeves said. "I couldn't hold up my end and dropped it." He clenched his trembling hands in front of him.

"That isn't true. I lost my balance and tripped and caused Reeves to drop his end. I'm no good for anything. I'll be leaving, my lord. I know you can't keep me on." Coates strode toward the door.

"Well, I'm going too then. I should have retired long ago. I can't even hold a piece of wood." Reeves staggered up to Coates's side, his wrinkles stretching in an abject look of despair.

Meagan watched both men reach the threshold and cried, "You mustn't leave us. We'd be lost without you." Meagan shared a glance with Barrett. A scowl marred his face. She gave him her best pleading look.

"Yes," Barrett said, the word forced through a clenched jaw. "You must stay."

Coates and Reeves turned around, wide smiles on their faces.

"We shan't disappoint you, my lord . . . my lady." Reeves executed a graceful bow.

"We'll do our best." Coates raised his chin, some of his confidence already returning.

"See about cleaning this mess up." Barrett strode over to Meagan and put his arm around her waist.

"Yes, my lord," Coates and Reeves said at the same time.

Tessa and Lyng smiled at them; then they shared an intimate glance.

Barrett guided Meagan from the room and didn't speak until they were almost to his chamber. "Do you know what you just did down there? Your act of kindness could be signing our death warrants."

"Coates just needs some confidence. And Reeves—well, if he retired, he wouldn't have a reason to keep living. I just couldn't let that happen. Thank you for letting them stay. You're the most understanding, kind, lovable—"

"Lovable?" Barrett cocked a brow at her. "That's stretching it a bit too far, isn't it?"

"I don't think so." Meagan reached up on tiptoe and kissed Barrett. The hard line of his lips softened. She twined her fingers in his thick blond hair and pressed her body against his chest.

"Perhaps I can change your mind when I show you how ruthless I can be," he said against her lips.

"My opinion shall still stand firm."

He swept her up into his arms and carried her into his room, slamming the door with his foot. When he laid her on the bed, caressed her breasts, and kissed her, Meagan decided his ruthless side was the most lovable of all.

Later that afternoon, Barrett heard a knock on the study door. He dropped a bill in his hand and said, "Enter."

Tessa gingerly stepped into the room, looking sheepish, her plump cheeks stretched in a smile. She bobbed a curtsy. "Begging your pardon, my lord."

"What is it?"

"I just came to say thank you."

"For what?"

"For making my mistress so merry. I don't know what you've done, but I've never seen her in such high gig, laughing and smiling. I thought you'd only hurt her, but I was wrong. You've made her happy. I ain't seen her this contented in her whole life, and I've known her since she was born. Living like a hermit wasn't likely to ever make her happy, now was it?" Tessa's smile widened.

"I suppose not." Barrett felt a growing sick feeling in his gut. He had to tell Meagan the truth and soon.

"I always admit when I'm wrong, and I was wrong about you. I hope you can see your way clear to forgiving me."

"Of course," Barrett said, forcing the words past the bars of his conscience.

"And I've another matter to ask of you."

"Ask it."

"Well, it ain't for me to ask." Her cheeks turned the color of Barrett's burgundy waistcoat. She poked her head out the door and said, "You can come in now."

Lyng appeared in the door, his expression slightly unsure.

"Lyng, what is it?"

"We want to marry, my lord, and we need your permission."

Barrett leaned back in his chair, a stunned and equally amused expression on his face. "Tessa, leave us for a moment," he said, eyeing Lyng.

"Yes, my lord." Tessa shot Lyng an uncertain look.

Barrett waited until she left the room; then he said, "If I had not heard the words out of your mouth, I wouldn't have believed them."

"They are true."

"So you've decided to marry the dragon."

"The dragon is not so bad." Lyng smiled at Barrett for the first time since they'd met. His eyes disappeared in his cheeks.

"If you're sure, then I say go to it, old boy."

"Thank you, my lord." Lyng's smile faded back into his serene countenance. "My path is set. What about yours? Have you unburdened your soul?"

"Not yet, but I shall." Not wanting to discuss Meagan, he frowned and said, "You are dismissed."

"The deeper the well, the harder it crumbles when shattered." Lyng shot Barrett a sage look, then left the room without a sound.

Barrett stood, fearing he had waited too long to tell Meagan the truth. It was pure selfishness on his part. He liked seeing her eyes glow when she looked at him, the affection she bestowed on him so willingly, the closeness he shared with her that he'd never shared with anyone in his life. She completed him. His happiness, his world, his life were tied to her. Later he would tell her the truth and ask her to marry him. But at the moment, he couldn't ruin the peace he'd found with her. If only he could get that look on Tessa's face out of his mind as she thanked him for making her mistress happy.

An hour later, standing in the ring at Jackson's, Barrett still felt the sting from his conscience. He eyed Bone Crusher, his opponent. B.C., so dubbed by his friends, had wounded many a man in his fifteen-year career in prizefighting. Barrett had engaged B.C. as a sparring partner in order to forget the lie he was living. It wasn't working. Barrett threw a punch and hit his opponent's ribs.

B.C, a behemoth of a man with a neck and physique that matched his name, merely grinned at Barrett. "That all ye got, governor?"

"Never fear. I'm just getting started." Barrett threw a right.

B.C. danced back, still grinning, and Barrett's punch hit air.

A crowd of gentlemen had gathered around. They were calling out encouragement to Barrett, while making bets among themselves how many minutes he'd last.

"What's the matter? You tired?" B.C. threw a left. It grazed Barrett's chin and sent him staggering back.

The bystanders went wild, their calls carrying around the gym.

Barrett shook the blow off and charged again. This time he struck quickly with a left, faking right. The punch caught B.C. square in his face.

He stood there staring at Barrett, appearing not to feel a thing, while blood trickled from his nose. "Pretty good, for a blue blood, but not good enough." B.C.'s face turned determined. He lunged at Barrett.

Barrett danced back, dodging fists as large as hammers. Out of the corner of his eye, he caught sight of his father in the crowd.

B.C. saw his opening and hit Barrett in the gut with such force it lifted him up off the floor.

Barrett sailed through the air and landed flat on his back, the wind knocked out of him. One side of his ribs felt as if they'd met with cannon fire.

"One . . ."

He heard the referee counting. He tried to sit up, but his father stepped over to the ring and pushed him back down.

"Two . . ."

"What are you trying to do? Kill yourself?"

In a ragged voice, Barrett said, "I don't need one of your lectures."

"No, you need a damned doctor."

"Three . . ." The referee called the fight.

Cheers went up, even as money exchanged hands.

"I'm fine." Barrett knocked his father's hands aside, grabbed the ropes, and pulled himself up. He saw his father grimacing at the scars on his back and turned so his father couldn't see them.

Looking hardly the worse for wear, B.C. lumbered over to Barrett and said, "Good fight. You lasted the longest. Gotta admire you for that. Soak in hot water. You'll feel like new."

"New . . ." Barrett echoed the word. Then he stood up straight and grimaced.

"One might be broken." B.C. thumped Barrett's rib cage with one of his ape-size hands and smiled when Barrett flinched. "I didn't hit you fast enough to break 'em all."

His father raised a brow at B.C. "Something can be said for your compassion."

Barrett grimaced at his father and stepped out of the ring. "Why are you here?"

"I need to talk to you." The Duke of Kensington made a great show of handing Barrett his shirt and coat.

Barrett's brows shot up in surprise and disbelief. Through Barrett's whole life, he could not remember one instance when his father had favored him with his attention. Not one. They could hardly stay in the same room without an argument. What had come over his father?

"If it's another lecture, I'm really in no mood to hear it." Barrett finished buttoning his shirt and slipped on his coat.

His father handed Barrett his cane. "Can you walk me out?" The words hadn't come out as a command, but as a request.

Barrett noticed an imploring quality in his father's expression that he had never seen before. It made him mutter, "Very well."

He followed his father outside. Thick white clouds masked over the earlier sunshine. A cold wind blew across Barrett face. In spite of the chill in the air, people moved down Bond Street in a steady stream. Greenery and bows swayed along the windows. Wreath-covered doors jingled as people moved into and out of the shops. The excitement of Christmas electrified the air, and shone on the faces of the shoppers. Barrett felt the need to buy Meagan an expensive Christmas gift—even if she might not want it. Perhaps it might assuage some of his guilt.

"How are you and Meagan doing?"

His father's voice broke into Barrett's thoughts. Barrett eyed his father skeptically. "That isn't the reason you came looking for me. What is the real reason? Why did you come back to England after all these years?" Barrett gripped the edge of his cane and kept his eyes on the door to Jackson's.

His father remained silent for a moment and he stared pensively at Barrett. Finally he said, "I confess at first it was to stop your marrying Meagan. But after meeting her, I realized she could change you and teach you a valuable lesson about loving and caring for someone.

"You think me incapable of loving someone?" Barrett grew defensive. "I suppose I am. I had a good teacher." He glanced at his father.

Peter gripped his own cane and struggled with his temper. After a moment, the hardness melted from his face and laid bare the emotion there. "I know I wasn't the best father to you. But you also have to admit you did everything you could to punish me for it."

"I can't deny that." Barrett stared down at his cane.

"I should have had more patience with you and not sent you away to boarding schools, but in order to have peace in the household I had to decide between you and Vedetta. I hated to make the decision. I loved you both, but—"

"You chose her." Barrett's words held a wealth of regret in them.

Peter's lip trembled slightly as he spoke his next words. "I'll tell you something I've never told you. I had a loveless marriage with your mother and I wasn't about to have a second. When Vedetta could not control you or your resentment for taking your mother's place, she told me I had to make a choice. It was either her or you. If you find fault in me for choosing love, then I can't blame you. I know it was selfish of me, and I know I have no right to try to be a father to you now that Vedetta is dead—"

"You're correct. You don't." Bitterness laced Barrett's voice.

His father's shoulders flinched at Barrett's words. He remained silent a moment; then his voice softened. "I can only hope you care for Meagan and it will help you realize what it's like to love someone. Perhaps you might understand why I was forced to raise you the way I did. I hope you can forgive me." His gaze dug deep into Barrett's for a moment.

When Barrett didn't speak, Peter said, "Better get those ribs bound, my boy." He turned and strode down the sidewalk.

Barrett watched Peter's regal bearing, the stiff back and shoulders, the way he swung his cane with arrogant confidence. As a child Barrett had felt awe and a certain dread at seeing his father, for it meant he'd be punished for some of his devilish mischief, yet as a man, as he watched his father walk away from him at this moment, he felt only pity and loss. He didn't want things to remain as they had been between them. It was a feeling he wouldn't act on immediately, but perhaps in time he might.

The footman opened the door to his father's carriage. Without looking back, the Duke of Kensington stepped inside. The black brougham pulled out behind a hack and disappeared into the bustling flow.

Barrett started across the street when James rode up beside him. He glowered at Barrett. "You had no bloody right to disable my men!"

"I didn't think you'd appreciate that." Barrett cocked a brow at him.

"This is my operation!"

"It may be, but you have a leak in your ranks and I'll not have Fenwick's life in danger."

"I've worked with those men for years. I'd trust any of them with my life. The leak is not one of them."

"I couldn't take that chance."

James's dark eyes took in the bruise on Barrett's cheek. Some of the anger left his expression as he asked, "You haven't told Meagan the truth yet, have you?"

"No."

"Well, you'd better tell her soon. This case is almost over."

"Over?"

"Yes, I've finally discovered the identity of the leader."

CHAPTER
TWENTY-EIGHT

"How did you find out?" Barrett watched James's fist tighten around the reins.

"I got lucky. I searched Coburn's and Fields's flats. In Coburn's place I found a singed corner of foolscap in the fireplace. I assumed if they'd received a message from their leader protocol demanded they burn it. Hence, there was enough paper left to trace the manufacturer to Winslow Printing."

"That must have taken some doing."

"You know me. I never give up." James's eyes glistened with an unyielding light. "I studied the list of all the customers until I came to one person and the name jumped out at me. At first, I brushed it off, but the more I thought about it, the more I realized this was our man. I dug through some old files on Thistlewood and found his name. He's young, an extremist, and very good at acting. He more than likely took Fenwick to one of Arthur Thistlewood's rallies before the Cato Street Conspiracy, then started the Devil's Advocates on his own."

"And who is it?"

"You won't believe it," James said, adding unaccustomed drama to his voice.

"Try me."

"Your wife's friend, Lochlann Burrows."

"Bloody hell!" Barrett mumbled and felt an uneasy feeling clawing at him.

Across town, Meagan slipped out the servants' entrance of Pellam House. Stratton and Hastings were not at their usual post by the door. She sighed with relief. This was a perfect time to sneak away. Barrett wasn't here, and all the servants seemed preoccupied—especially Tessa and Lyng. After Meagan had congratulated them on their upcoming nuptials, she left them holding hands and walking Nuisance in the garden.

Meagan hurried down to the drive's gates, clutching the note Lochlann had sent her. He had said it was urgent she meet him. He also mentioned some of the Devil's Advocates were following him and it was imperative he keep a low profile. They must believe Lochlann could take them to Harold. She feared for his safety.

The wind had picked up from the north, swirling the hem of her dress around her legs. She glanced overhead and felt the first few flakes of sleet on her face. Shivering, she hurried through the gates that were left open during the day, then strode past a stand of white populars. Lochlann stepped out from behind one of the trees and startled her.

"Geminy! You scared the life out of me," she said.

With a worried look on his face, he said, "I'm sorry. We have to hurry." He pulled her toward a carriage parked near the trees.

"Can't we speak here?"

"No. We'll go for a ride and talk. You don't mind, do

you?" Lochlann didn't wait for her answer, just smiled at her, his pewter eyes gleaming with an impenetrable light.

Meagan noticed the driver, an old bearded man with no teeth and a patch over one eye. He wasn't Lochlann's usual driver. Meagan didn't like the way he looked at her, and she gazed away. Lochlann opened the door and helped her inside.

He slammed the door closed, sat beside her, and called up to the driver. The carriage lurched forward. Meagan hit her back against the seat and asked, "Why are the Devil's Advocates after you?"

"I've found out who the leader is and they want to kill me."

"You must hide until Sir James and Barrett stop them."

"Yes, Sir James . . . " Lochlann's expression hardened.

Something withdrawn and strange in Lochlann's manner forced her to say, "You needn't worry. Barrett and Sir James will see them all arrested and hanged."

The preoccupied aspect left his face; then he turned and looked at her. "That doesn't do me a lot of good at the moment. Perhaps I should flee the city as Harold did."

"You know Harold left?"

"Yes. I heard Coburn and Fields speaking about him. Where did he go?"

"I'm not really sure. He's in Scotland somewhere."

"Are you sure you don't know where he is? I'd like to join him."

"No, I wish I knew. I've been worried about him." Meagan gnawed on her lower lip and wondered why Lochlann wanted to know where Harold was. She quickly changed the subject. "You said you knew who the leader was. Who is it?"

"That would be me." Lochlann wore a pleased expression.

"You!" Meagan blinked at him in disbelief.

"Close your mouth, my dear Meagan. It's very unbecoming."

In a barely audible voice, she said, "All these years, I thought we were friends. I thought I knew you."

"I was under the impression I knew you too until you went and married Waterton."

"I did it to save your life, but I can see now that fumbling with the gun and pretending to be frightened was all an act. You were trying to kill Barrett and me, weren't you?"

"I admit I was very miffed by your defection to Waterton."

Meagan remained silent a moment, digesting his words. "When you pulled out the pistol the first time and dropped it and put a whole in my bonnet—was that an accident or were you trying to kill me?"

"I started to but changed my mind at the last minute. I decided to use you to find out what you knew."

"And the second time at the duel, when you fired prematurely at Barrett, why didn't you kill Barrett instead of shooting him in the arm?"

"My aim was off that day. It's very hard to look like a bumbling idiot and shoot straight."

"I suppose it was you who shot at Harold from the window in the Foreign Office."

"Yes, that was me. My aim was off that night too—thanks to Waterton." He frowned.

"And I suppose you came to the ball and Pellam House as a way of trying to get into my good graces so I would tell you what I knew."

"Yes, how very astute of you." A cunning smile stretched his lips.

"What happened to you?" Meagan stared hard at him as if trying to look inside his mind and figure him out. "I had no idea you felt so strongly about government issues. You never once mentioned it to me."

"I knew you wouldn't be interested." The gray in his

eyes turned the color of steel. "And I didn't really get involved until I heard Thistlewood speak."

"He was an extremist and died for it."

"I admire him. He died for a cause."

"So you're willing to kill an old friend"—Meagan pointed to her chest—"and countless others, even yourself, for this same cause?"

"I'm fed up with the way this country is being run. Thistlewood was right. The only change we make will have to come through force. I want to make a difference. I don't want to be like my father and his father before him. They grew rich off the sweat and blood of their tenants. They hardly lived better than slaves. I couldn't live with myself if I didn't try to change it. Don't you see?" He turned and grabbed her arm.

Meagan felt his fingers dig through her cape and the sleeves of her dress, and she winced. "I know this is not the way to change things. You're changing things by the school you started."

"You'll never understand!" He dropped her arm and leaned back in the seat. "It isn't enough. Don't you see? You know nothing of the world. You've sequestered yourself at Fenwick Hall with your books and telescope. What do you know?"

"I know you're insane."

He laughed viciously. "Hardly. It's not insanity to want to leave my mark in the world. People will remember me in years to come. When I kill the king tonight, I'll get everyone's attention. There'll be chaos and revolution will follow. I'll be the head of the New World Order Party."

"The king . . ." Meagan felt the blood drain from her face.

"Yes, the king."

Meagan knew she had to get away from him and warn Sir James and Barrett. She steeled her courage and leaped for the door.

Lochlann grabbed her. Her fists flying, Meagan fought him. He easily pinned her back against the seat.

"I'm sorry, but I can't let you go." He grabbed her throat and squeezed and squeezed . . . .

A strangled gasp escaped her mouth. Her last thought was of Barrett; then everything melted into darkness.

Barrett pulled up to Pellam House and glanced over the backs of his grays at Stratton and Hastings. They held their heads and staggered toward the front steps. Barrett's heart banged against his ribs. He pulled back on the reins and leaped down. James reined in and followed on his heels.

Barrett ran up to the footmen. "What happened?" He glanced between the two.

"A message came for her ladyship," Stratton said, holding the side of his head.

"A message?" The wrinkles in Barrett's forehead deepened with worry.

Hastings rubbed the back of his neck and grimaced. "Aye, some young lad brought it, but he wouldn't say who sent it. We thought it might be from that Burrows character, and after you said you didn't want him in the house again, we wouldn't let the boy in."

Stratton continued. "After we sent the boy away, we heard someone yelling for help. When we ran to see who it was, somebody hit us from behind."

James shared a glance with Barrett, his expression apprehensive. "No doubt our man."

"Bloody hell! I hope she's here." Barrett ran into the house and took the stairs two at time, his pulse throbbing in his ears. A feeling he might not ever see Meagan again clawed at his insides.

*   *   *

Near the docks, Slip followed behind the carriage. It slowed and rolled into an alley behind several large warehouses—right where he expected it would stop. He waited at the alley's entrance, his eyes darting up and down the street.

The docks looked fairly deserted for an afternoon. A long line of ships rocked in the wind and creaked, their sails flapping. On a sloop closest to the alley, a hand swabbed the deck, while the crew loaded the hull.

Slip dismounted, kept his face low, and pretended to examine his horse's front leg. There was an art to blending in, and he was a master at it.

Burrows wasn't half bad either, but Collins? He was too cocky and stupid by half; Slip knew that from trailing the gentleman.

He watched the carriage creep down the alley and stop. The driver, a middle-aged man with a full beard, jumped down and heaved open one of the massive doors to the warehouse. Then he grabbed the trappings of the horses and guided them into the building.

When he didn't see anyone observing him, Slip tied his horse to the bough of a tree and slipped down the alley, his footsteps whisper soft on the cobblestones.

He peeked through the door at the driver and Burrows pulling Lady Waterton's limp body from inside the carriage. Was she dead? At that thought, his brows narrowed. Sir James wouldn't like it if the lady he was supposed to be watching got done in.

Burrows glanced up and saw him.

For a moment they stared directly at each other; then Burrows waved him inside.

After one more glance around, Slip slithered past the door. Crates lined either side of the warehouse, leaving only a small pathway for a carriage to enter down the center. The smell of molding planks, salty water, and tar hung in the air.

Slip wrinkled his nose and paused near Burrows and looked down at the bruises on Lady Waterton's neck. "Why'd you kill her?"

"She's not dead," Burrows said indignantly. "I couldn't kill her. She's like a sister to me. Do you think me totally heartless?"

The driver chuckled and mumbled to himself. "Aye, you're a regular saint."

"I didn't pay you for your comments, old man." Burrow shot the driver a look that wiped the grin off his face.

"You sure you weren't seen?" Slip asked.

"I was careful. Open that door for us."

Slip brushed aside some straw and flung back a trapdoor. He gazed down the dark hole and heard female cries.

"Let us out!"

"Please don't keep us down here!"

Slip frowned and said, "You puttin' her down there?"

"Yes. Collins wants her for the next shipment. It will make an even twelve."

"You shoulda killed her." Slip's frown worsened. "A lady like that will never do as a whore. The others come from the street, but she's a lady."

"Collins said he'd break her in, then ship her to France with the rest. They'll bring a tidy profit for the treasury. We're running low." Burrows's eyes took on a fanatic's glaze. "I needn't remind you this organization doesn't run without money."

"Collins has a grudge against Waterton. You think after he's had his fun with Waterton's wife that she'll be alive. Ain't likely."

"When I want your opinion on something, I'll ask for it." Burrows narrowed his eyes at Slip.

He clamped his mouth shut and watched them lay Lady Waterton down near the opening. Burrows glanced at the driver. "Take her down, and be careful. I don't want her hurt."

"Aye, governor." The driver spat near an empty crate, hoisted the lady on his beefy shoulder, and descended down the ladder in the hole.

Burrows kept his eyes on Lady Waterton, a pensive almost rueful look on his face. "Do you have the invitations?"

"Yep, I got 'em." Slip pulled out the invitations and slapped them in Burrows's extended hand. "That'll get you and all the gents into the ball. Had to do an awful lot of bribing to get 'em too."

"You've done an admirable job." A black curl fell on Burrows's forehead as he gazed down at the invitations.

"Ain't no one ever said Slip don't do a job right."

"I'll remember you when we start our new order. I'm going to appoint you chief advisor for security."

"That's all well and good, but what about the money?"

Burrows fished in his pocket and threw a pouch of coins at him. "Here."

Slip caught it and opened it. He gazed down at the twenty canaries shining bright against the leather. Usually the sight of so many coins thrilled him, but as he looked at the pieces of gold a queer feeling rose in him, for he knew he'd betrayed his country for twenty sovereigns and a cause he didn't give a damn about.

Meagan woke and felt pain when she swallowed. Gently she touched the bruises Lochlann had left on her throat. She pushed herself up and felt a stabbing pain in her head. When she went to touch her head, the manacles on her wrist rattled. The sound pierced her like needles.

She tried to see through the pitch-blackness around her, but couldn't. The odor of damp earth wafted through the air. Cold air pressed in around her. She shivered and pulled her cape tighter together. Then she heard a movement, and someone coughed.

"Who's there?" She crouched away from the sound.

"We are. Who do you think?" a woman's Cockney accent came back to her.

"Who are you?"

"We're all prisoners. Being 'eld down 'ere agin' our will."

Meagan frowned in the darkness, trying to see them. "How long have you been here?"

Chains clanked; then someone said, "Two days. Some of us three."

"How many of you are there?"

"You make twelve, 'oney."

One of the girls said, "Hear her accent. They're gettin' mighty hard up, takin' ladies off the street."

Someone tried to laugh, but there was no mirth in it and the sound turned to a sob. Meagan's shivering grew worse. She knew it wasn't from the cold.

"Do you know what they mean to do with us?"

Another voice spoke. "I heard them talkin'. They mean to sell us as whores to the Frenchies."

How could Lochlann do this to her? Anything for his cause. She frowned bitterly into the darkness. When she moved, her back brushed something hard. She took off a glove and felt behind her. Her fingers ran over the cold, bumpy surface of bricks. They were in some sort of cellar.

A little more to the left, and she felt the ring her chains were attached to. She yanked on the ring, but only hurt her wrists.

"No need to try that, 'oney. They ain't likely to be givin' away this century."

Meagan slumped back against the wall and rested her head there. Something caused her to glance up. One dim beam of light barely pierced the darkness. It had to be the only way out.

In a fit of frustration, she cried, "Help!" Her voice

thudded dully against the thick walls. She cried out several
more times.

Silence answered her.

A prisoner near her said, "Ain't no use. We all done
yelled ourselves 'oarse."

Meagan thought of Barrett. What she wouldn't give to
have the comfort of his arms at this moment. "Oh, Barrett," Meagan whispered pitifully in the darkness and
hugged her body.

Compassion came through one of the voices. "Who's
Barrett, me lady?"

"My husb—" The sound of footsteps overhead cut off
her words.

The woman near her said, "Sounds like your husband
heard you."

"Barrett," she called frantically, her heart thumping
with relief and anticipation at seeing him.

The trapdoor opened. Bits of straw fell from the ceiling
and hit her face. A ladder edged down into the darkness,
then a lantern. For a moment the light blinded her. Meagan blinked and saw the other captives around her, all in
rags, all pitiful-looking young women held in irons.

She hooded her eyes and glanced up. The face she saw
made her cringe and her blood run cold.

"You needn't look so happy to see me. I know I'm not
Waterton, but I'm infinitely more amusing."

A malicious grin spread across Lord Collins's face as he
climbed down the ladder.

CHAPTER
TWENTY-NINE

At that very moment across town, Barrett paused on the steps of Burrows's town house and felt a horrible sensation move through him, a strange gripping fear. Not his own, but by some bizarre twist of fate he knew it was Meagan's fear he sensed. His blood ran cold, and his pulse roared in his ears.

James stepped out behind Barrett and slammed the door. "Well, he hasn't hidden her here. This is the last place we haven't looked." He saw the stricken expression on Barrett's face. "What is the matter?"

"I just felt Meagan's fear." Barrett could hardly get the words past the constricting feeling in his throat. He gripped the edge of his cane and felt the feeling wane. His desperation slipped into in his voice, "I've got to find her."

"We shall." James stared at Barrett, amazement and worry on his face.

"How are we going to do that?"

"I have my men on Burrows. They'll let me know something soon."

"They haven't contacted you. Burrows might have found them and killed them, or your leak might be one of them." Barrett glanced around him at the rows and rows of houses and shops on Curzon Street. She could be anywhere. The vastness of the city seemed endless.

A tall man with a mustache reined in his horse in front of Burrows's house. Barrett recognized him as one of the men he'd stopped on the road to Herschel's.

They glowered at each other; then the man turned and addressed James. "I left Tibbs down at the docks, sir. We saw Slip speaking to Burrows. They looked particularly friendly. We didn't want to make a move until we had word from you."

"Slip . . ." James gritted his teeth. "So he's the leak. What about Burrows?"

"We lost him down at the docks, sir." The man saw the stormy scowl on James's face and added, "He must have known we were on to him. He slipped into a tavern, took a wench above stairs, and disappeared."

"Bloody hell!" Barrett ran his hands through his hair.

"There's more, sir. Burrows took Lady Waterton down into some sort of underground cellar. Then he left. She looked"—the man shot Barrett a hard sympathetic glance, then turned back to his superior—"dead, sir."

His words hit Barrett. Every muscle in his body tensed as if he'd just been kicked in the gut.

The man continued. "We were about to investigate when Collins came on to the scene."

Barrett's gut clenched. He and James shared a glance; then Barrett said, "Are you thinking the same thing I am?"

"Collins is still dealing in the flesh trade," James mumbled. "Why else would he be down at the docks?"

Barrett bolted for his carriage, climbed in, and grabbed the reins and whip. James hopped up on the seat next to him. Barrett cracked the whip and sped down the street. He had to believe Meagan still lived. She must be alive.

The light from the lantern flickered an eerie yellow glow around the cellar. Lord Collins's face looked demonic. Meagan felt Lord Collins's eyes on her, while he waited as several men clamped the young women in irons. Meagan felt her whole body trembling as she watched the men. They were brawny sailor types with stubble on their faces. They shoved the women about as if they were slabs of meat.

"Please let us go," a pretty girl who looked no older than seventeen pleaded.

"Shut up, you!" One of the men backhanded her.

She cringed and grabbed her chin.

"Ye say we can break 'em in?" the other sailor said, his gaze raking over one brunette.

"They are yours, gentlemen, as long as you don't scar them," Collins said. "They are worth nothing to me if they are scarred."

The sailor who'd backhanded the young girl thumbed his finger toward Meagan. "What about that one?"

"I have something very special in mind for that one." Lord Collins moved. The light hit his brown eyes, making them glow with a crazed light.

Meagan cringed and glanced past Lord Collins, where a man stood at the ready with a pistol trained on the women. She had meant to make good her escape when they unlocked her, but she had a feeling Collins wouldn't unlock her right away—at least, until he'd had his sport.

With a pounding heart, she watched the men prod the women up the ladder. The man with the pistol waved it at Collins. "Ye need me to stay?"

Lord Collins glared at Meagan. "The things I have in mind for Lady Waterton will require the utmost privacy."

"Suit yerself." The man stepped past the lantern and climbed the stairs.

Each time his foot hit a rung, another muscle tensed inside Meagan. She pulled so hard on the iron manacles that her arms locked and her wrists ached. When he reached the top, he stepped up and slammed the door closed.

Meagan jumped, feeling the sound vibrate through every sense in her body. She blurted, "Please let me go!"

Lord Collins stepped toward her. "Tsk, tsk! I wish I could, but it gives me such pleasure to see you in irons. I would love to see Waterton's face if he could see you now." He bent and ran his hand along her cheek.

Meagan jerked back, a wave of nausea rising at his touch. "You won't get away with this."

"Won't I?" He grinned. "Waterton won't save you. I saw him speaking to Neville. No doubt they are off to find Burrows, thinking he has you. I'm free to do what I like with you. I arranged it this way so Burrows would be implicated and not me."

Meagan kept her eyes on his hand. "Then you've known all along Lochlann was the leader?"

"Yes. It was I who supplied him with the money for his little cause."

"Why are you involved? You don't seem like the type to care about politics," Meagan said, trying to keep him talking.

"No, but I do so enjoy keeping Neville and Waterton on their toes." His eyes glazed over and he looked past her, as if not seeing her. "Waterton destroyed my business interests here in England and tried to destroy my reputation as well. If I hadn't kept a little book of all the justices and heads of state who'd frequented my establishment, I would have been exported. But I stayed here, just to seek revenge on Waterton. He thought he was so clever, shutting down my brothels. Well, he'll pay."

"Why did you attack me at Sir Neville's town house?"

Collins gazed slithered over her. "I couldn't pass up an opportunity to irritate Waterton. And Burrows thought it might help to get Neville and Waterton off his scent."

"How long do you think you can keep me?" she asked. "Barrett will come for me."

"Yes, but it will be too late. I can't wait to see Waterton's face when he finds you in one of my whorehouses in France." Collins reached out and ran his hand along her cape. His hand paused near her breasts, and he slid his hand inside her coat.

"No!"

"You'll have to get used to men touching you, my dear." She felt his hand close over her breast and screamed . . . .

A noise sounded above. "Meagan!"

Collins turned at Barrett's voice and glanced up at the door. Meagan breathed a sigh of relief and opened her mouth to call to him, but Collins backhanded her across the mouth.

"Not a word from you, bitch!" Collins pulled a knife out of his coat pocket, snuffed the lantern, then hid in the darkness.

The door opened.

Her pulse pounded in her ears. A dim light pierced the darkness. Meagan could see Collins lurking in a corner, his blade raised. "Barrett, he's got a knife!" she yelled.

Barrett jumped down and wheeled around at the same time. Collins lunged. In one lightning-quick movement, Barrett leaped aside and knocked the knife from Collins's hand with his cane.

A cry issued from Barrett as he threw aside his cane and charged Collins. He hit Collins and rammed his back against the bricks; then he pounded the other man with his fists. Collins didn't stand a chance. Something drove Barrett like a madman. He pounded relentlessly on Collins, driving his fists home with every punch.

Collins collapsed and Barrett grabbed him by his cravat and still hit him.

"Barrett, stop!" Meagan called out.

Meagan's voice seemed to penetrate Barrett's anger. After one more punch, he dropped Collins in a heap on the ground and strode over to her, his chest still heaving.

"Did he harm you?" Barrett knelt beside her and crushed Meagan to his chest.

She could feel his sporadic breaths against her neck and anguish and relief in the way he held her. Her heart leaped. Though he had never come out and said he loved her, Meagan had proof of it in the way he held her now. He leaned back, devoured her lips in kiss, then drew back and searched her eyes.

"I'm fine, save for these." Meagan touched the manacles on her wrists. "The key is in Lord Collins's coat pocket."

Barrett stood and searched Collins. He found the key and unlocked her wrists. When he helped Meagan up, James glanced down at them from above. "I say, is everything all right down here?"

"Yes," Meagan said. "But they took eleven other women on board a ship bound for France—"

"Indeed, I've taken care of that, my lady." James smiled at her; then he looked at Barrett. "By the by, I found Slip on the same boat with a small fortune on him. He's trussed up nice and tight with the others. I'll send someone to pick them up later, but at the moment we've got to hurry. The ball starts in fifteen minutes." He shoved the ladder down for them.

Barrett pulled Collins's limp form over to the spot Meagan had occupied and clamped the irons around his wrists. "That should hold him."

"Come on. We should hurry." Barrett slipped his hand in hers and helped her up the ladder.

Hand in hand, they ran after James. When they darted outside, a wall of cold air hit her, bringing with it the musty, fishy smell of the Thames. Meagan shivered and let Barrett help her into the carriage.

"Lochlann told me whom he meant to kill," Meagan said, watching Barrett snatch up the reins with deft movements.

"Who?" James asked.

"The king."

Barrett glanced over Meagan's head at James. They shared a look. Then at the same time they murmured, "Bloody hell!"

Ten minutes later, they sped down Pall Mall toward Haymarket, Barrett driving to an inch, barely squeezing through the traffic. They missed the wheels of another speeding gig by a hairbreadth. Meagan closed her eyes and gripped the seat, hearing the gig rattle past them. They raced past a constant queue of carriages that stretched all the way to St. James's Street and curved around to Bond Street.

Carlton House, Prinny's home, finally rose up before Meagan. The mansion was pronounced by some as vulgar in its opulence and overdone with finery. The king had nearly bankrupted Parliament in remodeling it. She raised her brows at the long colonnade at the front. Coupled on either side by Ionic columns, it stretched the length of the mansion and led to two gateways.

The horses stomped to a halt behind a carriage just pulling up ahead of them. Meagan watched footmen dash forward to open doors, while countless numbers of people streamed toward the entrance.

Lanterns lit up the night and burned along the bowers and grottos of the gardens behind the palace. Candlelight glowed in windows decorated with wreaths. Where the warmth met the cold panes, a frosty halo of light circled the wide glass. Meagan could see ladies and gentlemen parade past the windows, the men in court dress, the women in elegant, shimmering gowns.

"What a crush," James mumbled, then leaped out of the carriage.

Barrett hopped down, turned, and shook his finger at her. "Stay put!"

"But I can find Lochlann."

"No. Stay here." Barrett leveled a determined look her way, then followed James to the entrance.

Meagan watched them hurry through the Corinthian portico, squeezing their way past the ballgoers at the front door. No one could spot Lochlann better than she. Perhaps she might be able to save his life. She could not forget all those years of friendship as he had so easily forgotten them. She jumped down and hurried around to the back.

Servants ran back and forth emptying slops and kitchen refuse, too busy to notice her. She slipped into a hallway and passed larders, sculleries, pantries and kitchens, finally reaching a set of stairs.

She recognized one of James's men standing guard at the top of the stairwell. He was a stern-faced man with watchful eyes. "Hello," she said, using her most authoritative voice.

"Lady Waterton!"

"Yes, I'm with my husband. I seem to have gotten lost."

His watchful eyes combed over the soiled hem of her gray dress, at the strands of hair hanging down around her shoulders. "Sir James said not to let anyone pass."

"Now see here, sir. I know Lord Burrows better than anyone. If he kills the king because you don't allow me inside—"

"Very well." He opened the door for her, yet didn't look happy about it.

"Thank you." Meagan moved down a long hall, staring at the intricately carved and gilded plaster ceilings and scarlet flock wallpaper. The smell of rich food made her stomach growl.

The orchestra struck up a waltz. Music drifted above the roar of voices. She paused at one of the back entrances of an astounding barrel-shaped domed room. It branched off and led to a double staircase. She knew from reading about the house that it led to the king's private apartments.

Christmas greenery and elaborately carved topiaries seemed to fill every available space. The room looked as if it had been swept clean of furniture to make room for guests. The only furnishings were chairs placed around the perimeter and several enormous brass Chinese urns and statues that filled the corners. She saw a holly wreath gracing the neck of a Chinese dragon.

A head taller than most gentlemen, Barrett and James were not hard to spot. They stood near a column scanning the room, while the king waltzed.

Meagan eyed the king. At one and sixty, Prinny looked closer to seventy. Overweight, overdressed, and ravaged by a life of dissipation and overindulgence, he looked almost comical as he tried to keep up with his nubile young partner, a pretty lady with long blond curls. When he stepped on her toes, she held back a grimace behind a polite smile. By his red face and glassy eyes, Meagan knew he was foxed.

Couples circled the floor and waited intently for the dance to end so they might partake of the next. She noticed Lord Kensington standing not five feet from her, speaking to the Lord Chancellor.

Where was Lochlann?

She spotted a footmen on the staircase and almost glanced away, but the man's pewter eyes held her. Lochlann. He wore the white wig and livery of a footman.

Meagan scanned the room and spotted Mr. Fields and Mr. Coburn in a corner. They too wore wigs and livery in the guises of footmen.

Barrett and James discovered Lochlann and the others

at the same time she did. Lochlann's gaze never wavered
from the king as he pulled out a gun from inside his coat.
Mr. Fields and Mr. Coburn had been waiting for his signal,
and they followed suit.

CHAPTER THIRTY

Everything happened at once.

Meagan screamed.

James ran for the king.

Barrett dove for Lochlann.

James's men appeared out of nowhere and tackled Mr. Fields and Mr. Coburn.

James rammed the king from the side, taking him and his partner down. The bullet whizzed over their heads. One of the musicians cried out. His violin screeched as he grabbed his arm. Then the music ground to a halt.

Meagan's gaze darted across the room toward Lochlann, who saw Barrett running up the steps after him. He bolted, pulled another pistol from his pocket, and shot at Barrett.

Meagan screamed, but the sound knotted in her throat and only a gasp left her mouth.

Barrett feinted and dodged the bullet, while he continued to run after his prey.

Lochlann reached the top of the staircase. Two of James's men were waiting, pistols drawn. Lochlann's gaze shifted between Barrett and the men. He seemed torn for a moment. Then he leaped over the side of the railing, yelling, "It's not over!"

Lochlann plummeted thirty feet downward. The crowd gasped in the silence.

Thud. He hit the floor.

Meagan cringed at the sound. Several ladies swooned, caught just in time by gentlemen. Lochlann had hit the floor and landed on his side. Meagan's eyes widened in surprise as Lochlann moved his arm and began to groan. James's men ran and grabbed him. They dragged him, limping and holding his arm, from the ballroom. Before he went out, he raised his head and looked at Meagan. Their gazes locked.

Tears stung Meagan's eyes as she again felt his fingers around her throat. The memories of the dirty-faced little boy with whom she'd played pirates, argued, and shared her darkest secrets flashed in her mind. He'd comforted her through her insecurities and bouts with her condition. He'd always been there for her. Through a wet blur, she watched as they carried him out. James's men shoved Mr. Fields and Mr. Coburn out behind him.

James pulled the king to his feet. James brushed off the king's coat and said, "Excellent dive, Your Highness."

"Pray, Neville, is it your custom to wait until the last minute to do your job?" Prinny straightened his wig, the intoxicated glaze gone from his eyes.

"In some circumstances it requires patience."

"I see. I'd expect such a showing from Waterton, but you surprise me." The King of England smacked James on the back.

James grinned. "We captured the jackanapes."

"Indeed. When you told me someone might get killed, I never suspected it might be me."

"I didn't know you were the target until minutes ago."

"Well, well, what is a king for if not to be made sport of?" Prinny's demeanor brightened behind his usual gregarious smile. He waved his hand at the crowd of stunned ballgoers and in a voice that carried through the room said, "You'll all be talking about this one for an age, by God. See here. Strike up that band. And get that poor fellow a leech. He's bleeding all over my floor."

One of the footmen tied a handkerchief around the arm of the violinist and escorted him out of the ballroom. Meagan peered over the crowd who'd run into the ballroom at the sound of gunshots. She saw Barrett swarmed by a crowd, every gentleman near him slapping him on the back for his bravery.

Prinny turned back to James. "That was a clever plan to feign a marriage. Would never thought of such a devious plan myself. I guess Waterton will suffer the wrath of his lady." He winked at James.

James smiled woodenly; then his face contorted in a frown.

Meagan felt the impact of Prinny's words. A nauseating feeling twisted her stomach into knots. Her shoulders hunched as she crossed her arms over her chest and hugged herself. Her pulse drummed in her ears and drowned out the noise of the room. A pain rose up in her heart and it traveled up into her throat, tightening . . . tightening . . . . She couldn't swallow. Couldn't breathe.

Meagan watched the crowd converging on James now. She hiked up the hem of her skirts, wheeled around, and staggered down the hallway. The scarlet wallpaper ran and blurred behind her tears. How could she have thought he loved her? He had used her to get Lochlann. Used her . . . The words repeated in her mind, tearing at heart.

* * *

An hour later, Meagan sat in Lord Upton's town house and managed to stop sobbing long enough to pull back from Holly's arms. "I'm making a fool of myself. I'm sorry."

Holly plucked off another handkerchief from a stack of them on a table. With a quick jerk of her wrist, she flapped it open and handed it to Meagan. "Of course you are not. Your heart is broken."

John, sitting in a chair opposite them, steepled his fingers and said, "I think you should at least see him."

"I don't ever want to see him again." Meagan wiped at her swollen eyes with a handkerchief.

Meagan glanced around the parlor. It was a comfortable room, done all in blue. The furnishings were old and the chairs didn't quite match. It was exactly the kind of parlor Meagan had envisioned Holly would have. And Meagan might have felt at ease in it had John not been scowling at her after her last statement, his dark brows forming a straight line over his strange gold eyes.

"You know he'll come after you." John's frown deepened.

"I hoped I could stay here until I get my belongings from Pellam House."

"I don't know." He looked torn between his loyalty to Barrett and letting her stay.

Holly shot John a heated glance. "You heard what he did to her. Of course she can't go back there. And I hope you'll do the honorable thing and see that he doesn't force his way into this house and harass her."

"Harass her? She's his wife!"

"You weren't listening to a word she said. They are not legally married. He has no right over her."

"I heard. She may not be legally married to him, but by damn he's taken her maidenhead. That gives him some rights." John gripped the sides of his chair in a whiteknuckled grasp.

"He lied to her. Why should that give him any rights at all?" Holly's voice rose to match her husband's.

"Because it does!"

"Now I suppose you're going to spout off about a man's honor and duty—"

"Please!" Meagan looked at both of them. "I don't want to cause trouble. I'll go and stay at an inn."

Holly looked at Meagan, her cheeks red with anger. "You're staying right here. And when we go to the country, you'll go with us."

"I couldn't possibly stay."

"Of course you can. And we'll invite your brother too. Say you will. Please—"

Bang. Bang. Bang.

Meagan jumped at the loud knock on the door and heard Dunn, the Upton's butler, call out a greeting to Barrett.

"Didn't take him long," John murmured, a satisfied grin spreading across his handsome face.

One caustic look from Holly and he quickly straightened his expression.

"I don't want to see him! I can't see him!" Meagan leaped up, glancing around the room for an escape route. Nothing. She ran to the parlor doorway and collided with Barrett.

Barrett grabbed Meagan's arms, his face a mask of anger. "What the hell are you doing here? I should throttle you for leaving the carriage. I've been all over the city looking for you."

"How dare you come after me! Don't ever come near me again!" She knocked his arms away and stepped back from, her eyes narrowing at him.

He studied her face for what seemed like an eternity. The anger melted from his expression, and in a ragged whisper, he said, "You know?"

"I heard the king speaking to Sir James."

"Let me explain."

"No! Just leave!"

Holly hoisted her protruding body off the sofa and shook her finger at Barrett. "I'm going to ask you to respect Meagan's wishes. I didn't think you capable of treating a lady in such a manner. I'm truly disappointed in you, Barrett."

John grabbed Holly's arm. "Come, my sweet. They need some privacy."

Meagan started to beg Holly not to leave her alone with Barrett, but she didn't want to come between a husband and wife, and John looked determined to give Barrett time alone with her.

Holly didn't pull away from John's arm. She glanced at Meagan and asked, "If you wish me to stay—"

"No, no. I'll speak to him." Meagan glowered at Barrett.

"See, my sweet," John said. "They want to be alone."

"You have some nerve calling me my sweet after the argument we just had."

"I love it when you get angry. It makes your eyes sparkle with fire." John led Holly out of the room and she didn't appear to notice. Their voices died away in the hall.

Barrett stepped toward Meagan. "Please. We need to talk."

"What is there to talk about? I know exactly why you pretended to marry me. You knew Harold was a member of the Devil's Advocates and you needed a way to befriend and watch him. You also knew you could take advantage of him because of his gambling sickness. I loathe you the most for that." Meagan couldn't bear to look at him. She turned her back on him and walked across the parlor and looked out the window. She watched the gas lanterns on the street flicking their dismally dim light over the cobblestone.

"You have every right to be angry—"

"Yes, I do." She leveled a glare his way. "Tell me, did

you mean what you said about deeding Fenwick Hall and the lodge back to me? Or was that a lie to entice me to marry you?"

"My solicitor drew up the deeds and a trust fund for you."

"I suppose that's an even exchange for using me with little more care than one of your mistresses."

In a deep voice laden with regret, he said, "I never meant to do that."

"Well, you did it." She dropped the curtain and turned to face him. "I have more hair than wit. What a stupid fool I've been. I thought you cared about me, but I was wrong. Wrong! You don't have a heart, so you can't feel anything."

He tensed as her words struck him. A harsh mask settled over his face. "You are quite right. I'm a ruthless black-guard. I've admitted that all along. It was you who wanted to believe I was someone I wasn't. If we are throwing bloody stones, let's throw some your way. I wasn't the only one with a lie. You knew of your brother's involvement with the Devil's Advocates and you said nothing to me. You went running to Burrows." He emphasized Lochlann's name with a snarl.

"I did tell you."

"A little late, weren't you?"

"Perhaps, but it was no worse than what you did to me," Meagan snapped back at him.

"We are even then."

"How dare you imply that? We will never be even. You seduced me under the pretense of being married to me. How can you call that even?"

"I don't think it was I who did all the seducing."

Meagan had no retort for that salvo. She'd tried to seduce him and they both knew it.

"I'm tired of arguing with you, Princess. Truth is, I've

taken your maidenhead and I'm going to do the honorable thing and marry you. You're coming home with me now."

"I shall not! Do you think for one moment I'd marry a man as merciless as you—especially to ease what little conscience you have. I won't make the same mistake twice. I hate you—do you understand that? I hate you! I never want to lay eyes on you again."

"I won't argue with you." In two long strides he stood in front of her. He grabbed her arms.

Meagan felt his long fingers clamp around her flesh and blurted, "Your father was right about you. I don't know why I couldn't see it before. I even defended you and believed in you. But he was right in the end. He said you'd hurt me and you have. Now you refuse to leave me alone and prolong my pain. I just want to forget this ever happened. I want to forget you ever existed and get on with my life. Now leave me alone!" She wrenched her arms from his grasp and slapped him hard across the face.

For a moment he stood there, stunned, the bright red marks of her fingerprints branded across his cheek. Meagan felt her palm stinging and looked at his face. Her first instinct was to reach out to him, but she remembered how he'd hurt her and quickly quelled it. Tears blurred her vision, and she blinked them back.

Barrett's lips tightened into a hard line. His blue eyes bored into her face for a moment. A fleeting moment of hurt and regret flashed over his face before a detached, unyielding mask covered it. He dropped his hands. "Very well, if you feel that way." He turned and strode out of the room.

Meagan watched his broad shoulders swaying, watched him turn the corner, a muscle twitching in his clenched jaw. He stalked past the doorway, his pounding footsteps following him out.

She stared down at her stinging palm. She'd find a way

to pick up the pieces of her life and live without him. She had to.

The door banged shut. Meagan jumped. A constricted feeling in her chest traveled up to her throat, to her eyes, tightening, squeezing until tears streamed down her cheeks.

CHAPTER
THIRTY-ONE

The next day, Meagan hibernated inside a chamber in the Lord Upton's town house, listening to the hiss of the fire in the grate. Through a blur of tears, she watched dust motes drift through a ray of sunshine that angled across the bed. Since her meeting with Barrett, she couldn't stop crying and she fought a recurring dizziness. She couldn't get over how he'd made her love him and how he'd betrayed that love. He must never have cared for her at all. How could she have been such a fool?

A soft rap sounded at the door.

She sat up and dabbed her eyes and cheeks with a handkerchief; then she smoothed back the hair that had escaped the bun at her nape. When she thought herself presentable, she asked, "Who is it?"

"It's me. Please. May I visit for a moment?"

Meagan recognized Ann's muffled voice and said, "Come in."

Ann strode into the room, smiling, but it was such a reflective expression that it hardly resembled a smile. Her dainty pink taffeta dress sported a wide pink bow tied at the waist and dirt and grass stains on the hem. She gazed at Meagan over the potted plant in her hands as she covered the length of the room.

Ann saw Meagan looking at her soiled dress and said, "I haven't changed from playing with my brothers."

"Indeed. It looks as if you had a wonderful time."

"I did once I got the better of them." Ann noticed the dust motes in the sun. "Oh! You have so many dust fairies in your room. Uncle Barrett must have hurt you terribly."

"Why do you say that?"

"Well, for one thing, fairies don't like to see people hurting and they try to cheer them up. And for another your eyes are all puffy and red—a sure indication you've been crying."

"I suppose it's very hard to hide red eyes from fairies or"—Meagan looked at Ann—"intuitive little girls."

"Yes, very," Ann said, her smile fading. She sat on the bed and handed the plant to Meagan. "I grow these shamrocks. I thought one would brighten up your room. The fairies will like them."

"Thank you very much." Meagan touched one of the four delicate leaves with her finger. "It's beautiful."

"Did you know fairies like toadstools and shamrocks? I believe they like shamrocks better."

"I didn't. How did you come by this knowledge?" Meagan asked, watching the halo of gold highlights in Ann's hair glistening in the sun.

"I've experimented with all sorts of plants to see which one they like best. It's the shamrocks, all right. You see, their leaves drop when the sun goes down and the fairies like to hide under them."

"I see. I'm going to put it right here by my bed so the fairies will have a place to sleep." Meagan set the brass pot on the nightstand next to a candle.

Ann touched Meagan's hand. "I hope you will cheer

up soon. I heard Mama tell Papa that Uncle Barrett did a horrible thing to you and that is why we must be kind and ignore it when you cry."

"You're right. He did do a horrible thing," Meagan said absently.

"Uncle Barrett shouldn't have hurt you," Ann said, worrying her bottom lip, looking lost in her own thoughts. "It isn't like Uncle Barrett to hurt anyone. He's very kind to me." Tears glistened in Ann's eyes.

"He never loved me."

"I had hoped he wouldn't be lonely anymore since he married you, but . . . " Ann's words trailed off and a tear slipped down her cheek.

Meagan realized she'd lost her train of thought. She glanced at Ann and saw the tears steam down her cheeks. "Please don't cry," Meagan said past the tightness in her throat.

"I can't help it." Ann wiped at her tears with the back of her hand. "I don't like to see you or Uncle Barrett upset."

"Please forgive me. I didn't mean to upset you." Meagan hugged Ann, feeling her fine blond hair against her fingertips.

"It's not only you that made me cry," Ann said, the weight of the whole world in her voice. "I'm worried about a lot of things, but mostly over my mama having a baby. I don't want anything to happen to her."

"You shouldn't be troubled over it. Your mama is very strong. She'll do well in childbirth."

Ann pulled back and wiped a tear from her eyes. "Thank you for trying to make me feel better."

Meagan forced an upbeat note into her voice. "Perhaps you can smile for me." Meagan tried for a smile of her own, but it hardly lifted the corners of her lips.

Ann pushed back a strand of blond hair that had fallen over her eyes and smiled, but sadly. "You are right. I should not be melancholy. Christmas is only a week away. It isn't allowed in our house to be unhappy at Christmas. We'll be going home to the country soon and Mama says you'll be going with us. I'm glad you're going with us. You'll like my grandmama. She lives there with us. She'll make us both smile.''

"I'm sure she will."

"And on Christmas Eve, I always send a Christmas prayer to Saint Nicholas. He's real—I saw him once, you know."

"Really?"

"Yes. He's jolly and round and his beard is like strands of silver. And he told me if I prayed every Christmas and the prayer was not a selfish one that it would be answered. This year I'll pray that you and Uncle Barrett find happiness together.''

Meagan thought of how Barrett had devastated her and torn her heart apart. That wasn't likely to change even if this dear little girl prayed to have it so. Tears stung her eyes again. She tried to blink them back but couldn't.

"I'm sorry. You're crying again."

"It will be all right." Meagan wiped her eyes with the handkerchief.

Someone rapped at the door.

"Yes?"

"It's me, miss," Tessa's muffled voice sounded out in the hall.

"Come in."

Tessa breezed through the door, an anxious expression on her face. "Oh, miss, are you all right? I've been worried so.''

Ann squeezed Meagan's hand. "I'd better go. I promised Mama I'd help her make cookies. She always burns them if I'm not in the kitchen with her." She gave Tessa a solemn greeting, then strode out of the room.

Tessa watched her leave, then hurried over to the bed.

"I packed up your things. I couldn't believe it when the master ordered it."

"Yes, well, I'll be going to the country with the Uptons; then I'm going back to Fenwick Hall."

Tessa's expression fell. "Oh, miss, are you never to be going back to the master?"

"You needn't look so glum, Tessa. There is no reason in the world why you should not proceed with your plans to marry Lyng."

"I've taken care of you all your life. I saw you being born. I couldn't leave you now."

Meagan saw the determined set of Tessa's mouth and said, "You will and shall. Do you hear me? You're going to marry Lyng. At least one of us will be happy." She eyed Tessa with her most stubborn look.

"But—"

"I'll listen to no excuses."

"I'll miss you." Tears swam in Tessa's green eyes.

"And I you." Meagan stood and hugged her. Why did love carry with it such a succession of pain? She had not only lost a man she'd thought loved her, but now she was losing a woman who had been more than a mother to her. Would the hurt ever come to an end?

"I wish you'd consider marrying him. He cares for you— I know it. You should have seen how he looked when he came home. I ain't never seen a man have such a case of the blue devils."

"He used me to get to Harold. I can't forget that. And I'm quite sure he doesn't care for me. He only wants to marry me because he's found a small portion of his conscience. He even told me once he was incapable of loving or caring about anyone. I didn't want to believe that. I even lied to myself about it, but now I know he wasn't lying. I was only a means to an end. It's finished."

"I hate to see it." Tessa's frown worsened.

Meagan forced an upbeat note in her voice. "If you

think about it, I'm better off now than before. I have wealth and property now."

"And what good will it do you? I know you. You'll go back to Fenwick Hall and live alone."

After Barrett had given her the confidence she'd lacked all her life, Meagan couldn't go back to her old existence, to the loneliness. So she said, "No, Tessa. You're wrong. I'm going to talk Harold into going abroad with me after Christmas. I need to get away from England and the scandal that will surely follow . . . . " A wave of dizziness struck Meagan and her words trailed off. She clamped her hand over her mouth and grasped the bed post.

"Oh, my!" Tessa grabbed a chamber pot managing to get it up in time for Meagan to retch in it.

After Meagan emptied her stomach and Tessa helped her to lie down, she said, "I know that look. Your mama wore it when she was expecting you."

"I must have eaten something bad or I'm coming down with something." Meagan rolled her eyes, feeling another wave of dizziness.

"The only thing you're coming down with is a baby."

"A baby?" Inadvertently, Meagan's hands went to her stomach. She thought of the life inside her and said, "Isn't life strange, Tessa? I've lost a husband I never had, yet gained something very dear in return."

"You're going to tell him, aren't you?"

"Absolutely not."

"You must."

She saw Tessa's scowl and said, "I won't be forced into marrying him because of a child. You have to swear not to tell him."

Tessa hesitated a moment, then sighed. "Very well, miss. It's your baby, but it don't seem right to me."

"I've made my decision, Tessa." Meagan clamped her arms protectively around her abdomen; then another wave of nausea caught her. She groaned and squeezed her eyes closed.

A week later brought Christmas Eve. Barrett paced in front of the fireplace, feeling the heat of the Yule log against his legs. He glanced over at Nuisance. The animal lounged on his back in a wing chair, soaking up the heat, his paws moving as he dreamed.

Barrett frowned at the dog and thought of Meagan. He reached up and felt the cheek she'd slapped. So many times he'd ridden past John's house. So many times he'd wanted to go to the door and see her. Then he had remembered she wanted no part of him. How could he blame her after what he'd done?

Pellam House had never seemed so empty. Every tick of the clock echoed through the drawing room, pounding against his eardrums. The crack and hiss of the fire sounded like a roar in his head. Silence pressed in on his chest like a hammer. He could feel the restlessness clawing at him again. He couldn't stand it any longer without her. Somehow he must win her back.

He took a step to leave, but footsteps sounded in the hall. Then James filled the doorway.

Nuisance woke, gave James a indolent look, then turned on his side and went back to sleep.

James covered the length of the room, firelight catching the shine on his black boots. "I let myself in. Where are those two butlers of yours?"

"They are putting up mistletoe, I believe. What do you want? I'm on my way out." Barrett cast James an impatient look.

"Are you going to see her?"

"Yes."

"Well, this might help win her back. Consider it an early Christmas present." James tossed a large envelope at him.

With one deft movement, Barrett caught it. He broke the seal and looked at his own marriage license. "I don't want this." He made a move to toss it into the fire, but James stilled his arm.

"I wouldn't toss that away. It's not a forgery."

Barrett stared at James. "I should kill you! Do you know how much hell you've put Meagan and me through?"

"I found out only a day ago Hibbert was not only an actor before he came to work for me, but an ordained minister as well."

"I don't believe you."

James stepped back, an enigmatic grin on his face.

"You planned this all along." Barrett took a swing at him.

James's fists shot up. "Hell and damnation! You should be thanking me. She's your wife. You can force her to come back to you now."

"Thank you very much!" Barrett swung and caught James in the eye. He had the satisfaction of seeing him stagger back a step.

James held up his hands. "All right, we're even."

Barrett dropped his fists, his anger ebbing behind a shrewd grin that matched James's. "No, we won't be even until I get you back."

James touched his eye and shot Barrett a wary glance. "All right, now that we've established that point, tell me if you have heard from Fenwick."

"I received a letter from him this morning. He's in Glasgow. I informed him the danger had passed and he could come home."

"That sews up the case, save for your marriage." James's eyes took on a contemplative gleam.

Barrett glowered at him. "Don't think to be interfering again. You have done enough. Be off with you. Go write your bloody reports and do your spying."

James grinned without it touching his eyes. "I intend to do just that. Happy Christmas."

"The same to you." Barrett watched James stride out of the room, then scooped up the marriage license that lay near his foot.

Across town, Meagan heard Holly cry out, the pitiful wail seeming to fill the whole town house. Meagan grimaced at the doorway of the parlor, still hearing Holly's cry ringing in her ears. She glanced at Dryden and Brock sitting at the card table opposite her. They looked at each other and made faces.

Inadvertently, Meagan laid a card on the table, her mind half on Holly and half on Barrett. If he cared for her in the slightest bit, he would have made some effort to humble himself and apologize. But he had not.

Dryden looked at it. "That's a queen of hearts."

"So it is." She picked it back up, hardly able to breathe for the heaviness over her heart.

Another scream wrenched the air.

Dryden glanced up at the ceiling. "It's getting close."

"She'll be cursing at Papa in a moment," Brock said, examining his cards.

Meagan frowned. "Cursing?"

"Well, ain't cursing so much, but she sure lets him know how she feels about lying in," Dryden said.

Brock laid down a king of clubs. "Last time she bawled at him it wasn't fair women had to give birth for a good thirty minutes."

"I hope she doesn't wake Lawrence," Dryden said, frowning. "He'll be bawling his head off all night."

Meagan swallowed hard and rubbed her belly. Would she be shrieking at Barrett when their child came? Definitely, after what he'd done to her. "Do you mind if I throw in? I can't concentrate on the game. I believe I'll go and find your sister.'' She laid down her hand.

"She's in the attic." Dryden tried to peek at his brother's cards.

"Stop it, cheater!"

"Was not cheating!"

"Were too!"

Dryden and Brock's bickering drifted away as she climbed the stairs. After four flights, Meagan reached the top. The door to the attic stood open, a dim halo of candle-light flickering along the scratches and dents on the door's edge. A draft drifted down the stairwell. Meagan shivered, rubbed her arms, and stepped up the last step into the attic. She passed hatboxes, an old chest of drawers with a broken chair on top, and a large chest, where a candle burned in a holder. Smoke spiraled up to the bare eaves overhead in a long stream.

She saw Ann standing in front of an open window, her elbows resting on the sill, her hands together in prayer. Moonlight beamed over her face and blond hair, the gray light enhancing her angelic features.

Ann raised her face and glanced up at the sky. "So you see, St. Nicholas, I would like to have a baby sister, but I don't really care anymore. I just want Mama to be all right. And if it's a boy, I'll be happy, for any boy born on Christmas Eve must be a blessing. Really, I shall be happy. I don't even mind that Mama couldn't make it to the country so we could have Christmas there this year. I'm sure you'll know where we are."

Ann sighed loudly and continued. "And the other thing about Lord Waterton and Lady Meagan. Well, everyone should be with the person they love. Don't you think? There's only one person in the world that is your soul mate. I'm sure Lord Waterton found his with Lady Meagan. They should be together. I know I'm asking for two Christmas wishes this year. I'll make up for it next year by asking for none— Well, I take that back. I'll be asking you to bring joy to the lives of all the children in the world—that is my wish year round. Does that count?''

Meagan had gone looking for Ann to comfort her, for she knew Ann was worried about the baby and Holly, but it was Ann who'd comforted Meagan. Her prayer touched something deep inside Meagan, and her despair somehow lightened.

"Hello," Meagan said softly so as not to startle Ann.

Ann glanced over her shoulder. "Lady Meagan, it's you."

"Yes, my dear, it's me." Meagan walked over to her, bent, and kissed her cheek.

"What was that for?"

"That was for being you. You are quite a marvel." Meagan smiled at her and touched the baby-fine hair on the top of Ann's head. "You'll not stay too long in front of the window. It's very cold. You might catch a chill."

"I won't stay long, but I like praying with the window open. It makes me feel closer to heaven. I'll finish in a moment."

Meagan smiled one last time at Ann, then strode toward the door. Before she left the attic, she saw Ann turn back toward the window and continue her prayers. "I've probably reached my limit on prayers, but could the baby come quickly . . . ?''

With a lighter step than when she'd climbed the stairs, Meagan reached the second floor landing. Footsteps thudded below her in the stairwell. Was someone bringing news of the baby? Grabbing the hem of her dress, she hurried down the steps. When she reached the first landing, she glanced down and saw Barrett.

He froze.

She froze.

For a whole minute Meagan drank in the sight of him. He wasn't wearing a cravat or a waistcoat and the top buttons on his shirt were open. Uncombed hair straggled down around his face, and several days' worth of stubble covered his chin. The dark circles under his eyes were back. She'd never seen him looking so haggard. Dear Lord, he was handsome!

His gaze searched her face, a haunted look in his eyes. Twenty steps separated them, but it wasn't the distance that Meagan felt between them, but a barrier of awkwardness. *Say something. Anything.* She waited, her heart pounding. All her insecurities came back to haunt her. Why was he just staring at her? Did he come to make her more miserable?

Meagan couldn't stand the silence any longer and asked, "Why are you here?" Her voice came out more abruptly than she'd wanted, and her words rang in the stairwell.

"I came to see you, Princess."

Hearing his deep voice whisper her pet name again made a lump form in her throat. She swallowed and said, "You've seen me. Now what? Have you come to tell me more lies?" With all her heart she wanted to hear him say he loved her. She wanted to know that he had suffered like her, that his heart had been wrenched into a thousand pieces.

His gaze searched her face. "I had hoped . . ." His voice trailed off. He turned to leave.

She was a fool! He didn't love her! Why had he come? Her mother had been right: She was not meant to ever have someone love her. Tears blurred Meagan's eyes.

Abruptly, he paused. "Bloody hell!" he ground out. Then he turned toward her and took the stairs two at a time. He paused near her and flung his arms around her waist, pulling her close. "I'm sorry, Meagan. I'll do anything to make it up to you. I love you."

Meagan's heart leaped at his words, but she kept her voice toneless as she asked, "Do you? How can I believe anything that comes out of your mouth?"

"I know I don't deserve your trust, but if you will let me, I hope I can earn it again."

She searched the blue depths of his eyes. The severely impassive facade was gone, and she glimpsed the sincerity and love gleaming in them. She found herself saying, "I might let you."

His expression hardened. "I'm not leaving here until you agree to come home with me. I won't go back to that empty house. I can't sleep. I can't maintain a coherent thought. I've gone mad without you."

"I hope so. You really do not deserve me, you know. You hurt me horribly." Meagan looked up at him behind lowered lashes, delighting in the feeling of his arm around her again.

"I know. I'm a blackguard." He captured her face between his large hands. "Please say you can forgive me." He ran his thumb over the corners of her lips.

"I suppose I can forgive you since I'm still in love with you, but it will take some doing." She wrapped her arms around his neck and smiled impishly up at him.

"I'm utterly and totally at your disposal, my dear, sweet princess." He bent and kissed her.

The instant his lips touched hers, Meagan felt her body grow weak. She hugged him, basking in the feel of him. It had felt like an eternity since he'd last kissed her, but in fact it had only been a sennight.

Meagan ran her hands through his mussed hair, feeling the crisp texture against her fingers. She felt his hand move to her breast and caress it. Heat and wanting poured through her.

After a moment, Barrett groaned deep in his throat and pulled back. "If we don't go home, I'm going to make love to you right here." He swept her up into his arms.

She smiled and wrapped her arms around his neck, running her lips along his chin. "We can't leave yet. Holly is having her baby."

"I thought I heard Holly cursing when I came in."

A gun blast went off outside, followed by loud, muffle[d] shouts. They looked at each other.

Meagan frowned and asked, "What was that?"

"If I'm not mistaken, that's John announcing to all an[d] sundry his child has arrived."

Footsteps pounded on the steps behind them. Ann ra[n] past them, her face radiant with a smile. "It's a girl! It's [a] girl! I heard Papa yell it. I have a baby sister!"

"Oh, Barrett, we have to stay. I want to see the baby." Meagan watched Ann dash down the steps, her hair bounc[c]ing against her back.

"We'll stay a few moments, but not for long."

"Thank you." Meagan kissed the frown line between his brows and decided she'd wait and tell him about their baby later.

Christmas morning, Barrett strode into the drawing room and found Meagan with her nose pressed to the window, listening to the symphony of church bells ringing outside. The air thundered with the din.

Dear God! She was gorgeous. And she was all his. She'[d] left her hair down, sweeping only the front back with a pearl-studded comb. Dark curls flowed down her back and shoulders. She wore a bright red-and-green-plaid dress that showed off her full bosom and figure to advantage. Barrett's fingers itched to hold her. He didn't think he'd ever be able to touch her enough.

"Good King Wenceslas" drifted in from the street as wassailers passed by, joining the bells' crescendo. Barrett listened to the clamor as he came up behind Meagan and wrapped his arms around her waist.

He nuzzled her neck. "Good morning."

"It is a wonderful morning." Meagan moved her head so he could kiss her neck.

"Why didn't you wake me?"

"I didn't dare. The way you were snoring, I thought you needed your sleep."

"How can I sleep with all this infernal racket?" He turned her around to look at him.

"It's not racket. It's Christmas." Meagan ran her hands over his bare chest, exposed at the top of his dressing gown.

"So it is." Placing his hands over hers, he relished the feel of her soft fingers touching him. He picked up her hands and kissed her palms. "Since it is Christmas, I have your gift." He pulled an envelope out of his pocket and placed it in her hands.

"What is this?" She eagerly cracked open the seal and pulled out their marriage license. She frowned down at the large print on it. "Is this your way of asking me to marry you?"

"Actually, we are married."

"What?" Meagan dropped the license.

He caught it and said, "James informed me last evening."

"I can't believe he didn't tell us."

"Yes, well, he'll regret it." A devious grin slid across Barrett's lips; then he bent and kissed the thin line of her lips. "I didn't tell you, for I wanted to surprise you this morning with it—along with this." He pulled a ring out of his pocket and slid it on her finger, next to the small wedding band he'd given her when they'd married.

Meagan held out her hand and looked at the gold ring. The belts of the solar system were etched around it. Diamonds took the place of the planets and were embedded in their proper orbits. "I love it." She flung her arms around his neck and kissed him.

He caressed her bottom and kissed her until his heart pounded in her chest and she felt a warm quickening in her. Even though he'd made love to her thrice last evening, he felt his loins aching for her. "Do you love it enough to come back to bed with me?" His gaze moved boldly over her body.

"Later," she whispered against his lips. "I have a little surprise for you. It's my gift to you."

"The only gift I want is to keep you in my bed."

"But I have to give you my gift."

Intrigued now, Barrett asked, "What is it?"

She took his hand and placed it over her abdomen. After a moment's hesitation, she said, "You're going to be a father." She bit her lip and looked at him with apprehension in her eyes.

Barrett hid his excitement behind a frown. "And you are just now telling me?"

"Yes, well, when I first found out, we were not speaking."

"I see."

"But I would have told you." Meagan reached up on tiptoe, wrapped her arms around his neck, and pecked him on the lips. "You're not angry, are you?"

"I don't know. It may take a whole day in bed before I decide." He swept her up in his arms. "We'll start now."

"But we cannot."

"Why?"

Reeves cleared his throat. "Begging your pardon."

"Yes." Barrett grimaced his displeasure at the elderly servant.

"Lord Kensington is in the parlor."

"That's the reason." Meagan smiled and kissed the tense line of Barrett's lips.

"What is my father doing here?"

"I invited him early this morning."

"I see."

"Please put me down." Since it was filled with sweet overtones, Meagan's demand almost sounded like a supplication.

With little enthusiasm, Barrett set her down and let her

rab his hand and pull him across the hall. His father sat
n the sofa, a mound of packages beside him. Nuisance
at his feet, sniffing his boots, the red bow around his neck
tark against the black leather of his collar. Coates leaned
ver a ladder, lighting the candles at the tree's base. He
ad lit all but three. An uneasy feeling clawed at Barrett
s he watched Coates struggling to keep his balance.

The Duke of Kensington stood and looked at them.
"Happy Christmas!" He hugged Meagan and pecked her
n the cheek. He turned to Barrett and searched his face,
s if he wanted to do the same to his son, but wasn't sure
bout it.

Barrett had never seen such raw emotion on his father's
ace before. It touched something deep inside him. After a
noment, he opened his arms and said, "Happy Christmas,
ather."

"It is, isn't it?" His father smiled and embraced him.

Barrett felt the Duke of Kensington's arms holding him.
He couldn't recall one time in his life when he had
embraced his father. Now he realized what he had missed.

Meagan gasped behind them. "Oh, my!"

Barrett stepped back from his father and followed her
gaze toward Coates. His hand wavered as it moved toward
the last candle at the top of the tree. Barrett took a step
toward him, sure of disaster, but Coates managed to touch
the candle in his hand to the wick. The top candle caught
and burned brightly, trailing a stream of smoke up to the
ceiling. Coates looked at the flame, his face beaming with
triumph.

Meagan clapped. "Well done, Coates. Well done indeed!"

"Thank you, madam." Coates descended the ladder, a
new air of confidence about him.

Reeves stood in the doorway, smiling as a proud father
might. Lyng and Tessa strode up arm in arm and stared
at the tree. Tessa began to sing "God Rest Ye, Merry Gentlemen." The Duke of Kensington slapped Reeves on the

back and belted out the song in a rich baritone. Everyon
joined in.

Barrett stepped near Meagan and wrapped his arm
around her. They shared a glance. He stared down at he
wide violet eyes, affection and love glowing in them, an
something warm and tingly flowed freely through him. H
knew it was happiness, real happiness. And love. He joine
in and sang the loudest of anyone.

Dear Readers,

I hope you enjoyed this story. Lord Waterton was so very wicked in *My Dashing Earl* that I had to tell his story. I had great fun making him fall in love with Meagan.

I hope you will look for my Valentine's novella "Cupid's Arrow," in Zebra's *Be My Valentine* collection. It is due out in January, 2000. It's about a poor young woman, driven to robbery. But when Brooke Lackland stops a coach and the local magistrate, Fitz Stanhope, steps out, things don't go quite as she expected—especially since she's had a crush on the magistrate all her life.

I love to hear from readers. Please write me at:

> Constance Hall
> P.O. Box 25664
> Richmond, VA 23260-5664
>
> E-mail: koslow@erols.com

Since this is the holiday season, I'd like to wish you a Merry Christmas and Happy New Year. May your holidays be filled with peace, joy, love, and above all, romance!

Constance Hall

BOOK YOUR PLACE ON OUR WEBSITE AND MAKE THE READING CONNECTION!

We've created a customized website just for our very special readers, where you can get the inside scoop on everything that's going on with Zebra, Pinnacle and Kensington books.

When you come online, you'll have the exciting opportunity to:

- View covers of upcoming books
- Read sample chapters
- Learn about our future publishing schedule (listed by publication month *and author*)
- Find out when your favorite authors will be visiting a city near you
- Search for and order backlist books from our online catalog
- Check out author bios and background information
- Send e-mail to your favorite authors
- Meet the Kensington staff online
- Join us in weekly chats with authors, readers and other guests
- Get writing guidelines
- AND MUCH MORE!

Visit our website at
http://www.zebrabooks.com